The
East End Girls

JEAN FULLERTON

The East End Girls

bookouture

Published by Bookouture in 2025

An imprint of Storyfire Ltd.
Carmelite House
50 Victoria Embankment
London EC4Y 0DZ

www.bookouture.com

The authorised representative in the EEA is Hachette Ireland
8 Castlecourt Centre
Dublin 15 D15 XTP3
Ireland
(email: info@hbgi.ie)

Copyright © Jean Fullerton, 2025

Jean Fullerton has asserted her right to be identified as the author of this work.

All rights reserved. No part of this publication may be reproduced, stored in any retrieval system, or transmitted, in any form or by any means, electronic, mechanical, photocopying, recording or otherwise, without the prior written permission of the publishers.

ISBN: 978-1-83618-526-0
eBook ISBN: 978-1-83618-524-6

This book is a work of fiction. Names, characters, businesses, organizations, places and events other than those clearly in the public domain, are either the product of the author's imagination or are used fictitiously. Any resemblance to actual persons, living or dead, events or locales is entirely coincidental.

To all the men and women from what was then the British Empire who travelled halfway around the world to defend the freedom we now enjoy.

PROLOGUE

MARCH 1942

With the nerve-shattering scream of a German bomb nosediving towards earth ringing in her ears and aching sadness in her chest, WAAF Corporal Effie Weston, of 906 Balloon Squadron of the Auxiliary Air Force, tightened her grip on the sodden rope.

Brushing the driving rain from her face, she looked up at Bessie, the huge, cigar-shaped barrage balloon tethered and hovering some two hundred feet above her head, just one of hundreds such pale inflatables glimmering above London as part of the city's vital air defence against the enemy. Searchlights' beams criss-crossed the night sky behind and ack-ack shells popped overhead, and Bessie's silvery-grey skin was alive with the red and gold reflection of the burning warehouses in Bermondsey and Southwark.

Satisfied that the nose of the balloon at least was aligned as it should be, Effie turned her attention to the half a dozen WAAFs around her, dressed in service-issue waterproofs and with sou'westers low on their brows, also hanging on to the balloon's guy ropes for all they were worth.

'Ready?' Effie screamed over the clanging of an ARP fire

engine's bell, the crackle of burning timbers and the rumble of collapsing masonry.

'Ready!' screamed Nell and Alice, lying practically horizontal on the concrete as they struggled to keep the balloon's tail from swinging out of alignment.

'Millie? Maeve?'

'We're grand,' the two WAAFs gripping tight to their respective side ropes yelled back.

'George?'

Standing by the engine block that controlled the balloon's cable winch, George raised a well-manicured hand.

'All fired up here,' she called, her clear-cut voice slicing through the racket around them.

Effie nodded. 'Then on my count—'

A deafening crash swallowed her words as, with a flash, a blinding light ripped across the sky.

There was a split second of absolute quiet, then the ground shook as the walls of the Colonial & Oriental warehouse to the east of King Edward's Memorial Park crashed to the ground, throwing tongues of fire and sparks upwards into the ink-black night sky.

As the acrid smell of cordite from the spent armament clogged her nose, Effie pressed her eyes and lips tightly together. Tucking her head in, she turned her back to the blast. The vacuum created by the burnt oxygen sucked at her bad-weather clothing and tugged at her hair, then, as the scorched air rushed to fill the void, a shower of pulverised brick and minute shards of glass rained down on her.

As the shower of grit and glass subsided, Effie looked up and shook the water from the brim of her hat.

'As I said, on my count. One, two, threeee!'

As they had practised for the past eleven weeks, until their backs ached and their hands blistered, the ten young women heaved as one on the ropes.

Caught in the gust of hot air as another bomb exploded nearby, Bessie strained at her tethers, and for a moment or two Effie feared she would tailspin down. But the cable drum whirled and the balloon righted itself and drifted up to the desired height of 300 feet.

After two and half years of war, the warehouses, businesses and homes of East London in and around Shadwell, Wapping and Stepney that clustered around London's docks had grown accustomed to the Luftwaffe's nightly visits. And there was little doubt that Effie and her newly fledged balloon girls would do the same in time. However, just now Effie welcomed her days of filled helium tanks, repairing and rigging ropes, checking cables and maintaining a temperamental diesel engine. In fact, she was grateful for any amount of back-breaking, exhausting work – it would numb her futile regrets and dull her yearning heart.

As an explosion rocked the earth beneath her feet, Effie gripped the rope tighter.

'One last pull and it should do it,' she shouted, as a dozen shells from the British Artillery ack-ack battery on Mudchute punctuated the sky in response to the aerial attack from the enemy.

Grateful for the rain to hide her tears, Effie looked up as the balloon rose a few dozen feet to its correct height. A flash of white light cut across her vision as another bomb found its target. The steeple of St Saviour's church, which had stood for three hundred years on the Rotherhithe shoreline, was silhouetted in the raw redness of the burning wharves for an instant, then it crashed to the ground, in much the same way that Effie's world had four days before.

CHAPTER 1

ELEVEN WEEKS EARLIER

Adjusting her hold on her suitcase, Euphemia Weston, known as Effie to her friends, placed her other hand on the top of her soft Women's Auxiliary Air Force cap and raised her eyes above the platform entrances to where one of the guards was putting up train times on the metal gantry.

'Oh dear, Effie, looks like you might be reporting for duty a little later than you planned.' Leonard, her fiancé of a year, stood next to her on the grand concourse of St Pancras station, watching as the railway official hooked a placard reading *Cancelled* beside the next train to Derby.

Although it was just after Sunday lunchtime, you'd have been forgiven for thinking it was the peak of the morning rush hour, though the vast majority of those milling around were, like her, kitted out in either khaki or air force blue, with a smattering of the navy blue of the senior service dotted among them. Whatever their calling, they were all wrapped up in scarves and hats against the frosty weather. On the far side of the station, a line of newly conscripted recruits, still in civvies, were being escorted onto a troop train by a barrel-chested sergeant major. As they marched on to their train on one side of the platform, a contingent of the pioneer corps were supervising the loading of what looked like prefabricated Nissen huts onto a goods train on the other.

Effie sighed. 'Well, I suppose it can't be helped,' she said, her breath visible as she spoke. 'There is a war on.'

'I know.' Leonard shrugged Effie's ten-pound kitbag from his shoulder. 'Wait here, my love, and I'll see if I can find out the time of the next train.'

He squeezed her hand, then marched off into the crowd towards the ticket booth at the far side of the station.

Effie put her case down next to her canvas sack and arched her back to ease the stiffness caused by the two-hour car journey to the station.

Someone knocked into her shoulder. Effie turned to see a young woman a few years older than herself, wearing in an ill-fitting dress, crumpled cardigan and a scarf tied round her head, standing beside her.

'I'm so sorry, luv,' the young woman said, her eyes darting frantically around at the people surrounding them. 'But I can't find my Johnny. 'E's only five. I had 'old of his 'and one minute and the next the little bugger was gone.' The young mother grabbed Effie's forearm. 'Do you think someone's taken him?'

'I'm sure he's somewhere around.' Effie spotted a police officer loitering by the WVS canteen trolley. 'There's a constable—'

The young mother let out a loud wail and her face crumpled.

'Wot's up, luv?' It was another woman, coming over to see what all the fuss was about.

'Her son's missing,' Effie explained.

'There's a little chap in a duffel coat wandering about over there.' The newcomer pointed across to the other side of the station. 'By that army truck.'

Still holding tight to Effie's arm and craning her neck, the young mother took a few steps forward.

'I wouldn't touch that suitcase if I were you, lad,' said a deep voice behind her.

Effie looked round to see a child of about eleven or twelve wearing a grubby shirt and short trousers, with his hand poised inches above the handle of her suitcase. He stared at Effie for an instant, then shot off towards the station entrance. The young mother released Effie's arm as she and the other woman suddenly disappeared into the crowd.

Effie stared after them for a second or two, then raised her gaze to look at her knight in shining armour, and her heart did a little double-step at the sight of the RAF officer gazing down at her.

He was probably a full seven or eight inches taller than her five foot five, and wearing a RAF greatcoat that fitted so well it had obviously hadn't come from the uniform store. He had a strong, angular face, light-brown skin and piercing sapphire-blue eyes. His cap was set at a jaunty angle on his very curly black hair, and he studied her from beneath its peak for a moment before a smile flashed across his face.

Effie, who realised she'd been staring open-mouthed at him like a loon, pulled herself together. 'Thank you so much.'

'My pleasure, miss,' he replied, in a Home Counties accent with just a trace of a faraway shore.

'Honestly, you must think me a country bumpkin to be taken in like that,' she said.

Unsurprisingly, given her rescuer's striking appearance, people surrounding them in the station's entrance hall were casting curious looks their way, even more so when he let out a rumbling laugh.

'Not so,' he replied, seemingly oblivious to the interest he generated. 'I was, to tell you the truth, about to offer to seek for the child myself when I spied that young'un eyeing your luggage.' Adjusting his kitbag across his powerful shoulders, he offered his hand. 'Flying Officer Nathan Fitzgerald.'

'Corporal Effie Weston,' she replied, more than a little proud of her recent promotion to the rank.

His long fingers closed round hers and Effie felt light-headed for some reason.

∽

Nathan had just heard about his train to Cambridge being delayed when he noticed her standing in the middle of the concourse. To be honest, with her slender figure, and her lovely chestnut hair glinting in the winter sunlight coming through the glass roof, how could he not?

En route to his new and cryptically secret posting in some obscure fenland RAF station, he'd allowed himself to appreciate the sight of her for a moment before deciding to seek out a cup of tea. It was then he realised that she was being set up by thieves, thereby giving him the chance to prevent her luggage disappearing and make the acquaintance of this stunningly beautiful young WAAF.

He bent down and picked up her suitcase. 'Which platform?'

'Actually, I don't know,' she replied, giving him a smile that stopped the breath in his lungs. 'I was supported to catch the two twenty to Derby, but it's been cancelled, and I'm waiting for—'

'Well, you've got time for a cuppa then,' he said, reluctant to bid her farewell so swiftly.

She smiled. 'I'd love to but—'

'Is this man bothering you, Effie?'

Tearing his gaze from the young woman in front of him, Nathan found a lean, clean-cut individual wearing a city suit and club tie and a look of thunder on his face. He was probably five or so years older than Nathan's twenty-six. As the WAAF standing beside him couldn't be much over twenty, he hoped this stuffed shirt was her brother. An odd reaction for him, to be sure, as he was usually easy-going.

'N...no, he's not, Leonard,' she replied. 'In fact, Officer Fitzgerald saved my case from being stolen.'

Leonard's eyes flickered over the narrow bands on Nathan's jacket cuffs.

'Thank you for rescuing my fiancée, Officer,' he said, looking down his narrow nose at Nathan. 'But don't let us keep you.'

'My pleasure,' said Nathan, answering the other man's hostility with a friendly smile.

He shifted his attention back to the young woman. 'It has been my pleasure also to make your acquaintance, Corporal Weston.'

She smiled up at him, causing an unexpected warm feeling in his chest, then Leonard snatched the suitcase from Nathan's hand.

'The stationmaster informs me that the two twenty to Liverpool stops at Bletchley, Effie, and you can connect to a branch line from there.' Turning his back on Nathan, he picked up her kitbag and took hold of her elbow. 'It's leaving from platform five in twenty minutes.'

He marched off, all but dragging Effie with him.

Feeling strangely bereft, Nathan watched her as she joined the throng heading for their train, but after a few steps she turned.

'Thanks again for saving my suitcase, Officer Fitzgerald,' she called, walking backwards.

'Don't mention it,' he called back. 'And perhaps next time we'll have that cup of tea.'

She grinned, and then she disappeared from view.

Nathan stared after her for a moment, then, shouldering his

own kitbag, turned away, feeling strangely disheartened that there was no chance of there being a next time.

∽

'Honestly, Effie,' said Leonard as platform five came into sight. 'I leave you for five minutes and you let yourself be picked up by some smooth-talking Brylcreem boy.'

Pulling her arm from his grip, Effie stopped walking. 'He's an RAF officer, Leonard, not a "Brylcreem boy". And I was not being picked up.'

'Well, it looked very much like it to me,' he replied. 'I'm not surprised; that sort are all the same.'

'Don't be silly,' Effie replied. 'I've met some very nice RAF officers.'

He gave her a tight-lipped look. 'Well, officer or not, from where I was standing it looked very much like he was getting fresh, and I'm afraid to say that it also looked like you were encouraging him.'

With annoyance bubbling in her chest, Effie thrust out her hand. 'My kitbag, Leonard.'

'Come on, don't be silly—'

'If you don't mind,' she cut in.

Leonard heaved a heavy sigh. 'All right, all right, you win, Effie. Perhaps I went a bit far, but you can't blame a chap for protecting what's his.' A contrite expression formed on his clean-shaven face. 'Let's not fight.'

Effie stood resolute for a second, then, feeling slightly guilty about her sharp words, she dropped her hand.

Perhaps she shouldn't be too hard on him. After all, they weren't going to see each other for over two months, and she knew that he would miss her just as much as she would miss him.

He smiled fondly at her and squeezed her hand again. 'That's the ticket. Now let's go and find your train, sweetheart.'

They showed their travel warrants and platform tickets to the rotund inspector as they walked through the gate, joined the other passengers on platform five, and, with the smell of coal filling Effie's nose and steam from the engine's boiler whirling around her ankles, they made their way down the platform.

'This one's free,' Leonard said, as they reached the second of the third-class carriages. He yanked open one of the doors and climbed in, and Effie did the same.

'Grab that window seat,' he said, as he heaved her rucksack up onto the mesh luggage rack overhead.

Effie placed her handbag on the seat and waited until he had finished tucking her suitcase in beside it.

'Well,' he said, as he turned to face her. 'I suppose this is it.'

'I'll be back in a few weeks,' said Effie, looking up at him with a smile.

'Not until after Easter,' he replied. 'When you've finished your training.'

'It will go quickly enough,' said Effie.

Leonard frowned. 'I wish you'd agreed to marry me two years ago when you turned eighteen rather than joining up. After all, your father was ready to give his consent and his bless—'

'You're the one who said let's not argue, Leonard,' Effie cut in. 'So let's not go over this again.'

He sighed. 'I know, but—'

A rolling whistle cut through the hullaballoo of the station and his words.

Taking her in his arms, Leonard pressed his lips to hers briefly before releasing her. He stepped back onto the platform and closed the carriage door.

Effie pulled the window down and leant out.

Doors along the length of the train clattered shut as the

train driver gave an answering toot, then with the screech of metal on metal, the train juddered.

'Bye, Leonard,' she said, waving, as the train rolled slowly forward.

'Don't forget to phone me,' he called, trotting along beside the train as he waved back.

'If I can,' Effie shouted back as the train picked up speed. 'But if I can't, I'll write.'

'I love you, Effie darling,' he yelled from the cloud of steam engulfing him.

'I love you too, Leonard,' she shouted back.

There was a tunnel ahead, and Effie pushed up the window, tucked her skirt beneath her and sat down. She rested her elbow on the window ledge, cupped her chin and gazed idly out of the window as the train picked up speed out of the station.

From nowhere, the image of the RAF officer with the dazzling blue eyes formed itself in her mind. With Leonard's kiss still on her lips, guilt clawed at her, but she pushed it aside and smiled. With a war raging around them and service personnel being posted hither and thither to all four corners of the realm, her encounter with Officer Fitzgerald was in fact the epitome of the phrase *ships that passed in the night*.

'Well,' said the WAAF with the mass of blond hair standing three feet above Effie in the back of the transport truck. 'At least we got here before the blackout started.'

'Only just,' Effie replied, glancing at the red and gold sky behind the trees at the far side of the airfield.

It was now four thirty and Effie, along with half a dozen other WAAFs who had also been on the train from London, had arrived at their final destination, Cardington.

The journey, which should have taken about two hours, had taken double that because they had sat in a siding for three-quarters of an hour outside Redbourn to let a goods train loaded with tanks pass. They had stopped for another twenty minutes outside Dunstable for no apparent reason, then finally arrived at Bletchley only to be told that the junction box had been burned to a cinder by an incendiary bomb two nights previously, so the points were having to be operated manually.

But she wasn't the only one who had to put up with the constant stop-start of the journey; after they had pulled out of St Pancras, a handful of giggling factory workers wearing boiler suits, colourful turban scarves covering their permed curls, burst in. They kept up a lively chatter, mostly about the dancing and men and a couple of smart-looking secretaries who had much the same on their mind. Still, Effie thought, at least she had a seat, because after only a couple of stops the train was so full that many newly embarking passengers were forced to sit on their suitcases or the floor in the corridors.

'Well, thank Gawd we're here, that's what I say,' said the blonde, throwing her haversack out and jumping down onto the gravel path after it.

She was dressed in exactly the same uniform as Effie, a year or two older and a little taller and broader than her.

'Ellen Reilly,' she said, swinging her kitbag up and across her shoulders. 'Call me Nell. We used to have an O in there but me grandpa thought it sounded too Irish. Like Reilly blooming well doesn't already.'

Effie laughed. 'Effie Weston.'

Nell's red lips widened into a friendly smile. 'Nice to meet you.'

'And you,' said Effie. 'Have you been on leave?'

Nell nodded. 'You?'

'Yes, a whole five days at home,' Effie replied.

'I only had a forty-eight-hour pass, which was just as well,'

Nell said, 'Cos any longer stuck with my lot and I swear I would have been had up for murder.'

'You don't get on with your family?' said Effie.

Nell gave her a cynical look. 'That's one way of putting it.' Her gaze flickered past Effie, and her eyes opened wide. 'Well, blimey, will you take a look at that.'

Effie turned to see what had caught her new-found friend's attention, and a look of amazement spread across her face too.

The runway ran diagonally across the site, with a couple of transport aircraft parked in front of hangars on the other side. A control tower faced the runway beyond them. To their left was the usual collection of unattractive concrete buildings you'd expect to see on any RAF station, housing the offices, repair shop, NAAFI and mess. However, beyond the runway in the frost-whitened landscape loomed up and blocking the last few rays of the setting sun, were two more, enormous hangars.

And in front of them, anchored to the earth by their metal cables and bobbing about twenty feet or so above the ground like so many fat, pale-grey cigars were the reason that Effie had volunteered to transfer to RAF Cardington: half a dozen barrage balloons.

'Don't stand gawping, you two. Snap to it!' said a clearly enunciated voice that any BBC announcer would envy.

Effie looked around and saw that not only had all the other WAAFs started heading along the path towards the accommodation block, but there was now a tall, fair-haired WAAF section officer standing beside her and Nell, the gilt bands on her cuffs that showed her rank bright in the fading light.

Effie snapped to attention and Nell did the same.

'Sorry, ma'am,' said Effie, saluting smartly.

'We was only admiring the balloons,' added Nell.

'You'll have time enough to do that tomorrow,' their superior replied, her grey eyes studying her and Nell from beneath the peak of her cap. 'Sergeant!'

Seemingly from nowhere, a rotund WAAF in her early thirties stepped up, her mirror-polished lace-up shoes crunching across pebbles as she marched over.

'Ma'am!' she bellowed, all but poking her own eye out as she snapped a salute.

'Show our latest Balloon Command recruits to their billet, then point them in the direction of the mess for some grub.'

'I don't know about you, girl, but I'm starving,' said Nell, and hooked her arm through Effie's. 'And if we're going to be hauling those buggers about, we'd better keep our strength up.'

CHAPTER 2

'Thanks, mate,' said Nathan, jumping down from the cab of the air force's six-ton fuel tanker. 'I hope I haven't taken you too far out of your way.'

'Don't mention it,' replied the driver. 'But I hope you can wake someone up to let you in.'

He had a fair point. After many mind-numbing hours loitering in the station's concourse, just as Nathan had been about to find a convenient wall to prop himself up on for the night, the announcement went up on the board that an all-stations train to Cambridge would be leaving from platform two at ten fifty. That was over two hours ago, and although it was too dark to see his watch, Nathan reckoned it must be well past one o'clock in the morning by now.

Nathan slammed the passenger door and the driver, his hooded headlights barely illuminating the hedgerow either side, revved the engine and drove on. The temperature was now well below freezing, and Nathan looked across at the wire fence intertwined with brambles surrounding RAF Tempsford in the waning moonlight and wondered, not for the first time, why he'd been posted to what looked to be an abandoned airfield.

He grasped the drawstring cord of his kitbag in his gloved hands, heaved it over his shoulder for what he hoped would be the last time today, and crossed the road.

When he reached the sentry post a young aircraftman, who didn't look old enough to vote, stepped out and brandished a Lee–Enfield rifle at him.

'Who goes there?' he asked, showing the usual surprise at Nathan's appearance.

'Flying Officer Fitzgerald.' Nathan extracted his papers from his left breast pocket and handed them over. 'Group Captain Donaldson is expecting me.'

The lad studied his credentials in the beam of his torch, then handed them back and saluted.

'Third hut on the left, sir,' he said, leaning on the metal weight beside him that raised the barrier.

Nathan returned his salute and continued through the barbed-wire perimeter fence into the darkened station. However, as he approached the third concrete building, a low rumble of a taxiing aircraft – a single-engine by the rhythm of it, possibly a Westland Lysander – rumbled out of the darkness, then whooshed low over Nathan's head and off into the black depths of the night.

When he reached the door, Nathan turned the handle and walked in. Glad of the warmth, he passed through the blackout curtains and found himself standing in front of a redheaded WAAF wearing round-rimmed spectacles, who, despite the late hour, was pounding away on an ancient typewriter.

For a brief moment, the image of the strikingly attractive WAAF he'd met on St Pancras station flitted through Nathan's mind, but then the young woman in front of him looked up. Her eyes stretched wide as she stared at him, then, noting the light-blue band round his cuffs, she stood up.

'Good evening, sir,' she said, saluting.

Nathan returned her salute. 'Flying Officer Fitzgerald.'

'Ah, yes,' she replied. 'Group Captain Donaldson is expecting you.' She gave him a tight smile. 'That's to say, he was some hours ago.'

'The train was delayed,' Nathan replied.

'Well, no matter,' she replied. 'He's left word that you're to attend the briefing at ten hundred hours tomorrow morning. I'll get someone to show you to your quarters.' She picked up the phone, waited for a second or two, then spoke again. 'Would you tell the officer on duty that I need one of his men to escort Flying Officer Fitzgerald to his quarters, please?'

The tinny sound of the telephonist's voice echoed out of the earpiece.

'Thank you, Kitty,' said the WAAF, sounding irritated, 'I do know what the time is, but Flying Officer Fitzgerald has only just arrived.'

She put the phone down. 'Someone will be along soon.'

She returned to her task, but after a few seconds the door opened again and a young airman with heavy eyes appeared through the blackout curtain and saluted him.

'Hazells, please,' said the WAAF. 'Cambridge Room.'

Nathan followed the airman back out to where a staff car was waiting. The junior airman took his kit from him and jumped in behind the wheel and Nathan settled himself into the passenger seat.

The car sped away between the small mounds of shovelled snow, only to halt five hundred yards later outside a moderately sized country house a mile away from the base's buildings.

'There we are, sir,' said the airman, jumping out and retrieving Nathan's kitbag from the back seat. 'Straight up the stairs and the Cambridge Room is to the left. The bathroom and khazis are at the other end of the landing.'

Nathan saluted. The airman did the same, then, turning on his heel, jumped back into the car and disappeared into the gloom of the night, leaving a smell of diesel in his wake.

Nathan adjusted his heavy kitbag on his shoulders, pushed open the front door and, leaving the frosty night behind him, stepped in. Having negotiated the blackout curtain, he found himself in a spacious, tiled reception hall, with stairs to the left spiralling upwards to the next floor. To his right there was a half-glazed door with the word *Library* painted in gold on it, and on his left he could see through an open door a handful of comfortable chairs dotted around. The large table and upright chairs in the room in front of him showed it to be the dining room, while the corner of a snooker table visible through the open door of the room adjacent to the library indicated the house's games room.

Although the house was mostly silent, there was the faint sound of male voices coming from behind the staircase at the rear, which Nathan guessed was where the officers' bar was located.

Yawning, he trudged across to the stairs and made his way up to the first floor and along to Cambridge Room. The distinct sound of male snoring could be heard from behind the door. Nathan took his pencil torch from his pocket, pointed it at his feet and switched it on. Using this, the equivalent of a single candle, he opened the door and stepped into the dormitory.

He guessed the room had been one of the main bedrooms, because it was both spacious and airy but now had two rows of cast-iron beds down either side of the space with a metal locker beside each one. Snug would now be a more accurate description. Mercifully, given he was now practically frozen to the bone, there was a small fire glowing in the ancient fireplace. There was one unoccupied bed at the far end of the room; the rest were taken by Nathan's new colleagues, huddled beneath their blankets. There was a table in the middle with four dining chairs arranged around it and a selection of magazines strewn across its surface.

Treading as lightly as he could on the creaking floorboards,

Nathan tiptoed between the sleeping airmen until he reached the last bed on the right.

Finally able to unburden himself of his rucksack, he put it on the floor, pulled the rope ties apart and took out his washing gear and pyjama bottoms. He flipped the towel over his shoulder and headed towards the washroom.

He emerged some five minutes later and then, having hung his uniform in the locker as best he could in the dark, pulled back the blankets and sank into bed. However, as sleep stole over him, the image of the WAAF corporal he'd met more than ten hours ago floated back into his mind. Which was both stupid and unsettling. Stupid because the chances of them ever meeting again were practically zero, and unsettling because for some peculiar reason Nathan didn't like the thought of that pompous fiancé of hers ever taking her in his arms.

CHAPTER 3

As the queue for breakfast shuffled forward, Effie put her hand over her mouth to cover her yawn and took another couple of steps.

'Keeping you up, are we?'

She turned to find Nell standing behind her.

'Not you,' Effie replied, stifling another yawn. 'But those blooming biscuits they call mattresses.'

'Ain't it the truth,' Nell agreed. 'You'd think seeing how we're saving the country they'd at least give us decent beds rather than three lumpy squares to sleep on.'

It was just after six in the morning and she, along with a dozen or so other WAAFS, trays in hand, were in a line leading to the serving hatch in RAF Cardington's NAAFI. With its stark plasterboard walls and exposed girders overhead, the canteen she and Nell were standing in was devoid of anything that could be described as homely. As with most navy, army and air force institutes, Cardington's clearly doubled up as a theatre and dance venue, because at the far end was a small stage with an upright piano at one side and grey curtains draped across the back. The noticeboard opposite the door had curling notices pinned on it. The only splash of colour, if you could call it that, was provided by the posters, one with a jolly-looking squaddie with a zip instead of a mouth telling them to 'Zip it' as careless talk cost lives, and another with *Dysentery and Diarrhoea* stamped in red across the top, which Effie decided not to study further.

The room was a sea of blue as around the three dozen wooden tables set out in three rows were the station's personnel, all eating their breakfast.

'Still at least there was no ruddy kit inspection this morning,' added Nell as the queue moved forward again.

'Right, me luvs, what'll it be?' asked the well-padded matron with red cheeks and wavy grey hair standing behind the counter. 'A bit of everything?' she asked, shoving the sleeves of her light-blue overalls up further.

'Too right,' said Nell.

The canteen assistant took a plate from the pile beside her, scooped up a lard-drenched fried egg and plonked it in the middle, shoved on two rashers of bacon, and handed it to Nell. 'Fried bread, toast and tea are at the end of the counter along with your eating irons,' she said. 'And margarine and jam's on the table along with the salt, if some ruddy bugger hasn't swiped it.'

She turned her attention to Effie. 'Same again?'

'No thank you, I'll just have a couple of rounds of toast,' said Effie.

'You sure, luvvie?' she asked, her motherly face a picture of concern. 'I mean, you've got a heavy day in front of you, so I'd keep my strength up if I were you.'

'Perhaps you're right,' said Effie. 'I'll have an egg to go with my toast.'

'That's the ticket,' the older woman replied. 'We don't want you fainting away halfway through the morning, do we?'

'I suppose not.' Effie laughed. 'It wouldn't look good on my first day, now would it?'

'I should say not,' the canteen assistant replied and offered her the plate.

Effie took it. 'Thank you, Mrs...'

'Elsie,' she replied, picking up another plate. 'Bone 'appy tit.'

Effie picked up her toast and joined Nell, who had added four triangles of fried bread to her egg and bacon while she waited.

'There's spare chairs over there,' said Nell, nodding towards a table with a lone WAAF sitting at it. They made their way over.

'Do you mind if we join you?' asked Effie when they reached it.

A portion of bacon poised on her fork, the young woman looked up and smiled.

'No, be my guest,' she replied. 'I'm glad of the company.'

Effie judged the woman opposite, with her auburn hair neatly pinned up off her collar, understated make-up and a trace of lipstick on her lips, to be a few years older than herself.

'Effie Weston,' she said, offering her hand.

The young woman put down her knife, took her hand and shook it. 'Alice Starling.'

'Nell Reilly, nice to meet you,' added Nell, placing her tray next to Effie's and sitting down.

'You were in the group that arrived last night, weren't you?' asked Alice.

'We were,' Nell replied. 'And bloody glad we were to arrive too after the journey we had from London.'

'I hope we didn't wake you,' said Effie. 'It was rather late when we arrived.'

Alice shook her head. 'I was awake anyhow.'

'I know, those blooming mattresses are murder,' said Nell, spearing a piece of rubbery egg.

Alice smiled but didn't reply.

'Where are you from?' asked Effie.

'Eastbourne,' Alice replied. 'What about you two?'

'East London, me,' Nell replied. 'Whitechapel to be precise. Where Jack the Ripper used to prowl.'

'You've had it pretty bad there these last few years,' said Alice.

'And still are,' Nell replied. 'While I was home on leave before coming here, a landmine landed on the block of flats opposite ours. Took the top two floors clean off and blew out all our windows. Mind you, I've heard it's been a bit fruity where you are too.'

'The Germans can practically see us across the Channel, so hardly a week goes by without a raid,' Alice replied. 'Still, at least now we have proper shelters. The council didn't bother at first because they thought the Germans wouldn't bomb a seaside resort. That's a joke. What about you?' She nodded at Effie.

'Waltham Abbey,' said Effie. 'My dad owns a hardware shop in the town. My mum's family owned it and he took it over when they got married. He's deputy churchwarden at the Abbey and my mum is in charge of the flower rota.' A shy smile lifted the corners of her mouth. 'And it's where I'll be marrying Leonard next April.'

Alice's eyes opened wide. 'You're engaged.'

Effie nodded.

'Show us your ring, then,' said Nell.

Hooking her finger beneath her shirt collar, Effie fished out the chain with her engagement ring dangling on it.

'It was Leonard's grandmother's,' she said, holding up the eighteen-carat gold band with a tiny cluster of diamonds.

'Is he in the services?' asked Alice.

Effie shook her head. 'He's reserved occupation because he runs the family livestock feed business, so he's regarded as an agricultural worker.'

'Is he very handsome?' asked Nell, sawing through a slice of bacon.

'Well, yes I suppose he is,' Effie replied, realising she'd not ever thought about it.

'And how did you meet him?' asked Alice.

'Well, I've sort of always known him because his family and mine are close friends, but because he's a few years older than me our paths hadn't really crossed,' Effie explained. 'But four years ago, when I was sixteen, my parents took me to the Conservative Party's Christmas dinner and dance. Leonard and I had a couple of dances, and we started to chat. A week later, he turned up at the house and asked my dad if we could start walking out, then six months later, on my seventeenth birthday, he proposed. War was declared four months later, and my mother was all for us getting married straight away.'

Alice gave her a querying look. 'Why didn't you?'

'Because I want to do my bit like everyone else, so I joined the WAAF,' Effie replied. 'Leonard wasn't happy about it and neither were my parents, especially my mum, so to keep them happy we settled on getting married next April the sixteenth as it's my parents' thirtieth anniversary.'

Alice's eyebrows rose. 'So in just over a year you won't be Corporal Weston, you'll be...?'

'Corporal Forester,' said Effie.

'A year, eh?' said Nell, laughing, through a mouthful of fried bread. 'A lot can happen in a year, especially with that lot here.' She pointed across the refectory.

Effie looked over to where a dozen or so airmen crammed into the doorway, grinning and blowing kisses at the newly arrived WAAFs.

From nowhere, the image of the flying officer with the easy smile and startling blue eyes that she'd encountered on the station the day before flashed through her mind, which then conjured up the scenario of him sitting across a table from her, actually having that cup of tea. She frowned and shook her head.

'WAAFs!' bellowed a voice over the racket of the NAAFI.

Effie looked up and her daydream was dispersed by the sight of the same spit-and-polish WAAF sergeant who had marched them to their barracks the night before.

'Parade in ten minutes and latrine duty for anyone late.'

She spun on her heel, marched back across the canteen and then, forcing two youthful-looking ground crew lads to jump aside, barrelled through the exit.

There was a pause, then the sound of dozens of chairs scraping across the canteen's floorboards sounded as the WAAFs stood up.

'Well, girls,' said Alice rising to her feet. 'As I doubt any of us want to spend the evening with our arms down the khazis, I suggest we get a shift on.'

'Copy that,' said Nell, wiping up a last smear of egg with a portion of bread and popping it in her mouth.

As her friends put their caps on and cleared away their crockery, Effie swallowed the last of her tea and followed suit. She rose to her feet, popped her hat on her head, grasped the edge of her tray and followed her friends.

Effie had only just finished buttoning up her jacket and setting her hat straight.

As the last few WAAFs got into line, the tall, fair-haired WAAF officer who'd caught her and Nell gaping at the balloons the afternoon before marched out from one of the office blocks. Hot on her heels were the sergeant who had interrupted their breakfast and another younger, slimmer one with bobbed light-brown hair. Both of the sergeants were carrying clipboards.

Seeing them approaching, the whole company stood to attention and looked ahead.

Stopping in front of them, the section officer looked them over briefly, then spoke.

'Good morning, girls,' she said. 'Stand easy.'

There was a shuffling of feet.

Her eyes ran over them again. 'I trust you slept well.'

'Ma'am!' the women on parade shouted.

'Good, good. I'm Section Officer Pemberton and these are Sergeants Marshall' – she nodded towards the younger woman with bobbed hair and a pleasant expression – 'and Dunbar,' she added, indicating the other sergeant flanking her. 'I have to tell you that you have a tough fourteen weeks' training in front of you, including three weeks at your balloon site, where you'll be assessed.' Her lips twitched a little. 'And believe me, after a couple of days getting a sixty-four-foot, six-hundred-pound barrage balloon up and down, you'll fall asleep on a bed of nails.'

There was a ripple of polite laughter.

'Although at present balloon teams consist of eight men, the top brass has decided that a WAAF barrage balloon crew will comprise ten women.' Pemberton's lips twitched again. 'You are the second cohort of WAAFs to be trained to operate the barrage balloons. The first balloon girls completed their training in September, but that cohort was made up of WAAFs who had been servicing and repairing the balloons, so already knew the ropes, so to speak. You girls are, I hope, the first of many WAAFs from all areas of the service who will take on this vital role of defending our country against enemy aircraft. However, despite our initial success there are still some in the Air Ministry who have argued that we aren't up to the job.'

Annoyance settled in Effie's chest and a murmur of exasperation went around the WAAF ranks.

'They say that weak women aren't up to the task.'

'Typical men,' muttered Alice, as another grumble went around the parade ground.

'But we'll show them, won't we, girls?' added Section Officer Pemberton.

The WAAFs cheered.

The commanding officer waited until the noise had subsided and then spoke again.

'Now you're going to be divided into two squads, A and B, for training, overseen by the two sergeants here. Within those sections you will be divided into crews comprising two corporals and eight aircraftwomen. In a moment they will be taking you to be issued with your equipment, after which you'll have free time until kit inspection at eleven. After lunch, Squad B will be in the classroom in the training block while Squad A are shown the balloon equipment until tea, after which you will change places until dinner at eighteen hundred hours. After that, your time is your own until lights out at twenty-two hundred hours.' A cool smile slid across her face. 'Now I wish you all a pleasant day and leave you in the tender care of Sergeants Marshall and Dunbar.'

After exchanging a salute with her two subordinates, the section officer turned and left the parade ground.

The younger sergeant, Sergeant Marshall, stepped forward and raised her clipboard for roll call.

'Those who I will call now for the next eleven weeks are Trainee Balloon Squad A,' said Sergeant Marshall when roll call was over. 'Arnold!'

'Ma'am!' shouted someone behind Effie.

'Baker!'

She continued to shout out names for a few moments, then shouted, 'Attention!' and there was a stamping of feet.

'Trust us to get old cod-face,' Nell muttered under her breath.

'At least us three are together,' Effie replied, through unmoving lips.

'Squad A,' shouted Marshall. 'Left face and step out.'

Four dozen pairs of RAF regulation lace-up shoes stamped on the gravel as those designated to Squad A turned.

'By the right, quick march.'

Leading with their right foot and swinging their arms, the first half of the WAAF intake marched off towards the equipment store.

Sergeant Dunbar stepped forward and, casting a jaundice eye over her charges, raised her clipboard.

'Now for Squad B. Appleton!' she barked.

'Sarge!' someone at the back replied.

'Smith, A.!'

'Sergeant!'

'Smith, E.!'

No one answered.

'Smith, E.!' bellowed Dunbar again.

'It's Smythe actually,' said a voice from behind Effie that made the king sound like a barrow boy.

From behind the ranks of WAAFs strolled a very tall, very elegant WAAF with rich auburn hair held off her collar in a snood.

With her smooth brow, impossibly high cheekbones and scarlet lips, she looked as if she should be on the front cover of *Vogue* rather than a damp parade ground. Although she was wearing the same uniform as all the other women on parade, hers fitted her slender figure like a glove, thanks most likely to a bespoke tailor in Savile Row.

'To be absolutely accurate, it's St John – pronounced sin-gen – Smythe with an e,' she added, towering over the flushed sergeant as she stopped in front of her. 'Sorry I'm late.'

Sergeant Dunbar raised her eyebrows. 'Late?! You should have been here yesterday!'

A cool smile spread across Aircraftwoman St John-Smythe's lightly powdered face. 'Well, there is a war on, Sergeant.'

Nell sniggered and so did a couple of others behind her. Feeling a smile gathering, Effie pressed her lips together.

Sergeant Dunbar's face took on an unhealthy hue, then she found her voice. 'Latrine duty for a week, *Smith*. Now get in line.'

The tall WAAF turned and strolled across. 'Budge up, girls,' she said, smiling at Effie and Alice.

They both took a step sideways and the aristocratic young WAAF slipped in between them, a whiff of perfume drifting up over Effie as she did.

'Morning, chaps,' said their new colleague. 'Turned out nice again.'

'So as you can see,' said Staff Sergeant Whittle in a broad Brummie accent, indicating the silver-grey barrage balloon bobbing above their heads, 'each balloon is anchored to the winch.' He nodded towards the truck parked some hundred yards in front of them.

It was now close to four in the afternoon and Effie, along with forty or so other members of Squad B, was standing on the edge of the huge tarmac area in front of Cardington's two massive balloon hangars.

Having pulled the short straw, Squad B had been allocated the classroom first, where Staff Sergeant Whittle, whose voice would have put a chronic insomniac to sleep within minutes, explained the development of barrage balloons from the previous war, when they had steel latticework strung between them like a giant metal net curtain.

The balloons the RAF were currently employing were

much the same but without the lattice curtain. However, the purpose was the same: to force the enemy aircraft to fly above them. This had three purposes. Firstly so they couldn't accurately pinpoint their target, secondly to prevent Luftwaffe fighters divebombing civilians and army installations and to force them into the range of the British guns which couldn't dip lower that a forty-five degrees. Or, if the Luftwaffe pilots were foolish enough to fly too low, they would entangle the aeroplanes' wings in the cables and bring them down. After this riveting introduction he'd gone on to explain how Barrage Command had been set up a year before war broke out and was divided into five groups, 30–34 inclusive.

After almost an hour and a half of stifling yawns and forcing their eyes open, Squad B was allowed a quick cup of tea and a tasteless biscuit before Dunbar marched them the mile or so across from the canteen to where they were now standing.

They stood in three lines and watched aircraftsmen, trainee balloon operators like themselves, grapple with a couple of uncooperative barrage balloons straining to escape their captivity in a brisk north-easterly wind.

'I tell you, if I stand here any blooming longer I'll turn into a block of ice,' said Nell, who was lined up on Effie's right.

'I know what you mean. But at least we've got our knicks on,' Effie replied, referring to their thick, standard-issue navy knickers in a hushed tone.

It had started snowing after they arrived the previous night, and the temperature was now hovering around freezing. If that wasn't enough to freeze the marrow in their bones, they'd been standing for two hours in the icy wind blowing across from the Fens and the North Sea. Along with the usual complement of shirts, collars and passion-killing underwear, they had been issued with all manner of new kit that morning. This included rubber boots, a boiler suit and a leather jerkin that made them look like coalmen. However, despite her new thick underwear and being buttoned up in her greatcoat, Effie could barely feel her fingers and toes.

'Each balloon is tethered by the main cable to the winch, which is under the metal cage shape of a dome on the back of the truck,' continued Whittle, pointing a chubby finger at the Barrage Balloon tender parked on the tarmac. 'Each balloon can go up to five thousand feet but the exact altitude you'll have to get them to when German bombers have been spotted is calculated by the observation corps, and a message will be sent to inform you. Each balloon is thirty feet high, twenty-five feet across and sixty-four feet long.' Showing a set of over-large teeth, he grinned. 'Which, as you girlies aren't very good with figures, is two buses high and three cricket pitches long and is—'

The latecomer to the morning parade, WAAF St John-Smythe, who was standing a few places down from Effie, raised her hand.

Whittle's grizzled eyebrows pulled together. 'Yes?'

'Is that three English cricket pitches or three Indian ones, Sergeant?' she asked in an artless tone.

There were a couple of sniggers and his scowl deepened.

'English, of course,' he barked. 'Why would I use a bloody Indian one, woman?'

'Aircraftwoman, actually, Staff Sergeant Whittle,' St John-Smythe replied. 'I was only wondering.'

'Well, don't,' barked Dunbar, who was standing to the right of their instructor. 'Unless you want to find yourself with your arm down the bogs for two weeks.' Her close-set eyes ran over the line of WAAFs. 'Thank you, Staff Sergeant Whittle,' she said, giving the beefy instructor an oddly girlish smile.

Acknowledging her intervention, he continued. 'Having our barrage balloons anchored above our towns and cities at about five thousand feet not only keeps the enemy aircraft in range of our ack-ack guns, but it means that the German pilots can't get an accurate fix on their targets or dive-bomb civilians.'

A strange whistling sound cut off his next words as the crew dealing with the balloon finally managed to get a grip on it and it slowly drifted upwards. Staff Sergeant Whittle watched for a second, then turned his attention back to the women in front of him and put his hands behind his back and stood with his feet apart. His critical gaze ran over them.

'To my mind, even twenty of you dainty-looking girlies couldn't handle a half-size balloon, let alone a proper one. But never mind. Sergeant Jones will soon toughen you up.'

'Sergeant Jones?' asked a freckle-faced WAAF towards the end of the row.

A fiendish smile spread across Staff Sergeant Whittle's less than attractive face. 'Cardington's PE instructor.'

Glancing at her watch for the third time in five minutes, Effie glared at the back of the redheaded WAAF on the other side of the small glass panel holding the receiver to her ear.

'How frikking long she been in there now?' asked the dark-haired WAAF waiting behind Effie.

'Too blooming long if you ask me, Dolly,' chipped in the WAAF standing behind her.

It was almost seven o'clock and Effie, along with half a dozen other WAAFs, was standing outside the public phone box opposite the officers' mess. There were two other public telephones fixed to the wall in the corridor outside the canteen but there was a queue, so Effie had strolled to this one instead.

Stepping forward, she banged on the glass.

The WAAF hogging the phone booth turned round and regarded them coolly through the glass panel.

'Oh, I might have guessed,' said the first WAAF. 'It's Lily Craven.'

'She's a friend of yours then?' asked Effie.

'Hardly,' Dolly replied. 'Me and Bridget were stuck with

her and all the sheep at RAF Aberffraw in Wales until she got transferred.'

'Never mind,' said Effie. 'I'm Effie, by the way.'

'Well, you want to pray Lily's not in your crew,' said Dolly, 'cos she's a blooming nightmare.'

'You phoning your fella?' said Bridget.

Effie shook her head. 'My mum. What about you?'

'Me sister, Mavis,' Dolly replied. 'She was evacuated to Oxford with her two nippers.'

The door of the telephone booth squeaked open.

'About blooming time,' said Effie as Lily stepped out. 'You've been in there almost twenty minutes.'

Lily shrugged and, turning her back on the three girls, she strolled away.

Effie grabbed the door and stepped in.

She placed her RAF-issue handbag on the shelf above the telephone books dangling from their anchors, opened her purse, found a sixpence and picked up the receiver.

There was a pause, then the tinny voice of one of WAAF telephone operators in the station exchange asked, 'What number, caller?'

'Waltham Abbey seven five two, please,' Effie replied. She sorted out a shilling from the copper pennies and halfpennies and pushed it through the slot.

'One moment please... Putting you through,' said the operator.

Effie heard a couple of rings, then as the line connected, she pressed the A button.

'Waltham Abbey seven five two. Mrs Weston speaking,' said her mother in her best telephone voice.

'It's me, Mum,' said Effie.

'Oh, thank goodness,' said her mother. 'I've had palpitations all day imagining that you'd been abducted or murdered. Why didn't you phone yesterday?'

'Because I didn't arrive until very late as my first train was cancelled,' Effie replied. 'But even so why on earth would you think I'd been abducted or murdered?'

'Well, Leonard told us you were almost robbed on the station, then accosted by some dodgy chap who looked like he was up to no good. I—'

'The man Leonard is talking about was in fact an RAF flying officer.' Effie frowned. 'And rather than trying to kidnap or murder me, he did in fact save me from having my suitcase stolen.'

'Oh, well, never mind that now,' said her mother jovially. 'You're safe and that's all that matters. What have you been up to, then?' Effie gave her a quick run-down of her day. 'Sounds like you got dreadfully cold,' her mother said when she'd concluded.

'I was. Look, Mum,' said Effie, catching a glimpse of Dolly and Bridget waiting outside. 'I need to get my kit ready before lights out, so I have to go.'

'Well make sure you ring Leonard before you do,' said her mother.

'I can't. There're others waiting to use the phone.'

'Well, if they say anything tell them you have to ring your fiancé. He's expecting you to,' her mother said.

'Tell him I'll ring when I can and I'll write to him tomorrow,' said Effie.

'But Effie—'

'Give my love to Dad,' cut in Effie. 'Bye, Mum.'

She put the phone down, then pressed the B button at the side.

A couple of pennies tumbled out and into the cup at the bottom. Effie put them back in her purse, hooked her handbag over her shoulder and pushed the door open.

'I hope I wasn't too long,' she said, stepping out.

'No, you're grand,' said Bridget. 'Will we see you in the NAAFI?'

'No, I think I'm going to turn in,' said Effie. 'Perhaps tomorrow.'

Leaving Dolly and Bridget to make their phone calls, Effie headed along the pathway between the flower beds sprouting carrot tops and onion leaves towards her wooden accommodation hut.

CHAPTER 4

'The old girl has had a complete refit including a new dress,' said Corporal O'Rourke, slapping the Lizzie, as the Westland Lysander Mk II fixed-wing aircraft was known, on its pitch-black fuselage. He grinned. 'All ready for you to pop over to France, sir.'

It was a few minutes after eight in the morning and, with the smell of engine oil tickling his nose, Nathan was standing inside the heavily camouflaged hangar on the edge of Tempsford's runway. Within the cavernous space was another Lysander as well as, at the far end, a couple of older aircraft. Along with two teams of aircrew mechanics in grease-stained overalls, there was the usual array of toolboxes and spare parts hanging on the walls.

Having finally fallen into a dreamless sleep, Nathan had been awake just after five, and after washing and dressing had made his way downstairs to the officers' refectory. After filling his growling stomach with a hefty portion of eggs and bacon and confirming his presence and recorded his pay book with the base's office, he'd wandered across to the hangar.

'Well,' Nathan replied. 'I'd say you've done a fine job.'

'Grand of you to say, sir,' said the engineer, standing a little straighter.

And it's you ground crew wizards who keep me flying, so "Skip" will do,' said Nathan. 'And carry on.'

O'Rourke and his team of half a dozen ground crew headed off towards the ancient Hawker Hector on the far side of the hangar.

Left to his own devices, Nathan clambered aboard the single-engine plane and into the cockpit. He settled himself into the pilot's seat and grasped the joystick, then ran his gaze over the array of instruments on the dashboard in front of him.

'You would be better off on the runway, if you want to take off!'

Nathan looked down. A young man of about his own age was standing next to the plane. He was wearing the same air force service dress as Nathan except for the addition of two pips on his collar, an ornate silver set of wings above his left breast pocket and the word *Poland* embroidered on his right shoulder.

Nathan rose from the seat, stepped out onto the wheel prop and jumped down.

Pressing his heels together, the Polish airman inclined his head. 'Lieutenant Wiktor Ostowicz, Ozzie to my friends.'

Nathan extended his hand. 'Flying Officer Nathan Fitzgerald.'

'I can see I'm not the only one not from this part of the world,' Ozzie said, taking it. 'Although I think you have travelled farther than I.'

Nathan laughed. 'From sunny Barbados.'

'Not so sunny Krakow,' Ozzie replied. 'But at least I'm used to this awful English weather.' He indicated the open hangar door, from where dirty piles of snow could be seen along the edge of the tarmac runway. 'When did you arrive?'

'Very late last night.' Nathan briefly ran through his protracted journey. 'I'm to report to Donaldson in a while, so I thought I'd take a little stroll around the place.' He glanced at his watch. 'Actually, I think I'd better head off towards the chief's office now, but perhaps I'll catch up with you later.'

'I will be in the officers' mess after dinner if you would care to join me,' said Ozzie.

Nathan gave his Polish counterpart a quick nod, then turned and marched out of the hangar as a Gloster Gladiator biplane taxied along the runway. Although it was a relic from the first war with Germany two decades before, with every plane fit for combat action deployed engaging the enemy the air force was being forced to use its ancient planes for training and courier duties.

With the putter-putter of the Bristol Mercury engine and the whir of the three-bladed propeller behind him, Nathan headed for the office block.

Walking in, he was again greeted by the sound of the same raw-bones typewriter he had heard the night before, but a different WAAF was sitting behind it. She paused in her task and looked up as Nathan walked in, then rose and saluted.

He returned her salute. 'Flying Officer Fitzgerald, for Group Captain Donaldson.'

'He said to send you straight through to the briefing room, sir,' she replied.

Leaving the young woman to return to her task, Nathan marched down the same corridor to the half-glazed door at the far end.

He knocked briefly and, hearing a gruff 'come', strolled in.

Like every other operational briefing room he'd ever been in, RAF Tempsford's had a raised platform with a pinboard propped up on an easel at the far end of the oblong-shaped space. In front of it were two lines of chairs, while behind there was a floor-to-ceiling map of southern England and northern

Europe with pins marking various RAF bases and radar stations across it. The wall to the right had several blackboards fixed side by side and a huge clock above. Instead of numbered squadron lists, individual aircraft were chalked up along with their captains and flight route. There was also a column with the letters OPA at the top, under which such names as Violet, Pierre and Bernarde were scrawled.

However, the room was dominated by the huge desk in the middle, with two black telephones, a green and a red one lined up on it. Around the desk, maps and notebooks spread out in front of them, sat three men. The ruddy-faced individual with an impressive sandy-coloured handlebar moustache was Group Captain Donaldson, with whom Nathan had served at RAF Syerston in 1940. However, the other two men round the operation table were unfamiliar to him.

On the group captain's left was a man in his mid-forties wearing a major's crown on his epaulettes, a thin line of service ribbon from the last war, and the rose and laurel insignia of the Intelligence Corps on his collar. Unlike Donaldson, with his leathery complexion and fair hair that the war was rapidly turning to steely grey, the major's colouring would probably have earned him the nickname of Ginger throughout his school years, and his dappled skin wouldn't have lasted for an instant in the West Indian sun.

However, it was the third man, the slim young man about the same age as himself, with matinee idol good looks, very blond hair, and a lofty expression, who had Nathan wondering. Not least because, along with the standard two lieutenant pips on his shoulder, stitched above his left breast pocket was the distinctive emblem of a parachute with wings – the newly formed and separate Special Operations Executive, who operated separately from the other Intelligence Service branches.

They all looked up from the map spread before them as he walked in.

Nathan stopped at the end of the table, stood to attention and saluted briskly. 'Flying Officer Fitzgerald reporting for duty.'

Without rising, Donaldson returned his salute. 'So you've finally arrived, Fitzgerald.'

'Sorry, sir,' Nathan said. 'There was a problem with the train yesterday.'

Donaldson's moustache twiddled back and forth a couple of times. 'Well, you're here now. Accommodation all right?'

'As good as the Ritz, thank you, sir,' Nathan replied.

A hint of a smile crinkled around the senior officer's eyes. 'And stand easy.'

Releasing his rigid stance, Nathan stepped his feet apart and clasped his hands behind his back.

'This here,' continued Donaldson, indicating the army officer sitting on his left, 'is Major Rawlings of the SOE.'

Nathan saluted again.

Rawlings touched his forehead briefly by way of reply. 'Fitzgerald, you say. Where are you from?'

'Barbados, sir.'

'Come to help the old mother country out, eh?' said Rawlings.

'Yes, sir,' said Nathan.

'Good show. Volunteering to fight for king and country,' continued Rawlings. 'For once the blasted Colonial Office made a sensible decision to let you lot help us beat the Hun.'

After a lifetime of practice, Nathan's respectful expression didn't falter as he let the remark roll over him.

'And for goodness' sake,' barked Rawlings, 'do stand easy, man. You're making my back ache just looking at you.'

Nathan resumed his previous position.

'And this,' continued his commanding officer, 'is Lieutenant Frazer Frobisher.'

As they were of equivalent ranks, Nathan acknowledged him with a nod, and received the same in return.

Frobisher's blue eyes regarded him steadily. Nathan matched them for a long moment, then his attention returned to his senior officer.

'I suppose you're wondering why you've been posted here,' said Donaldson.

'I assumed somewhere along the line I'd put someone's nose out of joint,' Nathan replied, as several incidents with other senior officers flitted through his mind.

Donaldson's moustache shifted back and forth again. 'I dare say you have somewhere, but this time you're here by request. My request, because you're by far the best pilot in the whole damn circus and a top-class navigator to boot.'

'Thank you, sir. But may I ask, sir,' he said. 'Where exactly is "here"?'

'The home of 161 Special Duties Squadron,' Donaldson replied. 'We moved here from RAF Newmarket a month ago.'

'We, that's to say F section of the SOE, are planning to step up our operations in France,' Rawlings added. 'As you might imagine, we have some of our people over there already, but... well, let's just say things haven't always gone the way we'd planned. However, we have learnt from our mistakes and have a better system up and running now for placing and retrieving agents behind enemy line. Therefore, we've decided to step up operations and set up small circuits of four or five men or women who will work as independent sabotage cells.'

'Is this with General de Gaulle's Free French?' asked Nathan, feeling increasingly excited at the prospect before him.

'Good God, no!' said Rawlings, looking at Nathan as if he'd suggested they engage with Hitler himself. 'Whatever made you think that?'

'Because it's their country,' Nathan replied.

'Well, they shouldn't have damn well caved in and raised

the white flag after just six bloody weeks, should they?' snapped Rawlings. 'France is riddled with communists, and we have credible intelligence that a number of their communist fraternities have been trained by the Comintern and receive their orders direct from the Russian secret service. No. The last thing we need is a bunch of bloody jumped-up red-flag-waving Frogs poking their noses into our operations.'

Donaldson cleared his throat. 'Yes, well. There will be two arms to our operation. The first is being handled by the 138 Squadron, who will be responsible for parachuting agents and supplies into occupied France. We in the 161 are tasked with dropping off SOE personnel and picking them up, and the odd stranded pilot, which is our job. That's to say *your* job, Fitzgerald,' he continued. 'It goes without saying all this is highly classified, hence the shabby look of the place, so as not to draw too much attention. And if the enemy get so much as a whiff of what we're doing then not only are the lives of SOE operatives on the ground in grave danger but the whole operation will be in jeopardy. Your role in all this will be flying low and landing your aircraft in rough fields and moorland.'

'That explains the Lysander that flew over me last night as I arrived,' said Nathan.

'Indeed,' Donaldson agreed. 'The best plane for short take-off and landing.'

'I take it you speak French, Fitzgerald,' said Rawlings.

'My mother is from Martinique.'

'And a thousand hours of night flying.'

'Yes, sir,' Nathan replied.

'Splendid. You'll be working with Frobisher,' continued Rawlings, indicating the younger man beside him. 'He's been instrumental in training our operatives and will be in charge of the operations here at Tempsford. Your job, Fitzgerald, is to ensure we get our people behind enemy lines without alerting the enemy.'

'Do you think you're up to the task, Fitzgerald?' asked Frobisher, in a clipped upper-class tone.

'I certainly am,' Nathan replied, holding the other man's cool blue gaze.

'Top show,' said Donaldson, his moustache doing a little shimmy again. 'You'll have a few weeks' training of course, to get yourself reacquainted with the old Lizzie, but I've every confidence you'll be up to speed by the time operations start.'

'And may I ask when that might be?' asked Nathan.

'About four weeks,' Frobisher replied. 'Actually, it's a bit of a cushy number for you pilots as we can only operate a week either side of the full moon, so you'll be twiddling your thumbs for two weeks out of every four.'

Nathan raised an eyebrow. 'Very cushy, except for the navigating across enemy lines to unmarked locations and landing under the noses of the Germans and French collaborators bit.'

Frobisher gave him a sharp look.

'Right, I think we've covered everything, so unless there's something else,' his commanding officer said, glancing at the two men either side of him, who shook their heads.

'Sykes!' bellowed Donaldson.

The door opened and the group captain's assistant marched in.

'Would you give Flying Officer Fitzgerald a quick tour of the base, then get him over to the NAAFI so he can be issued with his extra kit,' Donaldson said over his shoulder. 'After which, Fitzgerald, your time's your own, until o-eight hundred tomorrow in here. Dismissed.'

'Thank you, sir.'

Nathan gave him a quick salute, then turned on his heel.

'And make sure you show him the library, Sykes,' Donaldson called as they were halfway to the door. 'Fitzgerald here is a great reader.'

CHAPTER 5

'Come on, ladies,' Corporal Makepeace bawled across the field. 'Put your bloody backs into it.'

Flexing her right hand inside her leather glove, Effie grasped the rope a little higher up and, using her body as leverage, rocked back on her heels.

'Buggery thing,' grunted Nell, who, red-faced and sweating, was grasping the next rope along.

The buggery thing her friend was referring to was the fat, grey whale-like object bobbing in the stiff westerly above their heads that seemed hell-bent on ripping their arms out of their sockets.

It was just after three thirty on a blustery Wednesday afternoon halfway through Effie's third week at Cardington.

She was standing in the middle of the field in front of the shed along with eight other WAAFS who were having their first practice at working with a balloon. Like them, she was wearing her newly issued serge working suit and gumboots, plus the leather gauntlets they were all given to protect their hands.

That morning both groups had been split up into crews of ten. She had been assigned corporal of no. 3 crew while Millie

Tyler was put in charge of no 9. Thankfully, Alice, Nell, Maeve and George were in the crew too, along with Dolly, and two girls from Squad A called Peggy and Rose, who were from Halifax and Cambridge, respectively. Unfortunately, the final two WAAFs allocated to their crew were Lily and her chum Maureen.

As this was their first hands-on experience working with a balloon as a crew, four barrage balloons had already been filled with helium and floated up to a couple of hundred feet before they arrived in the practice area.

'Take that slack out of that bloody cable, woman,' bellowed Makepeace. 'Or it'll take someone's head off.'

He was one of the four field instructors allocated to Squad B that afternoon after another mind-numbing morning of being instructed on how a barrage balloon was constructed.

As always, they had a mere half an hour for lunch, after which Sergeant Dunbar had marched them out onto the freezing-cold open space in front of the hangars to put theory into practice. They had been allocated one of the bobbing balloons tethered to the back of a lorry with an instructor, Corporal Makepeace, standing beside it.

In his early thirties, with the buttons on his battle jacket stretched to their limits and his fatigue trousers so tight it was a wonder the seams held together, he looked like a khaki balloon himself. He also had a pair of ears that would have been a gift to any playground bully.

'Wind the winch half a turn,' shouted Dolly, on the back of the specially adapted Fordson truck.

'Half a turn, coming up,' shouted George, who was sitting in the driver's seat beneath the metal cage.

As she was one of the few to put her hand up when they were asked who had ever been behind a wheel, George had been designated as the crew's driver. However, part of their training would involve a short driving course, which pleased

Effie no end. She'd asked her father to teach her a year ago, but her mother had vetoed it as not ladylike.

George revved the winch engine and cable drum to roll slowly, taking the slack out of the wire cable.

'That's it,' shouted Makepeace. 'Now hold it steady as we're going to bring it down.'

That command was for the eight WAAFs holding the guy ropes attached along the side of the balloons halfway up. As had been explained to them at some length as they huddled around the model of a balloon and its rigging set up on one of the benches, it was essential for everyone's safety that the balloon be raised and lowered in a controlled manner. Given that it weighed just off five hundredweight, should the balloon start crashing about in the wind someone, most likely one of the ground crew manning it, would be seriously injured or even killed.

'Come on girls, show us your muscles,' shouted one of the trainee balloon airmen loitering about outside the hangar.

'Yeah,' called another. 'Show us what you can do.'

A couple of wolf-whistles rang out across the open space and Nell frowned.

'I'd like to ruddy well show you what I can do with my fist,' she said, beads of sweat springing out on her forehead as she strained on the rope.

'Let's save our energy for getting this balloon down,' said a red-haired young woman holding one of the ropes further toward the rear.

Effie's shoulders screamed as the balloon she was holding tugged at its bonds again.

'Right, reel it in,' shouted Makepeace, raising his head and looking at the balloon.

'Reel it in,' shouted Effie.

'Copy,' George shouted back, revving the engine again, and the cable drum slowly cranked round, taking the cable with it.

'Steady, steady. Keep those guy ropes tight,' shouted Makepeace.

Slowly, like a whale being landed on the shore, the puffy monster hovering over them descended.

'Right, that's enough,' shouted Makepeace, as the cable reached the cut-off marker.

With the balloon secure and hovering just ten feet above them, Effie and the rest of her crew set about tying off their guy ropes, but as she pulled her sheepshank knot tight the balloon suddenly bucked.

'Oi, you, Starling,' shouted Lily, who was hanging on to a rope at the rear. 'Get a bloody grip, will you?'

'I'm trying,' Alice shouted back, heaving on her rope.

'Well, try a bit harder,' Lily called back. 'Me and Maureen are doing all the sodding work back here.'

'I'm doing my best,' shouted Alice, repositioning her hands on her own tether.

'Bloody useless, that's what you are,' Lily called back. 'Bloody useless.'

'And you're a bully,' said Effie.

Tying off her guy rope securely and satisfied that the front half of the balloon was hovering safely ten feet above them, Effie stepped across to Alice.

Grasping the guy rope higher up, she added her weight to Alice's and between them they pulled the tail of the balloon into line.

'I'll hold it while you tie it off,' shouted Effie, as her shoulder muscles screamed again.

Alice looped the tether through the anchor weight and whipped the end round a couple of times.

'Thanks,' she said, pulling it tight.

'Don't mention it,' said Effie.

'Oi, you two!'

Effie and Alice looked round.

'This ain't a bloody muvvers' meeting, you know,' shouted Makepeace. 'Get those ropes stowed so we can put this balloon to bed.'

Effie rolled her eyes.

'Thanks again,' said Alice, as Effie ducked back under the balloon and resumed her position on the other side.

'Right then, now we're all done having a chat, let's move this great balloon thing back into the hangar. Steady as you go, driver!'

George crunched the gears and the truck rolled forward.

'Not too fast,' bellowed Makepeace. 'You're not competing in the bloody Grand Prix.'

Team A were a little way in front of them with their silvery-grey beast, so George steered number four truck in behind them, with Dolly standing on the back to keep an eye on the cable and the winch it was attached to.

The remaining eight women in Effie's crew fell in line behind their charge as the other trucks and balloons that made up Squad B followed after.

Suddenly carried in the wind and over the rumble of the lorry engines came the sound of female voices drifting across from Squad A.

Tilting her head, Nell, who was walking beside her, took a deep breath.

'We're going to hang out the washing on...' she sang in a strong clear voice.

'The Siegfried line...' sang Effie and others around her.

'Have you any dirty washing, Mother dear,' sang out her fellow WAAFs who were bringing up the rear.

With the silvery barrage balloon bobbing overhead in the late afternoon breeze and the sound of women singing ringing out over the practice area, Effie and the rest of trainees headed for the hangars.

. . .

Standing in front of the eight-by-ten-inch mirror fixed to the inside of her locker door, Effie ran her brush through her slightly damp hair. She twisted it into a bun, took one of the hairpins she held between her lips and jammed it in. Holding tight to the knot, she took the remaining pins and threaded them through.

According to the clock fixed above the dormitory entrance it was now twenty to seven, two hours since Sergeant Dunbar had dismissed her and the rest of Squad B, after a very long hard week.

Having got back to her hut, Effie had stripped off her working fatigues, grabbed her towel, washbag and dress uniform, then, using her raincoat as a dressing gown, raced across to the ablution block situated between the rows of accommodation huts. Thankfully, she was one of the first in line for the showers, so the water was still relatively warm. After lathering away the dirt, sweat and grime from an afternoon of heaving a barrage balloon back and forth, she wrapped her raincoat round her again and returned to her barrack.

Satisfied that her wayward locks couldn't escape, she turned her attention to her tie. After straightening the knot, satisfied that she was properly dressed, she closed the door.

'You ready, Nell?' she asked, looking across at her friend, who was packing her washing kit back into her locker.

'Almost,' Nell called back over her shoulder. 'Are my seams straight?'

Effie studied her friend's shapely calves. 'The left one could do with shifting in a quarter of an inch.'

Nell twisted around and fiddled with her navy-blue lisle stocking. 'Better?'

'Perfect,' said Effie. 'Now let's go and eat. I'm starving.'

. . .

Outside their hut, they joined a stream of freshly showered WAAFs also heading for their evening meal along the base's main road, and within a few moments they were pushing open the main door.

The two WAAFs' messes were separate from the regular male aircrew ones. Although there had been WAAFs at Cardington before, it was only a handful. However, with the influx of sixty or so of WAAF trainee balloon operators who were either airwomen first or second class or one of the handful of corporals, the base had had to rethink their off-duty facilities. Some in the air force thought having WAAFs take over balloon operation was doomed to failure, but Effie guessed that her intake was likely to be followed by many more. Obviously, someone in the Air Ministry thought the same thing, because smack-bang next to the WAAF officers' mess a brand-new junior ranks' one had been set up – and, judging by the lingering smell of paint, just in the nick of time, too.

As she stepped through the door of the NAAFI canteen, the smell of meaty stew and boiled cabbage filled Effie's nose and set her stomach rumbling.

Unsurprisingly, the canteen was packed, and being off duty they could have changed into civvy attire, but, without exception, every WAAF in the room was wearing her service uniform. And why wouldn't they? With civilian clothing soon to join the list of items for which you needed ration coupons, whatever you had in your wardrobe since last June needed to be preserved.

Having picked up a tray each from the stack, Effie and her friend joined the end of the queue.

'It's fish and chips,' said Effie, peering along the counter to where the WAAF catering division were ladling food onto outstretched plates from huge metal baking tins.

'Yeah, but perhaps you should be wondering to yourself,

"what sort of fish?"' said the redheaded WAAF standing in front of Effie.

'Well, I bet a pound to a penny it ain't cod,' said Nell.

'Whereabouts in Ireland do you come from?' asked Effie, noting the redhead's soft Irish lilt.

'Newry,' Maeve replied, as they shuffled forward. 'Right on the border.'

'My gran was a Reilly from a village outside Cork,' said Nell as they reached the front of the line.

'I'm Effie by the way, and this is Nell.'

'Maeve. Maeve Lynch,' she said.

'What sort of fish is it?' asked Nell of the young girl standing behind the counter holding a serving slicer aloft.

'The sort that swims in the sea,' the girl replied, giving her a long-suffering look. 'If you don't want it, I'm sure your mates will be happy to have yours.'

'That'll be grand,' said Maeve, taking a plate loaded with fried fish, chips and dull green peas the size of aniseed balls and, for dessert, a bowl of something disguised under a blanket of custard.

Effie and Nell placed their dinner on their trays and moved away.

'The place is fair heaving,' said Maeve as she surveyed the room for a seat.

Effie's gaze ran over the heads of the women eating their evening meal.

'Over there,' she said, spotting Alice sitting by herself at a corner table. 'Quick.'

Dodging between the tables, Effie, followed by Nell and Maeve, made their way over.

'Do you mind if we join you?' Effie asked.

Alice looked up and smiled. 'Be my guest.'

Effie slid into the seat beside her while Nell and Maeve

took the chairs opposite. Picking up her cutlery, Effie introduced Alice to Maeve.

'Have you girls got anything planned for this weekend?' asked Alice as they tucked into their evening meal.

'Sleep,' said Nell, cutting into her fish with her knife.

'I've to write home to me mammy,' Maeve replied.

'Me too,' said Effie. 'And my fiancé.'

Although she'd promised Leonard to write him a letter each day, after four hours in the classroom and five hours hauling a barrage balloon around, she'd only managed a quick couple of lines last week, and even less this.

'You're engaged?' said Maeve.

Effie nodded. 'We're getting married next year. What about you?'

'Oh, I was walking out with a chap a while back but, well...' Maeve shrugged. 'You know how these things go.'

'Well, I'm waiting for the Americans to arrive,' said Nell, through a mouthful of fried fish. 'Then I'm going to grab meself a long-legged cowboy and ride off into the sunset.'

'That sounds like a fine plan,' chuckled Maeve. 'But will you ask him for me if he's got a friend?'

They all laughed.

'What about you, Alice?' asked Effie, looking at the woman sitting beside her.

'Married.' Sadness crept into her smoky grey-green eyes. 'I mean, I was married until Arthur stopped a German bullet at Dunkirk.'

Nell frowned. 'Bloody Germans.'

Alice nodded. 'Arthur had become friends with a chap called Peter,' she said. 'He came to see me. He told me that they were about to board one of the rescue boats when a wretched Stuka dived at them, firing both barrels. Arthur saw it coming and pushed Peter out of the way. Poor Peter was in tears, telling me how Arthur saved his life,' she continued. 'That's why I joined up.'

'I'm so sorry,' said Effie, knowing her words wouldn't scratch the surface of the other woman's pain.

There was a heavy silence, then Alice forced a bright smile.

'Anyway,' she said. 'Who's for a cuppa?'

After taking the girls' tea orders and stacking her dirty plate and bowl on her tray, Alice left them and made her way across to the tea urn set up next to the serving hatch.

Nell offered Maeve the packet and she took one.

'Poor sod,' said Nell, shaking out the match flame after lighting her cigarette.

'Well. She's not the first and nor will she be the last to lose a sweetheart before we're done,' said Maeve.

Nell blew a stream out of the side of her mouth. 'Cor blimey, Irish. It's being cheerful that keeps you going.'

Maeve laughed. 'That it is, London.'

They smiled at each other.

Between their heads Effie saw the canteen door swing open as a familiar figure strode in. Stretching her neck, she peered over the heads of the WAAFs milling around.

'George,' Effie shouted, waving.

Maeve turned. 'Is that the highfalutin filly with a name that could cover a half a page?'

'Yeah,' said Nell. 'But she's all right.'

'What-ho, girls,' George said, sliding into the chair next to her. 'How are we all this fine evening?'

'Knackered,' said Nell. 'Aren't you getting any grub?'

'I will but only after you try and guess what I've found out that will make your eyes light up with joy,' George replied.

'Dunbar is being transferred,' said Nell.

'Nope!'

'Makepeace has lost his voice?' offered Maeve.

'If only.'

George looked at Effie. 'I don't know. We're all being promoted to air commandants.'

A wide grin spread across George's aristocratic features. 'There's a dance at the Corn Exchange in Bedford on Saturday night.'

Maeve and Nell's faces lit up.

'With a band?' asked Maeve.

George nodded.

'And men?'

'Well, as there are at least five RAF bases around the town plus a couple of army camps, I'd say there's a fair chance there'll be some fellas there, too,' George replied.

'I thought you were waiting for the Americans to arrive,' said Maeve.

'I am,' Nell agreed. 'But that don't mean I can't get a bit of practice until they do. Count me in.'

'Me too,' added Maeve. 'If I'm invited.'

'The more the merrier.' George looked across at Effie. 'You in?'

An image of Leonard's enraged expression when he found her standing with Nathan loomed into her mind. 'I'm not sure... I don't think my fiancé would like me going.'

'Don't tell 'im then,' said Nell.

'You're only dancing,' said Maeve. 'And sure to God, after the devil of a week we've all had what sort of man would begrudge you for having a bit of fun—'

'Or a couple of G&Ts,' added Nell.

Biting her lip, Effie looked across at her fellow WAAFs.

'All right,' she said, and laughed. 'You've twisted my arm. I'll go.'

'Splendid!'

'But how are we going to get there?' she asked.

George gave her an exaggerated wink. 'Leave it to me.' She

stood up. 'Now, as the butler seems to be having a night off, I'd better get myself some dinner before it all goes.'

She strode off back across the canteen and joined the queue just as Alice returned to the table.

'Go where?' she said, placing the tray of tea on the table.

'To the dance in Bedford Saturday night,' Nell replied.

'Why don't you come along, Alice?' asked Effie, taking one of the mugs without a spoon sticking up.

'It'll be a great laugh,' added Nell.

'I'm sure it will be and thanks for inviting me, but perhaps next time.' Alice stood up. 'I'm going to take my tea through to the lounge as there's something on the wireless at eight that I want to listen to. Will you excuse me?'

'Of course,' said Effie, giving her a friendly smile. 'I'll be coming in myself for the nine o'clock news, so I'll see you later.'

Giving them a friendly smile, Alice headed off towards the refectory's entrance.

'So,' said Nell. 'What about us having a little wager on who dances with the most men tomorrow? You both in for half a crown?'

CHAPTER 6

With the first streaks of the mid-January dawn breaking over the eastern horizon and the sleepy fields of Kent 1,500 feet below him, Nathan gripped the leather-bound ring atop the joystick and turned the Lysander northwards.

Although the sound of the three-blade propeller whirring in front of him filled his ears, flying high above the earth with only the wind and twinkling stars in the icy winter air gave Nathan a sense of peace. He checked his instruments and, satisfied that they were as they should be, looked down. Through the perspex lenses of his goggles, he studied the fields of ripening wheat, hedgerows, oast houses and stone-walled farmyards below him as they awaited the dawning day.

When he'd taken to the sky to defend Britain a year and a half ago, he'd done so wearing pretty much whatever the store sergeant at Biggin Hill could scrape together. However, having presented himself to the NCO in charge of equipment and uniforms the day after he arrived, Nathan now cut a dash in the RAF's latest kit.

Now he soared into the clouds in grey full-length flying suit instead of a set of white twill overalls. His pre-war lifejacket that he'd painted yellow in the hope he'd be spotted if he had to ditch in the sea had been replaced with a yellow Mark 2 one, inflated by a gas cylinder within. Even his goggles and mask had been upgraded, the latter to one that regulated the oxygen rather than just pumping it through. He'd declined the new flight boots the RAF had introduced the year before and had opted to keep his old well-worn, sheepskin-lined ones as they fitted his size eleven feet perfectly.

Something flashed in the corner of his eye and brought him abruptly back to the here and now. He looked around and saw a dozen or more Hurricanes to the east of him, heading south towards the coast. Perhaps they were on their way to intercept a formation of enemy planes that had been spotted by coastal defence, or perhaps on a routine patrol along Britain's southern flank.

Mindful that they could have been a group of enemy bombers, Nathan refocused on the task at hand.

He pulled out the map from the top of his right boot and glanced at the lines he'd marked up prior to setting out four hours before. Satisfied he was smack-bang above where he should be, he turned the craft northwards. The plane's wings, which sat across the top of the fuselage, dipped to the left then back again as Nathan plotted the course.

Within minutes the dark, shadowy snake that was the lower reaches of the Thames east of London came into view along with silvery barrage balloons bobbing above the odd cloud of black smoke from the previous night's raid. Even at this distance and in sparse light, the destruction that two years of almost daily bombing had visited on the city was clear to see.

Pulling back the joystick, Nathan climbed to 2,000 feet to clear the barrage balloons tethered over Canvey Island and Tilbury Docks, then turned the aircraft a few degrees west and headed for his base.

The wheels of the Lysander touched the ground as the first

inch of sun cut through the trees at the end of the base. Slowing the plane to a walking pace as he reached the end of Tempsford's grass runway, Nathan adjusted the tail and flaps on the aircraft, taxied it towards the camouflaged hangars and brought it to a halt just in front of the first. After doing the final check of the systems, he switched off the engine. As the propeller blade did its final couple of turns, Nathan grasped the handle over his head and slid back the perspex canopy above him.

He unclipped one side of his oxygen mask, stood up and squeezed himself out of the confined space of the cockpit, then made his way past the two passenger seats through to the back.

'I thought you'd got lost, Skip,' said O'Rourke as Nathan jumped down from the ladder fixed to the port side of the plane.

'Nope, I found the site in Gloucester easy enough,' said Nathan, pushing his goggles up onto his leather flying helmet. 'And took the scenic route home over this green and pleasant land, Corporal.'

'A bit different to from where you come from, I imagine,' the mechanic replied.

He grinned. 'Just a bit.'

'All coconuts and beautiful maidens in grass skirts, eh?' chuckled O'Rourke.

Nathan sighed inwardly.

Considering Barbados was one of England's oldest colonies, when he'd first arrived in England back in the summer of 1939 he'd been surprised to find how little people knew about it and the West Indies in general. Most people he'd encountered seemed to think the king's subjects who lived on the British Caribbean islands lay around under palm trees eating pineapples all day and playing bongos. They often didn't know where on the globe the Caribbean actually was or that the West Indian and African colonies were completely different. They were also genuinely surprised to be told that Barbados had several public schools that had been founded three centuries before and sent scholars, like him, to Oxford and Cambridge each year. At first he'd done his best to enlighten people about his home, but now he let remarks like O'Rourke's go.

'Flies like a dream though, doesn't she?' said the corporal, stroking the aircraft's black fuselage fondly.

'She certainly does,' Nathan agreed. He yawned. 'I'm going to get myself some breakfast, then hit the sack.'

Leaving the airman checking the plane, Nathan unclipped the crotch straps of his parachute, then made his way across to the pilots' locker room. There were a couple of 109 Squadron Hercules pilots kitting themselves up for the day. They greeted him as he stripped off his flight suit and hung it in the tall metal cabinet with his name on it before changing into his workaday khaki denims.

Nathan shrugged on his sheepskin jacket over his khaki flight suit against the frosty January morning and headed along the path to Hazells Hall.

Although it was only a little after six o'clock the officers' mess was in full swing, with orderlies already tidying up the hall and lounge.

The sound of male voices echoing down the stairwell from above told him that most of his fellow officers were already up, which was good news as the bathroom and showers would be free by the time he got to them.

His stomach growling, Nathan turned towards the refectory. After loading a tray with a bowl of porridge, two slices of toast and a mug of tea, he looked around and, seeing Wiktor at a table by the window, strolled over.

'The wanderer has returned,' he said as Nathan placed his tray on the table and sat opposite him. 'How far did you venture?'

'The West Country,' Nathan replied.

Wiktor took a sip of his coffee. 'I'm glad you've happened by before seeking your bed because I want to know if you have any plans for this weekend?'

Yawning, Nathan shook his head. 'Nothing except sleep.'

'Well, that is where you are wrong, my weary friend.' Wiktor sat forward. 'There is a dance in the nearby town on Saturday night and the rag-tag brotherhood are going.'

Nathan looked confused. 'Who?'

'Us foreigners,' Wiktor explained. 'The two Vikings are coming, and so is Pierre. Surely you are not going to let those big blond Scandinavians and that smooth-talking Frenchman have all the fun?'

Nathan scooped up a spoonful of porridge. 'I don't know.'

The Polish officer placed his right hand over his heart.

'It's your duty, sir,' he said in a solemn tone. 'Your duty, I tell you, to save the good women of Bedford from Sven and Karl crushing their toes all night.'

Nathan gave him a weary smile. 'Well, if it's my duty then...'

'Splendid,' said Wiktor. 'What is it the English are fond of saying?' He glanced up at the ornate plastered ceiling. 'Ah, yes. "All work and no play make Flying Officer Fitzgerald a very dull boy".'

CHAPTER 7

'So you're training as one of those balloon girls they've been writing about in the papers,' said Rodney, the freckle-faced corporal swirling her around the dancefloor to the strains of 'You Are My Sunshine'.

'I am,' Effie replied.

He laughed. 'I thought you were all supposed to be beefy types.' He tweaked her waist. 'Not pretty little things like you.'

Effie forced a smile.

It was a few minutes before nine on Saturday evening, and Effie was in the middle of Bedford's Corn Exchange dancefloor along with dozens of other couples, predominantly dressed in their service uniforms. There were civilians among them, young women from the town, many of them wearing flowery dresses, but for the most part the assembly hall was awash with air force blue and khaki with the odd black uniform of ARP wardens.

They'd arrived as the town hall clock on the other side of St Paul's Square had struck quarter to seven. Somehow, George had persuaded the transport officer on the camp to provide them with a lift to town. Effie, along with twenty or more WAAFs, had squeezed into the back of the truck. And a squeeze it was, because the benches either side were only designed to take twelve apiece and at least double that number piled into the back of the truck, all desperate to get off the base for a few hours.

'So, you're in the transport regiment,' said Effie, glancing at the flash at the top of her dance partner's sleeve with RCT embroidered on it.

He nodded. 'Go all over the country, I do, on my motorbike. But mostly to London and back.'

'Are you based in the town?'

'Naw. Six miles away in Bletchley,' he replied, as they narrowly avoided colliding with another couple.

Thankfully, the closing bars of the tune blasted across the heads of the dancers and Effie's partner swirled her to a stop.

'Thank you,' she said, letting go of his hand to clap the band.

'I hope I didn't tread on your toes too much,' he said.

'No, not at all,' she replied, her still-throbbing little toe calling her a liar.

The band struck up for an old-fashioned waltz and couples around them started drifting off the dancefloor.

'Perhaps I can catch you for a quickstep later,' he said, looking hopeful as they stopped at the edge.

Effie smiled non-committally. 'I hope you enjoy the rest of the evening.'

He left and Effie made her way off the dancefloor and back to where Maeve and Nell were sitting.

'I got you a G&T,' said Nell, sliding it towards her.

'Thanks, I need it.' Effie grasped the glass, swallowed a large mouthful, then looked balefully at her friends. 'I thought you said this would be fun.'

Maeve and Nell laughed.

'Oh go away with you,' said Maeve. 'Sure, even dancing with your man with two left feet is better than sitting alone in the lounge listening to the wireless.'

Effie couldn't disagree. 'Where's George?'

'Over there by the bar,' said Nell, tapping the ash from her cigarette into the ashtray in the middle of the table.

Shifting her attention to the far side of the dancefloor, Effie saw George standing between two RAF officers with a glass in one hand, a cigarette in the other and a devil-may-care expression on her face.

'Well, you can't say she's not enjoying herself,' Nell added.

The band master brought his small orchestra to order and the opening bars of the next dance drifted across as couples started to take to the floor again.

'Oi, oi, aircraft approaching,' Nell said as two airmen sidled over.

'Evening, ladies,' said the taller of the two as they stopped at the table. 'Would you give us the pleasure of taking you for a turn round the ballroom?'

'What do you think, girls?' said Maeve, looking sideways at the others from beneath her eyelashes. 'Should we take a chance with these fine-looking fellows?'

'Perhaps we should take pity on them, Maeve. Effie?' said Nell.

'I've already got company,' said Effie, raising her glass.

Nell and Maeve stood up and the two airmen led them onto the dancefloor.

Effie took another mouthful of drink and idly watched the dancers glide around the sprung dancefloor.

'Well, well, Corporal Weston,' said a deep voice behind her. 'Fancy meeting you here.'

Effie turned and her jaw dropped as she found herself staring into the smiling face of Flying Officer Nathan Fitzgerald.

The scene behind him seemed to fade somehow as the ground shifted beneath her feet. Although he was dressed in the same dress uniform as at least half the men in the room, on Nathan's broad chest and shoulders the cut of it was snugger, and the brown of his throat emphasised the crisp whiteness of the shirt beneath.

Captured by his incredibly blue eyes, Effie stared up at him for a moment, then found her voice. 'I thought you were catching a train to Cambridge.'

'And I thought you were travelling to Derby,' he replied, his rich voice washing over her.

The melody of 'I'll Be with You in Apple Blossom Time' drifted across the room as the string section moved to the next tune in their repertoire.

Nathan's smile widened. 'Corporal Weston, would you do me the honour and take a turn around the dancefloor with me?'

He offered her his hand.

Matching his smile, Effie rose to her feet.

'I'd love to.' She took his hand, and the ground shifted again. 'And as neither of us are on duty, it's Effie.'

With his palm against hers and long fingers curled around her own, Nathan led her to the edge of the dancefloor.

Ignoring the curious glances directed at them, Effie placed her hand lightly on his shoulder as his arm slipped round her waist.

Sending a thrill through her, Nathan gathered her to him. He stepped off on the beat and Effie followed him into the waltz.

'Where are you then?' she asked.

'Tempsford,' he replied. 'About five miles east. You?'

'Cardington,' she replied. 'I'm one of the intakes of WAAFs training on the barrage balloons. I started last Monday.'

He looked impressed. 'How has it been?'

She gave him a grim smile. 'I don't think there's one muscle in my entire body that doesn't ache but I'm enjoying the work. Certainly a lot more than my last post at Boscombe Down where I spent all day typing, filing and answering the telephone. The girls are from all over but they seem decent enough.'

As they circled the dancefloor Effie gave him a quick rundown on the Balloon Training Unit's no. 3 crew.

'To be honest,' she concluded as they executed a sidestep. 'Given that we all come from completely different backgrounds, I didn't think we all get on as well as we do.' She laughed. 'In fact, I'd go as far as saying that we're all going to be firm friends by the time we've got through all this.'

'It's the same at Tempsford,' Nathan said, as holding her a little closer as he turned them across the floor. 'Except we're the rag-tag squadron, from all over the world.'

'And what are you doing there?'

'Oh, flying, you know,' Nathan replied. His muscular leg brushed against hers as they sidestepped again.

Effie smiled. 'Of course. Careless talk cost lives.'

He gave her a charming smile.

The band played the closing bars of the tune and Nathan turned them to a stop. He released her and they stepped apart.

'Thank you,' said Effie, clapping lightly.

Although other couples were drifting off the dancefloor, they stood staring at each other for a moment. Then Nathan cleared his throat. 'I'll walk you back to your seat.'

As the band blasted out the opening chords of the next dance, Effie headed back to the table, acutely aware of Nathan just half a step behind.

As George was still downing G&Ts at the bar and Nellie and Maeve were bobbing around the dancefloor with an ARP warden and auxiliary fireman respectively, their table on the edge of the dancefloor was empty. As they reached it, Nathan stepped round her and pulled out her chair.

'Still my gallant knight in shining armour,' she said, tucking her skirt under her as she sat.

'Always,' he said, his gaze taking hold of hers. 'And as such, can I fetch you a goblet of mead?'

Effie laughed. 'A glass of gin and tonic would go down better.'

Giving her a half-salute he turned and headed for the bar, which gave Effie the opportunity to notice, slightly guiltily, that he was both taller and had broader shoulders than Leonard – not that such things mattered to her, of course.

∾

Nathan left Effie and made his way between the tables towards the bar at the other side of the room, glad that the time it took to get there was sufficient to let his heart return to its regular rhythm.

When he'd spotted Effie across the room earlier that evening, he had thought he was hallucinating. Given that the memory of their meeting on St Pancras station had returned to his mind on more than one occasion in the past week, that was a real possibility, but when she smiled up at him it was clear that he wasn't going insane. However, when she placed her hands in his, Nathan thought he was about to lose his mind as several emotions he'd never experienced before and couldn't name washed over him.

Squeezing his way past a group of land girls who were chatting to some soldiers, Nathan reached the bar. The stout barman, red-faced from exertion, spotted him and waddled over.

'What'll it be, chief?' he asked, extracting a none-too-clean handkerchief and mopping his sweating brow.

'A G&T and a pint of bitter, please,' Nathan replied.

The landlord returned his handkerchief to his trouser pocket and went off to get Nathan's order.

''S'not right,' muttered someone under their breath standing behind Nathan. 'Against nature, that's what. Everyone knows it.'

'Yeah,' someone else replied in the same hushed tone. 'That sort should stick to their own kind.'

'Well, I know what I'd do if my sister brought someone like him down 'ome,' said the first voice. 'Cos any woman who goes with one of them is nothing more than a—'

'Nothing more than what?' asked Nathan, turning sharply.

Behind him, dressed in ill-fitting Home Guard uniform, were two youths, neither of them were more than five foot seven. One had angry-looking acne pustules on his cheeks and forehead while the other had a dark shadow across his top lip.

'I said, is nothing more than a *what*, soldier?' Nathan repeated as his eyes bored into them.

They held his gaze for a few seconds, then both of them lowered their eyes.

'I can't remember,' muttered the pimply-faced one, studying his toecaps.

'Is there a problem?' asked the bartender as he returned with Nathan's drinks. He placed them on the bar.

'No, just a difference of opinion,' Nathan replied as the boys shuffled on the spot. 'And shouldn't you salute a superior officer, lads?'

The youth with acne shot him a resentful look but they stood to attention, saluted and then skulked away. Nathan turned back to the bartender.

'What's the damage?'

'Two and three,' the landlord replied.

Nathan put his hand into his pocket, pulled out a handful of coins and handed over half a crown.

'I don't think they meant anything by it,' said the barman, handing Nathan his thruppence change.

'They never do,' Nathan replied.

Popping the thruppenny piece into the jar with the image of a Spitfire stuck on it, Nathan picked up his drinks and, having taken the froth off the top of his pint, made his way back to Effie.

A smile lit up those lovely eyes of hers as he approached.

'There we are, one G&T for m'lady,' he said, placing it in front of her. 'May I?'

'Of course you can.' She laughed. 'Was there a problem with those lads?'

Taking the seat beside her, Nathan shook his head. 'Nothing worth talking about.' He raised his glass. 'Cheers.'

'Now,' she said, copying his gesture and then taking a sip from her drink. 'If you can't tell me about what you're doing at your base, I'm sure you won't be breaking the Official Secrets Act if you tell me about yourself.'

'All right,' he said, resting back and enjoying the view. 'What do you want to know?'

'Where's home?' she asked.

'The West Indies,' he replied. 'Barbados, in fact. What about you?'

'Waltham Abbey,' she replied. 'It's in Essex, not far from Epping Forest...'

Nathan allowed himself the pleasure of watching her mouth as she described her hometown and family. 'My mother didn't want me to join up but... well, I wanted to do my bit, like everyone else. Did you sign up at home?'

'Not exactly. I worked as solicitor's clerk for a couple of years, then got a grant to study here for the bar. I arrived in August '39 to train as a barrister but when I arrived war was looming, so I signed up with a dozen other Barbadians who had sailed over to do the same.'

'A barrister,' said Effie, looking suitably impressed.

'I was lucky enough to go to Harrison College, the most prestigious school on the island, and then a scholarship to Codrington College where I got my law degree,' he explained.

'Who sponsored you?'

'The West Indian Anglican Society,' he replied. 'Why do you ask?'

'Because my dad's on the Friends of Africa Mission Society and they provide grants like that, too.' She laughed. 'Wouldn't that be a coincidence?'

'It certainly would,' Nathan agreed, oddly lightened by the knowledge.

Effie's attention shifted past him.

Nathan turned to see the two young women she'd been sitting with earlier standing on the edge of the dancefloor with three keen-looking airmen hovering alongside.

Laughing, Effie shook her head and, raising her glass, pointed at it.

The two girls pulled faces and gestured for her to join them as the opening bars of a quickstep filled the hall.

Effie gave him a little smile and stood up. 'I'm sorry, I ought to—'

'Don't apologise.' He rose to his feet. 'Lovely to meet you again.'

'And you,' she replied. 'Thank you for the drink.'

'Thank you for the dance,' Nathan replied.

'Perhaps we'll run into each other again sometime,' she said.

'I hope so,' he replied fervently.

She gazed up at him with those lovely eyes of hers for a long moment, then she started towards the dancefloor.

Taking his beer, Nathan strolled back to the bar. Wiktor was deep in conversation with a fair-haired Red Cross nurse at the other end, and his Norwegian comrades were energetically bobbing about on the dancefloor with a couple of auxiliary fire-women, so Nathan tucked himself into the corner and looked across at the dancers. Well, not the dancers, but Effie.

CHAPTER 8

〆

'That's right,' bellowed Makepeace, his voice echoing around the vast aircraft hangar. 'A bit at a time or you might miss something, then where will you be if you're told to get your balloon up?'

Effie dutifully slid her hands along the rubberised seams of the half-inflated barrage balloon.

It was the middle of the morning on Monday at the start of their fourth week of training, and she, along with her no. 3 crew, all looking like car mechanics in their newly issued navy boiler suits, were inside one of the vast hangars on the southern edge of the airfield. The other two crews in Squad B were in the hangar next door learning the correct way to unpack and repack barrage balloons for transportation.

Effie's crew, now crawling around on hard concrete groping for holes and tears, would be having that pleasure after lunch.

'Anything?' asked Maeve, who was standing behind her.

'Not yet— hang on, I think I've found one,' said Effie as she felt some frayed fabric. 'Hand me a patch and get the pot.'

Keeping her fingers on the tear, Effie reached behind her, and Maeve handed her the glue brush.

'God but doesn't it stink to heavens,' she said as Effie dabbed the glutinous goo around the damaged fabric.

'Where's George?' asked Nell, who was groping around on the balloon's fins a few yards in front of her.

'Helping Alice on the other side of the of the balloon,' said Maeve.

'I thought Alice was paired up with Lily,' said Effie.

'Last time I saw Lily she was sneaking off to have a quick ciggy,' said Dolly, who was holding a glue pot for Nell.

'Well, I 'ope as how Makepeace catches her anyway – she's always skiving off,' Nell replied.

'Having another bloody mothers' meeting, are we?'

Makepeace was standing a few yards away from them, with his hands behind his back and his stomach testing the strength of the thread securing his tunic buttons.

Putting her hands in the small of her back to ease the ache, Effie straightened up.

'No, we were—'

'—just remarking on what a fine figure of a man you are, Corporal,' said George, giving their instructor her cool aristocratic smile. 'Weren't we, girls?'

Alice and Dolly nodded, Nelly tittered, and Maeve turned away suppressing a smile.

A flush appeared above their instructor's too-tight pale-blue collar.

'I think we've found all the damage,' said Effie, purposely not looking at her sniggering friends.

Makepeace waved them aside. 'Not bad,' he conceded, running his hands along a few of the seams until he got to the tail end. 'Now you, you, you and you' – he pointed at George, Alice, Maeve and Effie – 'inside. And you two' – he indicated Nell and Dolly with a nod – 'start at the nose and repair patches on the outside.' He gave them a patronising smile. 'Go on then, toddle off.'

Leaving Nell and Dolly, Effie and her three fellow WAFFs made their way to the vent halfway along the body of the balloon.

'If me and George get in first,' said Effie, 'then you two can pass the workbox and glue through to us.'

Crouching down, she grasped the edge of the vent, then threw it over her head and wriggled up the tube and into the dusky, grey world lit only by a couple of hurricane lamps on the floor the belly of the beast.

The smell of rubber filled her nose, bringing back memories of the black mask at the dentist. Reaching back through the tube, she took the equipment, and George clambered after it, followed by Dolly and Maeve.

The four of them got themself into some semblance of order and made their way to the nose of the balloon.

'We're ready for the first one,' George said, tapping on the taut shell.

'I didn't see much of you yesterday,' said Alice, handing a brush clogged with glue to George. 'So I haven't had a chance to ask you how it went on Saturday night.'

'It was grand, so it was,' said Maeve, 'Wasn't it, Nell?'

'It certainly was,' agreed Nell through the balloon wall.

'You'll have to come with us next time, Alice,' said Maeve encouragingly.

'Maybe,' said Alice.

'It was certainly a night to remember,' agreed George, moving on to the next rent in the fabric.

'The way you were knocking drinks back with those RAF officers at the bar, George, I'd be surprised you remembered anything about Saturday night,' said Nell from the other side of the balloon.

'I was just being sociable,' George replied, taking back the glue brush.

'Yes, you looked to be getting very sociable indeed with those airmen, George,' said Maeve, winking at Effie.

George raised a haughty eyebrow. 'And doing my bit for the war effort by keeping the chaps' spirits up.'

The girls laughed.

'I 'ope as how you're not mucking about in there,' barked Makepeace through the grey fabric wall.

'No, Corporal,' the girls chorused.

'Anyway,' said George in a loud whisper as they moved along again. 'What about you, Effie? Staring into the eyes of that handsome stranger.'

'What's this?' said Alice, looking at Effie.

'I had a dance and a drink with a flying officer from Tempsford air base, that's all,' said Effie, her heart doing an unexpected little double-step.

'Oh, but not any old flying officer, I'll have you know, Alice,' said Maeve. 'But some very tall, handsome flying officer who looked good enough to eat in that uniform.'

'Oh, yes,' said George, covering a long gouge with a length of fresh cladding.

'For goodness' sake, he wasn't the only chap I danced with,' Effie replied, trying to dispel the unsettling image of Nathan forming in her head.

'Be that as it may,' Maeve replied, giving Effie a knowing look, 'sure, no woman alive would be blaming you for spending the night gazing into his dark brown eyes.'

'Actually,' said Effie, taking the brush from her, 'his eyes are blue.'

'Wo-ho,' laughed George, as Nell wolf-whistled from the other side of the stretched canvas.

Thankful that the shadowy interior of the balloon hid her glowing cheeks, Effie turned and dabbed the glue around a hole, then passed it back to Maeve, who handed her a repair patch in return. Effie pressed it on, ran her hand over it a couple of times and, satisfied that it had stuck, stood up and turned round.

'Right, Nell,' she called, ignoring the barely concealed amusement on her friends' faces. 'Where's the next one?'

An hour later, her stomach rumbling, Effie stowed the balloon repair toolbox back on the shelf in the maintenance cupboard at the back of the hangar. She returned to the line of WAAFs standing at ease in front of Makepeace and their sergeant, Dunbar, and tucked herself in at the end of the second row alongside Alice.

'Well, the corporal here tells me most of you girls made a decent job of it,' Dunbar said. 'But you'd better get used to it as you'll have to do the same in all weathers when you get to your practice site in a few weeks.' Her close-set eyes ran along the ranks lined up before her. 'Attention!'

The WAAFs snapped upright.

'Left turn!'

Thirty pairs of wellington boots slid around on the concrete floor of the hangar.

'By the right. Quick march.'

Having suffered the usual catcalls and wolf-whistles from the male aircraft crew as they passed, Effie and the rest of the crew headed across the balloon practice area towards the WAAFs' mess.

Dunbar brought them to a halt and got them back into four lines again. 'Right,' she said. 'I want to see you back on the parade ground at thirteen hundred hours, sharp. Dismissed.'

The women turned to the left again, then broke ranks. Nell and Maeve wandered over to join Effie.

'Where's she off to?' asked Nell, nodding towards George, who was striding off down the pathway.

'She said she was going to phone her mother,' Alice replied. 'Come on, girls, we've only got an hour.'

There was already a sizeable queue lined up in front of the refectory's serving hatch by the time Effie and her friends arrived.

'I wish to heaven they'd get a bit of a move on up there,' said Maeve, stretching her neck to see the front of the line. 'Me belly's so empty I could eat a horse, so I could.'

'Funny you should say that,' said Nell, her face a picture of innocence. 'Cos I the way I 'eard it one of the nags from next door's farm has gone missing.'

Horror spread across Maeve's face for an instant, then she shoved Nell.

'Here she comes,' said Alice as George strode across.

'How's your mum?' asked Effie, as she joined them.

'My moth—' George looked puzzled for a second, then the penny dropped. 'Oh, she wasn't in. The post was, so I picked ours up on the way.'

She handed one letter apiece to Nell and Alice, and a postcard with a green stamp depicting Ireland to Maeve.

'And these are for you,' she said, handing two letter to Effie. 'One, strangely, from an animal feed company.'

Taking them, Effie laughed. 'That's from Leonard. He's using up the old company stationery.'

'Leonard?' asked Alice.

'Her fiancé,' Nell explained, as the queue shuffled forward.

George raised an eyebrow. 'And what colour eyes does he have, I wonder?'

Effie gazed down at the scribbled handwriting on the front of the envelope and was surprised to find that she couldn't actually remember.

CHAPTER 9

With the low buzz of the Lysander's propellers in his ears, Nathan checked the altitude and speed. Satisfied both were as they should be, he switched on the mute light concealed beneath the plane's fuselage and pulled out the map from the top of his right boot.

A hand grasped his shoulder from behind.

'How we doing?' Frobisher shouted through the leather of Nathan's leather flying helmet.

Keeping his eyes on the horizon and his right hand on the joystick, Nathan gave him the thumbs-up with his left.

It was somewhere close to two o'clock on Thursday morning and, according to the map and Nathan's calculations, he was skirting past Abbeville in northern France and twenty or so miles from the village of Elevage D'ilac in Picardy.

Behind him in the two passenger seats were Frobisher and a sandy-haired, heavily built individual referred to by both Rawlings and Frobisher only as Jacques. Frobisher and the SOE officer they were delivering behind enemy lines wore rough working clothes, while Nathan was dressed in his uniform. However, tucked under his seat in case he was forced to land was an emergency haversack containing civilian clothing with its tags removed, along with a stack of French franc notes, a map printed on a silk scarf, a fishing hook and line, and food tablets. These items, along with his compass, revolver, fighting knife and photos of himself for forged identity papers, were all he had to aid him in evading capture, should he be forced to land. Hopefully, they would never be needed.

After three days of waiting for favourable conditions and the precise location of where they were heading, they had got the word to go at 2300 hours and Nathan had lifted the aircraft's wheels off the runway twenty minutes later. He had turned westwards after crossing the Thames, glistening in the moonlight, then turned his plane towards Hastings, thus avoiding the Luftwaffe's favourite flight path into London. With the white cliffs of England's south coast behind him, he flew over the English Channel towards occupied France.

That had been three and a half hours ago. There had been some clouds dotted about when he'd taken off but now over France it was a clear winter sky. Above him, stars twinkled in the silence and the waxing moon bathed the fields and villages below in a silvery glow. Looking down on the silent countryside of France from 500 feet, you wouldn't have known a war raged below.

Peering down through the perspex hood of the cockpit, Nathan checked a couple of landmarks below, then raised his left hand.

'Ten minutes,' he hollered over the sound of the engine.

Frobisher tapped him twice on the shoulder in acknowledgement.

Nathan adjusted the flaps, took the plane down to 400 feet and, with his eyes searching the field, continued towards his destination. Then he spotted it.

Out of the gloom a light flashed the signal he was looking for: *dot dot dash dot*. 'F' in Morse code.

Using the switch fixed on the dashboard, Nathan signalled the same back. In the gloom, three lights set out in an inverted L-shape flickered on. Adjusting the flaps and trimming the rudder, he brought the Lysander in line with the two lights.

The plane bumped a little as the wheels made contact with the earth, but then almost immediately Nathan taxied round to line his nose up with the single light at the other end of the field.

With the engine idling, Nathan gave Frobisher the thumbs-up again.

Frobisher shoved the rear hatch back and the stuffy smell of the cockpit was replaced by the icy chill of the frigid air.

As the SOE operative and Jacques clambered down from the plane, Nathan released his oxygen mask. He drew a deep breath, memories of the dance the Saturday before flooding back into his mind. He now knew that Effie was stationed less than ten miles away from him, but he'd travelled halfway round the world to do his duty to king and country, so romance – unlikely anyway, given her current engagement – would have to take second place. At least, that was what he'd repeatedly told himself every time his imagination conjured up images of her.

There was a thump on the fuselage.

Nathan looked round, expecting to see Frobisher climbing back up the ladder, but instead the lieutenant was standing on the ground below him.

'I'll be back in a jiffy,' he called up, then sprinted off into the shadow of the trees.

Nathan looked at his watch and then raised his gaze eastwards. The horizon was still deepest black, but in a few hours the first pink and blue streaks of the coming day would be lightening the sky. It would be tight, but Nathan had plotted a course home that, cruising at 500 feet and doing a steady 150 to 200 miles an hour, would have them back across the English Channel and within British coastal air defence before sunrise. However, that was on the basis that he would only be on the ground for five minutes at most, not that he'd be sitting in a field in occupied France for goodness knows how long while Frobisher went off on a frolic in the woods.

Feeling his temper rise, Nathan forced his shoulders to relax and rechecked his dials, then glanced at his watch again. Five past six!

For pity's sake!

A movement in the bushes caught his eye. Reaching forward, he took the revolver strapped beside his control panel from its holster.

With the blood pumping through his ears almost deafening him, Nathan flipped off the safety catch and waited.

Out from the foliage sprinted Frobisher, thankfully not with half a dozen Germans following him. He took something from beneath his jacket, threw it into the back of the plane, then scrambled up the ladder.

Nathan turned in his seat. 'What the hell was that?'

Frobisher smiled, his teeth white in the fading moonlight. 'Cheese.' He patted Nathan on the shoulder. 'Come on, old chum. Chocks away.'

Nathan glared at the grinning lieutenant, then, turning round, pressed his foot on the pedal and then pulled back on the throttle. The plane's wheels lifted. Nathan skimmed the tops of the trees, banked the aircraft northward and, with blind fury choking him, headed for home.

The next morning, after only four hours' sleep, Nathan all but yanked the door to the main command building off its hinges and marched in, his lips pressed tightly together.

The dark-haired WAAF pounding on the typewriter looked up.

'Officer Fitzgerald,' she said, as he barrelled across the reception. 'The chief is in the—'

Without breaking his stride, Nathan marched straight past her. He reached the solid door at the end of the corridor a few moments later.

He knocked, but burst in without waiting for a reply.

Donaldson, with his counterpart Major Rawlings, was already bending over the table poring over the map spread before them, but both men straightened up when Nathan strode in. He stood to attention and saluted, which the two senior officers returned.

'Spot on time as usual,' said Donaldson. 'Get yourself a coffee and join us.'

Nathan removed his cap and hooked it on the coat stand by the door, then crossed to the grey metal cabinet where a tray with cups and a coffee pot was sitting.

Only too aware of his lack of sleep, he poured himself a strong black coffee and added three sugars. Returning to the table, he sat down on the same side as his commanding officer.

Donaldson looked at his watch.

'You did tell Frobisher eleven hundred hours, didn't you, Major?' said the group captain, regarding his army counterpart from beneath his abundant eyebrows.

Rawlings's eyes narrowed, but he didn't reply.

As the second hand on the clock above the operational blackboard on the far wall ticked its way round the dial, Nathan relaxed back in the chair and took a sip of coffee.

With nothing requiring his attention, his thoughts started to wander back to Effie Weston. However, alongside conjuring up her beautiful face and alluring form, his mind returned to the seemingly insurmountable problems of meeting her again.

A knock on the door and his senior officer's gruff response brought Nathan's attention back to the present. The handle rattled, then Frobisher strode in.

Thanks to his orderly in his accommodation, the creases in

his dress uniform were sharp, but that couldn't be said about his eyes, which had dark shadows around them.

Nathan raised an eyebrow but didn't comment.

'Perhaps we can make a start,' said Donaldson, as Frobisher made his way across to the refreshments. 'Your report, Fitzgerald.'

'Other than spotting the usual RAF coastal patrols I encountered no problem getting across the Channel,' said Nathan as Frobisher, cup in hand, seated himself opposite him. 'And once I did so it was more or less plain sailing, or, should I say, flying, across Picardy to the touchdown coordinates, where I landed without incident.'

'Why, then, were you back an hour later than you were supposed to be?' asked Donaldson.

'Perhaps, sir, you should ask Lieutenant Frobisher,' said Nathan, looking pointedly at the army officer lighting a cigarette on the other side of the table.

Blowing a ring of smoke skywards, Frobisher shrugged. 'You're the bloody pilot,' said Frobisher.

Donaldson looked at Nathan.

'After our package had been safely delivered, instead of getting back into the plane Lieutenant Frobisher decided to go for a little frolic in the woods for almost twenty minutes,' said Nathan.

Frobisher snorted. 'I was gone no more than ten.'

'Gone where exactly?' asked Nathan. 'You never did say.'

'It's top secret, I'm afraid, old boy,' Rawlings answered.

'And was the cheese top secret, too?' Nathan replied, glaring at Frobisher.

'Cheese! What bally cheese?' yelled Donaldson.

'Maroilles – a local speciality, I understand, sir,' said Nathan, without taking his eyes off the man opposite.

'Just a little present from our grateful allies,' Frobisher explained.

Nathan's senior officer turned his attention to his army counterpart.

'Lieutenant Frobisher had orders to meet a contact,' Rawlings explained.

'And you didn't think to mention it at the mission briefing,' said Donaldson.

'The information came through very last-minute,' Rawlings replied. 'The contact should have been waiting at the designated spot when you landed but he was—'

'Running late?' suggested Nathan.

The major gave him a sharp glance but let his insubordination go.

'Look here,' said Frobisher, tapping his cigarette against the already full ashtray on the table. 'I don't know what all the damn fuss is about. The packet was dropped off as planned. I was gone longer than I anticipated meeting the contact, that's all.'

'And what if a German trooper had spotted you?' asked Nathan.

'Well, he would have ended up in a ditch with my bullet in his brain, of course,' Frobisher replied.

'In case you've forgotten, Flying Officer Fitzgerald,' snapped Rawlings, 'the Germans are the enemy and this operation has taken months of planning at the highest, and I mean the *highest*, level.'

'I can almost smell Churchill's cigars,' chipped in Frobisher.

'The SOE operatives you will be dropping behind enemy lines in this operation have been training for months,' continued Rawlings. 'They know the protocols and safeguards inside out, whereas you, Flying Officer Fitzgerald, as Lieutenant Frobisher has already pointed out, are just the bloody pilot.'

'On top of which,' drawled Frobisher with a sneer, 'if you haven't got the nerve for the job then I'm sure we can find a British-born pilot who has.'

Struggling to keep a grip on the fury rising in his chest, Nathan let a slow smile spread across his face.

'You're right,' he said. 'I'm only the bloody pilot, but let me spell out for you how stupid and reckless Lieutenant Frobisher's actions were last night. Firstly, if you had left a dead German lying in a ditch then every village within a five-mile radius would have been overrun with stormtroopers. The SS would no doubt have rounded up a dozen or so inhabitants and shot them as reprisal. Hardly something that would endear us to the very people we are supposed to be helping. Secondly, when the Germans found that it was a British bullet in their countryman's head it would have put them on alert, thereby endangering both the operative and anyone helping him.'

'Have you finished?' asked Rawlings, an unhealthy mauve hue creeping up his jowls.

'Not quite,' Nathan replied. 'In addition, with every German patrol in the area on high alert you would have lost the use of a perfectly good landing site. Lastly, I was wearing my uniform last night, so had we been captured I would have been deemed to be a legitimate combatant and therefore protected by the Hague Convention 1907, viz Laws and Customs of War, and the 1929 Geneva Convention. Lieutenant Frobisher on the other hand was dressed as a civilian and would have been treated as a spy. I imagine the Gestapo would be cracking open their looted champagne if they'd discovered they had captured not only an English spy but a member of the British Secret Service to boot.' As he looked Frobisher squarely in the eye, a cynical smile lifted the corner of Nathan's mouth. 'And as to nerve, Lieutenant Frobisher, I hope yours holds when they start shoving hot skewers under your fingernails.'

Red-faced, his eyes burning with rage, Frobisher leapt up, knocking his chair backwards to the floor. Regarding his fellow officer's look of burning rage coolly, Nathan swallowed the last mouthful of his coffee.

'Thank you, Flying Officer Fitzgerald,' said Donaldson, his voice slicing through the palpable tension. 'Is there anything further?'

Nathan shifted his attention to his senior officer. 'No, sir.'

'Major Rawlings?'

The army officer gave a sharp shake of his head.

'Well, in that case, Fitzgerald, dismissed.'

Nathan rose to his feet and saluted, then, retrieving his hat from the peg as he passed, marched out of the room, feeling Frobisher's angry blue eyes burning into the space between his shoulder blades all the way.

'How's she looking?' Nathan asked, looking up at O'Rourke in the plane's cockpit.

'You were right,' the RAF mechanic called back. 'The left flap was a bit sticky so I've dabbed plenty of grease on it. You shouldn't have no trouble with it now.'

'Thanks,' said Nathan. 'It wasn't much, but I'd rather not have to struggle to get both wheels down at the same time in a high wind.'

He was standing in the hangar next to the Lysander, half an hour after leaving the debrief in Donaldson's office.

'Ah there you are, Nathan,' said Wiktor, strolling over.

'Morning, Wiktor,' Nathan replied as O'Rourke clambered out of the plane and toddled off to his next task.

'I missed you at breakfast,' said his friend.

'I got back later than planned,' Nathan explained. 'So I decided to skip breakfast in favour of another hour in bed.'

'A very sensible decision,' his friend replied. 'The bacon this morning could have soled shoes. However, I am surprised to see you inspecting your plane – your name isn't on the duty board for tonight.'

'It isn't,' Nathan replied. 'But like a good Boy Scout, I like to be prepared.'

Wiktor gave a short laugh. 'And was your missed breakfast also why you were marching so purposefully around the runway earlier, to build up an appetite?'

Laughing, Nathan shook his head. 'I'm already starving but I just needed a bit of fresh air to clear my head.'

His friend gave him a sympathetic look. 'I take it the debrief of last night's mission didn't go well?'

'It went very well as far as *I* was concerned,' Nathan replied.

'Hey you!'

Nathan looked round.

'Of course, others might not agree,' he added wryly, as Lieutenant Frobisher stomped across the hangar towards them.

'What the bloody hell do you think you were playing at in the briefing room, Fitzgerald?' he barked as he reached them.

'I was asked to give my report on last night's mission, which is exactly what I did,' Nathan replied, smiling coolly at him. 'And it's Flying Officer Fitzgerald.'

'Don't give me that,' Frobisher spat out, a faint whiff of whisky accompanying his words. 'You were just trying to make me look bad in front of the old man.'

Nathan gave a hard laugh. 'You don't need me for that – you managed pretty well all by yourself.'

'Now then, gentlemen, please,' said Wiktor. 'We are supposed to be fighting the enemy, not each other. We're all on the same side. No?'

Ignoring the Polish officer, Frobisher took a step forward.

'Now you listen to me, you jumped-up bloody bastard,' he said, jabbing his finger at Nathan. 'The prime minister himself has given us full authority to carry out our mission as we deem necessary.'

'And my job is to get you there and back again in one piece.

And in case you didn't know, like the captain of a ship, in the air I'm the one who calls the shots.' Nathan's eyes bored into Frobisher's. 'And if you don't get that finger out of my face, I'll break it.'

The lieutenant stood stock-still for a second or two and then let his hand drop.

'That gung-ho stunt you pulled last night was both foolhardy and dangerous,' continued Nathan, holding the other man's belligerent gaze. 'Not only did it jeopardise us but the ordinary people on the ground who are risking everything to liberate their country. If you're looking for Germans to shoot, I suggest you get yourself transferred to Tobruk. Now, if you've nothing else to say, I'd like to continue my conversation with Lieutenant Ostowicz.'

Frobisher's eyes flickered from Nathan to Wiktor and then he pulled the front of his jacket down sharply. He turned and stormed past the handful of mechanics who were pretending not to have heard the fracas by busying themselves around the planes.

'I don't think Lieutenant Frobisher will be sending you a Christmas card this year,' Wiktor remarked as the SOE officer disappeared out of the doorway.

Nathan laughed. 'Nor I him.'

'What are you going to do about him?'

'Nothing much I can do,' Nathan replied. 'Donaldson and Major Rawlings know what happened last night, so he's their problem. Thankfully, most of the time my only passengers will be the SOE operatives, so I won't have to suffer his company in the air too often. Anyway, were you after me for something?'

'I was indeed,' Wiktor replied. 'I've heard that there is a concert of Vivaldi's sublime *Requiem* in the main church in Bedford on Saturday afternoon. Myself and couple of the others from the crew are going, so I wondered, if you are around, would you like to accompany us? Perhaps we could treat ourselves to a civilised tea in one of the hotels.'

If he wanted to take up that place in Lincoln's Inn after the war was over, he ought to catch up on some reading, plus there were still the unanswered letters from his mother and sister and truthfully, calypsos and soulful voices were more his cup of tea than a classical recital, but perhaps it would do him good to get off the base for a while. Nathan smiled. 'Ozzie, I'd love to.'

CHAPTER 10

Jumping off the bus as it drew to a halt outside Bedford's Midland Road station, Effie glanced at her watch.

'Don't fret yourself, Effie,' said Nell, as she leapt down behind her.

'Nell's right,' agreed Maeve, joining them on the pavement. 'He'll be so dazzled by the very sight of you all else will flee his brain.'

It was Saturday at the end of Effie's sixth week at Cardington – Valentine's day, in fact. After she and her friends wolfed down a plate of liver, onions and lumpy potato they'd scooted across the site only to emerge from number 1 gate onto London Road as the 130 bus disappeared down the road, leaving a cloud of black smoke in its wake. After they'd cooled their heels for twenty minutes at the bus stop the next bus had arrived, packed to the gunnels with locals heading into town for an afternoon's stroll along the embankment or a matinee performance at the Picturedrome or the Plaza.

However, that was three-quarters of an hour ago and now Leonard's face loomed in Effie's mind. His train had arrived a full twenty-five minutes earlier.

She forced a smile.

'Where are you taking him?' asked Nell.

'The Swan,' Effie replied.

Her two friends looked impressed.

'Very swanky,' said Nell. 'We're off to the WVS canteen before queuing up at the Plaza for the matinee. They've got an orchestra from one of the local schools playing. It's in aid of the children evacuated from London and the town's Spitfire fund.'

'Plus, they always do a grand selection of cake,' added Maeve.

'Well, you enjoy stuffing your faces while I take more refined refreshments,' said Effie with a laugh. 'And I'll see you back at base this evening.'

'You have fun with Leonard, too,' Maeve called over her shoulder as the two friends headed off.

'But not so much that you find yourself up-the-you-know-what!' Nell winked.

'Cheeky,' Effie called after them.

The two WAAFs linked arms and joined the crowds heading into the town centre.

Smiling, Effie watched them go, then she glanced at her watch again. Twenty past! Blast.

Adjusting her cap so it sat squarely on her head, she side-stepped a mother pushing a grizzling toddler in a pushchair in front of the town hall and hurried into the railway station's ticket hall.

As usual the concourse was packed with people, mainly ARP personnel or, unsurprisingly with at least four RAF bases within ten miles of where she was standing, men and women dressed in the same uniform as herself, plus a sprinkling of farmers and locals.

Scanning the throng milling around in the concourse, Effie spotted Leonard sitting on one of the benches next to the ticket office. Adjusting her handbag on her shoulder, she made her way over to him. He spotted her and, glancing at his watch, rose to his feet.

'Ah there you are, darling,' he said, giving a light laugh as she halted in front of him. 'I was beginning to think you'd stood me up.'

'Sorry, Leonard,' she replied, catching her breath.

'Well, you're here now.' Bending forward, her gave her a kiss on the cheek. 'And these are for you.'

He handed her a quarter-pound box of Dairy Milk.

'Thanks,' she said, squeezing it in her handbag. 'And for the card. It arrived yesterday.'

'I'm pleased to hear it,' he replied. 'Shall we go?'

Effie took his arm, and they headed for the exit.

'I know how you hate waiting, so I'm sorry I was late,' she repeated as they strolled out into the pale winter sunlight. 'We had planned to catch the one thirty bus but we missed it.'

'We?'

'Me, Maeve and Nell,' she replied. 'I told you about them.'

'Of course,' he said, smiling benignly.

'They're in the same balloon crew as I am, along with Alice, Dolly and...' Effie named the rest of the WAAFs she was working alongside as they headed past the shops and businesses of Midland Road. 'And of course there's George.'

'George?' asked Leonard, as they stopped to let an ARP lorry go past. 'I thought you said your crew was all women.'

Effie laughed. 'We are. George is Georgina. Georgina Hermione Matilda St John-Smythe. She's very upper-class and her family own half of some county or another, but she's a great laugh. She's off for a jaunt in the country with an officer friend of her brother's.'

Leonard frowned slightly. 'She sounds a bit flighty.'

Irritation niggled in Effie's chest. 'She's not. In fact, she's a very good sort and pitches in with everything. Also, although she hasn't said as much, I get the impression she's recently been let down badly by some man.'

Leonard's smile returned. 'Well, that's something you'll never have to worry about, will you, my dear?' He patted her hand. 'Although I must say it's a pity you haven't got a chap in charge of your balloon team, group, company or whatever it's called to make sure you girls don't get yourself in tangled in the ropes. Still, I've come all this way to see my lovely fiancée' – he patted her hand again – 'so why don't we forget all about balloons for a while and enjoy a nice afternoon together.'

'Well, everyone in the business is up in arms,' said Leonard, taking the last sardine sandwich from the plate in the middle of the table. 'Given that Hudson has a commercial background, you'd think he'd realise that fixing feed prices would cripple the industry.'

As she had done since the waitress arrived with a tray load of sandwiches, cakes and bone china crockery half an hour ago, Effie maintained her attentive expression. It wasn't easy – there was only so much talk of oats and rye a girl could take.

It was now close to four in the afternoon, and they were sitting in the Swan Hotel's restaurant. Around them were a couple of dozen well-heeled citizens of the town also enjoying afternoon tea.

The hotel had once been the town's main coaching inn, and sat on the north side of the River Ouse at the bottom of the high street. Their fellow afternoon-tea-drinkers reflected the lack of armed forces vehicles in the car park as; apart from Effie and a couple of army and RAF top brass, everyone else in the room was dressed in civvies. What with the sea of best suits, smart dresses, extravagant hats, fur stoles and the string quartet on the small stage playing a selection of classical pieces in the background, it was easy to forget the country was in a fight for its very survival. That was until you noticed the gummed paper criss-crossing the tall Georgian windows, stirrup pumps in each corner and the gas masks tucked beneath customers' chairs.

'Instead,' continued Leonard, 'he's acting like Attlee, Morrison or that rampant socialist Cripps.'

He bit a chunk off the corner of his sandwich.

'Well, I suppose we all have to make sacrifices,' said Effie, raising her cup to her lips.

'So they keep telling us,' Leonard replied through his mouthful. 'If you ask me, I'd say it's a blooming excuse to slide communism into this country through the back door. "A fair day's wage for a fair day's work." My eye! I'll pay my men a fair day's wage when they decide to put their backs into a fair day's work.'

Effie stifled a yawn. 'How's your mum?' she asked, hoping to move on before Leonard got fully onto his favourite political hobby horse.

'Busy as ever,' he replied. 'The rector's wife had to go and care for her sister and new baby, so Mother's taken over running the WVS relief centre.' He gave a dry laugh. 'I'm not sure the good ladies in green appreciate having a new broom quite like my mother. You know what she's like.'

Effie did, and pitied the gentle ladies of Waltham Abbey's WVS.

Leonard polished off his last mouthful of sandwich and swallowed what remained off his tea.

'Any more in the pot?' he asked, wiping his mouth with his napkin.

Effie lifted the silver-plated Mock-Regency teapot and shook her head.

Raising his hand, Leonard clicked his fingers. 'Waitress!'

A young girl, no more than a child really, wearing a black dress two sizes too big, a white apron that could have gone round her twice and a frilly cap, hurried over.

'Another round of tea,' Leonard told her, circling his finger over their used crockery. 'And another plate of sandwiches.'

'Please,' added Effie, giving the youngster an encouraging smile.

The waitress bobbed a curtsy and darted back to the kitchen.

'Well, if you'd excuse me, my dear,' Leonard said, placing his crumpled napkin on the table beside his empty plate, 'while we're waiting, I'm off to the little boys' room.'

He rose to his feet, turned and walked across to the door leading to the hotel's lobby.

The lead violinist played the opening bars of a Viennese waltz. A handful of couples took to the dancefloor. Effie watched them for a minute, then took a sip of tea and turned and looked between the strips of gummed tape at the people strolling along the embankment in the sun.

'Well, hello, again, Corporal Weston.'

Effie looked up into the blue eyes and handsome face of Flying Officer Fitzgerald, a face she had to admit had been drifting into her mind quite a bit since their encounter at the Corn Exchange dance three weeks ago.

'Flying Officer Fitzgerald,' she said, hoping only she could hear the quiver in her voice. 'What are you doing here?'

∼

As he walked through the door behind Wiktor and spotted Effie sitting gazing out of the window, Nathan had to suppress the urge to shout hurrah and do a samba round the dancefloor.

All the way into town in the back of the supply truck he and Wiktor had cadged a lift in, he'd repeatedly told himself that it was impossible that he would run into Effie. After all, the county town was crowded with service personnel, refugees who had fled London to escape the bombing, hundreds of evacuees, and farmers and factory workers from miles around in town for the Saturday market. However, logic and mathematic probability couldn't stop his heart from harbouring a little flicker of hope. And now here she was.

Ignoring his pounding pulse, Nathan fashioned his features into a casual expression and answered her question.

'The same as you, by the look of it,' he replied, indicating the cups, saucers and empty plates on the table.

'By yourself?' she asked.

'With a friend.'

An expression he couldn't quite interpret flashed across her face, then she gave him a bright smile. 'One of the WAAFs from your base?'

Nathan gave her a crooked smile.

'No. Ozzie,' he said, trying not to read too much into her words. 'Or Lieutenant Ostowicz, of the Polish air force.'

He glanced across to Wiktor, who had bagged them a table next to the French doors.

'You?' he asked.

'My fiancé,' said Effie. 'He's just popped out.'

Hiding his disappointment, Nathan widened his smile. 'How is it going with the balloons?'

Effie puffed out her cheeks and blew. 'Exhausting. But I think I'm getting the hang of it. Although my fingers are raw from the wire-splicing class yesterday.'

She turned her small hands over and held them out.

He took one, enjoying the feel of her small hand in his large one. He studied her palms for a moment, then his attention returned to her face.

'That does look sore,' he said, his thumb gently rubbing her fingertips.

As her lovely hazel eyes locked with his, Nathan had the urge to sweep her up into his arms and press his lips against hers.

The string quartet behind them struck up a foxtrot and couples took to the floor again.

'Would you like to dance?' he asked, willing her to say she would so he could take her into his arms again.

For a second he had the impression that she was about to say yes, but then her gaze flickered past him.

'There you are, Leonard,' she said, a dazzling smile lighting her lovely face.

Nathan turned and looked at Effie's fiancé.

Wearing an expensive suit, starched collared shirt with a club tie at his throat, Leonard looked very much the pompous individual that Nathan remembered from the first time they had met.

'You remember Flying Officer Fitzgerald, don't you?' Effie said as the two men eyed each other up.

'I can't say I do,' Leonard replied stiffly.

'Of course you do.' Effie laughed. 'He kindly came to my rescue on St Pancras station.'

'Oh, yes, I do now you mention it, my dear,' Leonard conceded.

'Well, I do stand out in a crowd,' Nathan said, answering the other man's hostile look with an artless smile.

He offered his hand and after a moment's hesitation Leonard took it. Unlike his own, rough from handling engine parts and armaments, Effie's fiancé's hand was soft and smooth. They shook once, then Leonard let go. A brittle smile lifted the corner of his lips.

'Well, nice to meet you again,' he said in a tone that indicated otherwise. 'But don't let us keep you.'

Raising an eyebrow, Nathan his attention shifted back to Effie.

'Lovely to meet you again, Corporal Weston, and I hope to see you again some time.' Looking into her eyes, Nathan let a warm smile spread across his face. 'Perhaps for another turn round the dancefloor.'

Without looking at the man seething beside her, he turned and, hands in pockets, sauntered across the room to Wiktor, who was sitting with a pile of sandwiches, cake and china on the table in front of him.

'Was that the WAAF from the dance a few weeks back you were just oozing all over?' his friend asked as Nathan settled himself in the chair opposite.

'Yes, it was,' Nathan replied, his eyes still on Effie. 'Lovely, isn't she?'

'Very,' Wiktor agreed, pouring their drinks. 'Who was the klutz with her?'

'Her fiancé,' Nathan replied. 'But don't worry, my friend, she's not going to marry him.'

Wiktor's reddish eyebrows shot up. 'Is she not?'

'No,' said Nathan. 'Because she's marrying me.'

∽

Taking a sip of her tea, Effie studied Leonard as he sliced into a rather dark-looking slab with his pastry fork.

'That ginger cake looks tasty,' she said.

He grunted but didn't look up.

She studied her fiancé's downturned mouth, then put her cup back in the saucer. 'Are you going to sulk all afternoon?'

'I'm not sulking, Euphemia. I'm furious.' Raising his head, he glared at her across the table.

There was no point asking why because Effie already knew.

The words 'I'd love to' had hovered on her lips in response to Nathan's suggestion of a dance, but thankfully she'd caught a glimpse of Leonard outside the restaurant entrance. She only just managed to snatch her hand back before he strode across the restaurant towards them.

'I leave you for a couple of minutes,' he continued, 'and come back to find you flirting with some bloody stranger.'

'Leonard!'

'I'm sorry about my language,' he replied. 'But honestly, it's enough to make a saint swear.'

Effie matched his unyielding gaze. 'Well, firstly, you weren't gone "a couple of minutes" but almost ten.'

'There were two chaps in the lobby with Farmers' Union lapel badges moaning about the prices their local grain supplier was offering, so I introduced myself and gave them my card,' he explained.

'Be that as it may,' continued Effie. 'Secondly, and more importantly, I was talking, not flirting, and Flying Officer Fitzgerald isn't "some stranger", but, as is self-evident by his officer's uniform and the insignia on it, an officer in the RAF. And if you remember, he saved me from having my suitcase stolen on St Pancras station.'

Leonard's expression shifted from peeved to sullen. 'What about "another turn round the dancefloor" then?'

Memories of the dance at the Corn Exchange flooded back into Effie's mind.

'There was a dance in the town a few weeks ago,' she explained, trying to keep the memory of Nathan's hand cradling hers and his arm round her waist at bay. 'So me and my friends went.'

'And you danced with—'

'Flying Officer Fitzgerald,' Effie cut in. 'Yes, I did, and several other service and ARP chaps, in the same way as you dance with women at the Conservative Club dinners and those tedious council dances.'

'That's different.'

'I don't see how,' Effie retorted. 'And it's called being sociable and the reason it's called a "social dance", Leonard – because people dance with each other.'

'Yes, but not with...' He shot a glance across the room. 'What do you think people will say about you dancing with a... you know...'

Anger flared in Effie's chest and her mouth pulled into a hard line.

'I'm only thinking of your reputation, sweetheart. That's all,' he added.

Effie regarded him with a glacial look, then her eyes flickered to his cup.

'Don't let your tea get cold, Leonard.'

He opened his mouth to speak but then wisely thought better of it and clamped it shut.

Spearing the last bit of cake on his plate with his fork, he opened his mouth and shoved it in.

Effie watched him munch away at the piece of ginger cake, his eyes fixed on the crumbs on his empty plate, for a moment, then, reminding herself that he had travelled half a day to see her and that he was the man she'd agreed to marry in less than a year, she picked up the teapot.

'Would you like another?' she asked, holding it aloft.

He glanced up. 'Yes, please.'

'Look,' said Effie after another few seconds passed. 'If you're going to sit there brooding all afternoon, I suggest you catch an early train home so I can go and join my friends at the cinema.'

He didn't reply but reached across and took her hand. 'It wasn't my intention to upset you, Effie.'

'Well, you have,' she replied. 'I've had an utterly exhausting few weeks, and I was looking forward to a nice afternoon in the best hotel in the town instead of a stewed mug of tea in the NAAFI. Instead of which, you've—'

'I'm sorry, darling.' He contorted his features into that scolded puppy-dog face of his.

Effie remained stony-faced for a moment, then her shoulders relaxed and she smiled.

'That's my lovely Effie,' he said, as the quartet played the opening bars of 'I'll Be with You in Apple Blossom Time' Leonard gulped down the last mouthful of his tea and put the cup down. 'Now we're friends again, my darling, what say *we* have a little turn round the dancefloor?'

Standing up, he held out his hand.

Effie rose to her feet and took it.

Leonard led her out onto the dancefloor and turned her towards him but as they stepped off Effie realised three things. Firstly, that her fiancé wasn't as tall or broad as Nathan, secondly that his shoulder muscles under her fingertips weren't as firm, and lastly that she had to guiltily admit that she would have preferred to be gliding around the floor in the arms of the man sitting near the French doors wearing an RAF uniform, watching her with his very blue eyes.

CHAPTER 11

Banking slightly to the right and with the moonlit beaches below him, Nathan tracked along the coast of France for ten minutes, then, easing his joystick forward, guided the nose of the Lysander into the wispy cloud cover on the marshes below.

He checked the map in the clear pocket on his thigh and half turned in his seat.

'ETA ten minutes,' he called over the noise of the engine.

His passenger gave him the usual two taps on the shoulder by way of acknowledgement.

It was a little after three in the morning on the last Wednesday in February and he was flying 2,000 feet above Nazi-occupied northern France. It had been over a month and a half since Nathan had arrived at Tempsford.

This was Nathan's third nocturnal excursion into France, but his first time carrying a young woman. She was French and had been referred to only as Simone. She was about the same age and height as Effie but with corn-coloured hair instead of Effie's rich chestnut brown. She, like all the other operatives he had ferried across the Channel, had been training for months with the SOE in Gibraltar Farm Barn on the perimeter of the airfield. Like them, she carried a small brown suitcase that had a shortwave radio concealed beneath a false bottom, covered by her more everyday belongings.

Usually, apart from the operative he'd been tasked to deposit safely on French soil, he'd carried no other passengers. Unfortunately, tonight he did – along with the young woman he also had Lieutenant Frobisher, SOE's arrogant head of operations.

Of course, for security reasons the pilots assigned to the missions were never included in the SOE's pre-mission briefing, which made perfect sense as then if you were captured you couldn't tell what you didn't know, even under torture. However, from the odd word Rawlings let slip and Donaldson excessive moustache-twitching at the operational meetings, it was clear that SOE operations didn't always run smoothly. Which was another reason why, after Frobisher's stupid cheese stunt, Nathan was less than thrilled to have him sitting behind him.

Nathan checked his map again and, satisfied that they would soon be a few miles from their landing site, moved the joystick forward once more and flew below the clouds.

'Can you see them yet?' Frobisher shouted from behind his left shoulder.

In the intense blackness of the arable landscape, Nathan trained his eyes on the horizon and then checked his bearing.

'Yes,' he bellowed, pointing into the far distance. 'Over there.'

Banking right, he adjusted the angle of the plane, then headed for the field on the other side of a country lane. As usual a light at the far end flickered on and off briefly, but Nathan frowned. 'The signal's wrong.'

Frobisher shifted forward and peered over Nathan's shoulder. 'What do you mean?'

'They've signalled four dots for H,' Nathan yelled back.

'Are you sure?'

'Of course I am,' he yelled.

'Signal back.'

'What and show them their mistake?' Nathan replied. 'Not—'

The light from the hedgerow flickered again, this time sending three dots and a dash for V, the mission's correct code.

'Satisfied?' Frobisher bawled in Nathan's ear.

'Not really,' Nathan replied. 'I still think we should abort.'

'Don't be a bloody coward. Signal them back and then get this plane down,' Frobisher screamed.

Pressing his lips together, Nathan flicked the light in his cockpit to return the signal, and the three lamps ignited in the field in front of him.

He circled round once, then, lining up the plane's nose between the two furthest flickering lights, pushed the joystick forward again. Within a few minutes the Lysander's wheels were bumping over the rough ground of the makeshift airstrip.

Leaping up, Frobisher flipped the lid off, letting a rush of warm night air into the stuffy cockpit. He and Simone scrambled out.

'I'll be taking off in five, so don't go shopping,' Nathan shouted over the whirl of the propeller.

Frobisher sent him a hateful look, then he and Simone, the young woman clutching her case, ducked beneath starboard wing and headed towards the signal.

Pressing on the left pedal, Nathan circled the plane round and lined the Lysander up ready to taxi back down the runway. And then he saw a movement in the trees and the outline of approaching men.

'Frobisher!' he screamed, standing up in his seat and waving his arms.

The lieutenant and the young woman stopped running and turned.

'It's a trap!' Nathan yelled.

Darts of light flashed at the end of the hedgerow as a burst of machine-gun fire tore apart the silence. Frobisher and Simone froze for a second, then, under fire from all sides, they dashed back towards the plane.

German soldiers emerged from the foliage and added the crack of rifle fire to the rat-a-tat-tat of the machine guns.

Frobisher, unhindered by having to carry a heavy suitcase, outpaced the young woman and reached the plane first.

'Get this bloody thing off the ground,' he shouted as he scrambled up the ladder and tumbled into the rear seat.

Simone still had ten or so yards to go before she reached the plane. But then she screamed, pitched forward and collapsed onto the meadow grass.

Frobisher punched Nathan's shoulder. 'I said to go.'

Ignoring him, Nathan snapped open his buckle and stood up.

Frobisher grabbed his arm. 'What the blue blazes are you doing?'

Giving him a look of loathing, Nathan shook him off, jammed the aircraft's engine into neutral and jumped down.

'Leave her,' Frobisher shouted as bullets pinged off the metal wheel arches. 'She's probably dead anyway.'

Ignoring him and crouching low, Nathan sprinted across to the injured young woman. He grabbed her hands and, holding them in his large ones, he hoisted her up and across his shoulder in a fireman's lift.

She groaned as Nathan adjusted his hold and jogged back towards the Lysander.

Grasping the ladder fixed to the side, he planted his flight boot on the first rung and heaved himself up.

'There's a first aid kit under your seat,' he shouted, as he pitched her unceremoniously into the back seat.

He jumped back down and placed his boot on the step

above the wheel arch but, as he sprang up and into his seat, biting pain ripped through his left shoulder. Gritting his teeth, Nathan grasped the joystick's ring and adjusted the flaps and rudder, then, with shots piercing the canvas fuselage, picked up speed before pulling back hard on the throttle as he passed the solitary landing light. Mercifully, the plane soared into the air and skimmed across the tops of the hedgerow, leaving the enemy patrol firing into empty air.

Donaldson and his counterpart Major Rawlings, both with expressions on their faces that would curdle milk, were already sitting in their usual chairs when Nathan strode in.

He saluted and his superiors returned it.

'How's the shoulder?' asked Donaldson.

'Aching like billy-o,' Nathan replied. 'But the doctor says I'll live to fight another day and should be back in action in a few weeks. How is Miss Simone?' he added.

'She's got a punctured right lung and a few broken ribs, but although she lost a lot of blood she'll make a full recovery,' Rawlings replied. 'Get yourself a coffee.'

Nathan hooked his cap on the coat stand, then dragged his weary aching body across to the cups and coffee pot.

It was the morning after the aborted mission and, after spending two hours being stitched up and bandaged in the infirmary, he'd only managed a couple of hours in his bed. Not that he'd got much sleep, between his colleagues banging and crashing around in the dormitory and his throbbing shoulder. Hoping that a shot of caffeine would make him feel at least half human, Nathan spooned in three sugars and carried his coffee to a seat alongside Donaldson.

Donaldson, whose moustache did its usual shimmy across his top lip, looked at his watch and then at Rawlings.

With the ticking of the clock above the blackboard breaking

the silence, Nathan eased himself carefully back in the chair and took a sip of coffee.

Actually, what the RAF doctor had really said was that had the bullet gone through his shoulder an inch further to the left it would have punctured the subclavian artery and he would have bled to death. He'd also said that Nathan should be resting up for a few weeks before returning to flying duty.

The other thing the good doctor couldn't have diagnosed was that, as a result of his brush with death, Nathan was even more determined to make Effie his wife.

Of course, how he was going to achieve this he had yet to figure out.

A rapping on the door returned Nathan's mind to the present. Frobisher entered the room. Unshaven and with bloodshot eyes, he looked as bad as Nathan felt, but the faint whiff of spirits that floated in with him made him suspect the SOE officer's groggy manner was due to something other than lack of sleep.

Clearing his throat, Donaldson made a show of looking at his watch.

'Sorry,' said Frobisher, making his way across to the refreshments. 'I'm running a bit late.'

'As always,' said Donaldson.

Anger flashed across Frobisher's face briefly.

'Shall we make a start?' said Rawlings.

'Well, can we start with what the bloody hell went wrong,' barked Donaldson.

'The Germans were waiting for us,' said Frobisher, returning to the table. 'There was no way we could have anticipated that there was something amiss as we approached the drop-off—'

'Except that I did,' interrupted Nathan.

He gave the two senior officers a quick recap of his heated exchange with Frobisher over the incorrect signal.

'So why did you land?' asked Rawlings.

'Yes, why did we, Frobisher?' asked Nathan, giving him a severe look across the table. 'When I distinctly told you the first signal was the wrong one.'

'I thought the resistance chappies had made a simple mistake,' Frobisher replied. He turned to his superior officer. 'And you know yourself, sir, how vitally important this mission was.'

'Important enough to risk your life along with two other people's?' asked Nathan.

Frobisher surreptitiously pulled out a hip flask and poured what looked like brandy into his coffee. 'I thought it was worth taking the chance. And anyway, we all returned in one piece, didn't we.'

'No thanks to you, Frobisher,' Nathan replied.

'All our operatives know the risks,' said Rawlings. 'And our operations are more important than any one person.'

'I know as much as anyone the risks involved in flying these missions,' said Nathan. 'But I take some of the responsibility for last night's fiasco as I ignored my gut instinct that something was wrong and landed.'

Tucking the hip flask back where it had come from, Frobisher gave Nathan a condescending look down his long aristocratic nose. 'Look, Fitzgerald, as I said before, if you've lost your nerve for the job then—'

Nathan sprang to his feet. 'You've got a bloody cheek to talk about nerve when you're the one who lost it completely when the Germans appeared.'

'Are you calling me a coward?' shouted Frobisher, leaping up.

'Well, it wasn't me screaming to leave a young woman bleeding to death in a French field and take off, was it?' Nathan snapped back, throbbing shoulder adding to his rage. 'And just in case my words aren't permeating that drink-soaked brain of yours, let me say it clearly – yes, I am most certainly calling you a coward. A reckless bloody coward.'

Frobisher kicked his chair aside, dashed around the table and grabbed Nathan's lapels.

'How dare you, you jumped-up bastard!' he screamed, his sour breath full in Nathan's face. 'My ancestors fought at Waterloo and in the Crimea.'

'I don't care if your ancestors fought alongside William the Conqueror at Hastings, you're still a bloody coward,' Nathan replied, his shoulder screaming its protest at the rough handling.

With his face turning a dull puce, Frobisher drew back his fist. Planting his feet firmly and turning to protect his injured arm, Nathan braced himself for the blow but, when Frobisher's fist was inches from his face, another hand grabbed it.

'As you were, Lieutenant!' bellowed Donaldson.

Glaring blindly at him, Frobisher struggled against the group captain's grip, but the older man held firm.

'I said, as you were,' Donaldson repeated firmly.

Frobisher's angry, red-rimmed eyes glared into Nathan's icy-blue ones while the clock ticked off another few seconds. Then the SOE officer stepped back. Still scowling at Nathan, he returned to his side of the table and threw himself back in his chair.

Nathan resumed his seat, resting his arm on the table to ease the pain.

Donaldson turned and looked pointedly at his army colleague.

Rawlings cleared his throat.

'Well, I think it's clear that things didn't go as well as we'd hoped last night, for a number of reasons,' he said. 'Have either of you got anything further to add?'

Nathan shook his head while Frobisher continued to fume at him across the table.

Rawlings stood up and Nathan and Frobisher rose to their feet.

'Very well,' Rawlings said. He tapped his papers together and shoved them into the briefcase on the table next to him. 'Fitzgerald and Frobisher, I'll expect full statements from both of you on my desk by nineteen hundred hours tonight, after which I will be sending my report of the incident to Whitehall.'

'Sir,' said Nathan and Frobisher in unison as they saluted.

'See you in the mess later, Donaldson.' He picked up his briefcase and headed out of the room, with Frobisher a couple of paces behind him, but when he reached the door he stopped. 'Just so you know, Fitzgerald. Having spoken to Miss Simone this morning, I'll be entering your name into dispatches for bravery in the face of the enemy.'

'Thank you, sir,' said Nathan, resisting the urge to glance at Frobisher.

The two army officers left and as the door clicked shut Nathan resumed his seat.

'How's the arm now?' asked his senior officer.

'It could have done without being manhandled,' Nathan replied.

'You haven't made yourself any friends with the bloody brown squad,' said Donaldson. 'Calling one of their number a coward.'

Nathan shrugged. 'Well, he was. I dread to think what horrors that young woman would have suffered at the Gestapo's hands if she'd been captured. I only hope the SOE's top brass realise that Frobisher is a loose cannon who is likely to get someone killed.'

'Well, let's hope it's not one of our pilots, eh?'

'Amen to that, sir,' Nathan replied.

Leaning back in his chair, Donaldson rested his elbows on the arms and steepled his fingers.

'Now, about you being out of action for a few weeks,' he said, regarding Nathan steadily.

'Well, the flight window around the full moon finishes in two days,' said Nathan. 'So I'll be ready to go back up when operations start again at the end of the month.'

'I'm sure you will be,' said his senior officer. 'But it's the next two weeks I'm worried about. You and Frobisher are unlikely to become lifelong chums, and the two of you stuck here together with time on your hands sounds like a recipe for disaster.'

Nathan couldn't disagree. Frobisher was obnoxious enough sober and two weeks of propping up the bar wouldn't improve that.

'I'll try to avoid him,' he said.

'I've got a better idea to keep you and Frobisher from killing each other,' said Donaldson. 'The wing commander at Cardington telephoned. One of his instructors is out of action and he asked if we could send an officer with knowledge of aerodynamics to help train their WAAF balloon operators.'

A thousand bells started ringing in Nathan's head. 'Help with—'

'I know it's not ideal,' continued Donaldson. 'And not something I'd expect a pilot of your experience to do, but it's only for a few weeks, so...'

'No, no, sir, that's fine.' Images of Effie dancing around in his mind, a broad smile spread across Nathan's face. 'I'd be more than happy to spend a few weeks at Cardington.'

CHAPTER 12

As she clambered over the rustic stile, Effie spotted George hanging on to the five-bar gate at the other end of the field.

'What's the devil's up with your woman over there?' Maeve asked, following her over and landing squarely in the same freezing mud puddle Effie was ankle-deep in.

It was Monday the second of March , about a quarter to ten in the morning and some five hours since they'd been woken up by the base's morning bell.

Effie and the rest of the second contingent of 'Balloon Girls', as everyone called them, were now two weeks away from being sent to their practice site for assessment. As was not uncommon, they had lost a handful of women along the way, mainly to injury and illness, the most serious being a young woman from Squad A who'd suffered a broken leg and cracked ribs when she got dragged along the ground by a balloon. Effie's crew had lost a young woman from a village in Leicestershire, who had been carted off to hospital with suspected appendicitis and subsequently found to be five months pregnant. As motherhood and the WAAF did not mix, she'd been sent packing. Thankfully, Peggy had been moved over from no. 5 crew to replace her.

After the first few weeks of not knowing where everything was and where she should be, for the past month Effie's days had settled into a familiar routine. Leaping out of bed, she would grab her washbag and towel and dash to the ablution block in order to avoid having to wait in line for a free sink. As the boiler was only lit for an hour each morning, after a lukewarm wash, using her precious sliver of soap sparingly, she headed back to the stark Nissen hut to get dressed and be ready for kit inspection with Maeve and Nell. They were accustomed to rising early, Maeve having been raised on a farm and Nell having worked on her family's fruit and veg stall opposite the London Hospital on Whitechapel Road, known locally as the Waste, since she was a child. Alice would generally join them a few minutes later. George was usually the last to drag herself out of bed and get to the wash block, mainly because she often sneaked into bed just as the first streaks of light were cutting across the horizon.

After a hurried breakfast in the WAAFs' mess they would be standing by their beds ready for Sergeant Dunbar to stride in at six forty-five precisely.

Wearing a face like she'd eaten half a dozen lemons for breakfast, their dour sergeant would poke and prod the kit they'd spread out neatly on the dun-coloured blankets and stick her head into each locker, before dismissing them to attend their first lesson of the day.

Unfortunately, as if to punish them for having had the weekend to themselves, the working week always started with two hours with Sergeant Jones, the base's utterly mad physical training instructor.

The sadistic Welshman had decided, for reasons of his own, that this morning after a full hour of bending and stretching the girls in Squad B should run the perimeter of the camp twice.

Dressed in white singlets, blue shorts and black plimsolls, and splattered from head to foot with mud, they were halfway round the second lap when they spotted George at the five-bar gate.

'We'd better go and see if she's all right,' said Effie. As a couple of other WAAFs scaled the gate behind them, she and Maeve trotted across the field to where George leant white-faced and red-eyed on the lichen-covered gate.

'Are you all right, George?' said Effie as she reached her.

'I'm just having a breather—' She clamped her hand over her mouth, then turned and threw up into the bottom of the hedge.

Effie took her handkerchief from her pocket and handed it to her friend. 'Do you want me to take you to the infirmary?'

George shook her head. 'What, and give Dunbar an excuse to put me back a group to the cohort of trainees behind us? Not bally likely.'

Twisting aside, she heaved up again. WAAFs trotting past gave them odd looks.

'But if you're ill...' Effie persisted.

George shook her head again. 'I'm not ill, I'm—'

'You're not in the family way, are you?' cut in Maeve.

George gave a hard laugh. 'No, I'm ruddy not. Believe me, I wouldn't get caught like that agai—' An odd emotion flitted across her face and she cleared her throat. 'No, the only thing I've got in my belly is a bottle of whatever it was that rather handsome group captain kept pouring in my glass last night.' She looked balefully at the mess soaking into the soil. 'And if that sadist Jones hadn't made us run around right after breakfast, it still would be, too.'

'Can't you remember what you were drinking, George?' asked Maeve.

Despite her pasty expression and dark smudges under her eyes, George mustered an indulgent smile.

'My sweet innocent child,' she said, placing a hand on Maeve's arm. 'I can barely remember what happened after he opened the second bottle. Although I can remember he had strong broad shoulders and a great deal of stamina. And now I come to think of it, lovely eyes.'

From nowhere an image of Nathan's strikingly blue eyes flashed into Effie's mind. And although a young woman with a fiancé shouldn't think such things, Effie couldn't help remembering the pleasing feel of his broad shoulders under her fingertips, too.

Nell, Alice and Dolly jumped over the stile.

'Come on, you slackers,' shouted Nell as they puffed by. 'Shake a leg or Dunbar will have you all scrubbing the khazis for a month.'

Splashing mud up their legs as they passed, Effie's three friends headed off towards the finish line at the end of the field.

Leaning heavily on the post, George straightened up. 'What have we got next?'

'Working with helium followed by the aerodynamics of barrage balloons, in number three classroom,' Effie replied.

'Thank God. I can park myself in the corner and snooze until midday chow.' Despite her sickly appearance, George managed a grin. 'Now come on, girls, last one back buys the first round in the NAAFI bar tonight.'

Swaying slightly, she set off after the half a dozen girls who had just passed them.

'Do you think this chap George was out with last night plied her with strong liquor and had his wicked way with her?' Maeve asked as their friend started off again.

A half-smile lifted Effie's lips.

'No, I don't. If you ask me, I'd say if anything it was the other way round,' she replied, pondering how precisely a well-brought-up young woman, say like herself, would go about doing that.

. . .

'Hydrogen is highly combustible,' said Sergeant Whittle. 'So, make sure you girls all remember that when you're on your practice sites in a fortnight . And also remember: unless you want to suddenly find yourself on St Peter's roll call at the pearly gates, never – and I mean never! – light a cigarette when you're operating a balloon or anywhere near one. Do you understand?'

'Yes, Sergeant!' a chorus of voices replied.

Effie and the rest of Squad B were sitting in number three classroom and had been for the past forty-five tedious, mind-numbing minutes, while Whittle once again explained in his monotonous nasal tone the perils of handing the volatile gas.

After finishing the murderous run around the air force base Effie had dashed into the changing room to swap out of her PE kit and back into her WAAF uniform. Having washed the mud from her legs under the freezing-cold showers and dressed, she'd grabbed a quick cup of tea in the NAAFI and arrived in the classroom two or three minutes before Sergeant Whittle walked through the door.

The room itself was situated at the east end of the base in the road behind their accommodation huts. With its worn wooden floorboards, rows of desks and raised platform at one end featuring a blackboard on an easel, it could have been any classroom in any senior school in the land. Except that, instead of posters on flora and fauna and kings and queens hung around the walls, there was one with the silhouettes of enemy aircraft and another with diagrams showing various knots.

The cold shower had brought her round for a while but now, listening to their instructor drone on, she was hunched over with her elbows on her desk and her chin cupped in her hands, trying to look as if she was paying attention.

'Does anyone have any questions?' asked Whittle, and the collective wish that no one would speak hovered in the air.

Mercifully no one did.

'Now, as you may have heard Corporal Makepeace came off his motorbike in the blackout last week after an unfortunate encounter with a stray cow on the St Neots road,' continued Whittle as he shuffled his lecture notes back into their manila folder. 'He isn't too badly hurt, just a broken wrist and some bruising, but he will not be returning to duty for a few weeks and—'

'What about the cow?' Maeve piped up.

Whittle frowned. 'What about it?'

'Is it all right, too?' asked Nell.

There was some sniggering and the instructor's perplexed expression deepened.

'How do I know?' he barked. 'And that's not important because—'

'Well, I doubt the farmer would be agreeing with you there, Sergeant,' Maeve chipped in.

'Because,' continued Whittle, glaring at her, 'it means you will have a temporary instructor for the next couple of weeks as you prepare for your practice site. He should be here any mome—'

The door swung open.

Effie's jaw hit the ground in utter disbelief as the man who had lately been creeping into her thoughts both day and night marched into the room.

Dressed in his officer uniform, with his cap sitting at a slightly jaunty non-regulation angle on his black hair, Flying Officer Nathan Fitzgerald looked every inch the RAF officer. However, in addition to his dress uniform he was also sporting a sling supporting his left arm. Before she could stop it, her heart did a little double-step, then galloped off.

Chairs scraped back as forty-plus WAAFs stood to attention and saluted.

Nathan stopped next to Whittle and faced the class.

'As you were,' he said, and returned their salute.

A murmur went around the room as they resumed their seats.

'Oi, oi,' said Nell under her breath, nudging Effie in the ribs. 'Look 'oo it is.'

Nathan's bright-blue eyes skimmed over the assembled WAAFs but, when they reached Effie, an emotion flickered in them. They stared at each other for a few seconds before Nathan's gaze moved on.

'Girls, I'd like you to meet...' As Whittle ran through their tall, strikingly handsome temporary instructor's credentials, Effie stopped listening.

Staring mindlessly at Nathan, she wondered why she'd never experienced the unfamiliar emotions now swirling inside her when she looked at Leonard.

'So now I'll hand you over to Flying Officer Fitzgerald, who will be running over the theory of aerodynamics as it applies to barrage balloons,' concluded Whittle, dragging Effie's mind back from its wandering. 'Until lunchtime, after which he will be with you on the practice ground this afternoon to make sure you're applying the principles correctly. Any questions?'

No one spoke.

'Well then,' continued Whittle. 'I'll leave our balloon girls to your tender care, Flying Officer.'

'Thank you, Sergeant.'

Whittle left the room.

As the door clicked closed Nathan turned and looked at the class. 'Good morning, ladies.'

'Good morning, sir,' said forty female voices in unison.

Nathan smiled. 'Shall we begin?'

. . .

'So,' said Nathan, tapping the chart behind him with the long pointer. 'Remember, the way to ensure the barrage balloon holds steady and at the right height is to treat it in the same way you flew a kite as a child. Keep it tilted at a thirty-six-degree angle into the oncoming wind and the main cable taut.'

He was standing on the raised platform at the front of the class, and had been for the past forty-five minutes as he ran through the physics surrounding flying a balloon. Effie was doing her best to concentrate on the matter at hand, but her attention was constantly dragged off the topic and on to the person delivering it. As Nathan spoke about the Beaufort scale Effie tried not to notice the way his trousers fit snugly around his long legs. Instead of focusing on barometric pressure, Effie scandalously found herself imagining what it would feel like to have his dexterous hand holding hers, and, as the rest of the class got to grips with meteorological terms, Effie was trying to fathom why she was light-headed and dry-mouthed every time Nathan's gaze meet hers across the room. Mind you, judging by the dreamy looks some of her fellow balloon students were casting in his direction, she wasn't the only one having trouble concentrating.

'This will give it lift and control while the air-filled side fins give the balloon its stability.' He shifted the pointer to the bowed cylinder at the side of the fat grey balloon on the diagram. 'It will also minimise the risk of personnel on the ground being entangled in slack anchor ropes. Holding it steady ensures your balloon remains in formation with the others over the protected area. Are there any questions?'

'I've got a few,' said Dolly, sitting behind Effie, under her breath. 'But not about wind velocity.'

'And I wouldn't mind having a go at inflating his balloon,' said someone else in the same hushed tone.

'Good,' said Nathan. He glanced at the clock above the door. 'Then class dismissed, and I'll see you on the practice ground at thirteen thirty sharp, when we will put theory into practice.'

Chair legs scraped on bare wooden floorboards again as the class stood up and, while Nathan collected his lecture notes together, the WAAFs filed out of the classroom.

Effie waited until most of the rows behind her had trooped out, then followed Nell along to the end of the row. As they moved towards the door, Nathan stepped out from behind the desk.

'Hello again,' he said, as she reached the front.

'Hello,' she replied, and stepped a little closer to let Maeve and Alice pass her.

Her three friends were waiting for her at the door, out of Nathan's eyeline, blowing silent kisses and rolling their eyes.

Effie was about to say that she ought to go or some such thing, but then all other thoughts left her head as Nathan's eyes captured hers.

Gazing up at him, she was vaguely aware that she and Nathan were the only two left in the classroom.

'We seem to be developing a habit of bumping into each other, don't we?' he said after giving her that roguish smile of his.

'We do.' Effie laughed.

That was certainly true because, as well as running into him at the Swan Hotel three Saturdays before with Leonard, their paths had crossed again last Wednesday evening when she Nell and Alice were lining up outside the Plaza for the matinee. In fact, when she and her friends had been milling around Bedford's Saturday market two days before, Effie had actually found herself oddly disappointed that he wasn't there.

Effie glanced at the sling. 'What happened to your arm?'

'Just a slight accident,' he replied. 'Nothing serious. But obviously I won't be flying for a bit, which is why I was sent across to Cardington to cover for your injured instructor.'

'Lucky you.' She laughed.

Something she couldn't fathom flitted across Nathan's face. 'Yes,' he replied, in a low rumbling voice. 'Lucky me.'

Effie's mind went blank again, but after a few seconds lost in his gaze she dragged it back. 'I ought to get to the mess before...'

'Yes, sorry, I'm holding you up.'

'No, you're not,' Effie replied. 'And I don't mind.'

'I'll walk across with you.'

Nathan picked up his folder, but as he did a handful of the papers inside it slipped out. He managed to catch most of them but two glided to the ground. Putting the folder back on the desk, he reached down to retrieve them from the floor.

Effie had also automatically bent down to catch them. She reached them first, but a second later Nathan's fingers closed over hers as he also grasped the wayward notes.

She raised her head and found herself gazing into Nathan's eyes, just inches away. A second or perhaps it was an hour or possibly eternity passed, then Effie let go and they both stood up.

Slotting his papers back in his folder, Nathan looked down at Effie, and her heart did another little double-step. Oddly, she had the ridiculous impression that he was about to put his arm round her and kiss her. Then the classroom door burst open.

Tearing her gaze from him, Effie looked round as Alice's head appeared round the doorframe.

'Sorry, Effie,' she said, 'But George's stuck in the ladies bog being er...' Her attention shifted from Effie to Nathan and back again. 'Unwell, and she's wedged herself in one of the cubicles.'

'Is George all right?' asked Dolly, as Effie placed her tray on the long refectory table. It was half an hour later.

'Well, she's still in the land of the living,' Alice replied, taking the empty seat next to Maeve.

'Even if she looks like she's been dug up from her own grave,' added Effie, settling herself in the space between Nell and Dolly.

They had just arrived in the canteen, and it was already halfway through their hour-long dinner break. Their friends had saved them a place, thankfully – as usual, the WAAFs' canteen was heaving.

'Your drunk mate still in the bog, is she?'

Effie turned to see Lily and a couple of her friends sitting a few places down.

'Mind your own business,' said Dolly.

'She'll be kicked out if Dunbar gets wind of it,' added Lily, her red lips curled in a sneer.

'And if she does, we'll know who blabbed, won't we, girls?' Nell replied.

Effie and her four friends gave Lily and her chums a hard look and Lily turned her back on them.

'Has she gone over to the quack?' asked Maeve, leaning across the table and lowering her voice.

Effie shook her head. 'We've given her a couple of aspirins and poured NAAFI coffee down her. We said we'd pick her up after break when we head across to the practice area.'

'I can't understand why George drinks so much,' said Alice, slicing determinedly through a lump of unyielding liver. 'I mean, she's got money, expensive clothes, and men gravitate to her like bees to nectar, so—'

'It's because of some bastard bloke,' chipped in Nell. 'I'll lay you a quid to a tanner that it's some fella's done the dirty on 'er somewhere along the line.'

'Sounds like some fellas have done the dirty on you, too, Nell,' said Dolly.

Nell mopped up a smear of gravy with a chunk of grey National Loaf and popped it in her mouth. 'Just the one.'

There was a long silence, then Alice stood up. 'Can I get anyone a cuppa?'

'Yes please,' said Effie, spearing another portion of streaky bacon.

'Talking about fellas,' said Maeve, as Effie and Alice munched their way through their liver and bacon casserole. 'What are we thinking of our new instructor, then?'

At the mention of Nathan, Effie's heart thumped in her chest as the memory of him walking into the classroom returned to her mind.

'Well, he's easier on the eye than Makepeace, that's for sure,' said Dolly.

'Yes, but did you hear anything he said?' asked Alice.

Nell winked. 'I don't think Effie did, although she certainly gave our tall handsome instructor her full attention.'

The girls laughed and, as four pairs of eyes turned in her direction, Effie's imagination conjured up the captivating expression on Nathan's face as his gaze rested on her across the classroom.

'We're being sent off to our practice site in a few weeks, so obviously I was listening,' she replied, hoping only she could hear the slight tremble in her voice.

Dolly raised a pencilled eyebrow. 'Is that so?'

Feeling her cheeks burning, Effie didn't reply.

'And not to mention,' continued Nell, 'that our dangerously handsome instructor couldn't keep his eyes off our Effie either.'

'His lovely blue eyes, no less,' added Maeve. 'Sure, isn't the man himself sin on legs.'

'Hark at them,' said Lily, her voice harsh as it cut into their conversation. 'Going on about that flipping pilot like he's Clark Gable or something.'

'I thought I told you to mind your own business,' said Nell.

'It is my business when she' – she jabbed her finger at Effie – 'is going to give us all a bad name,' Lily spat back.

'If you're worried about your good name, Lily Craven, you want to stop shagging that ginger corporal who works in the supply store,' Nell replied.

'Is she?' asked Alice, looking shocked.

'That she is,' confirmed Maeve. 'Now that your fella with the buck teeth from transport depot has been posted elsewhere.'

Two splashes of colour appeared on Lily's overly made-up cheeks. Giving them a look that could have cut paper, she stood, picked up her tray and left.

'At least now we can eat our dinner without getting heartburn,' said Nell as she watched Lily storm off across the refectory.

Mindful of the time, the girls turned their attention back to their meals. However, as Effie dug her spoon into her spotted dick and custard, the image of Nathan leaning on the desk as he taught them floated into her mind. Although she might not be in danger of indigestion now, that didn't mean there wasn't an odd burning in her heart.

CHAPTER 13

'Are you all right, Effie?' asked Alice, looking across the refectory table at her. It was two weeks later.

'Just a bit of a headache, that's all,' Effie replied. 'I didn't sleep too well.'

'I'm not surprised,' chipped in Nell. 'That hut was like a blooming ice box last night.'

Effie gave her friends a wan smile.

Now it was the second Friday in March . With the Spring just around the corner they had hoped that spring might start to show its face a little but instead, for the past week they'd had near-Arctic conditions blowing across from the fens to the east. However, the ice forming on the insides of the Nissen hut windows was not the reason for Effie's lack of sleep; it was something very different that made her, in contrast, feel oddly warm.

Ever since he strode into her classroom four days ago, every time she'd tried to close her eyes at night her mind was filled with images of Nathan, his mouth as he spoke, the shape of his hand as he held the pointer, the sound of his voice. She'd finally fall into a fitful sleep, only to be woken as the sun peeped over the horizon. And if that wasn't enough to give her a headache, she had a niggling feeling of guilt hovering over her that never once had Leonard featured in such a dream. In fact, if she was honest, she had to admit that recently she went days without giving her fiancé a thought. It was very perplexing, especially as all these unfamiliar and, frankly, unsettling emotions she'd been experiencing whenever she saw or even thought about Nathan now had her questioning her true feelings for Leonard.

Putting the problem to the back of her mind, Effie returned her thoughts to the here and now.

'Remind me what we've got after lunch?' she asked.

Setting down her knife, Alice pulled her timetable from her boiler-suit pocket. 'As Makepeace is still off sick, Writtle's down for doing knot practice again,' she replied, then returned the tatty piece of paper whence it came.

Placing her spoon in the bowl of her barely touched pudding, Effie stood up. 'I think I'll take a little walk to clear my head.'

'Good idea,' said Alice. 'Leave it,' she added as Effie started tidying her used crockery. 'I'll wash it.'

Effie gave her a grateful smile and, leaving her friends to finish their midday meal, buttoned up her greatcoat and made her way outside.

Although it was still icy, the pale sun overhead was doing its best to warm the asphalt pathway outside the WAAFs' mess as Effie emerged. She headed towards the open practice area, making her way past the administration offices and the social hall.

Skirting around the edge of the open area, Effie headed for the small clump of bare-limbed trees at the far side, which someone had thoughtfully put an old bench beneath. She wrapped her coat around her and pulled her scarf up over her ears, then tucked her nose in its front fold and closed her eyes.

Away from the balloon hangars and maintenance shed, the

sounds of the Bedfordshire countryside held sway. Tucked in her greatcoat cocoon, birds chirping in the branches above, the tight band circling Effie's head started to ease and she felt herself dozing off.

'Hello.'

Effie's eyes snapped open, and her heart did a little double-step.

There, buttoned up in his greatcoat and scarf as she was, stood the man responsible for her restless nights.

'Officer Fitzgerald.'

'Out here all by yourself?' he asked.

'I needed some fresh air,' Effie replied.

'Me too. Do you mind if I join you?' He frowned slightly. 'Because I wouldn't want to disturb you...'

'You're not disturbing me,' Effie replied.

She shuffled along the bench and Nathan sat down beside her. Stretching his long legs out, he crossed them at the ankle.

He tilted his face to the weak winter sun and Effie's eyes ran over his strong profile. She'd noticed it before but, unlike Leonard's sparse jaw bristles, Nathan's were as thick on his cheeks as they were on his chin. He also had a kink along the top of his ear, which for some odd reason made her smile.

'Lovely day, isn't it?' he said, his blue eyes gazing up through the leafless branches above.

Effie laughed. 'It's blooming freezing.'

'But I'm sure I can feel a hint of spring in the air,' he said.

'I think you're being a tad optimistic,' Effie replied. 'But at least it doesn't look like it's going to snow yet.'

'Do you know,' he continued, still contemplating the sky. 'I'd never seen snow until I arrived in England two and a half years ago.'

'I can't remember a year when we didn't have snow, sometimes for weeks on end,' said Effie, suppressing the sudden urge to snuggle into him.

Nathan gave a great rumbling laugh. 'You should have seen me and the other West Indians and Africans in our training camp, jumping around and throwing snowballs like a bunch of kids.'

She turned, and Nathan's mesmerising eyes locked with hers. Something changed in his expression – she couldn't name it but whatever it was it started an odd fluttering sensation circling her navel.

'Although,' she continued, forcing her brain to work. 'I suppose our summers are more what you're used to.'

Nathan's lips widened into a grin. 'In some ways, but what you consider a heat wave here is what we have on the island almost every day in the summer. The thermometer regularly hits the nineties. Even in the winter it still tops eighty sometimes. But of course, it's not all sunshine. We have a hurricane season too from the late summer until October or November. They crash in from the Atlantic, ripping up the cane fields, tearing roofs from houses and branches from trees.'

'My goodness,' said Effie. 'It sounds frightening.'

'You get used to it,' Nathan replied. 'And we know when it's coming, so we batten down the hatches. The tropical storms usually follow, which can flood villages and wash away roads.' He gave another rumbling laugh. 'However, most of the time it's ocean breezes and unending sunshine. On hot days me and my friends would dash down to the nearest stretch of sand as soon as the end-of-school bell rang and dive in the sea, or set up three sticks as stumps for an impromptu game of cricket.' Nathan's striking features pulled into a grave expression. 'I have to tell you, Effie, that we Barbadians are completely cricket mad, by the way.'

'Sounds like paradise.' Effie laughed, enjoying the sound of her name on his lips.

'We have our problems like everywhere else, but even so...' A hint of sadness crept into his blue eyes.

'It's home,' said Effie.

He nodded and his smile returned.

'Do you have any family?' asked Effie, resisting the urge to reach out and straighten his greatcoat collar.

'Do I have family?' Nathan's smile widened. 'I most certainly do. There are three of us boys, of whom I'm the eldest. I also have an older sister, Esther, plus Jacob, Joshua, Miriam and Sarah, who are younger.'

'Gosh,' said Effie. 'Being an only child, I always hoped to have a large family one day. But Leonard isn't keen. He says two is more than enough,' she added, her heart squeezing a little.

A small frown creased Nathan's brow for a second, then his cheery expression returned.

'And you all have biblical names?' Effie continued.

'Let me tell you, we are a God-fearing island,' Nathan replies. 'And my mother has the hats to prove it.' He laughed and the swirling sensation in Effie's stomach started up again. 'I sang in the cathedral choir until my voice broke.'

'I'm sure you looked perfectly angelic in a pie-crust collar,' said Effie, trying to imagine him thus.

Nathan raised an eyebrow again. 'I doubt that's what Father MacPherson called me. I think he, along with my teachers, thought I had the devil in me sometimes as a child. But to give him his due it was his supportive letter that helped me win the island scholarship to Harrison College, the top private school on the Island. And when I set sail for England in August 1939, nearly everyone in our neighbourhood and St Michael's Anglican Cathedral congregation came down to the dock to wave me off.' He chuckled. 'Probably to make sure I was really leaving.'

'I'm sure that's not true,' said Effie. 'What about your parents?'

'My father started as a junior clerk in Government House and is now the assistant to Sir Henry, the governor of Barbados and the Windward Islands,' he replied. 'When he's not mired in the running of the island you can find him at the parish cricket club, where he's president.' His serious expression returned. 'Did I mention that on the island we are crazy wild about cricket?'

Effie laughed. 'I believe you did.'

'And my mother's a headmistress,' he added.

'It must have been quite a wrench to leave your home and sail to a totally alien country,' said Effie, noting the warmth in his voice.

'Well, the thick fog at Blackwall Docks when I arrived and, as I said, the snow, were some things I've never experienced before,' Nathan replied. 'But other than the heat and storms, Barbados is very similar to England in lots of ways. We have the same parliamentary system, law and education as over here, so for me England is a home from home. That's why hundreds of us from the British West Indies have signed up. But I do miss the cricket.'

'Just cricket, or perhaps a special—' Effie pressed her lips together.

Nathan turned and his mesmerising gaze scrutinised her face for a moment, then he smiled. 'There's no one waiting for me, if that's what you're asking, Corporal Weston.'

'I'm sorry. I didn't mean to pry I just wondered.' Lowering her gaze, Effie brushed a non-existent speck of dirt from her trouser leg. Then her eyes returned to his face. 'Will you go home when the war is over?'

'One day I might. And I do miss my family and friends, but I'm very glad I came to England. After all' – the emotion she'd glimpsed before flashed across Nathan's face – 'had I not, I would never have met you.'

Effie's heart thumped a couple of times as her eyes locked with Nathan's.

From nowhere the urge to throw her arms round him and

press her lips onto his swept over her so forcefully that it caught her breath. Then a two-tone wolf-whistle rolled across the practice area.

They both looked round.

The two gas lorries, weighed down with thirty cylinders apiece, had arrived from the storage area at the other side of the base. Corporal Writtle, red-faced and sweating, was waving his arms around frantically in an attempt to get the consignment of hydrogen in position before the start of the afternoon's practice.

'I'd better go and lend a hand.' Nathan rose to his feet and straightened his collar. 'It's been a pleasure talking with you, Corporal Weston.'

'You too, Officer Fitzgerald,' Effie replied. 'Barbados sounds wonderful. I hope one day, when the war's over, I will see it for myself.'

'I hope you do, too,' he said in a low voice, his eyes looking deeply into hers.

Effie lost herself in them for a second, then pulled herself back to the here and now and smiled.

Nathan smiled back, then, leaving her sitting on the bench, he made his way in long-legged strides towards the commotion on the other side of the practice ground.

She'd lied, of course.

When she'd opened her eyes and found Nathan standing not three feet away from her, Effie had been very disturbed indeed. Understandably really, because the plain truth of the matter was that, from almost their first meeting, the sight of Flying Officer Nathan Fitzgerald sent her head reeling and senses tingling every single time she laid eyes on him. And try as she might, she could no longer deny it. For better or for worse, to her Nathan Fitzgerald was not just a ship passing in the night.

CHAPTER 14

'Let it out another ten yards,' shouted Effie, ignoring her aching shoulders and holding fast to the rope.

'Fifty feet,' bellowed Maeve from her vantage point on the tailboard of the truck.

George gave her the thumbs-up and, revving the winch engine, released the cable as instructed. The fat grey balloon bouncing around above their heads drifted up a little higher.

It was now the middle of Thursday afternoon on their final week before their three-week practical assessment at a war site. Effie and the rest of no. 3 crew were halfway through their final supervised run-through of getting their barrage balloon up from scratch. And it was quite a task, too.

Having taken the massive canvas and rubber grey skin out of its bag, they had to unfurl it ready to be filled. The next task involved securing it to the winch cable before attaching one end of the articulated gas pipe to the inlet valve on the side of the balloon's main chamber and the other to the first of the cylinders on the back of the supply lorry. A task made more difficult for her crew because all of them were wearing RAF-issue gloves at least a size too big, not just against the biting cold but to prevent their flesh being burned to a crisp by any escaping gas. This had to be done in double-time as, when they were deployed to their war site, their balloon and thousands like it would play a vital part in protecting Britain's cities from the Luftwaffe's attack.

They'd achieved the first half of the task without any hitch in thirty minutes flat, and now they were engaged in the much tricker and potentially dangerous undertaking of actually getting the unwieldy, oversized bag of gas airborne, to the correct height and at the optimum angle within the air defences array.

This took both skill and concentration.

The skill had been drummed into them for the past eleven weeks, the concentration, however – in Effie's case at least – was in short supply this afternoon. The reason for this was that standing alongside Writtle on the edge of the practice ground was Flying Officer Nathan Fitzgerald.

Listening to Nathan talk about his home and family the week before as they sat on the bench had changed something deep within her. All she had to do was figure out what.

'How are we doing?' shouted George from beneath the winch truck's arched protective cage.

'Not so bad,' Maeve replied. 'I'd say we could go another fifty before we can get it on an even keel.'

'Stand ready.'

Effie tightened her grip on the rope.

'Stand ready,' she shouted over her shoulder to Nell, who was in charge of the middle section's rope.

'Ready,' shouted Alice and Dolly, taking up the slack on the other side of the balloon from Effie.

''We 'eard,' snapped Lily who, as always with her chum Maureen, had opted to take up the tether ropes at the rear of the balloon.

'She's only saying,' Alice replied, leaning back to add her weight to the rope.

'Showing off in front of that flying officer, more like,' Lily shot back.

Ignoring her, Effie dug her rubber boots into the practice ground's gravel. George revved the winch engine again and released a further length of the main steel cable.

'Hold it steady at the back,' screamed Nell as, caught in a sudden gust of cutting wind, the balloon tugged violently against its anchor.

'What do you think I'm blooming well doing?' Lily screamed back.

Out of the corner of Effie's eye she saw Nathan looking in their direction for a moment. He said something to Writtle, next to him, then strolled over.

'Everything all right over here, ladies?' he asked, stopping a few yards behind Alice.

'That we are, sir,' Maeve replied. 'Just making sure we've the beast into the wind.'

Nathan looked up and cast his eyes along the fat, grey, cigar-shaped balloon floating overhead.

'You need to tighten the rear guy ropes to give it more upward lift,' he said to Lily and Maureen.

'Yes, sir,' said Lily, giving him a syrupy smile. 'Right away, sir.'

He gave her a cool look, then watched as the two young women heaved on their respective tethers.

The rope in Effie's hand slipped half an inch within her leather glove as the balloon's tail-end angle adjusted, then it settled again.

'Much better,' Nathan shouted over the noise of the winch engine. 'Remember what I said about the balloon being like an oversized kite and you'll be fine.'

'Yes, sir. Thank you, sir,' said the crew said in unison.

'Carry on, ladies,' said Nathan.

From beneath his cap peak his gaze locked with Effie's, and his eyes softened, sending the now familiar ripple of excitement through her.

He stood there a few moments longer, then returned to his place beside Makepeace.

'Yes, sir. Thank you, sir. Three bags full, sir,' said Lily in a falsetto voice. 'You lot are such a bunch of teacher's pets.'

'Why don't you put a sock in it,' shouted Nell.

'Why don't you make me,' Lily replied.

'For the love of Mary can we just get this bloody thing in the air and have done with it?' shouted Maeve.

'Good idea,' said Effie, twisting round and giving Lily and chum a hard look.

'Are you ready?' bellowed Maeve from the back of the lorry.

'Ready,' the rest of the crew chorused back.

Puffing out a cloud of diesel from its exhaust, the winch engine revved again.

'Twenty. Thirty. Forty,' Maeve shouted as the drum let out the balloon's metal cable.

Keeping an eye on the balloon angle as it floated upwards, Effie let out the tether rope inch by inch. The rest of the crew did the same until the balloon was bobbing 160 feet above them.

'Another forty,' called Maeve, circling her arm, her eyes fixed to the bloated grey underbelly. 'That's it almost—'

'Watch out,' screamed Alice, cutting across her friend's words.

Effie's head snapped up.

The side fins, which kept the balloon on an even keel, had yet to fill with air. They flapped against the side, allowing a gust of wind to catch hold of it.

'Hold it steady,' shouted Effie, her feet skidding over the gravel as the rope she was holding slid from her grip.

Gritting their teeth, Alice and Dolly wound their ropes round their wrists and leant back as the silver-grey cylinder swung wildly back and forth.

With sweat springing out on her forehead and her arms being pulled from their sockets, Effie hung on for dear life.

'Get the back down,' shouted Maeve.

'We're ruddy trying,' Lily shouted back. 'But I can't hold the bloody—'

A loose guy rope cracked past Effie, missing her nose by inches, then flailed about on the ground. The balloon pitched downwards, the nose almost hitting the truck, before soaring skywards.

Effie's feet left the ground, causing her to stumble before what felt like an iron hand encircled her right ankle. She flew into the air for a couple of seconds, then landed with a thump.

A flash of air force blues darted in and out of her vision as she gasped for air.

'Get hold of those ropes,' a deep voice bellowed.

Gasping for air, Effie tried to get up but instead found herself bumping across the gravel, dragged by an unknown hand. Mercifully, the balloon above her finally stopped bucking and she came to a halt.

Blinking to clear the black fog crowding her vision, she looked up. The balloon had stabilised and was now bobbing peacefully above her, with its cable fully extended and side and tail fins filled with air.

'Are you all right, Effie?' the same resonant voice asked, from what seemed like a long way away.

Her head whirling, she looked up.

Nathan, an anxious look on his handsome face, stood looking down at her. Behind him, looking equally worried, stood Alice and Nell.

'Effie?' he repeated, his blue eyes scrutinising her closely.

'Just a bit shaken, sir,' she replied, forcing a smile. 'That's all.'

'Can you stand?'

'I think so,' she replied.

He offered her his hand. She took it, and his fingers closed round hers. Gripping on to him tightly, Effie managed to get to her feet.

'I think we should take you to the quack,' Nathan said.

'No, honestly.' She shook her head, and regretted it instantly. 'I need to catch my—'

The black cloud framing her vision suddenly crowded in and her legs gave way. However, as she sank to the ground, a pair of strong arms surrounded her.

∽

'Can I help you, Officer?' asked the Princess Mary's RAF nurse, smiling up at him from behind the reception desk of Cardington's small infirmary.

She had hair greying at the temple and comfortable motherly roundness, and Nathan guessed she was a few years younger than his mother's fifty. She was probably one of those who had seen service on the front as a young nurse in the first fight with the Germans, but like many other armed service veterans had opted to defer their well-earned retirement to do her bit this time round.

'I'm enquiring about Corporal Weston,' Nathan replied, the pungent mix of carbolic and surgical spirits filling his nose. 'She was bought in a couple of hours ago after a training accident. I am one of the instructors.'

The nurse looked down and consulted her clipboard, then raised her head.

'Well, she escaped quite lightly, considering,' she said, her jolly, round face beaming from beneath her starched, white triangular cap. 'A few scrapes and bruises, but Doctor wants to keep her in tonight just to make sure.'

'Could I see her?' Nathan asked.

'She's supposed to be resting for the shock,' the nurse replied. 'I don't—'

'Only for a moment or two,' added Nathan, giving her his widest, friendliest smile.

She hesitated, then nodded. 'Very well. She's in the ward on the right at the end of the corridor.'

'Thank you, Sister,' he said.

She indicated which of the two corridors she meant, and with his cap tucked firmly under his arm, he set off.

'But ten minutes, no longer,' she called after him.

When Nathan reached the ward he pushed the door open and walked in.

Although there were only ten beds on the ward, they were laid out like any other hospital with a row down either side. There was a nurses' station at the far end, behind which were two doors, presumably to the treatment room and sluice respectively. At the other end of the small ward were a couple of single-bed cubicles with windows looking out onto the main part of the ward.

The young nurse sitting behind the desk looked up briefly as Nathan entered, then returned to writing her notes as he cast his eyes along the rows of beds.

There was a young woman he didn't recognise in the bed in the corner by the treatment room, and the only other bed that was occupied was the last one in the row opposite under the window. As he looked at its occupant, Nathan's heart swelled.

Effie was lying on top of the pink counterpane with her hands across her stomach and her eyes closed. Nathan let his eyes enjoy the sight of her for a second or two, then a half smile lifted his lips.

How on earth could a woman look so ravishingly beautiful

dressed in RAF-issue striped winceyette pyjamas, a dressing gown at least two sizes too big and a pair of grey woolly service socks? But then to be fair she also looked unbelievably gorgeous in a baggy boiler suit. In fact, as far as he was concerned, Effie Weston would look as stunning as any woman in the land in an old potato sack, as he'd realised as he held her in his arms on the dancefloor weeks ago, because he loved her, and had done so almost from the moment he'd first laid eyes on her. Which raised the question as to what on earth he was going to do about it.

As if sensing him watching her, Effie opened her eyes and smiled.

'Officer Fitzgerald,' she said, attempting to sit up.

'As you were,' said Nathan, crossing the space between them in a few long strides.

She let out a long sigh. 'Thank you.' She sank back into the pillows.

Taking the chair from the foot of the bed, Nathan placed it alongside her. He put his hat on the small bedside locker and sat down.

'I've just popped in to see how you are,' he said, enjoying the sight of her unbound hair curling over her left shoulder.

'Battered and bruised, and I've been reminded how much iodine stings,' she replied. 'But thankfully, no bones broken – but my head! It feels like I've done six rounds with Joe Louis.'

Nathan laughed. 'I'm not surprised after the way you hit the ground.'

'Did you see what happened?'

He nodded. 'A gust caught your balloon before it was stable. You and your crew had only just got it back on the right alignment to the wind when the WAAF behind you let go of her rope. Your foot got tangled in it and it dragged you across the ground. I'm only thankful that I was close enough to help.'

'Yes, thank you for stepping in like that to help a damsel in distress, again.'

'Call me Sir Galahad,' Nathan replied.

Effie laughed, then gave him a shy glance from beneath her lashes. 'And for catching me.'

'My pleasure,' he replied, remembering the delight of her head resting on his chest as he held her in his arms.

'Matron said you carried me all the way over here,' she continued.

'You were very pale,' he replied. 'And I didn't want to wait for the base's ambulance.'

His gaze rested on her small hand on the infirmary bedspreads and he wished he had the right to take it in his. Resisting the urge, he returned his attention to Effie's face. She smiled and her lovely hazel eyes softened, swelling Nathan's chest and setting his heart off at a gallop.

They stared wordlessly at each other for a moment, then, to stop himself from blurting out something stupid, Nathan cleared his throat.

'So, you and your crew are off to your war site on Monday,' he said.

'Yes, we're all looking forward to it,' said Effie. 'It's at a place called Shadwell alongside the Thames. Apparently, being so close to the London Docks, it's been in the thick of it since the start.'

'I suppose you're all going to have a bash in the WAAFs' mess on Saturday before you set off,' said Nathan.

'Some are, but me and a few of the others are going to the BBC concert they're broadcasting from the boys' school,' she replied. 'It's going to be Mendelssohn's Scottish symphony, which is one of my favourite pieces.'

'What a coincidence,' said Nathan. 'I'm going there with a couple of friends myself.'

Actually, that wasn't quite true. Wiktor and the two Vikings were going and had asked him to join them but he hadn't committed to going.

'Perhaps I'll see you there,' he said. 'I understand there are refreshments afterwards, so maybe we can even get that long overdue cup of tea?'

Effie's lovely face lifted in a wistful smile.

'I'd like that very much, Officer Fitzgerald,' she said softly.

'So would I, Corporal Weston,' he replied, holding her gaze.

They stared wordlessly at each other, then a bell rang in one of the side rooms and the nurse at the desk stood up, and, tearing his eyes away from Effie, so did Nathan.

'I ought to go,' he said, not making the slightest move to do so.

'It was good of you to come and see how I am,' she said, her eyes bright as they looked up at him.

'Not at all. It was the least I could do.' Nathan picked up his cap from the locker and tucked it firmly under his arm. 'I hope you feel better after a good night's sleep.'

'I'm sure I will,' she replied.

Although he knew he should go, Nathan just couldn't. Instead, rooted to the spot, he stared down at the woman he was hopelessly in love with, bundled up as she was in a faded, dressing gown.

The words 'Effie, I love you' formed themselves in Nathan's brain and started to make their way to his vocal cords but as he opened his mouth to speak them the sound of the ward door swinging open cut them off.

He turned as the older nurse who had been sitting at the desk poked her head round the door. 'Officer Fitzgerald?'

'Yes, sorry, Sister,' said Nathan. 'I'm about to leave.'

'I'm sure you are,' she said. 'I'm not here to scold you about your timekeeping but to tell you that RAF Tempsford telephoned through to the main office asking you to return their call urgently.'

Her head disappeared again, and the door squeaked shut. Nathan's attention returned to Effie. 'Sorry, I'd better...'

'That's all right,' she said. "And I'll see you on Saturday.'

'You most certainly will,' Nathan replied.

He took in the sight of her for a second or two longer, then flipped his cap on, turned and marched out.

It was two days until Saturday. Just two days until, even if she laughed in his face or despised him as a scoundrel for disregarding the fact she was engaged, he would tell her straight that he loved her, and ask her to marry him.

CHAPTER 15

'Good of you to come so swiftly,' said Donaldson as Nathan walked into the briefing room.

As the blackout had come into force twenty minutes ago, at six fifteen, the blinds at the control room windows were all down tight, which had plunged the nerve centre of the 161 Special Duties Squadron into a murky gloom lit only by the harsh strip lighting buzzing overhead.

As usual there was a map of northern France spread across the central table that Donaldson was sitting at, but all the other chairs round it were empty.

'Matron said it was urgent,' Nathan replied, closing the door and saluting.

The group captain's considerable eyebrows pulled together. 'Matron? Not your shoulder, I hope.'

'No, that's tip-top,' Nathan replied, which was as near to the truth as damn it. 'I was at the infirmary checking in on one of the trainees who was injured. You said it was urgent, so I gathered my kit as instructed and dumped it at Hazells Hall on my way across.'

'Good,' said Donaldson, beckoning him closer. 'Because you're transferred back here with immediate effect.'

'Has something happened?' asked Nathan, praying one of his fellow 161 squadron pilots had not been captured or killed.

'Not as such,' Donaldson replied. 'But Whitehall are pretty pleased with the SOE's operation to set up their own networks behind enemy lines, so the top brass have decided to give SOE the thumbs-up to step up their activities. This means there's likely to be a couple of our chaps flying every night we're able. On top of which, we still have our stranded pilots lying low with the resistance who need picking up, so it's all hands to the pump, Fitzgerald.' His bushy moustache lifted at the corners. 'Or perhaps that should be "all hands to the joystick".'

Nathan acknowledged the quip with a small smile. 'So what am I on the board for?'

'Collecting two pilots a few miles north of Le Mans.'

Nathan raised an eyebrow. 'That's one hell of a flight, Skip, even with the extra fuel tank on the Lysander.'

'I know, I know,' agreed Donaldson. 'You'll have to stop at Tangmere to top up before you set off across the Channel.'

'When?' asked Nathan.

'Tomorrow!'

Nathan breathed a silent sigh of relief. Thank goodness. He'd be back in time for the concert with Effie.

'And it has to be tomorrow,' continued Donaldson, cutting into the images of Effie entwined in his arms dancing in Nathan's head, 'or we'll be moving into the moon's last quarter. I know it will be a bit of a scramble to get your prep done, but I'm sending you, Fitzgerald, because frankly I wouldn't entrust it to anyone else. So wheels-up twenty-one hundred tomorrow, eh?'

Nathan stood to attention. 'Yes, sir. And thank you, sir.'

He saluted and Donaldson returned it.

Nathan turned on his heels and, leaving his commanding

officer poring over the maps strewn across the table, marched out of the briefing room.

Duty and stranded pilots came first, of course, but, having resolved to tell Effie how he felt, he was relieved he'd be back in the early hours of Saturday morning and in good time to meet her at the concert that night. And then who knew...? Didn't Father MacPherson always preach about living in hope?

CHAPTER 16

～

Holding the pencil torch between his teeth, Nathan checked his compass and watch, then, after doing a quick computation in his head of both, he checked his map. Satisfied that he was on the right trajectory and within a few miles of his landing site, he adjusted the Lysander flaps and took the Lizzie down 100 feet.

There before him was spread the Normandy countryside, dotted with farmhouses and the occasional village, all shades of grey in the pale light of the quarter-moon.

It was now a little after one thirty in the morning and some three and a half hours since he had filled both his main and reserve tanks to the brim with aviation fuel. Nathan raised his head and glanced at the flight instruments in front of him and the hint of a smile lifted the corners of his mouth. Thanks to his keeping the brisk westerly on his tail, the fuel still showed a little over half full.

A river shimmered below him, indicating that his intended landing site was coming up fast. Nathan adjusted the circular joystick and took the plane down a further 100 feet, then spotted a small copse on the horizon and a light flashing *dot dash dot dot* for L. Nathan reached forward to the button on the right of the cockpit and replied with the same, and the inverted L of the three landing lights flashed on.

Nathan circled low once, then lined up the nose and brought the Lizzie down almost within the plane's own body length. As four figures emerged from the hedgerow he taxied to the end of the pair of lights, then wheeled round and lined the aircraft up with the third, ready to take off: an operation that should take three perhaps four minutes at most.

Sliding back the cockpit canopy to dispel the stale air, Nathan took a long breath. Glancing over the edge of the aircraft, he noticed that one of the figures was hobbling and being held upright on either side by two others. The other one of the four, a middle-aged man wearing a shapeless jacket and trousers and with a Sten gun slung across him, was running towards the plane.

'I am afraid we 'ave three who must go,' he called up over the rhythmic whoosh of the propeller blade.

'Three might be a problem,' Nathan shouted back.

'I know, monsieur. But Jack was betrayed to the Gestapo by collaborators and shot making 'is escape,' the partisan shouted back.

Nathan studied the three standing figures in the gloom. One of the airmen was about the same height and build as him, so probably weighed in around twelve stone; however, the other pilot could have weighed no more than ten stone, and the youth they held between them couldn't be more than eight stone, very likely less.

Given that he was at the limit of the Lizzie's flight range, squeezing in another passenger would put them all at risk, so by rights he should refuse, but...

'Get in,' he shouted.

The slightly built pilot clambered on board, and did the usual double take when he saw Nathan's face beneath his leather flying helmet. Reaching down, he lifted the injured young man up, followed swiftly by the second pilot.

With a wave of acknowledgement, the resistance fighter melted back into the night.

'Best to lie him on the fuselage shelf in front of you,' Nathan called over his shoulder as he bumped along the improvised runway. 'There's a flask of brandy next to the first aid box – you might want to give him a swig.'

Picking up speed, Nathan adjusted the flaps and rudder, then he pulled back on the throttle and the plane soared up over the trees of the wooded copse into the ink-black midnight sky.

'How is he doing?' Nathan shouted over the drone of the engine.

'Better,' the first pilot called back.

'I'll call in once I'm in range of our air defence and have the medic standing by,' Nathan said.

'What about you?' asked the other pilot.

Nathan gave a thumbs-up.

That was more or less true.

Other than the odd puffy cloud lingering around, the night was crystal clear, and flying at 5,000 feet Nathan could clearly see the French coast below him, so knew without consulting his map that he was on the right course.

Nathan continued on, skimming over the silent land and riding a couple of bumps of turbulence as the warm air rising from the land mingled with the cold air sweeping in from the sea as they approached the coast of Brittany. With the first hint of dawn lightening the eastern sky he spotted the craggy east coast of the Cherbourg peninsula, so, taking the Lizzie down, he was just about to turn north to head back to Tangmere when to his right in the distance he spotted the distinctive shape and black-and-white double-cross fuselage markings of a Focke-Wulf Fw 190 heading his way.

'Bandit at two o'clock,' the pilot behind him shouted, but Nathan had already banked hard to the left.

He took the plane down to about a hundred feet and skimmed above the crashing waves, hoping the soaring cliffs would conceal his unarmed plane from the guns of the Luftwaffe fighter plane. However, as Nathan banked left to avoid a rocky spur the Focke roared over the edge of the cliff above.

The enemy plane high above them circled round, then came up behind the Lysander. As he had in his Spitfire during the Battle of Britain, he banked left and then right in rapid succession as a burst of machine-gun fire spat past them.

The Luftwaffe fighter copied his moves and wheeled round again, but this time instead of returning to its previous position at the rear it disappeared back over the top of the cliff.

Still hugging the shoreline, Nathan held his breath and waited for the enemy aircraft to reappear. However, after several agonising minutes it was clear the Fw 190 wasn't going to. Nathan let out a long sigh.

He glanced at the fuel gauge and, noting that the needle had suddenly dropped to below the quarter, pressed his lips together. A bullet from his encounter with the Luftwaffe aircraft had clearly punctured the reserve fuel tank beneath the Lysander.

Damn!

There were still two and a half hours of flying into a head wind until he was in sight of the British mainland and the safety of the coastal air defences. Even before his encounter with the Fw 190 he would have been flying the last few miles to Tangmere on fumes. But now...

Gritting his teeth, Nathan opened up the engine's throttle and, mindful of the inflatable dinghy beneath his seat, headed northwards towards the English Channel. It wasn't ideal by any means, but if he had to land in the drink then the nearer to

England he was, the more likely that the navy's coastal patrols would pick them up.

An image of Effie and the life they might have flashed across his mind.

He'd been in tighter spots before and survived, and, with the hope of a life with the woman he loved burning in his chest, Nathan was going to make damn sure he survived this one.

CHAPTER 17

As the last strains of Mendelssohn faded the whole audience erupted in excited applause.

'Marvellous, wasn't it,' said Alice, clapping enthusiastically beside her.

'Electrifying,' Effie replied.

And it had been.

However, although she dutifully acknowledged the skill of the musicians performing the classical piece, as Nathan had not arrived a cloud of disappointment still hovered over her.

'I think they were better than when I heard the piece performed at the Albert Hall in 'thirty-six,' said George.

The orchestra rose to their feet at the conductor's invitation and the applause rose again. People stood up and Effie followed suit, taking the opportunity to skim her eyes across the audience behind her.

'Shall we get a cuppa?' asked Alice.

'If we get a shift on we'll have first dibs at the cake,' said Nell. 'You lot coming?'

'I could very well murder a cuppa,' said Maeve.

'Me too,' said Alice.

Pushing aside her gloom, Effie put on a bright smile. 'Count me in.'

'George?' asked Nell.

'I'll join you in a mo,' said George. 'I've just spotted Buzzer Beasdale, my brother's old friend from Eton.'

'Buzzer!' Nell rolled her eyes. 'Don't your lot ever use your proper monikers?'

George gave her a serene smile, then gathered up her handbag, sidestepped out of the row and headed for a knot of army officers standing by the door.

Nell and Maeve followed her and then joined the crowd filing into the school's refectory.

Effie's gaze strayed back to the group of airmen from the gallery who were now in the queue for refreshments, and guilt clawed at her chest. With Leonard's engagement ring on a chain round her neck and a wedding booked in the Abbey for next April, her head knew it was wrong of her even to look at another man, but somehow her heart didn't seem to share that opinion.

'Shall we join them before Nell scoffs all the cake?' said Alice.

Forcing aside her gloom, Effie hooked her arm in her friend's. 'W-what-ho, old thing, let's bally well do just that.'

Alice laughed. 'Right you are, old bean. Tally ho!'

Effie took her cup from the motherly-looking WVS woman in her forest-green uniform on the other side of the serving hatch, thanked her and stepped aside.

George was at the back of the hall, talking in her usual animated fashion to a slightly built army captain with a sandy-coloured toothbrush moustache and receding chin. True to her stated aim of marrying an American, five-foot-nothing Nell had cornered a six-foot-plus GI.

Maeve and Alice had gone off to locate the Ladies and had yet to return, so, balancing her fern-coloured cup and saucer in her hand, Effie made her way across to one of the empty tables by the long casement window.

Taking a sip of her tea, she looked across at the half a dozen or so RAF officers standing towards the back of the room. As always, given their dashing reputation among the popular press and the cinema newsreels, there was a cluster of female admirers gazing adoringly up at them.

The truck would be taking them off to their war sites tomorrow and she doubted that Nathan would still be at Cardington when she returned. Of course, there could be any number of reasons why he hadn't turned up at the concert.

She sighed. Perhaps, as she had a wedding planned for next April, it was for the best.

'Well hello there,' drawled a voice behind her. 'We meet again.'

Effie turned and found herself face to face with a tall, slim young army officer with a blunt chin, chiselled features and pale-blond hair. However, despite his evident attractiveness his pale-blue eyes had an expression in them that could only be described as leering.

'Do we?' said Effie, giving him a cool look.

'I'm sure we've met before,' he replied. 'As I never forget a pretty face.'

'And how many times have you used that pick-up line?' Effie asked.

'Come on, don't be like that,' he said. 'I'm only trying to be friendly. I tell you what, why don't we start again with a little drink?'

Delving into his trouser pocket, he pulled out a silver hip flask. He flipped off the lid and offered it to her.

'No, thank you,' said Effie. 'In case you missed it as you

came in, there's a noticeboard by the door that says no alcohol allowed on school premises.'

'What the eye doesn't see the heart doesn't grieve over.' Winking, he took a swig. 'Besides, I'm a bit of a rebel.'

'Are you?' said Effie.

Raising the flask to his lips, he nodded.

'I have to be, in my job,' he continued, smacking his lips. 'Because I'm with...' He tapped his aquiline nose with a long index finger. 'Frazer Frobisher, by the way. Lieutenant, obviously.' He indicated the two pips on his epaulettes. 'So where are you based then, Corporal...?'

'Weston,' Effie said. 'And I'm part of Balloon Command at Cardington.'

Frobisher clicked his fingers. 'I knew I'd seen you before. About a few months ago at the dance at the Corn Exchange. You were dancing with that bolshie Fitzgerald.'

'Do you know Nathan?' Effie's asked, her heart thumping in her chest.

Frobisher's mouth twisted into an ugly line. 'Yes, I know him, more's the pity. He's a bit too free with his opinions. I've pulled him up more than once for not knowing his place. Not that he takes much heed.' He raised an eyebrow. 'And Nathan, is it? Well, well. I suppose he does hold a certain... appeal for some women.'

Effie bristled. 'I found him to be a perfect gentleman. And a very good dancer.'

'Well, I doubt he's dancing anywhere now,' Frobisher replied.

Effie stared at him. 'What do you mean?'

'He's been reported as missing in action,' said Frobisher, pouring a generous measure of spirits into his tea.

The tiled floor under Effie's feet tilted for an instant, then returned to its rightful place. With her head reeling and the blood pounding in her ears almost deafening her, she stared dumbly at the man beside her.

'He was sent on a mission two days ago and no one has seen or heard from him since,' Frobisher continued, in a voice that seemed to be coming from a long way away. 'Of course, he might turn up, but...' He pulled a face and shrugged. 'Shame of course,' he added, oblivious to the scream rising in Effie's throat. 'He was a decent pilot, I'll give him that, but there it is.' Studying her closely, he offered the flask again. 'You sure you don't want a drink?'

Her heart crashing in her chest, Effie shook her head. 'If you'd excuse...'

She sidestepped round him and, squeezing through the milling crowds, hurried across to where Alice was standing.

'My goodness, Effie, are you all right?' her friend asked, concern written large across her face.

With tears pinching the corners of her eyes, Effie shook her head. 'I have to go.'

Placing her half-drunk cup of tea down on the nearest table, Alice put her arm round Effie. 'Let's find a taxi.'

Listening to the soft snoring coming from the WAAF in the bed four down, Effie lay with her arms on top of the grey RAF blanket, staring blankly up at the iron girders of the hut's roof. She reckoned it was about four in the morning now, and Dunbar would be in to wake them at six to ensure they were watered, fed and packed before the transport trucks started arriving at nine. Not that it mattered, because now Effie's mind was clear.

She peeled back her blankets, swung her legs out of bed and placed her bare feet on the floorboards. Crouching down, she reached beneath her bed and pulled out her personal box, and extracted the Basildon Bond stationery her aunt had given her for Christmas and the fountain pen lying beside it.

Effie pushed the box back, grasped her pen, paper and envelopes and, in her baggy navy-striped WAAF pyjamas and dressing gown, tiptoed across to the table next to the unlit stove. She placed her writing equipment on the desk and slid into one of the chairs, then spread a sheet of light-blue paper before her. She fished beneath her pyjama top and, finding her engagement ring dangling on its chain, slipped it over her head.

Effie studied it nestled in the palm of her hand, then, laying it on the table, picked up her pen and unscrewed the top. She took her pencil torch out of her pocket, laid it on the desk, then in the pool of muted light from its beam, pressed the nib to the paper.

Dear Leonard,

I wish I could say what I have to say face to face but as I'm off to my war site in a few hours I won't have the opportunity. I am very sorry, Leonard, but I cannot marry you...

CHAPTER 18

'Right, here we are, ducks,' said Mrs Granger, beaming at Effie. 'This here's the lounge. Back there' – she indicated over her shoulder with a red nail-polished thumb – 'is the kitchen and there's five rooms up top with two beds. There's a box room too with a single, plus bathroom and lav on each floor. The linen's all clean and there's two blankets and an eiderdown bedspread on each bed, plus a wardrobe and chest of drawers in all the rooms.'

Effie and the rest of no. 3 crew were standing in the first-floor front room of the Maid of Norway, a century-old four-storey gin palace squatting on the corner of Glasshouse Fields and the Highway a stone's throw from the Thames and overlooking their war site.

Although it was just after midday, their new landlady, a voluptuous redhead with bosoms threatening to spill out of her figure-hugging navy dress, looked as if she was about to enjoy a night out. However, her heavily mascaraed blue eyes were warm and her cherry-red lips had a friendly smile.

The main living room of the public house accommodation

was a decent size, although judging by the faded flock maroon wall the room hadn't been decorated for years.

However, the heavy furniture had been polished, the chandelier sparkled and the Indian carpet that covered most of the floor, although worn, had been recently swept. The sofa and chairs were a little threadbare in places but had an assortment of brightly coloured knitted blankets draped over them. Also, given that winter had yet to loosen its grip, the small heap of coals glowing in the cast-iron fireplace grate were very welcome.

'I hope it's all right,' continued Mrs Granger, cutting across Effie's thoughts.

'Thank you, Mrs Granger, it looks very comfortable,' said Effie.

'It's an absolute palace compared to the freezing hut we've been in for the past eleven weeks,' said Alice.

'It's Florrie, ducks,' said Mrs Granger. 'And I say it's the least we in the Shadwell WVS could do for you all, seeing how you girls are here defending us. In fact, we've adopted you as our crew.'

'That's grand,' said Maeve.

Florrie's powdered face lifted in a friendly smile. 'We girls have to stick together, don't we?'

'I should jolly well think so, Mrs G,' said George.

'We've sorted out a family for you all to visit when you're off duty,' said Florrie. 'And of course we'd love you to join us at our rest centre in Highway School down the road from here if you're at a loose end any time. There's always a cuppa brewing and a bit of cake.'

'If there's cake going, count me in.' Nell laughed.

Florrie gave her a querying look. 'You from around here?'

'Whitechapel,' said Nell.

'My cousin lives up that way, in Alders Street,' said Florrie. 'Right opposite what's left of the old church.'

'We're in Thrawl Street,' said Nell.

'Well, tell 'em they can pop in any time,' said Florrie. 'That goes for the rest of you, too. You ain't banged up in barracks now, so you might as well make the most of it.'

'Thank you,' said Effie.

'Well, I 'spect you want to settle yourselves in, so I'll leave you to it,' said Florrie.

She left and her high heels echoed up the stairwell as she returned to the pub downstairs. Lily and her friend Maureen ran up the stairs to the landing above.

'I guess they're going to nab the best room,' said Maeve.

'Well,' said Alice. 'We might as well go up and sort out ours, too.'

Shouldering their kitbags, the five girls made their way upstairs to the floor above.

As they'd predicted, Lily and Maureen had taken up residence in what Effie guessed was the main bedroom, opposite the bathroom and toilet, so the unlikely duo of George and Nell took the slightly smaller one overlooking the rear of the pub, while Peggy and Rose took the double room next to them.

Effie, with the other two following, continued up to the third floor.

The rooms at the top of the house were in the eaves and had probably once been where the potman, skivvy and maid slept. Maeve and Dolly went into the one at the front, so Effie and Alice took the one at the back.

Florrie and her WVS chums had again worked their magic so, although Effie and Alice's room was smaller and had a partially sloping ceiling, both beds were covered with patchwork covers and there were rag rugs on the floor. The rooms at the top of the house were as welcoming and cosy as the rest of their accommodation.

Alice dropped her bag on the floor. 'Well, I'm going to unpack later because I'm desperate for a cuppa. Do you want one, Effie?'

'Thanks, Alice, I'm a bit whacked out so I think I might put my feet up for half an hour,' Effie replied.

Her friend gave her a sympathetic look. 'You do look a bit done in. You get forty winks, and I give you a shout when Florrie tells us that grub's up.'

Alice left the room and Effie sank back onto the bed, kicked her shoes off without untying the laces and closed her eyes.

Actually, she wasn't just physically done in but emotionally wrung out, too.

It had been almost five thirty by the time she finished Leonard's letter, and she had washed and dressed, then walked to the post box at the front gate before returning to the NAAFI. She had then phoned Tempsford's main office, only to be told, despite her hopes and prayers, that Nathan was indeed missing in action. Of course, plenty of men who were listed as such turned up, but...

Tears formed behind her closed lids and rolled down her temples into her hair.

How could she have been so naïve, so blind and so stupid as not to realise sooner that the breathless reaction and unsettling emotions whirling around inside her were in fact her deep and passionate love? Deep and passionate love for Nathan, who was goodness only knew where.

∽

The sound of two pairs of heavy boots and jangling keys woke Nathan from the light doze he'd drifted into as he sat propped against the tiled wall of the cell. Opening his eyes, he looked across at Flight Sergeant Hanson and Navigator Mills, sitting on the hard wooden bench fixed to the opposite wall.

It was now Sunday afternoon and Nathan and the two pilots he had rescued were sitting in this damp cell, and had been since they'd been picked up by a Home Guard patrol, who had held them captive as German spies since the Lysander belly-flopped into a ploughed field forty-eight hours before.

It was understandable really why the doughty retired general who led the motley contingent of rheumatic veterans and beardless youths should arrest them as spies. Although Nathan was still in his padded flight suit, thanks to the French resistance who had sheltered them, Mills and Hanson, unshaven and dressed in threadbare trousers and colourless jumpers, looked like a pair of Breton fishermen who had fallen on hard times.

'What do you think they want this time?' said Mills, his blue eyes looking expectantly at the iron door standing between them and the outside world.

'I have no idea,' said Hanson, running his chubby fingers through his Brylcreemed hair. 'We've told them who we are. I don't know what else they need.'

After a moment or two the footsteps stopped outside, and Nathan and his fellow inmates sat upright and looked expectantly at the solid century-old prison door.

The door swung open and revealed a sandy-haired RAF officer with two narrow blue bands on his epaulettes.

Nathan let out a long breath. Thank goodness!

He and the rescued airmen sprang to their feet and saluted.

'As you were, men,' said the RAF officer, striding into the cell.

They all stood easy.

'Lieutenant Lamont. Sorry it's taken so long to get this sorted out,' he said, glancing around at them from beneath his peak of his cap.

'How's Bellman?' asked Nathan.

'His knee's still a bit wonky but on the mend otherwise,' Lamont replied. 'What about you three?'

'Just glad it's all been squared up,' said Hanson.

'Good,' said Lamont, beaming at them. 'You can bunk down

with us at Warmwell until we can get you back to your units.' He turned to the stout Home Guardsman. 'I trust you've done the paperwork.'

'Sir,' he replied, saluting smartly.

'So can we get out of here now?' asked Mills.

'You most certainly can,' said Lamont. 'Follow me.'

The Home Guard captain saluted as Nathan and the two other airmen marched out of the cell and into a tunnel that appeared to be hewn out of solid rock.

'You're in the dungeons under Milton House,' Lamont explained as they walked through. 'It's been requisitioned by the army for the duration.'

After winding their way through a series of passages and up some well-worn stone stairs, they finally emerged into the bright early-morning glare of Sunday morning.

The once manicured lawns stretched out in front of them, now dotted with khaki USA army tents and GIs perched on crates and field stools playing cards and cleaning boots. Someone somewhere was playing a guitar. There were others in the far field playing what looked like rounders. While most of the American soldiers were at ease, a cluster of GIs could be seen, sponge in hand, washing the dozen or so jeeps with white stars painted on the bonnet.

Lamont's staff car, a Humber Snipe, was waiting for them in the sweeping driveway of the Palladian-style country house. A couple of the American soldiers gave Nathan a hostile look when he, as next senior officer, clambered in beside Lamont.

'What about my Lizzie?' asked Nathan as they sped away, the Union Jack pendant on the bonnet fluttering.

'It looks like you came down with a bit of a bang, old chap,' Lamont replied. 'Busted one of its wheels, I'm afraid. And the radio antenna looks as if it's been shot off.'

'That explains why I couldn't raise coastal control,' said Nathan.

'I'm afraid the old girl's going to take a few days before you can fly her back to base,' added Lamont.

'How long?' Nathan asked.

'You'll have to check with our grease monkeys in the engineering shed, but we've rung through to Tempsford to let them know you're safe and well,' he replied as they passed through the stone pillars of the estate and into a sleepy-looking village with honey-coloured houses topped with thatch. ' I'm afraid it's a bit of a drive to base but at least the mess bar will be open when you get there.'

An hour and a quarter later, after bumping along country lanes, and being caught behind a flock of sheep for twenty minutes, Lamont swung the steering wheel and turned in to RAF Warmwell. Recognising him, one of the base's senior officers leant on the barrier and it swung upwards. The car zoomed along the base's main roadway and stopped outside a row of accommodation huts. A couple of aircraftmen second class jumped forward as they stopped.

Nathan and the two other passengers, clutching what remained of their clothes and gear, climbed out.

'Ah, Stevens, Farmer,' said Lamont, returning their salute. 'Officer Fitzgerald, Sergeant Hanson and Navigator Mills are going to be with us for a day or two, so show them to their quarters and let them know where everything is, will you?'

The two junior airmen saluted again and headed off, with Nathan and the two others a couple of steps behind.

'And see if you can find them some temporary kit, will you?' Lamont called after them.

They trooped along the corridor of the officers' quarters. Mills and Hanson were allocated their rooms, and Nathan was shown into his accommodation a few doors further down.

'I'll bring you some wash kit – the showers are two blocks

over,' said the aircraftman as Nathan dropped his kitbag on the floor. 'And the mess is next to the offices on the main road. You passed it as you drove in.'

'Thank you...?'

'Stevens,' the young airman replied. 'Is there anything else?'

'Thank you, Stevens,' said Nathan. 'Could you just tell me where the nearest telephone is?'

CHAPTER 19

'Right girls,' called Sergeant Munroe, standing feet slightly apart, her uniform's polished buttons twinkling in the frosty morning sunlight. 'Now you've settled into your billet I hope you're all raring to go.'

'Yes, Sergeant,' chorused Effie and the nine other young women who made up no. 3 crew.

It was five to seven on Monday morning and they were on the first day of their three-week stint of being on active duty as a WAAF balloon crew.

Thanks to Florrie having fired up the boiler first thing, they were all washed, dressed and breakfasted well before Munroe, a well-built, fair-haired woman in her early thirties, arrived at half past six.

However, despite having been dead on her feet by the time her head hit the pillow at ten, Effie had spent most of the night staring up at the light bulb swinging from the flex above her, as her mind ran through almost every image it had of Nathan and every word he had spoken. Interspersed with this montage was her aching heart calling her a fool for not realising she was deeply in love with him until now.

'Line them up, Corporal,' continued the too-chipper sergeant.

Stepping out from her position at the end, Effie faced her crew. 'Parade!'

Much to the delight of those passing by, the young women of no. 3 crew shuffled into two lines, Lily and Maureen bringing up the rear as usual.

Happy with the formation, Munroe took up position at the front.

'By the left,' she hollered.

Effie's crew stepped off and marched across the Highway and down King David Lane, which ran south from Cable Street towards the River Thames.

'My goodness,' said Alice, as they passed a tall wall that was all that remained of a tenement building. 'Those poor souls. I read about the London Blitz in the paper but I never imagined it would be this bad.'

'It's been like that off and on around here for two and half years,' said Nell, who was marching in front of them alongside George.

'I don't know how anyone could stand it night after night,' said Maeve, gazing at a spiral of black smoke over one of the riverside factories.

'We're a tough bunch, us East Enders,' said Nell. 'It takes a bit more than a few bombs to break us.'

'It must be heartbreaking to emerge from the shelter one morning and find everything you own gone,' said Effie, as her gaze travelled over clothes, bedlinen, mangled bedsteads and smashed furniture among the still-smouldering rubble that had once been people's homes.

'Still, at least the pickers haven't been able to go through it,' added Nell.

'Pickers?' asked Effie.

'Looters,' Nell explained. 'Surely you've read about them in the papers. There's no point risking ending up at the pearly gates under a collapsed wall for a bit of crockery or a pair of curtains.'

'I thought children were supposed to be evacuated,' said Alice, watching a gang of boys scrambling over the rubble of a row of houses on the opposite side of the street.

'Some were as soon as the war kicked off,' Nell replied. 'But most of them were back by Christmas. Now most people round here hold the view that if they're going to cop it then they might as well all go together. That's how my lot up Whitechapel think, anyhows. Of course, now the ARP have taken over most of the schools for control centres and relief centres and their mothers are working double shifts in factories to put food on the table, kids are left to get on with it.'

'You're lucky to be stationed so near to your family, Nell,' said Maeve. 'Mine are in Newry, so God only knows when I'll see them again.'

'Lucky, am I?' Nell gave her a baleful look. 'I joined the blasted RAF to get away from the buggers!'

When they reached Wapping High Street, the troop of WAAFs paused.

A black ARP van, its wheels caked with ash, went by, a couple of lorries laden down with crates and sacks from the nearby docks close behind. An army truck with a dozen or so khaki-clad soldiers bouncing around in the back trundled by, with the usual accompanying wolf-whistles and catcalls.

Finally, after a fire engine had sped by, Munroe marched the crew across. They stopped in front of a low wall with a series of rusty holes along the top where, presumably, the railing had been, and a sign with *King Edward VI Recreational Ground* painted on it.

The park in front of them was a little lower than street level, with herbaceous borders and artistically shaped flower beds cut into the lawn. However, the display of brightly coloured spring and summer flowers had been given way to cabbages, onion tops and carrot fronds, and the area that had once clearly been the place for Sunday afternoon strolls was now completely taken up by the bloated silvery-grey balloon, hovering at fifty feet or so above them in 'close-haul' status.

Beneath it was a circle of gravel about eighty feet in circumference. At its centre were two blocks of concrete with hooks embedded in them, at the top of one of which were the steadying guy ropes. The balloon was tethered into place by a winch with the taut anchor cable embedded in a ten-foot-square block of concrete.

On the opposite side of the gravel balloon bed from the winch was a prefabricated Nissen hut with a half a dozen or so airmen lolling around outside. They were dressed in their parade uniform, with packed kitbags at their feet. As the current balloon's crew spotted their relief crew, they started buttoning up combat jackets and shouldering their kitbags.

'Well, here we are, girls,' said Munroe, turning round and beaming at them. 'RAF Balloon Command Station 312 balloon. As you can see, we're right on the banks of Old Father Thames. St Katharine Docks in Shadwell is about half a mile to the west.' She pointed upriver. 'And the Victoria and Albert Docks are in Canning Town, about two miles in the other direction. As you can probably guess from the location and the bomb damage around us, your posting will be in the thick of the action. Shall we go and say hello to Bessie?'

'Bessie?' asked Alice.

'That's what we call the balloon,' the sergeant explained. 'They've all got names. Usually named after singers or film stars, but sometimes other people. I believe there's one bobbing around Whitehall named Winston. Now, shall we go and get you settled into your home from home?'

Without waiting for a reply Sergeant Munroe marched

down the half a dozen steps and started across the gravel towards the balloon.

'Right, crew,' said Effie. 'Let's go and get sorted out.'

Falling into step behind her, the balloon crew followed Effie across to the Nissen hut.

The airmen had already started loading onto the transport, but on seeing the WAAFs they paused in their tasks to give them their usual greeting of wolf-whistles, which the WAAFs responded to with some long-suffering eye-rolling and exasperated looks.

As Sergeant Granger was chatting to her RAF equivalent, Effie and Millie Tyler, the corporal from number 9 crew, headed across to the Nissen hut.

Their RAF counterpart, standing outside, was a tall, slender chap in his mid-twenties, with very blond hair and a prominent Adam's apple. He gave them a friendly smile as they approached.

'Morning, ladies. Corporal Rogers,' he said as they reached him.

'Weston,' Effie replied. 'Nice to meet you.'

'And you,' said Rogers. 'Now let me show you around Wapping's very own stately home, Shadwell Hall upon the Water.'

He pushed open the door and the two young women walked in.

The rank odour of male sweat clogged Effie's nose, but as her eyes adjusted to the dim interior the full horror of what would be their on-duty accommodation came into view.

'Well, as you can see it's a pretty standard hut,' the RAF corporal said, seemly oblivious to the foul condition of the hut's interior. 'There's three sets of bunkbeds at the far end for those on call,' he continued, indicating the cast-iron frames, stripped down to their mattresses and without pillows. 'I'm sure you're already used to our creature comforts.'

Effie's attention shifted to the pot-bellied stove with its chimney travelling up to a hole in the roof in the middle of the hut, then in horror to its two hotplates, which had a pot caked with burnt food and a frying pan containing congealed lard sitting on top.

'We've had to improvise a bit with the seating arrangements.' He nodded at the three striped deckchairs and battered mud-coloured sofa. There was a circle of cigarette ash sprinkled on the floor around it. 'And the facilities are out the back,' he added. 'It might need a bit of a clean, but follow me and I'll show—'

'No, it's all right,' cut in Effie quickly.

'Anyway, there it is, oh, and I forgot to say the telephone's on the far wall above the desk.' He picked up a tightly packed kitbag from one of the faded deckchairs. 'It might need a bit of a tidy, but I'd best be off.'

His boots thumping across the wooden floor, Corporal Rogers strode out.

Effie and her fellow corporal stood there in silence staring after him, then Millie spoke.

'A bit of a tidy?' she said, her eyes wide with horror beneath the peak of her cap. 'I dread to think what kind of state the outside bog is in.'

'Which is why I thought it was too soon after breakfast to see what it looked like,' Effie replied, walking across to the nearest window and opening it. 'Still, we'd better see what Munroe's up to outside.'

After opening the remaining five windows, all criss-crossed with tape, they stepped out into the early-morning sunlight again, as the transport lorry pulled away leaving a cloud of black diesel smoke in its wake.

No. 3 crew were milling about outside, but pulled themselves back into formation when Effie appeared. Stepping into the space at the end of the front row, she clasped her hands behind her.

'Duty will be twelve hours on twelve hours off,' said Munroe. 'So you will be on duty until eighteen hundred hours today, when no. 9 crew, who are billeted in the Old Dispensary on the Highway, relieve you. This pattern will reverse next Saturday and every Saturday thereafter, with your corporal allocating time off and weekend passes. Understood?'

'Yes, Sergeant,' the two teams replied.

Munroe's pale eyes ran over them one more time. 'Dismissed.'

Effie turned to face her friends. 'Right, crew, you know what to do so let's get to it.'

'Thank God,' exclaimed Nell, as Effie pushed open the door into the Maid of Norway's rear entrance. 'I'm practically dead on my feet.'

'Just practically, is it?' said Maeve as they trudged up the public house's back staircase. 'We've been to purgatory and back today.'

Effie couldn't disagree.

It was now six thirty in the evening and she and the rest of her crew had at last returned from their gruelling first day's duty on 312 site. Apart from spending two nights staring at the ceiling instead of sleeping, imagining Nathan lying in a burntout crashed plane or behind barbed wire in a prisoner of war camp, from the moment Sergeant Munroe had left on Monday, Effie hadn't stopped.

And of course it wasn't only the balloon.

She had expected that she and her crew would have to completely check and recheck the balloon, gas tanks, winch and all the equipment in their on-site shelter and eating area –

however what they hadn't expected to have to do was tear down pin-ups, sweep floors and wash cooking utensils. Not to mention how long they'd spent cleaning and bleaching the toilet.

'Well, we're finished now,' said Alice, unfastening the top two buttons of her serge working suit. 'Who's for a cuppa?'

'Tea?!' said George, flopping into one of the armchairs. 'What I need is a double Scotch.'

'Count us in,' said Alice, collapsing on the sofa between Dolly and Maeve, who were unlacing their boots.

'I'll give you a hand,' said Effie, following her friend as she headed for the kitchen.

The kitchen was spotlessly clean but pretty basic, with a single cold tap in an enamel butler sink with a wooden draining board attached to one side. The blackened stove must have come out of the ark, but had been recently cleaned, and all four of its gas rings worked. A generously sized kettle sat on one of them. There was a free-standing kitchen cupboard filled with crockery and a selection of goodies such as tea, boxes of porridge and cereals, plus a precious pot of jam. In the middle of the lino floor stood a table with a scrubbed top, and four mismatched chairs tucked beneath.

'Well, that's the first day out of the way,' said Alice as she filled the kettle up under the tap. 'Only twenty-one to go.'

Effie forced a smile.

She went to the dresser, opened the frosted cupboard door at the top and took out the large brown teapot, but she'd no sooner placed it on the table than Dolly's head appeared round the doorframe.

'There's a phone call for you, Effie,' she said.

Nathan's face flashed into her mind and her heart thumped painfully in her chest. Had he arrived back and heard that she'd telephoned that morning? But even if he had, why would he phone back? After all, as far as he was concerned, she was engaged and intended to walk down the aisle as a blushing bride next April.

Leaving her friend to make the tea and with her mind filled with hope and fear in equal parts, Effie made her way downstairs. The public house's telephone was fixed to the wall in the hallway leading from the bar.

Florrie, her bright-red hair swept up into a candyfloss pile on her head and her ample figure squeezed into a pencil skirt and frilly blouse, stood holding the black receiver.

'Oh, deary, you look done in and no mistake,' she said as Effie reached her.

'That's not the half of it, Florrie,' she replied, stifling a yawn.

Giving her a motherly look, the landlady handed her the phone. 'Never mind, ducks. Supper's in half an hour.'

Taking the roll-up from behind her ear, Florrie headed back towards the bar, her high heels striking the sawdust-sprinkled floorboards as she went.

Her hands trembling and her heart in her throat, Effie held it up to her ear.

'Corporal Effie Weston,' she said, her voice trembling as she spoke.

'Euphemia!'

Effie's heart sank. Although she recognised the trilled, shrill voice at the other end of the phone, she knew it wasn't going to tell her the news she'd been praying for.

'This is your mother,' continued Edna. 'What on earth do you think you're doing?'

'I guess you're ringing about my letter to Leonard,' said Effie, as tears of disappointment stung her eyes.

'Of course I am,' snapped her mother. 'What on earth is all this nonsense about you not marrying him?'

'It's not nonsense, Mother. I can't.' Effie took a deep breath. 'Because I don't love him.'

'Don't be ridiculous,' her mother scoffed. 'Do you think I loved your father when I married him?'

Effie's eyebrows rose. 'I'd always assumed so.'

'I was quite fond of him, naturally,' said Edna. 'But I married him because he was respectable, with the prospects to offer me a secure future, which is exactly what Leonard has to offer you.'

'But, Mother, I—'

'And what about how you breaking off your engagement to dear Leonard reflects on your father?' her mother cut in.

Effie frowned 'Father?'

'Well in case you've forgotten, Euphemia,' her mother's tinny voice snapped down the line, 'not only is your father the chairman of the Waltham Abbey and District Conservative Association, but, as our current MP is retiring at the next election, Leonard was adopted as his successor. How would it look to everyone if the man set to represent the constituency in the House of Commons had been jilted by you?'

'But—'

'And you know we've already booked the Abbey,' added her mother.

Effie frowned. 'Well, you'll have to unbook it, Mum, because I'm not—'

The nerve-jangling two-tone wail of the air-raid siren cut across Effie's words. Above her head there was a thumping of feet running back and forth across the floor.

'I have to go, Mum, an air-raid siren's started and I have to get to the shelter!' she shouted.

'Leonard said he will be coming down to talk some sense into you,' her mother huffed.

'Tell him not to bother because nothing he can say will change my mind. I don't love him and I'm not marrying him.'

'Love? You don't even know what it means,' her mother retorted.

Effie put the receiver down.

A door opened at the top of the stair and her crew, wearing their greatcoats and boots and carrying blankets, clattered down.

'Here you are,' said Alice, thrusting Effie's coat and handbag at her.

'Thanks,' she said, taking her heavy outerwear.

'Who was that?' her friend asked.

'My mother,' Effie replied, thrusting her arms into the sleeves. 'I've broken off my engagement.'

Alice looked surprised. 'To Leonard?'

'Yes,' said Effie. 'Because I don't love him, but my mother seems to think that doesn't matter.'

A sad expression flitted across Alice's pretty face. 'She's wrong.'

Effie raised her eyebrow. 'I know.'

Grasping the worn brass handle, Effie opened the public house's side door. As they joined the stream of people heading for the public shelter, her mother's words as she put down the receiver came back to her. She could say with absolute certainty that she knew what love was. And she could only hope that one day soon she would be able to tell Nathan.

CHAPTER 20

'For goodness' sake, Lily!' shouted Effie, gripping the rope she was holding more tightly with her gloved hands. 'If we don't keep it square into the airstream it's likely to take off.'

'I'm doing my best,' Lily bellowed back. 'But the bloody wind's picked up.'

She was right.

The dispatch rider from Balloon Control had skidded to a halt three-quarters of an hour ago with warning of a formation of enemy bombers heading in their direction and orders to get Bessie up to 5,000 feet. Since they raised it an hour before, station 312's barrage balloon had behaved perfectly – until ten minutes ago when the wind suddenly changed direction and started blowing up the Thames from the east. They needed to keep the nose pointing into the wind, so the side fins would remain fully inflated to balance the body of the balloon. To do this they had to lower the balloon in order to safely turn it, before letting it up again to the correct height.

With enemy planes arriving at any moment, it was vital that they get their balloon up and in formation with the hundreds of others already bobbing about every quarter of a mile over London.

'How's about tell your posh mate in the truck to roll the cable in a bit,' added Lily.

Effie glanced up at the silver underside of the balloon as it strained against its twisted metal leash.

'Dolly!' she bellowed. 'Get George to reel it in twenty feet.'

Dolly, who was standing next to the domed cage on the back of the truck, gave her the thumbs-up, then turned and tapped George on the shoulder.

The engine revved and a grey pall of diesel smoke billowed over them. Squeaking, the cable drum turned slowly a couple of times and when she looked up Effie saw the balloon above her head steady.

She turned her attention to where the rest of the crew were standing around the two anchor blocks of concrete.

'Right,' she yelled. 'Block teams, three paces. Right, go!'

Nell, Alice, Maeve and the three other WAAFs took up the strain and sidestepped to the right, taking the concrete blocks and their cables with them.

Caught by a gust, the balloon swung back and forth a couple of times, then settled down into the correct alignment.

Effie's shoulders relaxed. 'Well done, everyone. Dolly, let it back up to five thousand feet again.'

The engine roared and the drum squeaked again as the balloon floated majestically up to its assigned height.

'Oi, oi. 'Ere comes the calvary,' said Nell, looking past Effie's left ear.

She turned, and breathed a sigh of relief.

Making their way across the recreation ground towards them were the WAAFs who made up no. 9 crew.

'Evening, playmates,' said Corporal Millie Wheeler as she reached Effie. 'How's it been?'

Effie filled her in about the looming Luftwaffe attack, then cast her eyes over the WAAFs who had just arrived and were now taking over from her crew.

'You're a bit light in numbers, aren't you?' she said.

'Ruby and Winnie had the shepherd's pie for dinner round the British Restaurant and now they both have the squits,' said Millie. 'But the RAF crew only had eight men, so we should be all right as long as no one else starts dashing to the bog.'

'I'll leave you to it then,' said Effie. 'The kettle's filled and a couple of the Shadwell WVS dropped off some cakes earlier. They're in the Mackintosh's toffee tin.'

Effie gathered together the rest of no. 3 crew and they headed across the park and back to their billet.

With weariness washing over her, Effie pushed open the Maid of Norway's side door and stepped in. However, she'd only taken a couple of steps when the grubby curtain dividing the back hallway from the bar was pulled aside and Florrie appeared, wearing her usual behind-the-bar slinky outfit.

'Our barmaid Daisy took a phone call earlier from some chap saying he was coming to talk to you,' she said. ''E did say 'is name but she'd forgotten by the time I got back. Sorry.'

'Don't worry,' said Effie, as an image of Leonard loomed in her mind. 'I know who it was.'

'Says he's catching the first train and will be here later,' added her glamorous landlady over her shoulder as she high-heeled it back into the bar.

Taking a deep breath, Effie turned and started to make her way up to the floor above.

'Who's coming?' asked Alice, peering down at Effie from the top of the stairs.

'Leonard,' Effie replied. 'My mother said he'd be coming to "talk some sense" into me.'

When she reached their room, she sat on the bed and, after removing her boots, collapsed back and stared up at the ceiling.

'Well, he must care about you if he's coming all this way to try and change your mind,' said Alice.

'Lucky me,' muttered Effie.

Feeling tears gathering in her eyes, she shut them.

'What's wrong, Effie?' asked Alice.

Effie lay there quietly for a second or two longer, then opened her eyes and looked across at her friend.

'The reason I broke off my engagement to Leonard, Alice, is because I'm in love with Nathan.'

Alice looked puzzled. 'Who's—' Her friend's grey-green eyes opened wide as the penny dropped. 'You mean the dishy flying officer who covered for Makepeace.'

Effie nodded.

Alice's eyes stretched even wider. 'You and him were carrying on?'

'No, we weren't,' Effie replied. 'More's the pity.'

'Effie!'

'I know, I'm a little shocked myself,' Effie replied.

Actually, that was a bit of a lie. Truthfully, she was more surprised than shocked at some of the things she yearned to do with Nathan, as she had never had the slightest desire to do them with Leonard.

'Does he know?' asked Alice, cutting across her thoughts.

Effie shook her head. 'I only realised how I felt myself last week. He's always been polite and sociable when we meet, but honestly I have no idea if he feels anything other than friendly towards me, and now perhaps I'll never find out because he's missing in action.'

'That doesn't mean anything,' said Alice. 'Plenty of airmen go missing in action and then turn up fit and well a few weeks later. Maybe there was a problem with his aeroplane, and he's had to bring it down in some remote field or he's had to bail out over the Channel. Have you telephoned his station again?'

'Yesterday, but the operator said the telephone exchange at

the other end wasn't answering, so...' An image of Nathan flashed across Effie's mind and tears again pinched the corners of her eyes.

Alice stood up and came across to sit next to Effie on the bed. She laid her hand on Effie's. 'You rest up there while I make us both a nice cup of tea.'

She forced a smile. 'Thanks. I'll do the same for you one day.'

Giving Effie's hand an affectionate squeeze, Alice stood up.

'See if you can nick a shot of George's Scotch to go in it,' Effie called after her. 'I need a bit of Dutch courage to face Leonard when he arrives.'

The piercing wail of the air-raid siren through the window brought Effie out of the sleep she didn't realise she'd drifted off into. In the light from the spotlights criss-crossing in the sky, she noticed a cold cup of tea on her bedside table and the alarm clock showing a quarter past eight.

Sitting up, she swung her legs off the bed and, after pulling the blackout curtains across, switched on the lamp on the bedside dresser. Feet clad in her socks, she padded out into the hallway and down to the floor below.

Dot Wilcox, from no. 9 crew, dressed in an oversized sheepskin jerkin, wellington boots and wearing her helmet, was standing in the middle of the lounge talking to Alice.

'What's happened?' Effie asked.

'Harriet and Jane have got the lurgy now too, so we're four men down and it's blowing a hooley out there, so—'

'Tell Millie we'll be there in five minutes,' said Effie, already rebuttoning her boiler suit.

Dot shot off and down the stairs.

'Right, everyone get togged up and call the others, Nell,' said Effie.

Nell ran upstairs and came down a few moments later carrying the flying jacket she'd acquired from a GI airman along the way, with Maeve, Dolly and George shrugging on their cold weather gear close behind.

'Lily and Maureen have gone out,' said Nell as she handed Effie her boots, jerkin and tin hat.

'Never mind,' said Effie, sitting down on the sofa and pulling on her boots. 'You go, I'll be right behind you.'

Nell trooped down the stairs after the other three.

Having laced her boots tightly, Effie sprang up and, shoving her arms in the sleeves and with the siren screaming in her ears, she hurried after them.

As she burst through the side door of the public house into the blackness and driving rain, a stark beam from the nearby searchlight cut across the sky. Effie looked up. Captured in the glare was an RAF Hurricane darting across the sky to engage the enemy. From nowhere, images of Nathan and his magical blue eyes flooded into Effie's mind. Tears welled up as pain gripped her heart. She stood frozen for a couple of seconds then, pressing her lips tightly together, she wiped her face with the back of her hand and sprinted down the road.

∽

As an explosion rocked the earth beneath Effie's feet, she gripped the rope tighter.

'One last pull should do it,' she shouted, as a fork of lightning streaked across the sky.

Effie and the rest of the WAAFs had been wrestling with the barrage balloon for an hour as bombs fell all around them.

However, regardless of the grit-spattered faces and ragged hair she and the handful of no. 3 crew WAAFs had arrived in the nick of time. When they reached the balloon's launch area the metal tether was running free on the drum as the barrage balloon pitched back and forth, ropes flailing dangerously in the aftermath of every blast and vacuum created by the German armaments.

Although it was edging towards midnight now, and despite the blackout, Effie and the rest of the crew had no trouble seeing what they were doing thanks to the fires raging on the other side of the river and illuminating the opposite bank. Another bomb crashed to earth somewhere slightly to the west of them, its flare of white and red in the sky showing the hollowed-out, bomb-damaged buildings.

'Olive, Lena. Take up the strain!' bellowed Millie at two members of her crew, their galoshes skidding across the gravel, hanging on to the thrashing rear of the barrage balloon for dear life.

'Everyone ready?' shouted Effie, as the smell of cordite and sulphur filled her nose.

'Copy!' shouted the dozen or so young women anchoring the balloon.

Another explosion rent the air, sending a factory warehouse half a mile east of them crashing to the ground. Effie flexed her frozen fingers and, gripping the rope, took a deep breath.

'Ready. Steady. Heave!' she screamed, as the vacuum following the explosion whipped her hair around her face.

Holding the bucking balloon, the young women leant back.

'George!' shouted Effie.

George, in her usual position in the driving seat of the lorry, revved the engine. There was a burst of smoke as the winch gears engaged the drum and it started to let the balloon up slowly to the correct height and alignment, as the blessed sound of the all-clear screamed across the rooftops.

'Thanks, Effie,' said Millie. 'We couldn't have done it without you all.'

Effie grinned. 'You don't have to thank me. After all, I don't think either of us would want to have phoned Group to tell them that we'd lost a balloon.'

'Especially not in the middle of an air raid on our practice weeks,' added Millie. Her gaze shifted past Effie. 'What the hell is that lunatic doing out in this? Doesn't he understand that he should stay put in the shelter for ten minutes after the all-clear sounds?'

Effie turned and, in the red glow of the burning warehouse across the water, saw who Millie was talking about. With the urgent clang of fire brigade bells and the crackle and creaking of the burning warehouses filling her ears, she stood motionless for a second, her heart thumping painfully in her chest. Then she dashed towards the lone male figure walking across the water-logged lawn, and skidded to a halt a few feet from him.

Breathlessly and unable to believe her own eyes she gazed at him. 'Nathan!'

'Effie,' he said, dropping his kitbag on the floor as his blue eyes captured hers. 'I came as soon as I could because I have to tell you that—'

'I love you, Nathan,' she blurted out. 'I should have told you before, but I didn't realise. But I do. Love you, I mean. So much. I...'

Her words failing her, Effie threw herself into his arms and pressed her lips onto his.

There was a momentary pause, then, putting Effie's world back together in an instant, his arms closed round her, and he kissed her back.

CHAPTER 21

Although Nathan's left arm was prickling with pins and needles, he resisted the urge to flex his fingers. Truthfully, even if his arm fell off it would be worth the sacrifice just to have the utter joy of cradling Effie in his arms.

By the time they had returned to her billet the other WAAFs had disappeared up to their rooms to dry off, leaving him and Effie to their own devices. Effie was soaked to the skin. She had quickly changed into a skirt and jumper, while he had taken off his sodden greatcoat and uniform jacket and dried himself with a towel. Ideally, he would have taken his damp shirt off too, but as the house was full of young women he thought it best to suffer, removing his tie, unbuttoning his collar and turning back his cuffs. To be honest, with Effie in his arms and under his lips he doubted he'd notice if someone had thrown a bucket of water over him.

The storm had passed soon after they returned and, tired though they both were, they lay in each other's embrace on the not-too-comfortable sofa in Maid of Norway's upstairs lounge, talking about everything and nothing until Effie had fallen asleep.

Although weary himself after the train journey back from Dorset the day before and then immediately catching the train to London, Nathan forced sleep away and contented himself with holding the woman he loved in his arms and gazing down at her lovely face.

Effie was fast asleep on his chest. Strands of her hair were tangled in his early-morning bristles, and her hand on his chest felt as if it were on his bare skin, a sensation he longed for in reality, before too long. As his gaze moved slowly over her dark lashes, the curve of her cheek and the soft shape of her lips, love and happiness surged up in him.

As if sensing his eyes on her, Effie shifted slightly and, pushing the hair from her face, looked up.

He pressed his lips to her forehead briefly. 'Morning, sleepyhead.'

'Morning, handsome.' She smiled and Nathan's unfathomable joy returned.

Reaching up, she ran her hands over his face and through his hair, setting every nerve in his body tingling. They gazed at each other for a moment, then, stretching up, Effie pressed her lips to his. Nathan responded in kind, relishing the feel of her breasts pressing onto his chest and her slender legs sliding against his.

Finally able to flex his numb arm, Nathan grazed his finger over her sleep-flushed cheek. 'Do you still love me this morning?'

She shifted position and, placing a hand either side of his head, she looked down at him. 'Twice as much as I did last night. What about you?'

'Until the end of the earth and beyond,' he replied, wrapping his arms round her slender waist. 'And do you still want to marry me?'

Lowering her head, she pressed her lips onto his in a long hard kiss.

'Does that answer your question?' she replied, in a husky voice and looking deeply into his eyes.

Nathan swallowed.

'Completely,' he said, holding in check the urge to let his hands wander. 'How soon?'

Her lovely eyes held his for a second, then she gave him a brief kiss and rested her head back on his right shoulder.

'I've got three weeks until I'm back at Cardington the week after Easter and then a week until I finish, so perhaps we could get married a couple of weeks after that, say the 2nd May.'

'Sounds perfect,' Nathan replied. 'But what about your parents?'

Raising her head, Effie frowned. 'I'll ring and tell them our good news. I know they'll be a bit shocked at it being out of the blue, but I'm sure once they meet you and see how much we love each other they'll understand about our whirlwind romance. After all, they've always said all they ever wanted for me was to be happy.' Her expression brightened. 'I've got a seventy-two-hour pass at the end of my practice weeks, so if you can wangle one too, you can meet them. If we want to get married in May we'll have to get their consent as I'm not twenty-one until the thirtieth.'

A tiny niggle of anxiety started in Nathan's chest. 'I think perhaps you should warn them, Effie.'

She gave him a puzzled look.

'That I'm black,' Nathan explained.

'Oh, Nathan, don't be silly.' Stretching up, she kissed him again. 'I've already told you that they are lifelong members of the Friends of Africa Mission Society. My dad's even the treasurer of the Essex branch of the society. They won't give a fig, and will welcome you with open arms.'

'I'm sure you're right, sweetheart,' said Nathan. 'But I still think perhaps you should mention it when you speak to your mother.'

'All right, I will.' She stretched up and kissed him lightly. 'Right after I tell her you're the only man in the world for me.' Alarm flashed across her face and she sat bolt upright. 'What's the time?'

Nathan glanced at his watch. 'Four thirty. What time are you on duty?'

'Six.'

She laid her head back on his chest and Nathan gathered her in his arms again. 'I'll go at about half five but as I don't have to be back in Tempsford until tomorrow night I'll find myself a billet nearby and be back when you've finished your shift,' he said.

Effie tilted her face and gave him a lazy smile.

'Well, then,' she said, smoothing her hand slowly up his chest, setting his senses on fire. 'We'd better find something to do for an hour, hadn't we?'

That evening on platform 3 of St Pancras station, Effie stood on tiptoes as Nathan leant out of the carriage window and held her. With her eyes closed, Effie savoured the feel of Nathan's arms round her and lips on hers, but then all too soon he broke away.

'I'll see Donaldson as soon as I get back and telephone you tomorrow evening,' he said, looking down at her from the carriage window.

'I'll see you on Satur—' A rolling whistle cut off Effie's words.

Carriage doors slammed as the last few passengers jumped on board the eight twenty to Cambridge.

The guard standing alongside the last carriage blew his whistle again and waved his flag. Steam from the enormous engine of the London & North Eastern Railway train billowed out in a white cloud, filling Effie's nose with the tarry smell of coal. The sound of metal scraping metal jangled in her ears, then with a shudder the train moved off, spewing smoke and coal grit in its wake.

Stretching up, Effie took his hand, and trotted alongside the train until it picked up speed.

'Until Saturday,' he shouted, as his hand slipped from hers.

'Until Saturday,' she called back as the engine reached the end of the platform.

'I love you,' he hollered, leaning out of the carriage window.

'I love you, too,' Effie yelled back.

'And don't forget to phone your mother,' he bellowed, as the huge train, like a black snake, curled to the left and disappeared into a tunnel.

Feeling like Saturday seemed more like two years than two days away, Effie stared after it for a moment, then turned and headed back down the platform.

However, instead of heading for the Metropolitan Line underground entrance she made her way across to the line of six telephone booths next to the ticket office, just as a young woman in an ATS uniform stepped out of the one at the end.

Pulling open the wooden door, Effie stepped in. Rather than the smell of coal from the locomotive, the booth smelled of the spent cigarettes strewn across its floor.

Effie rested her handbag on the ledge, took out her purse and placed a thruppenny piece in the slot. She picked up the receiver and held it to her ear. There was a pause, then the line clicked.

'Waltham Abbey seven five two, please,' said Effie.

Picturing the telephone on the white doily on the hall table in her parents' home, she listened to it ring a couple of times at the other end of the line, then someone picked up.

'Good evening. Waltham Abbe—'

Gripping the receiver tighter, Effie pressed the coin into the slot. 'Mum, it's me.'

'Euphemia! Is everything all right?' asked her mother.

'Yes, it is,' said Effie. 'Better than all right actually, because—'

'You and Leonard have made up and you're engaged again,' her mother cut in. 'Your father will be so pleased to hear that when he gets back from the Friends of Africa Mission Society committee meeting. I told him you'd come to your senses, once you'd had time to think ab—'

'No, Mother, I'm not back with Leonard.' Effie took a long, deep breath. 'But I am engaged.'

There was a long silence, then her mother spoke again. 'I don't understand. If you're not engaged to Leonard, then who?'

'A flying officer named Nathan Fitzgerald,' said Effie. 'He's a pilot.'

'I gathered that, but—'

'He's from Barbados, where his father works for the Crown Commissioner and his mother is the headmistress of the local primary school,' Effie said, a little breathlessly. 'Nathan came to London just before war was declared to take up a position at the Inns of Court, but signed up for the air force instead.'

'Oh, so he's going to be a barrister,' said her mother.

'Yes,' said Effie, her shoulders losing some of their tension.

'Are his family members of a church?' asked her mother.

'They go to St Michael's Anglican Cathedral in Bridgetown,' Effie replied. 'Nathan and his brothers were choir-boys there when they were younger.'

There was another long silence.

'Mum?'

'I'm sorry, Euphemia, but last week you were going to marry Leonard,' her mother said at long last. 'And now this week you are marrying someone else. It's a bit of a shock, that's all.'

'It's a lot to take in, I know.'

'Leonard will be terribly disappointed,' her mother continued.

'I'm sorry about that and I'm very fond of Leonard, Mum, but I don't love him, I love Nathan, and he loves me,' said Effie, feeling the warmth of it deep within her.

'And he's going to be a barrister,' her mother continued.

'Once the war's over, yes,' Effie said. 'I'm sure Nathan will be happy to tell you and Dad about his family and plans for the future when I bring him up to meet you before I go back to Cardington in two weeks' time. I'm sure you'll both love him,' added Effie, praying silently that her parents would.

There was another long silence, then her mother heaved a heavy sigh down the phone. 'We'll just have to see, won't we?'

Effie caught sight of the station clock. 'Look Mum, I want to get back to my billet before the blackout starts. Give my love to Dad.'

'Goodbye, Euphemia,' said her mother. 'And stay safe. I do worry about you down there in London with all those bombs.'

'Bye, Mum, and I'll ring you next week,' Effie replied.

She put the receiver down and collected her handbag, then she pushed the telephone booth door open and, with a little smile lifting the corners of her mouth, stepped out onto the busy concourse.

CHAPTER 22

'This is all a bit sudden, isn't it?' said Group Captain Donaldson, his chair creaking as he leant back.

'I suppose it is,' Nathan replied. 'But that's love. Unpredictable.'

'Um!' responded Donaldson. 'I've been married twenty-odd years, so such things are a distant memory. However, I'm happy to sign your request, Fitzgerald.'

It was a few minutes after eight thirty in the morning the day after Nathan had caught the train back to Tempsford and he was standing in his freshly pressed uniform in his commanding officer's office, with an application for permission to marry on the desk in front of him.

'Thank you, sir.'

'Are you applying for married quarters?' Donaldson asked.

Nathan shook his head. 'Perhaps later when both our duties permit, but for now we're going to have to make the best of it.'

To be honest, Nathan would have like nothing better than to have Effie to welcome him home after a mission, but that joy would have to wait until the war was over. Needs must when the devil drives, and they wouldn't be the only married couple up and down the land who had decided to put duty before a home and a family life.

'So when are you and Corporal Weston planning to tie the knot?' asked Donaldson, cutting across Nathan's thoughts.

'On the eighteenth of next month,' Nathan replied. 'I am going to ask her father formally when we visit them in two weeks.'

Donaldson's generous moustache did a little dance under his nose for a moment, then he stood up and offered Nathan his hand. 'Congratulations. I wish you and your fiancée every happiness.'

Nathan took it. 'Thank you, sir.'

He stood to attention, saluted, then left the group captain's office.

Although it was still early, the airbase was already alive with activity. On the far side of the airfield, ground crew were already refuelling and rearming 109 Squadron's Wellingtons and 138 Squadron's Halifaxes ready for action.

Skirting past a troop lorry parked outside the main offices, Nathan headed along the path to the officers' mess in Hazells Hall.

With the spring sunlight warming the air and thoughts of Effie filling his mind, he arrived at the old manor house some fifteen minutes later. He strode up the handful of steps leading to the main entrance, stepped inside and was greeted by the welcome smell of fried bacon indicating that, as he had hoped, the catering staff were busy cooking up their usual hearty breakfast.

Nathan hooked his hat on the metal stand by the door and acknowledged a couple of his fellow officers coming down the hall's grand staircase, then headed across the black-and-white-tiled hallway towards the dining room.

The strains of Mantovani drifted from the brown wireless sitting on a heavy Victorian sideboard next to the ornate marble fireplace on the other side of the room. Nathan walked between the two lines of tables, joined the queue at one end of the serving hatch, and left at the other end a minute or two later carrying a tray loaded with a plate of scrambled eggs, sausage and bacon and a large mug of tea.

Glancing over the sea of air force blue, he noticed a couple of spaces on a table in front of one of the two long casement windows, and headed across.

He placed his tray down, unloaded it and took his seat, spread the white napkin across his thighs, then tucked into his breakfast. As he speared his second sausage, someone put down a tray down in the place opposite. Nathan looked up and smiled.

'Ozzie, when did you get back?' he said, as he sliced back and forth.

'About four hours ago,' his friend replied, flicking out his napkin. 'You?'

'Late last night.'

Wiktor gave him an enquiring look. 'And did your quest to win the fair maiden succeed?'

A smile spread across Nathan's face. 'We're getting married in five weeks.'

'Well done, my friend,' Wiktor asked. 'Did she need much wooing?'

Nathan's grin widened. 'She actually flew into my arms.'

Shovelling up a forkful of fried egg, Wiktor scoffed.

'No, truly, she did,' said Nathan. 'It seems she felt the same way about me as I did about her.'

'Well, love is a strange thing, but five weeks?' His friend let out a low whistle. 'That is speedy work.'

Nathan grinned again. 'Well, apparently there is a war on.'

They laughed and he took a slurp of tea. 'Of course, as

Effie's not twenty-one until the end of May we'll have to get her parents' consent. I'm going to meet them at Easter when she finishes her practice site training.'

'Well.' Wiktor extended his hand across the cruet set between them. 'Let me wish you and your future bride long life and good health.'

'Thank you,' Nathan replied, grasping it firmly. 'And I insist you act as my best man on the day.'

'Best man!'

Nathan looked round and saw Frobisher, with a couple of his regular drinking pals, standing either side of him. Although they were wearing uniform their ties were loose, shirt collars curled, and their jackets creased. He wasn't a betting man, but Nathan would put money on it that Frobisher and his dishevelled companions had spent the night slumped in the wingback chairs in the bar.

'Indeed,' said Wiktor, swivelling round in his chair. 'My good friend here is getting married.'

Shifting his attention onto Nathan, Frobisher raised his fair eyebrows. 'Married, you say, but who's the lucky lady—' His eyes lit up and he clicked his fingers. 'It's that little auburn-haired WAAF totty you were waltzing around with at that dreadful parochial dance in town a few months ago.'

Nathan's grip tightened on his knife as Wiktor gave him a nervous glance across the table.

'You're right, Frobisher. I am marrying WAAF Corporal Weston,' Nathan replied, in a glacial tone. 'But you will rue the day, if you ever refer to my fiancée in a derogatory way again.'

An irritable expression distorted the SOE officer's sublime aristocratic features. 'Are you threatening me, old boy?'

Leaning back casually in his chair, Nathan pulled his lips back in a brittle smile. 'Yes, I most certainly am, *old boy.*'

A scarlet flush crept up the SOE officer's throat.

Holding Frobisher's bloodshot eyes, Nathan waited for him

to leap across the table, but after a long pause Frobisher looked away. 'It's just mess talk, that's all. No need to take on so.'

Still regarding him coolly, Nathan didn't reply.

There was an uncomfortable pause, but then the army officer on Frobisher's left, a slim-faced individual with a youthful moustache, cleared his throat. 'We'd better go or we'll be late.'

Frobisher looked bewildered. 'Late?'

'For the briefing. You know,' the young officer said.

The SOE officer's puzzled expression remained for a second or two, then the penny dropped. 'Yes, the briefing.'

'But aren't you going to congratulate me?' Nathan said as the three men started to go.

Frobisher half turned. 'Congratulations.'

Nathan gave him an ingenuous smile. 'Much appreciated, Frobisher. I'll pass your good wishes on to my future wife.'

CHAPTER 23

'But that's only three weeks' time,' said her mother as she poured Effie a second cup of tea.

'I know it's quick, but we love each other and want to get married as soon as possible,' Effie replied.

'Be that as it may,' said her father, packing his pipe with fresh tobacco, 'I still don't understand why you're in such a rush.'

It was mid-morning on Saturday and a day after she'd successfully completed her three weeks on site. Effie was sitting in one of the two armchairs in her parents' front room, with her mother and father occupying the matching three-seat sofa opposite.

As they were meeting their future son-in-law, her parents were dressed very much the same as if they'd been off to church. In her mother's case this was one of her sober Sunday dresses, while her father was trussed up in his best suit and tie.

Unlike Effie, who had been given a blanket seventy-two-hour pass, despite his best efforts Nathan had only managed to secure a twelve-hour one. However, as there was no guarantee when they would be able to visit her parents again before the second May, he was travelling down from Sandy and catching the midday train from Liverpool Street to Waltham Abbey.

'Because we don't want to wait any longer,' Effie replied.

Her mother heaved a sigh. 'But it seems very quick, especially as you were quite content to have a long engagement to Leonard.'

To be honest, if she'd felt for Leonard a tenth of what she felt for Nathan she wouldn't have been.

'Still, I suppose it could be worse,' conceded her father, puffing cigar smoke towards the ceiling.

'It could, Father,' Edna agreed. 'From what Euphemia says, this young man of hers clearly comes from a respectable Christian family.'

'I would expect nothing less,' said her father.

'And he is obviously well educated and a member of a profession,' added her mother.

Her father nodded sagely. 'Very true. I don't know of anyone around here who has been to university, let alone has a degree. And having a barrister in the family is no bad thing. I could certainly introduce him to Roland Turnbull – I'm sure his law firm would be glad of a contact further up the legal tree in London.'

'But there's so much to organise,' said her mother. 'There's the Abbey and—'

'I've already telephoned Father Thomas,' cut in Effie. 'And Nathan and I are meeting him at the rectory later this afternoon.'

'What about your dress?'

'I've been saving my coupons, so I can treat myself to a new suit and hat,' Effie replied.

Edna took a sip of her tea and heaved another weighty sigh. 'I'd always dreamed of you walking down the aisle on your father's arm in a lovely white wedding dress, but...'

Reaching across, Effie's father put his chunky hand over

his wife's. 'If this Nathan is the man who will love and cherish our little Jellybean as much as we have, Mother, then we will be very happy to welcome him into the family, won't we?'

A soft expression stole over Edna's round face. 'Yes, we certainly will, Father.'

Her parents exchanged a fond look, then turned their attention to Effie.

'So,' said her father smiling across at her. 'What time did you say he would be here?'

Effie glanced up at the clock on the mantelshelf. 'Well, he's catching—'

The crack of the knocker striking the stud echoed down the hall, cutting off her words.

She sprang to her feet. 'I'll get it.'

Without waiting for her parents to respond, she dashed out of the room and streaked down the hall.

Feeling dizzy with excitement, Effie yanked open the front door, and her heart tumbled over.

Standing on the threshold, resplendent in his parade uniform, was Nathan.

He smiled at her, then, taking off his cap, he stepped in. Effie closed the door behind him, but as she turned his arms encircled her waist. He gathered her to him and lowered his lips onto hers. Savouring every nerve-trembling inch of his body pressed against hers, Effie melted into him.

After a heart-thumping minute he released her lips.

'God,' he said, in a low husky voice. 'I've missed you.'

'I've missed you, too,' she replied, feeling his muscles under her fingers as she hugged him to her.

In the mute light of the hallway Effie gazed up at him, then, running her hand through his curly hair, she pulled his face down to her and captured his lips.

Nathan responded in kind but after another pulse-racing

embrace he tore his lips from hers and gave her that quirky smile of his.

'Perhaps, Effie sweetheart, it would be better if you were to take me in and introduce me to your parents rather than them meeting me ardently embracing their only daughter in the hallway?'

Releasing him, Effie laughed. 'You're probably right. It wouldn't be the best way for them to meet their soon-to-be son-in-law.'

He took her hand and squeezed it. 'Not long now, Effie.'

'Yes. Not long now,' she replied, taking his hand and leading him through to the lounge.

∼

Effie's parents were standing in front of the sofa ready to greet him when Nathan walked into their lounge holding her hand.

From what Effie had told him, they looked more or less as he'd expected. She did favour her mother's side of the family but with her father's darker colouring and height. Like them, their home was tidy and comfortable, with a few little luxuries, like a radiogram and display cabinet crammed with ornaments. There were photos in silver frames on the mantelshelf of black children smiling happily as they gathered around white missionaries, presumably the members of the Friends of Africa Mission Society doing good works in some far-flung colonies. These, plus the Bible beside one of the chairs with bookmarks poking out, should have put Nathan at ease, but the looks on their faces as he entered the room told him all he needed to know about Edna and Albert Weston.

'Mum, Dad,' Effie said, gazing adoringly up at him, heedless of her parents' stunned expressions. 'This is Flying Officer Nathan Fitzgerald. My fiancé.'

Fixing a smile to his face, Nathan stepped forward.

'Pleased to meet you, Mr Weston,' he said, extended his hand and praying his assessment of the situation was wrong. 'Effie has told you so much about you.'

Seemingly rooted to the spot, her father didn't move; however, after a moment frozen in time her mother did, and sat back down on the sofa.

'What's wrong?' asked Effie, confusion written large across her face.

'We didn't realise,' her father said, his cheeks developing an unhealthy purplish tinge.

'Realise what?' asked Effie.

'That I was black,' Nathan replied flatly.

'But I told Mum on the phone that Nathan was from Barbados. Didn't I, Mum?' Effie replied.

'You did,' her mother agreed. 'But we assumed...' Pulling her handkerchief from her sleeve, she blew her nose.

'When you said he had a law degree and his father worked for the governor, we assumed he was... like us. Not a...' He gave Nathan a sideways glance but didn't finish his sentence.

'What word *would* you use, Mr Weston?' asked Nathan, regarding the older man coolly. 'Take your pick, I've been called all of them.'

Albert's bushy eyebrows pulled together tightly. 'There's no need to take that tone.'

'Hang on,' said Effie, taking a step forward to stand next to Nathan. 'You and Mum have supported missions all over Africa for years, even raised money to build schools and hospitals for black children and families. I don't understand why you're acting like this.'

'Why don't you explain to your daughter, Mr Weston?' Nathan said in an icy tone.

Albert turned his attention to Effie, standing next to Nathan.

'Firstly, let me say your mother and I are in no way colour

prejudiced. We sincerely believe that all men and women, wherever they come from and whatever colour they may be, are equals under God. We have always seen it as our Christian duty to do all we can help those less fortunate than ourselves, which is why we have devoted ourselves to the work of overseas missions. But the thing is, Jellybean, although we have nothing personally against Flying Officer Fitzgerald, who I'm sure is a very fine young man...' Reaching up, Effie's father rubbed the back of his neck. 'Well, without beating about the bush a-and to put it in a nutshell, the truth of the matter is that—'

'The truth of the matter, Effie,' repeated Nathan, looking her father square in the eye, 'is that although your parents are eager to bestow their largesse on people who have the same skin colour as me, they don't want their daughter to marry one.'

Effie's jaw dropped as incredulity spread across her lovely face. 'Is Nathan right, Dad?'

The blush on her father's jowls deepened but he didn't reply.

Effie's mother struggled up from the sofa. 'Your dad's only trying to protect you, sweetheart.'

'From what?' snapped Effie. 'Marrying the man I love? Being happy? Having a family?'

'And you know how people talk, so think what your friends and family will say when they hear you're marrying a coloured man,' pleaded her mother. 'And the rector.' Horror spread across her face. 'Goodness knows what will happen when he hears about all this.'

Effie looped her arm through Nathan's and he let out a breath he hadn't realised he was holding. He looked down and they exchanged a fond look, which steadied Nathan's pulse.

'So what you're both saying,' Effie said to her parents, tears gathering on her lower lashes, 'is that, while you're more than happy for Nathan to travel halfway across the world and risk his life every day in the defence of this country, he's not good enough to marry me.'

With his eyes bulging in his florid face, Effie's father chewed words for a second , then spat them out.

'No, he's bloody not,' he shouted. 'And if you marry a man like him your name will be in the bloody gutters and ours along with it.'

Edna blinked. 'Albert!'

'My pardon for the strong language, my dear,' he said. 'But having my only daughter, a gift from God after all our years of hoping, who I have loved and nurtured from the first moment she was put into my arms, tell me she wants to throw herself away by marrying a...' He waved his hand in Nathan's direction, then placed it dramatically, over his eyes. 'It's enough to make a saint swear.'

As Edna comforted her stricken husband, the clock on the mantelshelf ticked away half a minute. Nathan placed his large hand over Effie's small one on his forearm and cleared his throat.

'Mr and Mrs Weston,' he said, looking at his future in-laws. 'I love your daughter more than I can possibly explain and I promise to cherish and protect her with my life. She has also made me the happiest man on earth and my life complete by agreeing to be my wife. We hoped to marry on the eighteenth of April but, as you're obviously not going to give your consent, we will have to postpone the happy day until the sixth of June, the Saturday after Effie's twenty-first birthday.'

Mr Weston, who was arduously studying a point on the wall behind Nathan, didn't reply, while his wife responded by collapsing onto the sofa again.

'Now,' he continued. 'As I'm clearly not welcome in your house, I'll wish you both good day and leave.'

'And I'm coming with you,' said Effie, her voice quivering as she spoke.

Guilt clawed at Nathan's chest.

He squeezed her hand, and she looked up. 'Effie, are you sure you want to leave things with your parents like—'

'I'll go and pack my things,' she cut in, determination writ large across her face.

She left the room and her footsteps echoed up the stairs.

Effie's father ceased his contemplation of the wallpaper and glared at Nathan.

'I hope all this isn't because you've got my little girl in the family way,' he said, jabbing his finger at Nathan. 'Because I swear if she is, I'll—'

'She is not,' Nathan cut in, struggling to keep a grip on his boiling temper.

There was another long silence, during which Mr Weston glared hatefully across the Axminster carpet at him and Nathan returned the sentiment.

Mercifully, after what seemed like an hour, Effie's footsteps could be heard descending the stairs and within a few short minutes she walked back into the lounge carrying her weekend suitcase.

He took it from her and she slipped her arm through his as they faced her parents.

'I promise you, Euphemia, if you marry this man you will never be allowed over the threshold of this house again,' said her father.

'Oh, no, Albert, not—'

'I'm sorry, Mother,' he interrupted. 'But I'm the head of this house and that's my final word.'

Effie stood stock-still looking dumbly at her parents.

Nathan's heart thumped in his chest and he feared she'd changed her mind, but then she turned and with fat tears shimmering on her lower lids she smiled up at him. 'I'm ready when you are, Nathan.'

Stepping up to Waltham Cross's booking office window, Nathan placed Effie's suitcase at his feet. 'Two third-class singles to Liverpool Street, please,' he said, sliding a brown ten-bob note through the arch-shaped cubbyhole to the young woman on the other side of the counter.

Having collected their tickets and pocketed his change, Nathan took her elbow and guided her across the small concourse to the platform entrance.

'Can you tell me when the next train to London is?' he asked as the youthful guard at the barrier punched their tickets.

'In ten minutes at three twenty, sir,' he replied with an adolescent wobble in his voice.

Effie glanced up at the station clock.

How could it be that just two short hours ago she was sitting happily drinking tea in her parents' front room, and now...

A lump formed in her throat.

There were a dozen or so people waiting for the southbound train, but with the scene in her parents' front room playing over in her mind she barely noticed them as Nathan guided her along the platform.

As they halted next to the metal sign with the station's name painted on it, he turned and faced her.

'Perhaps we should go back, sweetheart,' he said, looking anxiously down at her.

Effie frowned. 'Go back?'

'Yes,' he continued, taking both her hands in his. 'To speak to your parents again. Perhaps when they—'

'Hello, Miss Weston.'

Effie looked round and saw her mother's daily help, Ivy Turnbull, standing beside her.

She forced a smile. 'Oh, Mrs T. Yes, hello. Are you off somewhere nice?'

'Visiting my sister in Broxbourne,' Mrs Turnbull replied. 'But I thought you were up all weekend visiting your parents.'

Effie nodded. 'I was, but...'

There was an awkward silence, then through the lenses of her spectacles Ivy's pale-blue eyes shifted onto Nathan. 'And who is this handsome young man you've got with you?'

Effie blinked and took hold of Nathan's arm firmly.

'This is Flying Officer Fitzgerald, Mrs T. My fiancé,' she said, looking boldly at the older woman.

To Effie's surprise, Ivy smiled warmly up at him and offered her hand.

'Nice to meet you, young man,' she said, her kindly tone reflecting her words.

'It's very nice to meet you too,' Nathan replied, taking her hand.

They shook and then Ivy's attention returned to Effie. 'I imagine you've been home to tell your parents your happy news.'

'We have,' said Effie. 'They were...' The scene in her parents' front room flickered through her mind and stopped her words.

'Surprised,' said Nathan.

Ivy studied them both for a moment, then her motherly smile widened.

'Well, congratulations to you both,' she said. 'I hope you'll be very happy.'

'Don't worry, Mrs Turnbull,' said Nathan. 'It's going to be my life's mission to make Effie happy.'

A thoughtful expression settled on Ivy's lined face, then, reaching out, she placed a work-worn hand on his sleeve. 'That's all any woman wants, young man.'

A shrill whistle cut between them, signalling the arrival of the London-bound train.

'Nice to see you, Mrs T,' said Effie as the locomotive rolled slowly along the platform.

'And you, Effie.'

Ivy turned and headed off towards the rear of the train.

'Let's see if we can find an empty carriage,' said Effie, as they set off in the opposite direction.

'This will do,' said Nathan as they reached the second carriage from the front. Turning the brass handle, he held the door open, and Effie stepped up into the carriage.

Nathan followed her in and put her suitcase on the luggage rack above their seats, then sat next to her.

Through the hissing steam billowing out from the engine, the shrill whistle of the train's guard rolled along the platform, followed by an answering one from the station's controller. The clank of metal filled the carriage as the couplings took up the strain and the train juddered.

Taking her hand in his, Nathan weaved his fingers through hers as Effie gazed blankly out of the window.

Within a couple of minutes, the last white-picket platform fence disappeared and was replaced by trackside shrubs as the train headed through the meadows and market gardens alongside the River Lee. Effie continued studying the scenery, before her father's anger, her mother's horrified expression and the ugly words they threw at Nathan forced themselves into her mind, and something akin to a ragged-toothed saw ripped deep into her heart.

With the rhythmic clackity-clack noise of the train speeding over the points in her ears, Effie stared numbly out of the window for a moment, then, with tears distorting her vision, she turned to Nathan and threw herself into his arms.

Holding her in his firm embrace, Nathan pressed his lips on her forehead as she sobbed helplessly on his chest.

CHAPTER 24

'Sorry, chum,' said the elderly man wearing a navy LNER uniform standing by platform seven's barrier. 'The army's taken everything on the Bedford line until after nine thirty. But you should be able to jump onto a passenger train after that.'

'Thank you,' said Nathan.

'Where are you going?'

'Bedford,' Nathan replied.

'Well, if you pop along to Euston there's one through Bletchley leaving at eight fifteen, if that helps you out at all,' the railway worker said.

'Thanks again,' said Nathan.

Nathan left the ticket collector to do his job, turned and, glancing at his watch, strode across St Pancras concourse to Effie.

She was sitting on one of the fixed benches with her weekend case at her feet and the forlorn expression on her face she'd worn the whole journey from Waltham Cross.

'Unfortunately, all the early evening trains travelling north on our line have been reassigned to the army,' said Nathan as he reached her. 'But the good news is there's one to Bletchley from

Euston in an hour. We'll catch the branch line across from there and a taxi at the station to your base.'

'But aren't you supposed to be back by midnight?' Effie asked.

'I'll phone them when we get to Cardington and cadge a lift from there. We've got an hour to kill, so why don't we grab a cuppa and sandwich,' said Nathan, indicating the Lyons teashop on the far side of the concourse with a nod.

Forcing a smile, Effie nodded.

Carrying her suitcase effortlessly in one hand and tucking himself in alongside her to prevent her being jostled, Nathan guided her through the bustle of the early evening station.

Unsurprisingly, with so many late arrivals and cancelled trains, the small refreshment area inside was heaving, but he spotted a vacant table on the other side of the counter and headed across.

He pulled out a chair for her and, tucking her skirt under her, Effie sat down.

He smiled. 'I won't be long.'

Nathan headed across to the counter and, seeing him approaching, a young redhead sidled over. Nathan ordered their refreshments, but as there were no sandwiches left under the perspex canopy he had to settle for two slabs of solid-looking cake.

'There you are, sweetheart,' said Nathan, placing a tin tray with two cups and two plates with a slice of cake in front of Effie. 'No sandwiches, I'm afraid, so we'll have to make do with pound cake. But I've refilled your flask with coffee for the journey home.'

He handed her the fern-green flask. Effie slipped it into the top of her suitcase, snapped it shut again, and picked up the teapot.

As Effie poured their tea Nathan sat down alongside her. 'How are you feeling, sweetheart?'

'I don't know really,' Effie replied, offering him a cup. 'Like my innards have been hollowed out perhaps.'

'You've had a shock.'

She shook her head in disbelief. 'Honestly, Nathan, I still can't quite believe their reaction.'

She broke off a piece of cake and popped it in her mouth. Nathan did the same. As he'd suspected, it was dense and tasteless but as, for obvious reasons, the afternoon tea with her parents hadn't happened, the slab on his plate at least placated his gnawing stomach.

'So,' he said, raising his cup to his lips. 'What do you want to do, Effie?'

She swallowed a mouthful of tea. 'Well, we'll obviously have to postpone the wedding until after I turn twenty-one.'

'I mean, do you want to wait a while to give your parents time to come round to the idea? I'd understand if you did,' he said, his heart sinking at the prospect.

Looking over the rim of her cup at him, Effie raised an eyebrow. 'Do you think they will come round?'

As much as he wanted to give her hope, Nathan didn't answer.

'Neither do I,' sighed Effie.

'I'm really sorry, Effie.'

'You've nothing to be sorry about, Nathan.' Her lovely eyes looked boldly into his. 'Actually, it isn't shock I'm feeling, but anger. Anger and shame. Anger for my parents' bigoted attitude but mainly deep shame for the way they treated you.'

Seeing her love for him blazing out of her angry eyes, Nathan's chest swelled. If they hadn't been sitting in a teashop surrounded by shoppers, ARP and army personnel he would have taken her in his arms and kissed her there and then. Instead, he contented himself with raising her hand and pressing his lips to her fingers.

There was a loud tutting and he looked round.

Sitting on the table next to them were two middle-aged women with shopping bags from both Barkers and Bournes & Hollingsworth gathered around their feet. They were wearing tweed suits, elaborate hats and sour expressions.

Nathan frowned. Perhaps he should have explained to Effie what she would have to suffer if she became Mrs Fitzgerald.

'Ignore them,' he said.

Effie's lips pulled into a hard line, and she glared at the two jowly women on the next table for a moment, then, reaching across, she grabbed his lapel. She pulled him to her, pressed her lips on his and gave him a noisy kiss, then released him.

Throwing back her tea, Effie stood up.

'Let's go and get our train, darling,' she said, loudly. 'We can talk about our wedding on the way.'

She held out her hand. Putting down his cup, Nathan grabbed her suitcase handle and rose to his feet. He took her hand and under the scrutiny of dozens of pairs of eyes they made their way out of the tearoom.

With his arm round Effie, who was sleeping peacefully with her head in the crook of his neck, Nathan was just at the point of sleep too when the train jolted to a stop.

Effie raised her head and blinked.

'Have we arrived?' she asked, looking adorably dishevelled as she pushed her hair from her face.

'I don't think so,' Nathan replied.

Kissing her briefly on the forehead, he stood and, reaching up, switched off the dim light illuminating their carriage. Turning to the window, he unhooked the blind. He let it roll up, then pulled down the window.

'Looks like we've stopped in the middle of nowhere,' he said. The breeze ruffling his hair as he stuck his head out and peered into the blackness.

'What time is it?' asked Effie.

In the light from the sliver of the moon overhead, Nathan looked at his watch. 'Half past eleven.'

By rights they should have arrived at Bletchley hours ago, but the eight fifteen train had turned into the nine fifteen and then the ten past ten.

Having piled into a half-empty carriage and found a seat at twenty past ten, they'd only been going thirty minutes when they'd been held at a red signal for half an hour before setting off again. A great number of their fellow passengers alighted at Watford Junction but again they were held at a red light while a goods train loaded with tanks rattled past. Thankfully, this was only for ten minutes. It was after they set off again that Effie had nodded off to sleep.

On hearing the compartment door opening behind him, Nathan pulled his head back inside. He turned round and found the train's guard, a portly middle-aged chap with ginger hair, standing in the doorway.

'Why have we stopped?' asked Nathan.

'There's a problem wiv the engine,' the redheaded railway worker replied. 'Hardly surprising really, considering the old girl's been chugging up and down this line since Queen Victoria was on the frone.'

'So what happens now?' asked Effie.

'Well, miss, I'm afraid you have two choices – you can either sit it out until the engineer arrives—'

'How long will that be?'

'I couldn't say, miss,' the railway worker replied. 'Or...'

'Or?' said Nathan.

'You can get out and walk to Bletchley, the next station,' the guard replied. 'It's only a couple of miles down the track. Shouldn't take you more than half an hour or so. It's up to you.'

He slid the door closed and moved on to the next compartment to give the occupants there the cheery news.

'Well, then,' said Effie, rising to her feet. 'It looks like we're going for a romantic moonlight stroll.'

Nathan pressed his lips together.

Unlike him Effie was wearing civilian clothes, which consisted of a maroon-coloured dress and lightweight jacket and a pair of black court shoes with heels the length of his thumb.

'Are you sure?' he asked, glancing at her feet.

'Of course,' she said, giving him a plucky smile. 'And you're already technically AWOL, so the sooner we get going the sooner we'll get there.'

She was right of course, but...

Nathan studied her for a moment or two longer, then, reaching up, took her suitcase down from the luggage rack. He opened the carriage's outer door and jumped down, placed the suitcase on the trackside gravel and held out his hand.

'Be careful, sweetheart,' he called up. 'It's uneven.'

Grasping his hand, she jumped down. He caught her holding her close and, in the darkness, kissed her, feeling her lips warm in contrast to the night chill.

All along the track other passengers were also starting their nocturnal ramble towards civilisation, crunching along as they made their way along the side of the train towards the locomotive at the front.

Nathan held Effie briefly, then took her case in one hand and held his RAF torch pointed at their feet in the other, and they followed the line of people heading for the next town.

Trying to walk where Nathan had, Effie stepped over a clump of earth, but as she put her foot down pain shot through the little toe on her left foot and she gasped.

Nathan turned to face her. 'Are you all right, Effie?'

'I'm fine,' she lied.

If she was going to be totally honest, her new shoes had

already been starting to pinch by the time she'd got on the train that morning at King's Cross.

In the faint light from their pencil torches, Nathan frowned. 'You're not fine, are you, Effie?'

Her shoulders slumped. 'No. My feet are killing me. The guard said it was only a couple of miles, so I thought I'd be all right. Plus you needed to get there to contact your base.'

'Then I'd better find somewhere we can stay until morning.' Nathan cast his eyes over the dark landscape. 'I think that's a farmhouse over there.'

Effie followed his gaze and saw the outline of a building in the next field over.

'Hopefully they'll have a telephone,' Nathan continued, 'and I can organise someone from Tempsford to fetch us. Failing that, I'll see if they can put us up for the night and sort everything else out in the morning.'

Putting her case down, he turned his back to her.

'Jump up,' he said, crouching slightly and holding his arms wide.

Effie stared at him. 'You can't carry me?'

'How else are you going to make it through a ploughed field in those shoes?' he replied over his shoulder. 'And if I'm not mistaken, it's starting to rain.'

'It's only a couple of spots,' Effie replied as a fat raindrop landed on her face. 'Even so, I—'

'Come on,' he cut in. 'You can't weigh more than eight stone. I was carrying that much from the cane fields before I started shaving. Now, as you said earlier, the sooner we get going the sooner we'll get there.'

Feeling more than a little foolish, Effie hesitated, then, putting her hands on his broad shoulders, she jumped up onto his back.

Nathan caught her. And ignoring the protest of his recently healed shoulder, hooked his right arm round her leg, then reached down with his right hand and picked up her case. He regained his balance and they set off across the field.

After twenty minutes or so of trudging across a potato field in the dark, and with the rain falling steadily, Nathan pushed open the five-bar gate.

'Here we are,' he said, and put her down on the farmyard's muddy flagstones in front of the solid, uninspiring brick-built farmhouse.

Given it was well past midnight and the blackout was in force, unsurprisingly there wasn't a light to be seen anywhere. The rusting farm equipment dotted about the place and the lack of sound gave the whole place a neglected feel.

'Let's see if we can rouse someone,' said Nathan.

He marched to the door and, as there was no knocker, banged on it with his fist.

'They won't thank you for waking them in the middle of the night,' said Effie as they waited.

Nathan grinned. 'Probably not.'

They listened for movement on the other side of the door for a second or two, then Nathan thumped the door again. Like the first time, the sound echoed through the house. He crouched down and, pushing up the letterbox flap, shone his pencil torch through it.

He let it fall, crossed to the window to the right and rubbed the glass with his elbow, the directed the beam of light through the grubby glass and peered in.

'Anything?' asked Effie, damp starting to seep through the shoulders of her jacket.

He shook his head. 'It's difficult to see properly but I think the place has been abandoned. But that looks a bit more promising.' He indicated the barn at the rear of the property.

Dodging between the puddles on the unmade track, they

hurried towards the outbuilding and found, in contrast to the dilapidated farmhouse, the barn was in good order. Housed in it was a fairly new tractor and trailer, standing in front of what looked like bales of hay, which filled the space with warmth and fresh country sweetness.

'We should be comfortable enough up there.' Nathan nodded at the neatly stacked bales at the back of the barn.

He strode across, pulled the ladder away from one of the walls and leant it against the stored hay.

'After you, m'lady,' he said, giving her an elaborate bow.

'Why, thank you, kind sir,' Effie replied.

She grabbed one of the rungs and clambered up.

The smell of sun-ripened sweetness was stronger on top and the drying grass was soft to the touch. It was warmer too, as the heat from below percolated upwards. Finding a comfortable spot, Effie took her slim torch out her pocket. She switched it on and the golden glow from it enhanced the peaceful feel of the space below the eaves. The ladder creaked and Nathan's head appeared.

'I've stayed in worse places,' he said he crawled across to join her.

'It's certainly better than spending the night in a railway carriage,' said Effie.

'True,' Nathan said. 'But we'd better make ourselves comfortable and try to get some sleep.'

They exchanged a loving look and, as Nathan shifted around bales of dry fodder, Effie slipped off her damp jacket.

'There we are, madam,' he said, patting a dip in the hay.

Effie snuggled down into it and made herself comfortable.

Nathan stood up and took off his greatcoat and tie and undid his jacket and a couple of shirt buttons, then joined her in the hay.

He lay down beside her and covered them both with his thick overcoat.

Snuggling into him, Effie placed her hand on his chest, and a rather pleasant feeling circled her navel. Wrapping his arms round her, Nathan kissed her lightly on the forehead. 'Warm enough?'

Enveloped in the heat of his body, Effie nodded.

'Good.' He pressed his lips on her forehead again. 'I can't have my darling fiancée catching a cold.'

She laughed and he hugged her.

'Actually,' said Effie, enjoying the sensation of his body against hers, 'I think it's rather romantic. Hero and heroine seek shelter in a barn on a rainy night. Thrown together by the elements, they realise they are in love. It's the sort of thing you'd read about in a romantic novel.'

Nathan chuckled. 'Well, I don't need to get stranded in a storm to know that I love you. In fact, I think I loved you from the first time I laid eyes on you.'

Lifting her head, she gave him a querying look. 'On St Pancras station?'

'It was love at first sight,' he replied, gathering her back into his embrace. Resting her head on his hard chest, Effie slipped her hands under his jacket and smoothed them around his body, setting off the pleasing sensation again.

Shifting slightly, she stretched up and pressed her lips on his briefly, then gazed up at him. In the dim light, Nathan's eyes changed in some way and his arms tightened around her.

Shifting onto his side, he lowered his mouth onto hers, starting a pulsing sensation south of her navel as she traced her fingertips across his back.

They stayed locked like that for a moment or two, then Nathan's lips left hers.

'We've had a long day,' he said, in a taut tone. 'So perhaps we should try and get some shut-eye.'

Effie nodded and laid her head back on his shoulder.

Reaching up, Nathan switched off the torch balancing on her suitcase, then his arm wound round her again.

Lying there in the dark in Nathan's embrace, Effie felt bothered and fidgety for some inexplicable reason, but as the unsettling feeling subsided, with the smell of the hay and quiet of the barn soothing her, she drifted off to sleep.

Nathan woke with a start to find Effie sitting bolt upright and holding her right foot.

'What's the matter?' he asked, sitting up alongside her.

'Cramp,' she replied. 'It happens sometimes when my feet get cold.'

Grasping the torch, Nathan switched it on, then shuffled round. 'Let me.'

He took hold of her stockinged foot and Effie rested back on her hands.

'Better?' he asked, as he gently massaged the sole and enjoyed the sight of her shapely leg.

She nodded.

Nathan rocked back on his heels, rose to his feet and stripped off his jacket. Kneeling beside her, he wrapped it lightly round her feet, then he straightened up.

In the mute light from the torch, Effie's gaze flickered over the open front of his shirt, and her eyes widened. Nathan's chest expanded as his senses started to respond, but he damped them down.

'That should keep you a bit warmer,' he said, brightly. He looked at his watch. 'It's almost three, so the sun should be coming up in an hour or two.' Lying down beside her, he pulled his greatcoat over them. Reaching up, he switched off the torch, then he tucked the coat round them both.

'Thank you,' she said. 'And sorry for waking you.'

'That's all right,' he replied, wrapping his arms round her

and kissing her forehead. 'That's what husbands are for, after all.'

Snuggling into him, Effie's hands slid over the thin fabric of his shirt and up his chest. 'And other things,' she said, in a throaty voice.

Excitement coursed through him, but as his body urged him on Nathan fixed his mind on running through the correct sequence of the pre-flight checks for a Lysander. However, as he started to visualise the fuel gauge Effie's hand continued its tormenting journey up his chest. Winding it round his neck, she pulled him to her and pressed her mouth onto his.

Desire pulsed through Nathan. With his love for her firing him, he rolled her over and then covered her with his body. Effie's hands went to the front of his shirt and fiddled with his buttons while, resting on one elbow, his free hand slid up her leg and beneath her skirt. She gave a small moan as she opened her legs and hooked them round the backs of his thighs.

Tearing his lips from hers, Nathan planted a trail of kisses across her cheek and down her neck, but as he reached her collarbone he raised his head and frowned.

Conquering his surging desire, he rolled off her and turned the torch back on.

'We shouldn't, Effie,' he said, forcing a serious expression on his face.

Lying in the hay with her skirt up above her stocking tops and her hair in disarray, Effie stared up at him for a second , then thankfully, as his resolve started to crumble, she sat up too.

'You're right,' she replied, her eyes dark and enormous as they looked at him. 'We shouldn't.'

He held her gaze. 'After all, it could result in... consequences.'

'Little consequences?' she asked.

He swallowed hard. 'Yes.'

In the mute light of her pencil torch Effie studied him for a few moments, then her hands went to the front of her dress.

'What are you doing, Effie?' he croaked, as she started undoing the buttons.

'Actually, Nathan,' she replied, yanking it over her head and throwing it behind her. 'I'm not altogether sure, but I'm hoping you might help me to find out.'

~

With Nathan's damp forehead resting on her collarbone Effie sighed and, opening her eyes, looked up at the rough-hewn rafter of the barn above her.

Twisting slightly, she kissed his left temple, the nearest bit of him she could reach, and received a small moan of acknowledgement in return.

She didn't know the time but with the dawn chorus chirping away in the trees and the spring sunlight now creeping into the barn, she guessed it must be somewhere around six in the morning.

Enjoying his weight on her, Effie basked in the glow of their lovemaking. Idly she watched dust particles dance in the light in the mute quietness of the barn, reliving every nerve-shuddering sensation she'd discovered in Nathan's arms.

He was right, of course, about the baby thing – but, as her parents had had to wait ten years before she arrived, she reckoned the odds were in her favour.

As if he was aware of her looking at him, Nathan's eyes opened.

'I love you, Nathan,' she said, looking down at him.

He gave her that lazy smile of his.

'I love you, too,' he replied, reaching up and tracing a path along her bare shoulder with his finger. He frowned. 'Are you all right, Effie? I hope I didn't—'

'I'm perfectly fine.' She looked into his concerned blue eyes. 'Never better, in fact.'

He frowned. 'I feel awful. Taking advantage of you like that.'

Effie raised an eyebrow. 'I think, Nathan, the boot was very much on the other foot.'

One corner of his mouth fleetingly lifted in a crooked smile, but then his eyebrows pulled together again. 'Even so, I wanted our first time to be special.'

Leaning over him, she took his face between her hands. 'It was, Nathan.'

She wasn't lying.

Somewhere between him massaging the cramp from her toes and him laying his greatcoat over them again, the sensation below her navel had shifted from a vague yearning into a trembling need. She hadn't understood it last night, but she certainly did this morning.

'And as to consequences,' she continued, pre-empting what she suspected might be his next niggle. 'My parents were married for ten years before I came along, and we're getting married in eight weeks.'

He opened his mouth to speak but Effie pressed her finger to his lips to stop his words.

'I love you and you love me, and that's all that matters.' Bending over him, she kissed him deeply. He hesitated, then his mouth opened under hers.

He wound his arm round her and rolled her on her back. Taking his weight on one elbow, he looked down at her, but as he did the sound of women's laughter cut through the silence of the barn.

Nathan looked up, then sprang to his feet.

Effie did the same.

They gathered their scattered clothes and hastily dressed.

Effie had just about got her underwear on and dress

buttoned up when the barn door opened and three land girls, wearing their brown cord trousers and green jumpers, strolled in.

Seeing them atop the bales of hay, they stopped dead in their tracks and their jaws dropped.

'Good morning, ladies,' Nathan said, tucking his shirt into his trousers.

'Morning,' they said, still staring up at them agog.

Nathan shrugged on his uniform jacket. 'Lovely day, isn't it?'

Open-mouthed, they nodded.

Nathan put his arm round Effie and a broad smile spread across his face. 'Any chance of giving me and my fiancée a lift to Bletchley station?'

CHAPTER 25

'Right girls,' shouted Sergeant Dunbar, her beady eyes skimming over them as she strolled along their ranks. 'Don't ask me how but it seems that all of you have passed your on-site weeks, so you are now full-fledged WAAF balloon operators.'

Effie, and the three lines of WAAFs standing in the mid-afternoon sunlight pulled their shoulders back a notch.

It was the second Friday in April and she, along with the rest of the January 1942 intake who had survived the gruelling fourteen-week course, were standing at ease in their freshly pressed number one uniforms in front of the north hangar.

'Now in a few moments' time the top brass from Stanmore will march out for your final inspection,' said Sergeant Marshall, her gaze running over their ranks. 'This will include the newly appointed wing commander of No. 30 Group, which covers London, where some of you are stationed.'

'Lucky us,' muttered Nell, who was standing behind Effie.

'At least after this we can say goodbye to all the square-bashing on Cardington's parade ground,' said Alice.

'And that unhinged Welsh PE instructor Jones,' added Maeve, who was standing next to her.

'And back to the bright lights of London, thank God,' added George, who as the tallest WAAF was on pole position in the line, next to Effie.

'Look lively, here they come,' said Effie, out of the side of her mouth.

'Attention!' bellowed Dunbar.

Four dozen feet did a double-step to attention and pressed their arms to their sides.

'By the left,' bellowed the rotund sergeant.

Raising their right arms, the lines straightened up, as half a dozen men and a couple of women marched onto the gravel parade ground.

Without moving her head, Effie ran her eyes down the line of senior officers, then her gaze rested on Nathan. On the basis that he'd been one of their trainers for a couple of weeks, he'd wangled himself an invitation to the parade.

Like his fellow RAF officers, Nathan was dressed for the occasion in his number one uniform, his broad shoulders and chest filling the jacket and the belt snug round his waist. Effie's heart squeezed in love while her stomach tightened for an entirely different reason, as she thought of their forty-eight-hour passes and a whole weekend to themselves.

Coming to a halt, the party of senior officers formed up into a line, then as they turned to face the WAAFs George's gaze fixed on the tall, slender officer with blond hair.

'What's that bastard doing here?' she snarled.

'Who?' whispered Nell.

'Wing Commander Percy Cuthbertson,' she replied. 'He's the bloody low-life liar who transferred me.'

Effie glanced across at her friend's angry face.

'Eyes front,' barked Dunbar.

Effie's head snapped back just as the officer George had been glaring at since the inspection party came into view stepped out of line.

Dunbar and Marshall marched across and stopped in front of him.

'Bastard,' George repeated, as the sergeants and wing commander exchanged salutes.

As the two sergeants marched back to their positions, he looked across at the assembled WAAFs.

'Well,' he said, surveying the rows with an aloof expression on his face. 'This is a momentous day for you as individuals and for the RAF, because today...'

The wing commander continued on about duty, service and king and country, the way senior officers always did on such occasions, as Effie and Nathan gazed across the parade ground at each other. Thankfully, after a few minutes Wing Commander Cuthbertson concluded.

Breaking away from the line of his fellow officers and with both NCOs in tow, Cuthbertson marched across to the WAAFs. Starting at the other end from Effie, he strolled along, wearing an indulgent expression on his refined features, until he reached George.

'Aircraftwoman St John-Smythe,' he said smoothly, a roguish glint in his grey eyes. 'Nice to see you again. How are you getting on?'

With a look that could have frozen boiling water, George gave him a brittle smile. 'Very well, thank you, sir. How's your wife?'

Although Cuthbertson's polished expression didn't waver, a crimson flush crept above his collar.

He and George eyeballed each other for a second, then he strolled past Effie and started to make his way down the second row of WAAFs.

Effie stole a quick look at her friend again. 'Are you all right, George?' she whispered.

'I'm fine,' her friend shot back through rigid lips.

The inspection continued until Cuthbertson had strolled

past all the newly qualified balloon operators, then he marched back to take his place in the parade party.

The two WAAF sergeants saluted the senior officers again, then marched back to their charges.

Forming themselves into an orderly line, the party of senior officers marched off the parade ground.

'Squad, dismissed!' bellowed Dunbar as they disappeared from sight.

In unison the rows of WAFFs stamped round half a turn, then broke ranks, laughing and chattering.

Feeling oddly emotional, Effie mingled with the women she'd worked with for the past three months and who were now off to balloon sites all over the country. After twenty minutes hugging them and wiping away the odd tear, she joined her friends.

'Well, there's no point hanging about, we'd better get ourselves packed up to enjoy our forty-eight-hour pass,' she said.

'Yer,' said Nell. 'Cos God alone knows when we'll get another one. Where's everyone off to?'

'I'm staying with my sister for a couple of days,' sighed Alice. 'What about you?'

'Back to Whitechapel to see my lot, God help me,' Nell replied. 'I'm guessing you're off to your castle to get drunk, m'lady.'

'I'm certainly going to get drunk,' George replied. 'But in Mayfair rather than some draughty country pile.' She looked at Effie and raised an eyebrow. 'And there's no point asking our corporal what she's doing, because we've just seen her weekend activity marching off to the officers' mess. Not that we blame you, Effie. The man's temptation on legs.'

'We're actually going to do some sightseeing in London,' said Effie, feeling her cheeks glow. 'And then seeing the priest at St Paul's along the Highway from the Maid of Norway about our wedding.'

'What are you bunch of princesses still doing here?'

Effie looked around and saw their formidable sergeant standing behind her.

'We're off,' said Effie. 'And thank you for all you've done.'

'Yes, well,' Dunbar said gruffly. 'And you can thank me properly by proving to the blooming top brass at Stanmore that WAAFs can operate a barrage balloon as well as any RAF crew.'

Effie grinned. 'Don't worry, Sergeant, we'll show them we can do it better.'

What could have been a smile hovered on the older woman's pale lips for a moment, then she cleared her throat, gave them a last once-over, and turned to march off the parade ground.

They watched her go, then they headed off to their draughty barrack hut for the last time.

Effie had just laid her freshly laundered shirt on the top of her kitbag when the young WAAF who worked in the station's reception hut put her head round the hut door.

'Corporal Weston?'

Effie looked round. 'That's me.'

'You've got a visitor,' she said. 'They're waiting in the sentry hut by the main gate.'

'Perhaps it's your dad,' said Alice, tucking her thick socks into her haversack.

A hope sparked in Effie's heart, but she damped it down and shook her head.

'Every time I've telephoned to talk to my parents they hang up before I can say more than a couple of words,' she said. 'And they haven't replied to my letters either.' She pulled the drawstring of her kitbag tight. 'I'd better go and see who it is.'

. . .

Effie headed along the path between the accommodation cabins toward the administration blocks and the front gate. Her heart sank when she spotted a green Austin 10 parked on the other side of the barrier gate, and a familiar figure leaning against it smoking.

She took a deep breath and squared her shoulders, then marched over.

'Hello, Leonard,' she said.

Throwing his cigarette away, he straightened up. 'We need to talk, Euphemia.'

He opened the car's rear door.

'If you have anything to say you can say it here,' she replied.

'In private,' he replied.

Effie regarded him levelly. 'I'm *not* getting in the car.'

'Very well.' He slammed the door shut. 'Let me say I was very upset when I received your letter a few weeks back.'

'I'm sorry, Leonard,' she replied. 'But I thought it best to be straight with you.'

'My first instinct was to jump in the car and drive here to talk some sense into you,' he continued. 'But knowing how stubborn you can be I decided that it would be better to wait until you realised your mistake. However, it's been a month now, Euphemia, and this nonsense has gone on long enough.'

She raised her eyebrows.

'There's no call for levity,' he snapped. 'Especially as your parents are distraught.'

'I'm sorry they are but they chose to throw me out,' she replied.

'And can you blame them?' he said. 'When you coolly announce that you're marrying a... a man like *him*.'

'I'm disappointed that you and my parents have such despicable, bigoted views, Leonard,' Effie said, giving him a hard look. 'But nothing and no one is going to stop me marrying the man I love who just happens to have brown skin.'

'And what about me?'

'I've already said I'm sorry,' Effie replied.

'Don't flatter yourself.' Grabbing her wrist, Leonard gave a hard laugh.

Effie tried unsuccessfully to free her arm.

'Let me go, Leonard,' she said, her heart thumping hard in her chest.

He tightened his grip.

'Understandably,' he continued, his nicotine-laden breath wafting over her face. 'Your parents have kept quiet about all of this, but once it gets out I'll be a laughing sto—'

'I'd advise you that, unless you want me to break yours, you release my fiancée's arm,' cut in a deep voice.

Effie's head snapped round and relief flooded through her as she saw Nathan walking towards them.

Leonard took half a step forward and pain shot up Effie's forearm.

'Don't you threaten me,' he snarled.

Nathan's mouth pulled into a tight line. 'Then let go of Effie's arm.'

Indecision flickered across Leonard's face, then he threw her arm from him.

Effie stepped across the space between them and slipped her arm through Nathan's.

'I think you'd better leave, Leonard,' she said.

'Don't worry, I'm going,' he barked.

He stomped to his car and tore the driver's door open, but as he got one foot in the car he turned and faced them.

'I'll tell you this for nothing, Effie,' he shouted. 'Now I know you're the sort of woman who'd throw themselves away like this I wouldn't marry you if you paid me.'

Climbing in, he slammed the door, then turned on the engine and sped off down the road.

Effie watched the rear of the Austin disappear round the corner and then she turned to Nathan.

'Are you all right, Effie?' he asked, concern written large across his handsome face.

Placing her hand on his chest, she stretched up and pressed her lips onto his briefly. 'I am now.'

He smiled. 'Just seven weeks until the big day.'

'Yes, just seven weeks until I can change my name to Mrs Fitzgerald,' she replied.

They exchanged a loving look, then, slipping her arm though his again, Effie smiled. 'I'm ready to go if you are.'

'I've done my duty by exchanging small talk with the bigwigs, so let's head off,' he replied, and they headed back down the base's main road.

'I have to pick up my kit,' she said. 'But as long as the quarter-to bus isn't late, we should be in time to catch the five thirty to London.'

Nathan grinned. 'I have a surprise first.'

'All right, but if we miss that bus the next one's not for half an hour,' Effie said as they continued along the path.

After a few moments they reached the back of the officers' mess and Nathan stopped by a burgundy-coloured Morris Eight standing with the handful of other vehicles parked there.

'What do you think?' he asked, as she stared open-mouthed at the four-door saloon.

'Is it yours?' she asked.

'It sure is, ma'am.' Nathan stepped forward and opened the passenger door. 'I picked up your gear from the hut and it's in the boot with mine.'

Laughing, Effie climbed in and settled herself into the leather seat. Nathan went round and got behind the wheel.

'Before we head into London to speak to Father James about our wedding, as you don't have to be back on balloon site 312 until Tuesday and I'm free until Wednesday, we're going to have a couple of nights in a hotel in a pretty village not far from here.' He switched on the engine. 'And' – he winked – 'another thing you might like to know about our new car is that the back seat is quite spacious.'

CHAPTER 26

⌘

'Is George all right?' asked Effie as Alice walked back into the Maid of Norway's lounge.

'She seems to be,' Alice replied, taking the empty seat next to Maeve.

'Thank Gawd for that,' said Nell, through a mouthful of toast and marmalade. 'When she stumbled out of bed an hour ago, she looked like she'd been dug up from her own grave.'

It was half past five on a Monday morning and they were sitting round the century-old dining table on an assortment of chairs. As she'd done since they left Cardington and returned to balloon 312 a month ago, as soon their tour of duty was over George had headed up west, not returning until the wee small hours.

'I hope your posh mate cleans that bog!'

Effie turned to see Lily and Maureen strolling into the lounge.

'What, like you did when you had the trots last week?' said Nell.

Lily gave Nell a scathing look, then turned her attention to Effie.

'You're supposed to be one of the corporals in charge around here, so why don't you report her?' she asked as she tied a red poker-dot scarf into a turban. 'After all, you were quick enough to report me last week and have them dock my pay.'

'Favouritism, that's what it is, Lil,' chipped in Maureen. 'One rule for 'er mates and another for the rest of us.'

'I reported you, Lily Craven, for persistent lateness, which is dereliction of duty,' said Effie firmly. 'But George hasn't broken any regulations.'

Lily glared at Effie, who gave her a cool look in return.

'Come on, Mo, we'll have our breakfast round the corner in the WVS canteen,' said Lily.

Picking up their gas masks and rucksacks, Lily and Maureen headed for the door.

'We're on duty at o-six hundred hours, so don't be late,' Effie called after them.

Giving Effie and her friends a caustic look as they went, the two WAAFs left the room.

The sound of a toilet flushing drifted down, followed by feet above their head padding across the floorboards.

'I'm worried about her, carrying on like this,' said Alice as they all looked up at the ceiling.

'So am I,' said Effie. 'But what can I do? No matter how much the worse for wear she is when she stumbles in, George is always ready for duty the next morning.'

'Yes, but it can't be good for her,' said Alice.

'You have the right of it there,' said Maeve. 'Sure, haven't I seen grown men turn yellow and die from the drink.'

'Well let's hope it doesn't come to that,' Effie replied, thinking of her friend upstairs.

'Morning, playmates,' said Dolly as she walked in carrying a mug and a plate of toast.

Those round the table mumbled their morning greetings as she took her seat.

'Was that George again last night?' asked Dolly.

'I'm afraid so,' said Maeve.

'Still, at least we know now it was that snooty Wing Commander Wotsit that did the dirty on her,' said Nell.

'You mean Cuthbertson,' said Effie.

Nell nodded. 'Bloody men.'

'What about bloody men?' asked George as she strolled into the room holding a mug.

Although she was dressed like the rest of them in her navy boiler suit and stout boots, her hair tucked in a snood, she did indeed look like a corpse. In fact, Effie had seen corpses looking healthier. As always, George's face was immaculately made up, but the light dusting of face powder and blusher couldn't disguise her pasty complexion beneath. Her grey eyes had both shadow and mascara applied but with the added colour of tiny red blood vessels.

'They can drive you to drink,' said Nell.

George raised an eyebrow, then looked at Effie. 'And how is our bride-to-be this morning, after your tryst with your beloved yesterday?'

'I hardly think two hours sitting in the back seat of the Morris along the Embankment qualifies as a tryst,' said Effie. Between her duties and Nathan's, they hadn't seen each other since their blissful weekend after her passing-out parade.

'Where's Nathan off to?' asked Bridget.

'I have no idea,' Effie replied. 'But he thinks he'll be back in a couple of weeks.'

'Well, as long as he's back in four weeks for your wedding,' said Alice. 'That's all that matters.'

Imagining Nathan standing beside her at the altar, Effie smiled. 'Yes, it is.'

She caught sight of the clock.

Throwing back the last of her tea, she stood up. 'Time to go.

Last one on site makes the tea,' she called over her shoulder as she grabbed her kitbag.

'How are we doing over there?' Effie called across to Maeve.

'Winch and brakes are grand and George is halfway through giving the engine the once-over,' Maeve called back. 'Although I have to be telling you we're running low on lubricant.'

'I'll order some from stores,' Effie shouted back.

Taking the pencil from behind her ear, she pulled the balloon's logbook from her boiler-suit pocket and made a note.

She and the rest of the crew had been on site for almost three and a half hours and had spent the morning, as they did every day, checking and doing routine maintenance to ensure Bessie was ready for action.

This included topping up the helium and checking there were no tears or holes in the balloon's fabric. Ensuring all the ropes and cables were sound, a task she'd allocated to Lily and Maureen at roll call. The task of repairing any guy ropes and cables that were found to be frayed or damaged she gave to Nell and Rose.

The balloon was floating in close-haul at 150 feet when they'd taken over from Millie's crew, but about ten minutes after they came on duty a dispatch rider from squadron headquarters at Stanmore arrived with their operational orders for the day.

This meant that before they could start any of their routine tasks they had to raise the balloon to 3,000 feet. With George – who by this time looked almost human – manning the winch engine, they let Bessie up and, after ten minutes or so of heaving and pulling, 312 balloon was bobbing about in the breeze above East London along with dozens of its fat silver chums.

The dispatch rider's motorbike had only just zoomed off when the truck arrived with their weekly supply of fresh helium. After Effie had spent twenty minutes with the driver checking the gauges to ensure they were correct, he departed with their empty cylinders.

Satisfied that everything that needed to be done was being done, now with her watch showing half past eleven, Effie made her way across to the hut.

Peggy and Nell were sitting, with coils of cable and rope around their feet, on one of the two park benches that she, Nell, Maeve and Alice had uprooted the day after they arrived and dragged across to the hut.

The other bench was at right angles, while the two faded, striped deckchairs they had found propped up at the back of the hut were set out next to it.

'Looks like it's going to be a nice day,' said Peggy.

'It's about time,' said Nell.

'Who's on chow duty?' asked Peggy, who was sitting outside the hut on a deckchair, splicing guy ropes.

'Alice,' Effie replied.

'Thank goodness it's not George,' said Nell. 'I know I'm not much shakes in the kitchen, but she'd burn a boiled egg.'

'Where *is* Alice?' asked Effie, looking around for her friend.

'In the hut making everyone a mid-morning cuppa,' said Rose.

Leaving them plaiting rope, Effie walked across to what was in effect a small garden shed.

She'd found out that when the station was allocated to balloon 312 the aircraftmen manning it were billeted in tents on site. However, after the terrible winter during the first year of the war, in order to stop balloon crews freezing to death, RAF Balloon Command started to look for more solid accommodation. Obviously this wasn't always possible on remote balloon sites, but it was much easier to find a suitable billet in large cities, for which Effie for one was eternally grateful.

Alice was taking the kettle off the two-ring Primus stove as Effie walked through the already open door.

'You've had a busy morning,' Alice said, as she poured the boiling water into the three-pint enamel teapot.

'I certainly have,' agreed Effie.

'At least the weather's brightened up at last,' said Alice.

'That's what Rose and Nell said,' Effie replied, pulling out one of the chairs by the table and sitting down.

'Still, I expect every day's a sunny day for you now,' her friend said. 'Have you finalised the wedding arrangements with Father James?'

'I'm going round to St Paul's vicarage Wednesday evening,' Effie replied. 'Nathan was hoping to be able to get a twenty-four-hour pass, but he can't, so I'll have to go by myself.'

'I'll come with you, if you like,' said Alice. 'And when you choose your dress.'

'Would you?' said Effie.

Alice nodded. 'Who wouldn't want to go shopping for a wedding dress?'

An image of her mother's shocked face flickered though Effie's mind. 'My mother, it seems.'

Stirring the tea, Alice gave her a sympathetic look. 'You still haven't heard from her?'

Effie shook her head. 'They are still hanging up the phone as soon as they realise it's me and still won't answer my letters.'

Alice laid the tea towel over the teapot, pulled a chair closer to Effie and sat down.

'Just give them a bit of time and I'm sure they will come round,' she said, placing a hand over Effie's.

Effie didn't reply. How could she? She was lost for words and hope. Tears pinched at the corners of her eyes, but she blinked them away and forced a smile.

'I take it you're off to see Mrs O'Toole this afternoon,' said Effie.

Florrie had been as good as her word, and her WVS team in Shadwell had found every one of Effie's crew a local family to adopt them. This meant that, in addition to their rather comfortable billet with Florrie in the Maid of Norway, they could visit local families when they were off duty for afternoon tea or an occasional Sunday dinner. It gave them a couple of hours to relax away from their balloon site and enjoy a bit of normality, which after all was exactly what they were all fighting for. Alice's family were the O'Tooles, who ran a scrap metal yard a twenty-minute walk away in Cannon Street Road.

'I certainly am' said Alice, as she set out the crew's enamel mugs on a tin tray with a faded image of Edinburgh Castle on it. 'One of Ma O'Toole's daughters had her baby last week, and I'm looking forward to having a cuddle. Are you planning to let Nell go to Mrs Baxter's this afternoon?' she asked, adding a splash of milk to each mug.

'I thought I would,' said Effie. 'As the house is only at the back of the children's hospital across the road, if we need her I can send someone across to fetch her. Although the Luftwaffe have been a bit—'

'You know it's bad luck to say the Q word, Effie, so don't,' cut in Alice.

Effie pressed her lips together and held them between her finger and thumb.

'That's better,' said Alice. 'Now make yourself useful and take out the tea.'

'Yes, ma'am!'

Effie gave her friend an extravagant salute and they both giggled, then, grasping the tray of tea firmly, Effie carried it outside. Alice followed after her with a tin of rock buns from the Shadwell WVS canteen that Florrie had dropped off on her way to the market.

In the fifteen or so minutes she'd been talking to Alice, the few puffy white clouds above them had scattered so the sun now shone down on them from out of a bright-blue sky.

Having completed their allocated tasks, nearly everyone was making their way back to the mess hut.

'Right,' said Effie, placing the tray on the upturned vegetable crate between the park benches. 'We'll have fifteen minutes for elevenses, then, while we wait for the chow box to arrive from base, we'll run through gas drill again.'

'This is the life,' said Dolly, who sprawled in one of the deckchairs, basking in the April sunshine.

'Too right,' said Nell, who was sitting on the other one with her face tilted towards the sun. 'Although I'd much rather be on Southend beach than here.'

'If I shut my eyes, I could almost imagine I was in St Tropez,' said George, who, wearing a pair of enormous sunglasses, was stretched out on one of the ground sheets, her hands behind her head.

After a chilly, wet and overcast couple of months the weather seemed to have woken up and realised it was supposed to be spring. Since they'd first arrived in Shadwell back in March for their final assessment, it had been getting progressively warmer and now, on this sunny afternoon, it was probably close to seventy-five degrees.

Effie sat on one of the two park benches rereading Dorothy L. Sayers' *Whose Body?* which she'd taken out from Shadwell library the week before. Maeve was sitting beside her knitting a navy balaclava to send to her brother on HMS *Valiant*. Rose and Peggy, who had joined the crew a few weeks before, were lounging with their feet up on the other bench in front of the hut. Lily and Maureen had dragged out the ancient sofa from inside the hut and were stretched out across it.

'Afternoon, ladies.'

Effie looked round.

Standing to the side of the hut was a slender young man a

few years older than her. He was about six foot or so with a mop of almost black hair, which was trimmed above his collar but sat in riotous curls above.

Although like most of the working men of the area he wore rough cords, a collarless shirt, a waistcoat and boots, there was a gold fob chain dangling from his waistcoat pocket to the middle buttonhole, and a weighty signet ring on his left hand. He also had a heavy toolbag slung over his left shoulder.

'Afternoon,' Effie replied. 'Can I help you, Mr...?'

'Charlie's the name, miss,' he said, his lean face lifting in an artless smile. 'Charlie Mulligan. And rather than you 'elping me, it's me 'oo has come to 'elp you lovely ladies.'

Effie gave him a puzzled look. 'In what way?'

'In the same way I did for the brave lads you lovely ladies have taken over from.' He placed the toolbag on the floor and, delving into it, pulled out a small bar of Lux soap. 'By ensuring you have those little things that will 'elp you fight Herr Hitler.'

He handed it to Peggy, who was sitting closest. He then pulled out a pack of digestive biscuits, which he passed to Lily, and a bar of fruit and nut chocolate, which he handed to Peggy.

'And finally...' he dived in again and this time pulled out a tin of Nescafé coffee.

George sat up and pushed her sunglasses up her head. 'My goodness.'

'A gift of appreciation to you brave girls from an 'umble punter, princess,' he replied, placing one hand dramatically over his heart as he placed the tin in her eager hands.

'Can I ask how you came by all this?' asked Effie.

'Course you can, Corporal,' Charlie said, his innocent smile widening. 'It's bomb-damaged stock that the council and shops flog off cheap. I've got a stall down Petticoat Lane but I thought, seeing 'ow you're defending king and country, I'd offer you girls what you might call a delivery service.'

'So, you'd be quite happy if I mentioned your visit to

Constable Clark, the beat officer from Wapping police station,' said Effie.

'Wot, you mean old Knobby?' Charlie laughed. 'Me and 'im go way back, so if you see 'im, give him my regards.'

'I don't suppose that by any chance you'd be having a pair of nylons in your bag of wonders there,' said Maeve.

'Not now,' Charlie replied. 'But I'll see what I can do. And do I detect a slight lilt from the Emerald Isle, sweetheart?'

'County Down,' Maeve replied.

'Sure, didn't my grandfather himself come from the old country,' Charlie replied. 'Didn't he used to tell me what a—'

'His grandpa came from Bermondsey but spent most his life in Dartmoor prison,' said Nell as she emerged from the other side of the mess hut. 'And no one knows who his other grandfather was, not even 'is grandma.'

Charlie looked across at her, his expression of bonhomie faltering a little. 'Hello, Nell, I 'eard you were back. How you doing?'

'A lot better before you turned up,' Nell replied.

'Come on, Nell,' he said. 'Let bygones be bygones.'

Nell gave him a glacial look. 'Don't let us keep you.'

She and Charlie eyeballed each other for a long moment, then, bending down, he picked up the toolbag and slung it over his shoulder again.

'Well, ladies,' he said, his convivial smile returning. 'It's been lovely to meet you all and I'll pop by another time with some more goodies.' His gaze shifted across to Nell. 'Good to see you, Nell. You look as lovely as when I last set eyes on you.'

Turning, he sauntered back across the park, Nell's gaze following him all the way.

'Sounds like you know Charlie well, Nell,' said Effie, as he disappeared from view.

Nell gave a hard laugh. 'Know him? I nearly married the bugger!'

CHAPTER 27

Effie slid back the curtain and stepped out of the changing room. 'What do you think?'

Alice was standing next to a mannequin modelling a utility suit, holding Effie's handbag and uniform jacket.

'That's perfect,' her friend replied. 'Especially if you add a veil.'

It was the last Friday in May, just before eleven. She and Alice were in the women's department on the first floor of Derry & Toms and had been for the past hour.

Like the rest of the country, the department store on Kensington High Street was doing its bit for the war effort. As well as the criss-cross gummed tape on the windows and glass display cabinets, between the counters and shopfloor display were dotted sand buckets and stirrup pumps. Along with summer dresses, jackets and suits the department store also stocked a range of siren suits, and there was a woman from the Ministry of Information by the stairs in the women's department giving demonstrations about how to take old clothes and make them into new outfits. It was understandable as to why there was an eager group of housewives clustered around her – the sparsely populated clothing rails in the women's department told their own story.

'Madame's friend is right,' said the middle-aged sales assistant wearing the shop's black livery, who was hovering nearby. 'Would madame care to step over to the mirror?'

'Go on, take a look,' said Alice.

Effie took a couple of steps across the lino shopfloor and stopped in front of the long mirror standing on an antique-looking frame by the coat rail.

Having dismissed a couple of suits, she was now working her way through the half a dozen dresses she'd also picked off the rails in the faint hope that if her parents did make an appearance at her big day at least they would see her in white. However, as she looked at her reflection she knew her search for her wedding outfit was over.

'What does madame think?' said the sales assistant.

'It's lovely,' said Effie.

'I'll fetch a veil.'

Without waiting for her to reply, the saleswoman hurried off.

'You look so lovely, Nathan will be speechless when he sees you,' said Alice with a sentimental look in her eye.

Effie laughed. 'I hope not, or he won't be able to say his marriage vows.' She twisted back and forth and pulled a face.

The shop assistant returned carrying a lacy veil in one hand and a small waxed apple-blossom headdress in the other. Standing between Effie and the mirror, she positioned the veil a few inches back from her hairline, then set the headdress in front.

'There,' she said, stepping back. 'Every inch a blushing bride.'

Effie studied her reflection. As Alice had said, the cream crêpe de Chine gown with a sweetheart neckline, bishop sleeves and mid-calf fluted skirt, with the elbow-length veil cascading over her shoulders, was indeed perfect, but...

Effie looked at the assistant, now standing by the mirror. 'And you say this is a thirty-six hip?'

'Yes, madame?' the assistant replied.

'What the matter, Effie?' asked Alice.

'It feels a little tight around the waist and the bust, that's all,' she replied.

'The gown is designed to show the figure to advantage,' said the assistant smoothly. 'I have a thirty-eight in stock, but not in cream, only in cerise and light blue. If madame would like me to fetch them I—'

'No, that's fine. As you say, it's probably the design,' Effie cut in.

However, as she gazed at herself in her bridal outfit in the mirror an image of her parents loomed up in her mind. How many times over the years had her mother talked about how happy she would be to see her only daughter walk her down the aisle in a bridal gown that they would have chosen together?

A lump formed in her throat, but Effie swallowed it down and looked at the woman standing expectantly beside the mirror.

'How much and how many coupons is the whole outfit, again?' she asked.

'That gown retails at three guineas and eleven coupons,' the shop assistant replied. 'The veil and headdress come to nine and six.'

Effie smiled. 'I'll take it.'

'There's one over there, Effie,' said Alice, heading off towards an empty table by the café's window.

With her WAAF handbag across her, the Derry & Toms

bag hooked over one arm and holding their two mugs of tea in the other, Effie followed.

It was now almost twelve thirty and they were in a small café halfway up Kensington Church Street along with several dozen other Friday shoppers.

'That was lucky,' said Alice, putting the tray on the table and sitting down.

'Yes, I'm not surprised it's busy though – now the weather's brightened up everyone want to get out in the sun,' said Effie, putting their mugs down and taking the seat opposite.

Shaking salt onto her lunch, Alice grinned.

'Haaappy the bride the sun shines on today,' she sang.

Effie laughed.

'Oh, and before I forget.' Alice delved into her pocket. 'I got you this.' She handed Effie a little package wrapped in tissue. 'It's for your twenty-first birthday tomorrow.'

'What is it?'

'You'll have to open it and see,' said her friend.

Effie unwrapped it and a blue silk and lace garter fell out.

'I made it myself, it's your something blue,' Alice explained, picking up her cutlery.

'Oh, thank you,' said Effie. 'That's so kind of you.'

'Well, your lovely dress is new, so what have you got for something old and borrowed?' asked Alice.

'My grandmother's cross and Maeve's silver dancing shoes,' Effie replied, tucking her present into her handbag.

'Well, you're all set then. Didn't you fancy the pie and veg?' Alice added, spearing a string bean.

Effie shook her head. 'I felt a bit off this morning from last night's liver and onion, so I thought it best to stick to jacket potato.'

'Good idea,' said Alice. 'We don't want you honking up in the bog, too.'

'No that's George's job.' Effie laughed, cutting into her potato.

'Although, thankfully she seems to have stopped drinking quite so much,' added Alice.

'I hope you don't mind me asking, Alice,' said Effie. 'But did you have a big white wedding?'

Alice nodded. 'Arthur's mother insisted on it and on inviting half the county. He was her only child and after his father died Arthur was her life.' Alice paused. 'She wasn't keen on him marrying anyone and I doubt the Princess Elizabeth herself would have been good enough for her "darling boy", let alone someone whose family worked the land. But since, to use her words, "your kind breed like rabbits", she put up with me in the hope of some grandchildren. But after five years...' Sadness flickered across her pretty face and she sighed.

'It never happened?'

Alice shook her head. 'And of course, his mother blamed me. Which was no surprise, because she blamed me for everything from the moment he took me home. If only she knew the...' Looking down, her friend buried her nose in her teacup. 'Anyway,' she continued, brightly. 'I'm sure my mother-in-law blames me for Hitler invading Poland. I know I said I joined up for Arthur's sake, but I also did it to get away from her sour looks and spiteful words.'

'Well at least now in London you're miles away from her,' said Effie.

Alice gave her a baleful look. 'I wish that were true, but my sister wrote to tell me she's moved in with her elderly aunt in Hampstead.'

'Even so,' said Effie, raising an eyebrow. 'I doubt you'll run into her in Watney Market.'

Alice's pretty face lifted in a smile. 'Very true.' They exchanged a fond look, then turned their attention back to their food. Effie finished her potato, picked up her mug, took a sip and then pulled a face.

'Does this tea taste funny to you, Alice?'

Alice swallowed a mouthful of hers and shook her head. 'Seems all right to me. I tell you what. As it's a nice day shall we walk back through Kensington Park before we head back to base?'

Effie nodded. 'Gloria Maskell's unit are manning one of the balloons in the park, so we could drop by and see how they're getting on.'

'Good idea,' said Alice. 'But first I have to spend a penny.'

'Me too,' said Effie. 'But there's a toilet down the street.'

Ignoring the mild metallic taste, Effie finished her tea and then they collected their bags and left the café.

Letting a jeep full of GIs pass first, Effie and Alice crossed the road, then walked the couple of hundred yards to the black metal railing with *Ladies* painted above the entrance.

They descended the steps and entered the echoey space with white tiles on the floor and walls. Opposite was a row of cubicles with half-length dark wood doors. Having done what needed to be done, Effie crossed the row of square Victorian sinks with swinging balls containing liquid soap fixed to the wall above them.

She turned on the knobbly brass taps and washed her hands, then turned to the pole fixed to the wall with a long-looped towel hanging from it.

As she pulled it down to find a dry section, Effie's gaze rested on the enamel advert screwed to the wall beside it. It featured a nurse in an old-fashioned uniform holding a packet, with the words *Every Lady Should Know* followed by *Southall's Sanitary Towels are a comfort, and convenience.*

Effie stared at it for a couple of seconds , then, as happiness spread through her, she laughed softly to herself.

There was nothing wrong with the tea and it hadn't been Florrie's liver and onions that had caused her stomach to churn that morning, but something quite different. In fact, something very, very wonderful.

CHAPTER 28

Nathan lifted the nib of his pen from the sheet of paper, sat back and read through the prose he'd spent the past half an hour writing.

It was almost eight o'clock on Tuesday the evening and having eaten dinner about an hour ago he was now at his usual desk in Hazells Hall's library. However, for once he hadn't had his nose in a law book but had been writing an overdue letter to his parents.

Overdue because with a two-week window of clear moonlit skies, there had been almost nightly SOE sorties across the Channel. Between flying and sleeping, he'd had little time for anything else. Sadly, as his heart and body constantly reminded him, this also included Effie, who he hadn't seen for almost two weeks and then for only for a day in London. Given that last Saturday had been a full moon and there were already several agents training in Gibraltar Farm, it would probably be busy as soon as the new operational window opened in a few weeks. The only consolation was that at least this particular phase would be over in a couple of days. He and Effie were getting married in four days, after which they would have seven blissful days together.

Memories of Effie in his arms, under him and clinging on to him in her passion the last time they'd been together rose up in Nathan's mind then he dragged himself back to the here and now and reread his letter.

Satisfied with what he'd written, he returned his pen to the paper.

Although I wish you, Dad and the rest of the family could be here for the wedding on Saturday, I will send you photographs. So, Mum, by the time you read this letter, I will be a married man. .

And who knows, perhaps in a month or two I'll be writing to you with more happy news?

All my love to you both and all the family.

God bless and keep you all.

Your loving son

Nathan

He screwed the cap back on his fountain pen, and had just slipped it back into his top pocket when the library door opened and Airman Wilson, one of the mess orderlies, appeared round the edge.

'Officer Fitzgerald, there's a phone call for you in the office,' he said.

'Thank you, Wilson,' Nathan said.

Hastily folding his letter, he slipped it into the distinctive RAF envelope he'd already addressed, then rose to his feet and left the room.

As he entered what had once been the butler's pantry and was now the mess office, the grey-moustached sergeant in charge of the day-to-day running of Hazells Hall stood up and, after saluting, left the room.

Nathan picked up the phone and held it to his ear. 'Flying Officer Fitzgerald sp—'

'Nathan, it's me.'

'Effie?' he said. 'Are you all right?'

'Yes, very,' she replied, brightly. 'In fact, I've never felt better. I hope I haven't pulled you away from one of your important briefings or something.'

'No, I was only writing to my parents,' he replied. 'I said we'd send them some photos of the wedding next time I write.'

'Oh, and thank you for my birthday card, it arrived this morning,' she said.

'Did you have a nice day on Saturday?' he asked.

'Well, I spent most of it hauling old Bessie up and down, but Alice made me a cake and we had a little celebration in the bar downstairs when we got back to our digs,' she replied.

'I'm sorry I couldn't be there,' he said.

'I know but that's how it is right now, but it won't be for ever,' she said. 'But as long as you're there on Saturday.'

'Don't worry I will be.' He laughed. 'Even if I have to walk all the way from Tempsford. I'm counting the days,' he went on. 'Is everything all right, Effie?'

'Yes of course. Why do you ask?'

'Well, you don't sound your usual jolly self.' Alarm niggled at Nathan's innards. 'You're not getting cold feet, are you?'

'No, no! Don't be silly.' Effie laughed. 'I can't wait to be Mrs Fitzgerald, it's...'

'What?'

'Oh, it's nothing that won't wait until Saturday.'

'That sounds very mysterious.' Nathan chuckled as the tension left his shoulders. 'Tell me.'

'No. You'll have to wait until Saturday, and all will be revealed,' she replied.

'I always look forward to you revealing all, Effie,' he said, in a low voice.

She gave a throaty laugh and the feel of her curled against him rolled through his body.

The wail of an air-raid siren echoed down the telephone line.

'The moaning Minnie's started,' shouted Effie.

'I can hear,' Nathan replied, picturing her standing in the hallway behind the Maid of Norway's bar with enemy bombers flying overhead. 'I love you, Effie.'

'I love you too, Nathan,' she hollered back over the howl of the siren.

'Four days,' he said.

'Four days,' she repeated. 'See you Saturday.'

The line went dead. Nathan placed the receiver back in the cradle, but as he did the door opened and Wilson's head appeared again.

'Sorry to disturb again, sir, but the guvnor wants to see you urgent like,' he said.

'With all due respect, sir, you must be ruddy well joking!' said Nathan, staring across the table at his commanding officer.

'I'm afraid not,' Donaldson replied. 'With Collins, Stalley and Goldmer all out of action and all the other pilots already earmarked for missions, you're the only one I'd trust to get the job done.'

It was some twenty minutes since he'd finished speaking to Effie and Nathan was now standing in the ops room across the table from his group captain.

'It's bad enough that the man's a law unto himself, but on top of that he's a bloody drunk,' protested Nathan.

'Be that as it may,' Donaldson replied. 'Whether we like it

or not, Lieutenant Frobisher is head of SOE operations here and he is insistent that he and he alone retrieve the agent.'

'Does he know it's me who will be flying him?' asked Nathan.

'Not yet,' his group captain replied.

'He won't like it,' Nathan said.

'It's not for him to like or dislike, nor you for that matter, Fitzgerald,' snapped Donaldson. He gave Nathan a hard look. 'And I doubt the agent hiding from the Gestapo likes it much either.'

Nathan stood to attention. 'My apologies, sir.'

The senior officer's craggy features softened a little. 'Yes, well. I've fed my misgivings about Lieutenant Frobisher up the chain of command, but you know how these things work.'

'Yes, sir.'

Donaldson sighed. 'Anyhow. Briefing at nine hundred hours tomorrow and chocks away twenty-two hundred hours, subject to a favourable weather report. All things being equal, you should be back guzzling bacon and eggs in the mess by the time the sun comes up on Thursday morning.'

CHAPTER 29

'Thirty minutes!' Nathan shouted behind him and received the usual light tap to his shoulder in acknowledgement.

It was about one o'clock on Thursday morning. According to the course he'd meticulously plotted on his map, he was almost at his landing coordinates just north of Rouen.

Behind him sat Frobisher and a slender youth referred to as Pierre, who was both very young and very nervous. As with all such operations, both the lieutenant and the operative were dressed like French labourers.

To be honest, as it was a straightforward drop-off and pick-up mission, he was a little surprised that the SOE lieutenant was accompanying him. Apart from exchanging perfunctory greetings and a couple of points regarding the actual mission, Frobisher had barely spoken to Nathan, which suited him fine. As soon as they touched down at Tangmere in a few hours' time they could return to their usual mode of communication, which was to totally ignore each other. To be honest, he had more important things on his mind, because tomorrow, or should that be later today, he'd be heading for London to book into the Aldgate Hotel ahead of his marriage to Effie on 6 June.

Nathan pulled the map from the top of his boot and, switching on his pencil torch, checked his coordinates again. Satisfied that he was bang on course, he adjusted the joystick, flew through the few wispy clouds and brought his Lizzie down to 500 feet.

Although, the waxing moon was bright enough for him to see the dotted farmsteads, streams and fields speeding past him below.

Scanning his eyes over the landscape, Nathan waited for a moment or two, then a light from the hedgerow flashed *dot dot dash dot* for F. Nathan flicked the switch on the dashboard and replied with the same.

The three lights in an L-shape came on in the next field, so he lined the plane's nose up in the middle of the furthest two and brought it down.

Nathan brought the Lysander to a halt a few feet before the two lights, altered the flaps and wheeled round to point the spinning propeller towards the single light some fifty yards ahead.

With the plane idling on the bumpy ground, he threw the canopy back to let in the night air. Unsurprisingly as they were in Normandy, the home of Calvados, the sweet smell of ripening apples wafted in.

Pierre leapt up and, gripping his case in one hand, scrambled down the side ladder and shot off towards the trees.

Nathan turned in his seat. 'Where's your operative?'

'He'll be here,' the lieutenant bellowed back.

'He'd better. Because its wheels-up in five. Understand?'

Frobisher gave him a hateful look, then clambered down after the youth.

Nathan checked his instruments in preparation for take-off as Frobisher stood by the aircraft waiting.

Pierre reappeared from the bushes.

'Un problem, Lieutenant. You must come,' he called, beckoning at Frobisher.

Unease prickled down Nathan's spine. 'I don't think—'

'No one asked you,' snarled Frobisher, starting off towards Pierre.

With his eyes on Frobisher, Nathan leant forward and took his Colt automatic revolver from its housing beneath the dashboard.

Frobisher took another couple of steps. Then Germans surged out from the hedgerow.

In what seemed like in slow motion, Frobisher froze for a split second, then turned and started to run back to the plane. Pierre dashed forward and grabbed him, pulling him back towards the enemy.

Flipping the safety catch off, Nathan aimed his gun towards the two men. Then he pulled the trigger. Pierre fell to the ground in an instant.

Staring at the youth at his feet, Frobisher froze.

'Frobisher!' Nathan bellowed, already taxiing the plane slowly forward.

A bust of gunfire brought Frobisher to his senses and he bolted across the field towards the plane as an armoured car with an anti-aircraft gun mounted on it burst through the foliage.

As Frobisher grabbed the ladder and hauled himself in, Nathan let out the throttle, leaving Frobisher to scramble aboard as the Lysander picked up speed.

With bullets ricocheting off the fuselage and artillery shells bursting around him, Nathan pulled hard on the throttle and the plane lifted off. However, as he crested the trees, an explosion rocked the plane and it started to lose height.

Struggling to keep the Lysander level, Nathan tried to adjust his rudder and tail flaps, but there was no response. Peering through the perspex of the cockpit canopy, he also noticed that instead of a right wheel there was just jagged metal at the end of the supporting bracket.

'What's wrong!' Frobisher yelled in Nathan's left ear.

'The tail's controls are damaged, and we've lost a wheel,' he shouted back, his arms tense as he struggled to stop the plane plummeting to the ground.

'But you'll get us back to Blighty, won't you?' the SOE officer shouted.

Nathan shook his head. 'I'll get as near to the coast as I can but then we'll have to take our chances.'

'Blast!' bellowed Frobisher, thumping the back of Nathan's chair in rage.

Indeed, thought Nathan, *and you're not the one getting married in two days.*

'Where are we now?' yelled Frobisher twenty minutes later as they skimmed over a small clump of trees.

'As far as I can tell, we've just flown over a village called Yerville,' Nathan shouted back.

'It's near the coast, though, right?' the SOE officer screamed, his voice tight with panic.

'I'm afraid not,' bellowed Nathan. 'And I won't be able to keep the Lizzie up for much longer, so you'd better prepare yourself for a bumpy landing.'

With the lightening eastern horizon heralding the approaching dawn, Nathan cast his eyes over the French countryside and spotted a field with a wooded area close by. He aimed the nose of the Lizzie towards the centre of the field and, slicing the tops off the surrounding hedgerow as they flew over, brought the plane down.

'Brace!' he yelled as the ground rushed towards them.

With his lips pressed firmly together, he took a deep breath and, his mind filled only with Effie, he crashed on to French soil.

Had it not been for his seat harness the impact would have jettisoned him through the domed cockpit. Mercifully, after he had been shaken back and forth like a rag doll in a dog's mouth for a few minutes, the Lizzie tilted to the right and, with the missing wheel support bracket ploughing the earth, the plane came to a halt.

Nathan ripped his flight helmet and goggles off and tossed them at his feet. He threw back the hatch, released his flight buckle and, grabbing the survival bag and revolver, sprang up.

Instead of gathering his things together, Frobisher was still fastened in his seat with a vacant look on his face.

Nathan grabbed the front of his flight jacket and shook him. The SOE officer blinked a couple of times as consciousness returned.

'Get up!' Nathan growled.

Frobisher went to stand, but screamed in pain. 'My knee.'

'Bugger your knee,' snapped Nathan.

Nathan grabbed the other man's survival haversack, slid down the side of the plane, then dashed to the small beech copse some fifty yards away. He threw their kit down at the base of a tree, then ran back to the plane.

Frobisher had managed to get out of his seat and was sliding down the sloping fuselage as Nathan ran across, but as Frobisher reached the ground he gasped.

'Can you walk?' asked Nathan.

'Not really,' Frobisher replied, leaning on the plane's wing.

'Well, you're going to have to.' Nathan grasped his wrist and tucked his shoulder into the lieutenant's armpit. 'Unless, of course, you want to wait for that German patrol to find us.'

Taking Frobisher's weight, he all but carried him into the wooded area, then sat him beside their haversack.

Nathan stripped off his boots and flight suit, rolled them

into a ball and stowed them, then shrugged on a faded shirt and moth-eaten jumper and stepped into a worn pair of brown leather shoes.

He picked up his bag and nudged the foot of the SOE officer's uninjured leg.

Frobisher opened his eyes.

'Let me see your knee,' Nathan said, shoving a wallet containing French banknotes and a couple of photos for forged papers into his back trouser pocket.

'I think I've broken it,' said Frobisher.

Nathan hunkered down next to him, took his knife from his belt, stuck it into the bottom of Frobisher's trouser leg and ripped it upwards, exposing his pale, hairy calf.

Thankfully, there wasn't any bone sticking through the flesh, and, although the lower leg was at an odd angle, the bones themselves were straight. Nathan took hold of the leg and, as Frobisher pulled a series of tormented expressions, gently probed around the knee.

'I think it's dislocated, not broken.' Taking the wallet from his back pocket, Nathan offered it to him. 'Bite on this.'

'What are you going to do?'

'Pop it back in, of course,' Nathan replied.

Horror spread across Frobisher's face. 'But surely that's a doctor's job.'

'It would be if we weren't in the middle of enemy-held territory with a German patrol looking for us,' Nathan replied.

'But... but...'

Nathan raised an eyebrow. 'I thought your ancestors fought at Waterloo?'

Frobisher opened his mouth to argue but then, glaring at Nathan, snatched the wallet and bit down on it.

Sitting on the leaves and twigs strewn across the ground, Nathan splayed his legs either side of Frobisher's injured one.

'I'd move your family jewels aside if I were you,' he said.

Frobisher covered his trouser flies with both hands.

Nathan wedged his foot at the junction between the lieutenant's hands and his thigh, grasped his calf below the knee, then pulled slowly. Frobisher moaned behind his clenched teeth and as the joint popped back into place he passed out and the wallet fell from his mouth.

With the lieutenant slumped insensible against the tree, Nathan gathered a few of the stouter bits of branch lying around him and, after tearing what remained of the lieutenant's trousers into strips, made an improvised brace to prevent the knee from moving.

Satisfied with his work, he caught his breath for a moment, then tucked his fighting knife into his belt, grabbed his discarded uniform and dashed back to the plane. He threw his clothes into the cockpit, took his knife from his belt and, after a couple of attempts, pierced the reserve fuel tank beneath the Lizzie, then took the packet of French matches from the inside pocket of the jacket.

Pausing, he regarded his old faithful Lizzie, then he struck a match and threw it at the trickle of petrol pooling in the grass beneath the fuselage. It ignited instantly, sending swirling blue and orange flames across the pool of petrol, then, as the smell of the burning tyres clogged Nathan's nose, the flame snaked upwards into the fuel tank above. There was a second of calm before the undercarriage of the plane burst apart in a blinding flash of red. The heat scorched Nathan's face and flames shot skyward. Nathan turned and ran.

As he'd expected, Frobisher was still propped up against the tree trunk, but he'd come to.

Nathan crouched down next to him. 'How's the knee?'

'Bloody painful,' Frobisher replied.

'That's a shame,' said Nathan, tucking the silk handkerchief with a map of northern France in his inside pocket. 'Because we're off.'

'Off where?'

'Towards the coast,' Nathan replied, shoving the lieutenant's survival kit into his own haversack.

He slung it over his shoulder and offered Frobisher his hand.

Frobisher regarded him steadily. 'You know, you could have shot me instead of Pierre. It would have achieved the same purpose. It was me they were after.'

'I could have, and by now I'd be flying over the white cliffs and looking forward to getting married in two days,' Nathan replied. 'However, I shoot traitors, not fellow officers. Now, are you getting up or waiting for the Germans?'

In the dappled dawn light filtering through the branches above them, Frobisher's blue eyes held Nathan's for a second, then he stretched up and grasped the offered hand.

Nathan heaved him up.

'Sorry about your wedding,' said Frobisher,

'So am I,' Nathan replied as Frobisher put his arm round his neck. 'But count yourself lucky, because I'm the best person to be stranded behind enemy lines with.'

'Why's that?'

'Because,' said Nathan, wedging his shoulder in the other man's armpit again, 'come hell or high water I'm determined to get home.'

～

'You'll look absolutely stunning when you walk down the aisle in that, Effie,' said Alice, looking at her across their shared bedroom.

Effie's pretty face lifted in a contented smile. 'Just think, by this time tomorrow I'll be Mrs Fitzgerald.'

Actually, to be truthful, as it was a little before nine on

Friday evening, by this time tomorrow she would have been a wife for almost ten hours.

Like Alice, Effie was wearing her shapeless RAF-issue pyjamas. She was sitting on the bed opposite, hugging her knees and gazing lovingly at the dress they'd bought in Derry & Toms, hooked over the wardrobe door ready for the happy bride to slip into tomorrow morning.

A small smile spread across Effie's face. 'And then seven whole days together...'

'Do you know where?' asked Alice.

Effie shook her head. 'Nathan won't tell me, but it doesn't matter.' She shifted her attention from her dress to Alice. 'Where did you spend your honeymoon?'

'The Grand Hotel in Eastbourne,' Alice replied, a sad, wistful expression settling on her pretty face.

'It sounds very luxurious,' said Effie.

'It was,' Alice replied, thinking of the silk counterpane and pile carpet of the honeymoon suite. 'But I'm sure wherever you and Nathan spend your honeymoon will be as lovely.'

'It will,' said Effie. 'Because all that matters is that we'll be married and together.' She sighed. 'And then of course, it's back to the old routine, with me heaving Bessie up and down and Nathan flying to who knows where. Three years, this war's been going on. Three bloomin' years! God, I wish this would end.'

'Don't we all,' said Alice. 'And perhaps it will now the Americans have joined us.'

'From your lips to God's ears,' said Effie.

Alice gave her an odd look.

'I heard a woman use the expression in the market the other day,' Effie explained. 'I hope you're right about the Americans.'

'Peggy said her sister wrote to say they are knee-deep in GIs in Cambridge and there's runways and Nissen huts being built over half the county,' said Alice. 'So hopefully the war will be over soon and we'll all be able to hang up our uniforms for good.'

'Well,' said Effie, a smile hovering on her lips. 'I might be hanging up my uniform a little sooner. I've missed two monthlies, so I'd say early in the New Year.'

Alice stared across at her for a moment, then her mouth dropped open. 'You're having a—'

'Shhh!' Effie got off her bed, crossed the faded rug between them and climbed onto Alice's. 'Not so loud.'

'Does Nathan know?' asked Alice.

Effie shook her head. 'I only realised myself when we were out shopping last week. I was tempted to tell him when we spoke on Tuesday, but I thought I'd wait until our first night.'

She frowned. 'You're not shocked, are you? I mean, I know you're not supposed to... you know... until you're married, but—'

'No, no, Effie,' interrupted her friend. 'I'm not at all shocked, in fact, if anything I'm a bit jealous.'

'Why?'

In the mute light from the 40-watt bulb overhead, pain flitted across Alice's pretty face but she forced a laugh. 'You and Nathan seemed to have managed in one night something that me and Arthur couldn't in five years of marriage.'

'Oh, Alice,' said Effie, seeing tears shining in her friend's eyes. 'I'm sor—'

'No, no, none of that, 'said Alice blinking them away. 'This is a happy day, so congratulations, to you and Nathan.'

Effie threw her arms round her friend's neck.

'Thank you,' she mumbled into Alice's hair.

She hugged her briefly and then Alice raised her head. 'But are you happy about it?' she asked.

'Yes, yes I am, except...' Effie frowned.

'Except?'

'Well, we both want a family,' Effie continued. 'A large one, but we hadn't planned to start one quite as soon.'

'Are you worried about what people will say?' asked Alice.

Effie shook her head again. 'Not at all, and I doubt I'll be the only bride getting married at the moment who will have to hold their bouquet high, but' – a sad smile lifted the corners of her mouth – 'I had hoped that me, you and our little gang would be seeing the war out together and celebrating when peace is declared.'

'And who says we won't?' Alice replied. 'You'll be living in Bedford, not the Outer Hebrides.'

'That's true,' Effie replied. 'And you will be godmother, won't you?'

Alice laughed. 'Do you need to ask? But be warned, I'll be spoiling Master or Miss Fitzgerald rotten.'

Effie's eyes widened as she placed her hand on the flannelette fabric covering her stomach. 'I wonder if it is a boy or a girl?'

'Or both,' said Alice.

'Two for the price of one.' Effie laughed.

'Effie, are you up there?' Nell called up from the floor below.

'Yes,' Effie called back. 'Is the cocoa ready?'

Nell didn't reply.

There was the sound of feet coming up the stairs, then the door opened.

Nell walked in followed by Sergeant Munroe, both with mournful expressions on their faces.

Effie stood up. 'Sergeant?'

With her heart hammering in her chest, Alice got off the bed and stood next to her friend.

Glancing at Effie's wedding outfit, Munroe cleared her throat. 'Corporal Weston. I'm sorry but I am the bearer of bad news.' Sensing what was coming, Alice took Effie's hand. 'I've received a telephone call from Group Captain Donaldson at

RAF Tempsford,' continued the section sergeant. 'I'm afraid your fiancé, Flying Officer Fitzgerald, is missing in action—'

Effie went white and crumpled onto her bed.

'When?' asked Alice, sitting next to her friend and putting her arm round her.

'Yesterday, over France,' Munroe replied. 'Group Captain Donaldson said he would have rung sooner but he didn't want to alarm you while there was a chance he might make it back in time for...' Her eyes flickered onto Effie's dress again. 'I'm truly sorry, Effie.'

Staring blindly at the rug, Effie didn't reply.

'Thank you, Sergeant,' said Alice.

Munroe hovered there for a couple of seconds, then left the bedroom.

As the door closed, Nell walked across and sat down the other side of Effie.

'Come on, Effie, chin up,' said Nell, taking her hand. 'Your chap went missing before and turned up fit and well a few days later, didn't he?'

Effie nodded, then an expression of dread replaced her stunned one. 'What if he's not, Alice? What am I going to do about—'

'We'll cross that bridge when we come it,' said Alice, as Nell gave her a questioning look. Frowning, Alice gave a small shake of the head, then her eyes darted to the door.

'I tell you what, why don't I go and make us a nice cuppa?' Nell said. She stood up and left the room.

'I ought to go round to St Paul's vicarage to tell Father James.' Effie went to stand up, but her knees buckled and she landed back on the counterpane.

'Never mind about Father James,' said Alice, rising to her feet. 'You've had a terrible shock.' Bending down, she hooked her arm under Effie's calves and lifted her legs onto the bed.

'Now I want you to put your feet up while I go and give Nell a hand.'

Effie nodded. 'I do feel a bit light-headed.'

She closed her eyes.

Satisfied her friend would remain where she was, Alice left the room and hurried down to the kitchen.

Nell was by the stove and Maeve and George, both in their service pyjamas, were with her. Closing the door behind her, Alice joined them.

'Nell's told us,' said Maeve. 'Is she all right?'

'For now she is, but she won't be if Nathan doesn't come back. In fact' – Alice gave them a very direct, very meaningful look – 'Effie will be in a great deal of *trouble*.'

Three pairs of eyes stared at her for a moment, then the penny dropped.

'Holy mother of God,' said Maeve, swiftly crossing herself.

George frowned. 'Effie's pregnant?'

Alice nodded.

'How far is she?' asked Nell.

'About two months, I think,' Alice replied. 'But we mustn't tell anyone.'

'Especially Lily and her pal,' added Maeve, putting a splash of milk in the five mugs set out on the central table.

George, who was leaning against the kitchen dresser, stood up. 'No, we can't. Look, chaps. Nathan has been missing for what? A couple of days, so there's every chance he'll make it back like he did last time.'

'George is right,' said Nell, as she stirred the pot. ''e's probably come down in some field in the back of beyond, or 'e's bobbing about in the drink waiting for the navy's bell-bottom brigade.'

'But what about if—'

George held up her hand. 'We'll deal with the "what ifs" when and if they occur.'

'I agree,' said Alice. 'For now, we have to look after Effie.'

'And the first thing we have to do is to make sure that this stays between ourselves. The more people who know the more likely it is that HQ will get wind of it.'

Maeve's eyebrows rose. 'And then Mary mother of God help us.'

'Help Effie, don't you mean?' said Alice, as Nell poured the tea. 'She'll be out on her ear if Munroe finds out. And then what? She'll have no job and no money and judging by what she's said she won't get any help from her parents.'

'Let's hope and pray it doesn't come to that,' said Alice.

'Let's not run ahead of ourselves,' said George, stretching forward to take a mug. 'As Nell said, Nathan's probably making his way back to Blighty somehow as we speak, but until he actually gets here we can't let Effie haul a ruddy great barrage balloon around, so we'll have to make sure she has lighter tasks, like chow duty, manning the engine or checking the gas cylinders.'

Alice picked up two hot drinks.

'Agreed?' she asked, holding them out.

George tapped hers against it, then Maeve and Nell took their tea and did the same.

'Good,' said Alice. 'Now let's go up to Effie.'

CHAPTER 30

With the hedgerow branches scraping his jacket, Nathan hurried down the side of the field. As dawn was yet to break, the Normandy landscape was still swathed in shadows. He reached the gate leading onto the farm and squeezed through the gap between the gatepost and the yard's stone wall, then headed for the barn in the far corner. The smell of hay and manure wafted over him as the three cows occupying the byre looked round briefly then buried their damp noses back into the trough as Nathan scrambled up the ladder to the loft.

Frobisher was still more or less where Nathan had left him an hour before, propped against a bale of hay with his legs stretched out in front of him, except instead of having his eyes closed he was now pointing his Webley .38 revolver at Nathan's head.

'And bonjour to you, too,' said Nathan.

Frobisher lowered the gun barrel and placed his weapon on the wooden floor. 'You've been gone a while.'

'There was a German convoy parked on the main road to the village, so I had to go the long way round. How's the knee?'

he asked, indicating the grubby splint strapped round the other man's leg.

'Still bloody painful,' Frobisher replied.

Nathan sat down cross-legged opposite, opened the haversack and pulled out the first two items.

Frobisher gave the two eggs with fluffy down still attached that Nathan was holding a hateful look, then took one.

Nathan took the knife from his belt and tapped the one he still held, then, tipping his head back, he twisted the shell open and dropped the slimy contents into his mouth.

After swallowing it down, he looked at Frobisher. 'If you don't want it, I'll have it.'

The SOE officer continued to glare at the egg, then broke the shell and swallowed it.

'God, I'll never eat anything but a hard-boiled one after this,' he gasped.

Nathan pulled out half a French stick and a chunk of cheese and offered them to Frobisher. 'These should go down easier.'

Frobisher grabbed the bread, tore off a chunk and crammed it in his mouth.

Nathan didn't wonder at his fellow officer's eagerness. He was starving himself – they hadn't eaten since yesterday morning.

It had been over two weeks since the crash. They had trudged day and night, living off their survival rations, for the first two days, without sleep in order to put as much distance as possible between themselves and the burning plane. After they had exhausted both themselves and their resources, they stumbled on an abandoned charcoal burner's hut among the trees. After a couple of days' sleep they had set off again. The locals would sometimes deliberately leave food somewhere that those on the run could find it – however, in order to keep them from starvation Nathan had to occasionally break locks and windows as they continued through German-occupied territory.

'What day is it?' asked Frobisher, breaking off a chunk of bread.

'Saturday,' Nathan replied, cutting a lump of cheese. 'And I should be a married man by now.'

'I'm sure she'll wait.' Frobisher snorted. 'Although you might have to tidy yourself up a bit or she won't recognise you.'

'It's not as if you're dressed for a dinner at Carlton Club either,' Nathan replied. 'And you stink.'

Actually, to be fair, they both stank like pigs and would both have benefited from a close encounter with a razor. They were now sporting two and a half weeks' worth of beard: a bushy, black one in his case and a sparse blond one in Frobisher's.

The SOE officer gave him a grudging smile, then bit into his cheese.

They lapsed into silence but after swallowing the last morsel of bread Frobisher spoke again. 'You do know, if you were alone, you'd have been at the coast by now.'

'I know, but if I was going to abandon you I'd have left you in the field with Pierre and flown off,' Nathan said. 'I hope given that you're an officer and a gentleman you would have done the same.'

Frobisher studied him ruefully for a second, then shifted his gaze onto his breakfast.

Nathan's mouth pulled into a tight line and in the slivers of light cutting through the wall panels he studied the top of the SOE officer's head. 'We'll be leaving at sunset.'

He stowed his canteen in the haversack, leant back on a bale of hay, draped his jacket across his shoulders and closed his eyes.

As it always did when not thinking of anything else, Nathan's mind drifted off onto the happier subject of Effie. He imagined her standing next to him at the altar and him slipping the gold ring he'd bought the day after she agreed to marry him, onto her finger. His imagination shifted to images of him holding their first baby, chasing toddlers around and, eventually, introducing Effie and their quiverful of children to his family back home.

He must have drifted off, because he was brought crashing back to reality in an instant by the roar of a vehicle.

Nathan's eyes opened and he saw Frobisher, dread painted across his face, staring wide-eyed at him.

'Hide,' he said, then sprang to his feet and strode across to the barn wall.

Pressing his forehead to the wood, Nathan looked through with his right eye. A Volkswagen Kübelwagen, the Nazi version of the GIs' jeep, drove into the cobbled farmyard below.

'It's a German patrol,' he reported as the four troopers, all with MG 42 machine guns slung over their shoulders, climbed out of the vehicle.

The farmhouse's front door opened and an old man wearing scruffy trousers and a shapeless jacket limped out.

'Are they heading this way?' hissed Frobisher.

'No, just laughing and joking with the farmer,' Nathan replied. 'It all seems very friendly and good-humoured.'

'Trust our bloody luck to be sheltering in the barn of a collaborator,' muttered Frobisher.

Nathan shifted around. 'Hang on, one of the soldiers is strolling towards the barn.'

'Shit!'

'No, wait, the farmer's wife's coming out carrying a bottle of beer in each hand,' said Nathan. 'The soldier heading our way has turned round and is joining his chums.'

'Thank Christ for that,' said Frobisher, with a heavy sigh. 'What are the Krauts doing now?'

'Guzzling beer,' Nathan replied, watching the four men passing the bottles of drink between them as they joked with the old couple. 'I think they're going,' he added as the German soldiers exchanged a Heil Hitler salute with their elderly hosts, then started piling back into their military car.

With the engine roaring, the car circled the farmyard once and then, with the troopers in the rear of the vehicle still swigging beer, it sped away.

Nathan sat down and leant against the barn wall.

'What do we do now?' asked Frobisher, looking anxiously across at him.

'The same as be—'

The barn door creaked open.

Nathan crept across on his hands and knees and grabbed his pistol from next to his kitbag.

Pressing himself against the bales of hay they were hiding behind and holding it against his chest, he peered round the edge.

Standing below was the elderly farmer's wife, carrying two milking buckets.

He pulled back and, looking across at Frobisher, pressed a finger to his lips. The cows below them started lowing as her clogs tapped softly on the beaten earth floor beneath them. Something scraped across the floor, followed by the bucket handle rattling.

'Bonjour, mes camarades,' the old woman said in a hushed voice.

Nathan held his breath.

'Êtes-vous anglais?' she asked in the same low tone. 'N'ayez pas peur. Nous allons aider.'

'She says she's going to help us,' Frobisher whispered.

With hope and suspicion whirling around in his brain in equal parts, Nathan stared blindly at a weathered beam for a second, then stepped out from his hiding place and, still gripping the gun, climbed down the ladder.

The old woman was sitting on a low stool, milking the brown and white cow in the first byre.

'Bonjour, madame,' Nathan said, raising his hands. 'Nous sommes des pilotes anglais et mon navigateur est blessé.'

She looked round and blinked in surprise.

'Most English speak my language as if they had a mouthful of marbles but yours, monsieur, is very good,' she said in French, as frothy milk spurted into the bucket below.

'That's to my mother's credit, not mine, madame,' Nathan replied. 'Madame...?'

'Barbier,' she replied.

'Flying Officer Fitzgerald,' he said, tucking the gun in his belt. 'But how did you know—'

'My daughter's baby woke up and she looked out the window and saw you heading for the barn,' she replied. 'You say your navigator is injured?'

'Yes,' Nathan replied. 'His knee.'

'Very well,' she said, pulling on the dangling teats. 'I will fetch a doctor when we can, but take this for now.'

She delved into her pocket, pulled out a small flask and gave it to him, then looked him over.

'I take it the plane burnt to a cinder outside Rouen two weeks ago was yours?' she said.

'It was,' Nathan replied.

Amusement lifted the old woman's weather-beaten face. 'You've done well to have made it this far, especially with that brute Lieutenant Schröder hunting you.' She spat on the dusty, straw-covered floor. 'You must keep out of sight and my daughter will bring you food later, but I will send word to our people. They will find you somewhere safer. Now go!'

Pausing in her task, she shooed him away.

Nathan placed his hand on his chest. 'Merci, madame.'

Leaving her to continue milking, he climbed back up the ladder to rejoin Frobisher.

'I take it you heard all that,' he said, sitting down.

Frobisher nodded. 'Do you trust her?'

'Not entirely,' Nathan replied. 'But she could easily have told that German patrol we were here but didn't. However, I suggest we hide anything that might indicate our real mission and stick with the stranded airmen story.'

'That sounds sensible,' the SOE officer agreed. 'Although I'm not sure I'm happy about you telling Madame whatshername I was your bloody navigator.'

'Would you rather me tell her who you really are?' said Nathan.

'Well, no but—'

'We're in civilian clothes behind enemy lines,' cut in Nathan. 'If we are caught, then after a bit of having electrodes fastened to our privates and our fingernails ripped off, as things stand, they will take us out and shoot us as spies. However, if they realise that they have captured the head of Special Operations in northern France you won't have to worry about a chit-chat with Waffen-SS, because I'm sure Himmler and Göring will be keen to entertain you themselves. Honestly, Frobisher,' he added, as he handed him the flask. 'As you're in the Intelligence Corps I thought you would have worked that one out for yourself. After all, I'm "just the bloody pilot".'

CHAPTER 31

Putting her hands in the small of her back, Effie arched backwards to ease the tightness in her lower spine.

'Are you all right?' asked Alice, who was securing one of the rear guy ropes to a concrete block about twenty feet away.

'A little stiff, that's all,' Effie replied.

That was a bit of an understatement – in fact after an hour crouched over, working the engine while the crew hoisted the balloon to the correct height, her back felt like it had been tied in knots.

'Plus, my stomach is still gurgling.' Effie wiped the beads of sweat from her forehead with the back of her hand. 'On top of which, why is it so blooming hot?'

Alice laughed. 'Well, what do you expect? It is the end of July.'

It was Wednesday the twenty-ninth of July, to be precise, and about three thirty in the afternoon. In ordinary times this would have meant flowery dresses, shorts, sleeveless blouses and straw hats. However, for Effie and the balloon girls it meant the same heavyweight old navy cotton boiler suits, with shirt and tie beneath.

Having looped the end of her rope round the concrete anchor, Alice came over and placed an arm round Effie's shoulder.

Tears pinched the corners of her eyes, something seemed to happen to Effie all the time now. According to *Expectant Motherhood*, the book she'd borrowed from the library, her constant tearfulness was caused by the baby growing inside her. However, she suspected it was more to do with the fact that Nathan had been missing for eight weeks, during which time her waist had grown from twenty-four inches to almost thirty-two. Perhaps then she should be thankful for her heavy drill boiler suit rather than moan about it, because its baggy shapelessness concealed her secret. However, the question that kept her awake half the night now, at four months pregnant, was for how much longer?

Seeing her forlorn expression, her friend squeezed Effie's shoulders.

'Now the Bessie's up, why don't you go and sit down? I'll finish off here and then I'll make us all a cup of tea,' she said softly.

Effie nodded and, leaving Alice to check the ropes, wandered across the balloon's dusty bed to the hut, where Nell and Maeve were already lounging in the deckchairs outside. They had taken their caps off and shrugged themselves out of the top half of their protective suits, along with removing their ties and unbuttoning a couple of shirt buttons.

'This is the life,' said Maeve, tilting her pale freckly face to the sun.

Effie gave her a wan smile. 'I can see Peggy playing with those kids by the gate but where is everyone else?'

'Lily buggered off to have tea with her family,' Nell replied. 'And Maureen went back to the digs because she was feeling ill. And Rose is playing a different sort of game with that tall, good-looking ARP warden.'

Effie's eyes shifted across to the tall, green-painted dome-topped cylinder by the park's entrance with *Warden Shelter* painted in large letters on it.

'At least we know where she is, if we need her,' said Maeve.

Thankful to take the weight off her feet, Effie eased herself down onto one of the park benches and took her cap off.

'How are you doing, Eff?' asked Nell, giving her a sympathetic look.

'My back's killing me,' Effie replied, feeling a bubbling around her navel start again.

'Wasn't my sister the same all the way through,' said Maeve. 'Something to do with the way the baby's lying.'

'Count me in,' said George, taking off her protective gloves as she joined them. 'All the cylinders are full and ready to go. So, there's nothing to do unless HQ rings through on the blower.'

She unfastened her boiler suit, peeled it down and tied the sleeves round her waist, then sat on the bench next to Effie.

'How are you feeling?' she asked.

'Hot and exhausted,' Effie replied.

'Yes, it is a bit of a scorcher,' George said.

'How are you feeling, Effie?' asked Maeve.

'Not so bad now the sickness has passed but...'

From nowhere panic surged up and Effie burst into tears.

'Now come on, old thing. Chin up,' said George, taking her hand. 'Your dashing young man will pitch up any day now, just you see.'

'George's right, Effie,' said Alice as she walked out of the hut carrying a tray of mugs. 'Any day now he'll telephone or turn up like he did last time, and you can book that wedding and put on that dress.'

'I doubt if it'll fit now,' said Effie, rubbing her tears away with the heel of her hand and attempting a smile.

'Well, Nell's good with a needle so I'm sure she'll make it fit,' said Maeve.

Effie placed her hands over her swelling stomach.

Nathan was not dead. That was something Effie knew for certain. And he would come back, but when? She had two, perhaps three more weeks and then even in her baggy boiler suit, her secret would be obvious to everyone.

Panic surged up again and threatened to overwhelm her, but Effie cut it short. She studied her friends' kind-hearted faces for a moment.

'Well, seeing as how you are all taking it easy, I think I'll join you,' she said. 'So, what I'm going to do is have a nice cup of tea and then put my feet up in the sun.'

'That's the ticket,' said George.

'It's a lovely day tomorrow,' sang Maeve in her clear alto voice.

Nell and Alice joined in.

Smiling, Effie stood up, but as she stepped forward to take a mug the ground beneath her feet shifted somehow, and her head swam. She staggered against the table and blackness crowded her vision.

'Effie!' a voice screamed from a long way away, as she pitched sidewards.

She put her hands out to stop herself hitting the ground, but other hands caught her under the arms and grabbed her ankle.

'She's going,' said another voice echoing around in her head. 'Get some water.'

She must have passed out because the next thing she knew she was resting back on the bench, with her boiler suit round her hips, no tie, and with shirt unbuttoned and open, exposing her brassiere and camisole top. Nell was waving the maintenance clipboard up and down in front of her face while Alice, sitting next to her on the bench, was holding a glass of water as Maeve and George crowded around her.

'She's coming round,' said George, standing alongside Nell.

'What happened?' asked Effie as she looked around.

'You fainted,' George replied. 'Understandable, really, in this heat. But I think you'll be all right once you've got some fluid in you and had a rest.'

'I thought perhaps this gurgling stomach I've had off and on for the past few weeks might have had something to do with it,' she said, taking the glass of water from her friend.

Maeve and Nell exchanged a knowing look.

'I don't think it's your stomach you're feeling there, my love,' said Maeve. 'But your wee babbie.'

With the glass poised halfway to her lips, Effie's jaw dropped, as her friend's words sank in.

She stared at her friends for a second or two then laughed. 'What an idiot I am for not realising it was the baby!'

'Baby? What baby?'

Effie looked round and saw Lily, in her dress uniform, standing by the hut.

Her eyes flickered onto Effie's expanded belly under the camisole and her mouth pulled into an ugly line. She spun on her heels and marched into the hut, and the command telephone dinged as the receiver was lifted off its housing.

'This is Aircraftwoman Craven, attached to balloon one three two,' Lily snapped. 'I need to talk to the section officer responsible for north-east London barrage balloons, urgently.'

∽

'So, Corporal Weston, have you got anything to say for yourself?' asked Section Officer Wright in a plummy voice, as the clock on the mantelshelf chimed eight o'clock.

'No, ma'am,' Effie replied, her eyes fixed on the point above the squadron commander's head.

They were in the Maid of Norway's front lounge with the

evening sunlight illuminating the room. Effie was in her dress uniform, which she'd changed into the moment she'd got back to the billet, two hours ago.

Her senior officer, an elegant-looking woman in her late thirties, was sitting at the dining table with an open file in front of her and Effie standing to attention on the other side.

'Is there still no news of your fiancé?' asked Sergeant Monroe, who was standing at Wright's right shoulder.

A lump formed itself in Effie's throat and she shook her head.

'Yes, well,' continued Wright. 'You sergeant has acquainted me with your situation, and you have my sympathies, but we are the front line in London's, nay England's defences.'

'Yes, ma'am,' said Effie. 'Sorry, ma'am.'

'Hardly the example I'd expect an NCO to set to her subordinates,' continued Effie's senior officer.

'No, ma'am,' said Effie.

'By rights, the four members of no. 3 crew who knew your condition and aided you in this deception should also be disciplined, but Sergeant Munroe has persuaded me otherwise, mainly because the crew's operation and effectiveness hasn't suffered.'

'Thank you, ma'am,' said Effie.

Section Officer Wright's hazel eyes softened a little. 'And I suppose we should be grateful that no harm has come to you and your baby, but you know the rules. Married? Yes. Pregnant? No. You are confined to your billet until payday on Friday, after which you are discharged from the WAAFs and are free to go. Dismissed.'

Closing the file, she looked expectantly at Effie.

Stunned, Effie stood rooted to the spot for a second, then gave a sharp salute, turned and marched towards the door.

'Good luck, Corporal,' Wright called after Effie as she walked out of the room.

. . .

Her four friends were sitting around the kitchen table, with mugs of tea in their hands. Their heads snapped round as soon as Effie walked in.

'What did she say?' asked Alice, getting up and coming across to her.

'Pretty much what I expected,' Effie replied, sitting down on a spare chair. 'I'm out the day after tomorrow.'

'Cow!' said Nell.

'What else could she do?' said Effie. 'And it was inevitable once Squad found out.'

'But they wouldn't have if Lily hadn't blabbed,' said Maeve, placing a fresh cup of tea in front of her.

'And looking so very pleased with herself to drop Effie in the soup,' George added.

Effie sighed. 'I couldn't have kept my condition secret for much longer. This week or next, it doesn't really matter.'

'I'm sure Nathan will be home any day now,' said Alice, sitting in the chair next to Effie.

Her friends nodded their agreement.

Effie clung to their assurances as something akin to ice water ran through her veins.

'But what if he doesn't?' she asked. 'I've got two weeks' pay plus thirty-three pounds in my Post Office savings. They might keep me going for a couple of weeks, but what the hell am I going to do when the baby comes?'

Effie's friends exchanged a couple of meaningful looks but said nothing.

They didn't need to. They all knew what happened to women who found themselves pregnant with no sight or hope of a husband.

'You have to go 'ome, Effie,' said Nell, after a long pause.

The memory of the last time she'd seen her parents surged back into Effie's mind. 'But my parents hate Nathan.'

'But they don't hate *you*, Effie, do they?' said Alice, taking her hand. 'They are your parents and you're their only child, so surely, once they've got over their shock, they will do what they can to help.'

'Alice is right,' said Nell. 'Even my old bag of a mother would do that much.'

'And at least Nathan will know where you are when he gets back,' Maeve added.

Effie studied her friends' kindly faces, and then she felt the bubbling around her navel again, and she smiled.

'You're right.' She took a sip of tea. 'Once they get over the shock, I'm sure they will do all they can.' She placed her hand on her rounded stomach. 'After all, this is their grandchild.'

'So let me get this straight,' said Albert Weston, looking across at Effie as she perched on the edge of an armchair. 'You've been dismissed from the WAAF.'

Effie nodded.

Her parents were sitting side by side on the sofa and Effie was in the armchair opposite them, in her mother's spotlessly clean and tidy front room. There on the coffee table between them was a tray with her mother's second-best tea set on it.

It was now a few minutes after eleven on Saturday morning the first of August and, after receiving her pay yesterday and saying a tearful goodbye to her friends in the Maid of Norway that morning, Effie had set out on the two-hour journey to Waltham Abbey. She'd arrived at her parents' house half an hour ago, wearing civvies instead of her WAAF uniform and clutching her suitcase.

Fearing that it would fuel neighbourhood gossip if she kept Effie standing on the doorstep, her mother had ushered her in.

'Dismissed for what exactly?' asked her mother now, a puzzled look on her face.

With her heart crashing in her chest, Effie drew in a deep breath. 'Because I'm pregnant.'

Her parents' jaws dropped, and they stared at her incredulously.

Her mother gave a strangled cry and clapped her hands over her mouth. 'You had relations with... with...'

Her father slammed his cup on a saucer so hard Effie was surprised it remained in one piece. He sprang to his feet and marched over to the bay window. Clasping his hands behind his back, he stared through the lace curtains and criss-crossed gummed tap for a second or two. Then he spun round.

'How many months?' he barked.

'Four,' Effie replied.

'Oh, Euphemia,' said her mother.

'Oh, Euphemia, indeed,' Albert yelled, stomping back across the room. 'Our daughter who got a gold star in Sunday school for her Bible knowledge has sinned with a ruddy—'

'It's not like that,' cut in Effie. 'Nathan and I are in love and were supposed to be married eight weeks ago, but a few days before he went missing behind enemy lines.'

'Missing or... dead,' said her father.

'He's *not* dead,' said Effie.

Her father waved her words aside. 'Either way, he's left you to deal with this... this...'

Clamping his mouth tight, he glared at her stomach.

There was a long silence, then Edna stretched forward and put her empty teacup and saucer back on the tray.

'What are you going to do, Euphemia?' her father asked.

'About the baby, your dad means,' added Edna. 'This is a small town and people talk.'

'Well, we could say that I'm a widow,' said Effie, as the small life inside her shifted around.

'Oh, we couldn't lie to people, could we, Albert?' said her mother.

'No, we couldn't,' her husband replied.

Effie stared at them in utter disbelief.

'I'm having a baby, *your* grandchild, for pity's sake,' she said, panic rising within her. 'And haven't you always told me how much you were looking forward to bouncing your grandchildren on your knee?'

'We are, Euphemia,' said her mother.

'But not like this,' added her father.

Edna pulled a handkerchief from the sleeve of her cardigan. 'Oh, Euphemia, if you'd only married Leonard none of this would have happened.' She started crying.

'How could you do this to your mother?' said Albert, jabbing a chubby finger at his weeping wife.

Feeling her temples start to throb, Effie slumped back in the chair.

'I'm sorry,' she sighed.

Pressing his lips together, Albert marched back to the window. He stood for several minutes staring out, then turned round.

'While we do not condone what you've done, Euphemia, the Bible tells us that we must forgive the transgressions of others. On top of which you are our daughter and, despite everything, we both love you.'

'Very much,' chipped in her mother, smiling at her with red-rimmed eyes.

'It will take me a few days, but I'll make the arrangements,' continued Albert.

'What sort of arrangements?' she asked.

He looked puzzled. 'A place in a home for unmarried mothers, of course. Somewhere discreet until the baby's born, after which the home will arrange for it to be adopted.'

The room shifted sideways as Effie's hands went to her growing stomach. 'But I want to keep Nathan's baby.'

He looked astonished. 'Keep it? Don't be ridiculous. As your mother said, people talk. And even if you did tell people that you'd been widowed, when they saw you in town pushing a pram around with a brown-skinned baby in it, your name would be in the gutter and ours along with it for not raising you better. We wouldn't be able to hold our heads up at church or at the Conservative Association.'

Shifting forward, her mother took her hand again and squeezed it. 'No one will know and once it's all over you can come home and forget all about it. It's for the best, Euphemia.'

'Don't worry,' continued her father, oblivious to the chasm opening up in front of Effie. 'It will only take a couple of days of phone calls, and until then you can put your feet up here with us.'

Effie stared in disbelief at her parents' faces for a moment, then stood up. 'Thank you, but I will never give up Nathan's baby. Either we both stay, or I go.'

'Now, now, Jellybean, you're letting your emotions get the upper hand,' said her father, giving her his don't-be-a-silly-girl look. 'How on earth are you going to survive by yourself with a baby?'

Uncertainty fluttered in Effie's chest. Damping it down, she squared her shoulders.

'I don't know,' she replied, looking resolutely at her parents. 'But I will.'

With astonished expressions on their faces, her parents' eyes followed Effie as she walked across the room and out into the hall.

She closed the door behind her and picked up her suitcase, then caught sight of the coat-stand mirror.

As she stared at herself, anxiety closed like a hand round her heart.

Nathan was not dead. She knew that as surely as she knew her own heart was beating. But where was he? And when would he return? Weeks? Months? Years? And how on earth was she, an unmarried woman with a baby born out of wedlock, going to survive in the middle of a war with only a few pounds to her name?

She didn't know. But one thing she did know was that she would never, ever give up Nathan's baby.

Turning back, she grasped the latch and pulled the front door open, then, with their child squirming around inside her, Effie walked out.

CHAPTER 32

Florrie Granger kicked off her high heels, sank into the ancient armchair beside the cast-iron range and put her feet up on the leather pouffe.

It was three forty on Sunday afternoon and she was in the room in the Maid of Norway that, as it served as both kitchen and parlour, contained not only a two-seater sofa and two chairs but a painted pine kitchen cabinet.

She, Ernie Moody, the Maid of Norway's elderly potman, who cleared away and changed the barrels in the cellar, and Daisy Driscoll, their dizzy-headed barmaid, had all given a sigh of relief when she'd called last orders three-quarters of an hour ago, as the dockside pub had been heaving since she'd opened the door at twelve. Before the war, of course, there would have been her husband Sidney and their sons Steve and Alex behind the bar. Now, with Sid pushing up daisies in the City of London Cemetery, Alex somewhere mid-Atlantic and Steve chasing the Germans in North Africa, it was just her, Ernie and Daisy holding the fort. Still, she shouldn't complain. With men called up and mothers and children evacuated during the first few months of the war, some weeks there was barely enough money to put a shilling in the gas meter, so perhaps it was better to be run off her feet serving drinks than leaning on the pumps looking across an empty bar.

Wriggling her toes, Florrie reached across and picked up the glass of stout from the table beside her. Savouring the cream bitterness of the dark liquid, she swallowed a couple of mouthfuls. She placed it back on the cork coaster and retrieved the ten-pack of Senior Service and the lighter from the pocket of her frilly apron.

She lit a cigarette and took a long drag. She let her head fall back, enjoying the sensation of inhaled nicotine tingling through her, but the clatter of the bead curtains hanging in the doorway interrupted her reverie.

She opened her eyes to see Ernie, wearing his black apron and an apprehensive expression on his hangdog face.

'I think you'd better come,' he said, then disappeared.

Florrie sighed and, wondering what disaster awaited her, swung her legs off the pouffe and stood up. Pinching out her cigarette, she stowed it behind her ear, then, ignoring her screaming feet, she put her shoes on and got to her feet.

As she walked through the hanging beads and into the bar, Florrie stopped dead.

Sitting in one of the booths was Effie Weston, with her suitcase on the floor on one side and a policewoman, her polished lace-ups planted firmly on the pub's floorboards, on the other.

Truth be told, Florrie had a soft spot for most of the WAAFs billeted in the pub's upper rooms, but she was particularly fond of Effie. Probably because, had she lived, her daughter Emma would have been the same age as Effie.

'Good afternoon,' said the policewoman. 'Do you know this young wom—'

'Effie,' said Florrie, hurrying across and sliding in beside her.

She started to cry, and Florrie put her arm round her shoulder. As Effie sobbed quietly, Florrie looked up.

'Where did you find her?'

'One of the ARP wardens at Liverpool Street station came across her sitting in the ladies waiting room at about three o'clock this morning,' the office replied. 'As she was obviously in shock and in the family way, he took her to the Old Street WVS relief centre. They called us and, when we asked her if she had anywhere to stay in London, she gave us this address, so we brought her to you.'

'I'm glad you did,' said Florrie, hugging Effie to her. 'Thank you, Constable, you can leave her with me.'

The policewoman left and Ernie bolted the door after her before wandering off to resume his tasks.

Effie raised her head. 'I'm sorry, Florrie. I didn't know what else—'

'No, no,' Florrie said, giving her another squeeze. 'Don't you fret none, ducks. Whatever 'appened, Florrie will sort it. Now what you need is a nice cup of tea.'

∼

A few minutes later, with Florrie's motherly arm still round her, Effie walked through the bead curtain into the landlady's private quarters.

'You sit yourself down there,' said Florrie, helping her into a chair with her half-drunk pint of stout still beside it. 'And I'll make us a cuppa.'

Weary to the bone from a couple of hours' fitful sleep on the relief centre's camp bed, Effie all but collapsed into the well-stuffed armchair.

'When I said goodbye to you on Saturday, I thought you were heading off to your parents,' said Florrie, lighting the gas under the kettle. 'So what happened?'

'Well, after their initial surprise at me turning up on their doorstep they were delighted to see me until I told them the reason why I'd been discharged from the WAAF and then...'

As Florrie made the tea Effie recounted the scene in her parents' lounge the previous afternoon. 'As I have no intention of giving up Nathan's baby, I couldn't stay.'

'But you're their own flesh and blood,' said Florrie as she placed a steaming mug of tea on the table beside Effie and sat in the chair opposite.

Cradling her mug, Effie blew across the top. 'I suppose being that Waltham Abbey is a small town, they felt they couldn't cope with all the finger-pointing and gossip.'

'I don't see 'ow a bit of poxy gossip would stop you 'elping your only daughter,' the pub landlady continued. 'But then what do I know about the way of some folks?' From under her mascaraed lashes Florrie gave her a measured look. 'I'm guessing you've had no word about your chap?'

Effie shook her head. 'But he's not dead. I know that.'

'Of course he's not,' said Florrie firmly. Her cherry-red lips lifted in a sideways smile. 'And won't he have a big surprise when he comes back?'

Her gaze flickered down to Effie's midriff.

As if knowing it was the subject of the conversation, the baby shifted around. Effie felt the weight of her situation pressing down on her, and tears welled up in her eyes again.

'Now there,' repeated Florrie. 'There's no need for that. Think of the baby.'

'I am,' said Effie, wiping a tear from her right cheek. 'And where on earth am I going to go?'

A puzzled expression settled on Florrie's powdered face. 'Go? You're not going anywhere. You're staying here. There's a single room on the landing below your old room and you can have that.'

Effie looked incredulous. 'But I've only got enough for a couple of weeks rent and food.'

'You used to work as a clerk, didn't you?' said Florrie.

'Well, yes at Waltham Abbey's town hall, but—'

'Well, you can pay your rent in kind,' Florrie cut in. 'I'm always getting the Ministry of Food's forms and brewery orders in a muddle, so you can pay your way by doing them. You'll have your friends around you, and you can book yourself in with the nurse at Munroe House. And before you ask, if your handsome flying officer hasn't returned by the time the baby arrives, then we'll all muck in. What do you say?'

Wide-eyed, Effie stared across at the Maid of Norway's colourful landlady for second, then her shoulders slumped.

'Thank you, Florrie,' she said and let out a long sigh. 'Thank you so much.'

The older woman gave a satisfied nod. 'Good. We look after our own around 'ere, we do. Now drink your tea and we can take your things up to your new room.'

CHAPTER 33

As he watched the raindrops cut a pathway through the dirty window of the skylight above, Nathan's stomach rumbled. Hardly surprising as the dawn sun had only just started to illuminate the grimy farmhouse attic he was lying in. He was propped up against one of the roof beams with a flea-bitten horse blanket beneath him and his service revolver resting on the haversack he'd taken from the Lizzie next to him.

This was the fourth safe house he and Frobisher had been hidden in since their encounter with Madame Barbier six weeks ago, and it was a whole lot better than some they'd been in. One had been little more than a dugout in a forest with a branch covering it, and another a cellar beneath the village slaughterhouse. However, Nathan wasn't complaining, firstly because after weeks spent in countryside crawling with German patrols they had somehow avoided being captured, and secondly, as the seagulls squawking outside testified, they were within a mile of two of the French coast and, please God, a boat back to England and Effie. It had been thoughts of her that had sustained him through all the hunger and pain since the crash.

A loud snort chased the images of Effie from Nathan's mind.

Frobisher, who had been sprawled on a faded bedspread under one of the roof beams and snoring softly, sat up.

'What, where...' he stuttered, grabbing his revolver.

'Stop waving that thing around. There's enough holes in this roof without you shooting more.' The drip-drip of water from the tiles above confirmed Nathan's words.

Frobisher placed his weapon back on the floor and looked at his watch. 'Damn.'

'It's almost six,' said Nathan, anticipating his next question.

'Thanks, I forgot to wind it,' Frobisher replied.

Nathan glanced at the empty apple brandy bottle lying among the dirt and rat droppings by the SOE officer's feet. 'How's the knee?'

'Still painful,' Frobisher replied. 'I hope I don't end up with a permanent bloody limp.'

'But think how distinguished you'd look, hobbling into the Carlton Club with a war wound and a walking stick,' Nathan replied.

Frobisher threw him a testy look, then, finding himself a support beam, leant back.

'God, all this waiting around is so bally tedious.' He sighed. 'You'd think they'd bring us a pack of cards or something.'

Nathan couldn't be bothered to answer.

Frobisher sat studying the wall opposite for a moment, then scrambled to his feet. Madame Barbier had given him a wooden crutch, which looked like a relic from Waterloo, and, tucking the top of it under his arm, Frobisher hobbled over to the skylight and peered out.

'I can't see any movement in the yard yet,' he said, craning his neck.

'I imagine, like the rest of the village, the blacksmith is still in bed,' Nathan replied.

Their host for the past three days was the village smithy. As far as Nathan could ascertain, he was a widower, whose daughter came to cook and clean for him each day.

Still scrutinising the yard, Frobisher didn't reply.

Resting his head back, Nathan closed his eyes again, and once more conjured up an image of Effie. He hated to think how anxious and worried she would have been these past weeks, so he would telephone her billet the minute he landed back in England and then rearrange their wedding. Better late than never, as they say.

In the glooming attic a smile spread across Nathan's face as his mind moved on from picturing her standing beside him at the altar to having her under him in their wedding bed.

'What-ho!' said Frobisher. 'That frump who skivvies for him is coming across with our breakfast.'

Within a couple of minutes the sound of heavy footsteps echoed up the attic stairs and a woman wearing a headscarf and a weary expression reached the top of the stairs, carrying a basket.

She was probably only in her early thirties, but, in a shapeless grey dress and shawl round her shoulders, looked a decade older, like so many of those who had lived under German occupation for the past two years.

'Bonjour, madame,' Nathan said, rising to his feet.

'Bonjour, monsieur,' she replied, handing him the basket. 'I have bought you and your friend petit déjeuner.'

'Merci, madame,' said Nathan, placing it on the floor.

'And a message,' she continued. 'As you might have realised, we are only a few miles from the coast. You will be collected this evening and taken to a waiting fishing boat in a nearby cove that will take you back to England, so be ready.'

'At last!' said Frobisher.

The woman gave him a sharp look, but Nathan took her hand.

'Thank you, madame,' he said, shaking it. 'We are very grateful for all you and your comrades have done.'

She nodded, then made her way back down the stairs.

Frobisher hobbled over, ripped off the red and white cloth covering the basket and pulled a face. 'Cheese and bread again.'

Taking the long loaf, Nathan tore it in two. He handed half to Frobisher. 'Well, they were probably out of quails' eggs and foie gras.'

He pulled the aluminium flask from the basket and opened it.

'What is it?' asked Frobisher.

'Milk,' Nathan replied.

Frobisher pulled another face and grabbed the bottle of wine poking out of the top of the wicker basket. 'I'll make do with this.'

Nathan took his half of the bread, a chunk of cheese and the flask of milk and returned to his horse blanket and, giving thanks that tomorrow he would be doing the same on English soil, he bit into his breakfast.

With the wind from the sea chilling his cheeks, Nathan lifted his head and drew in a lungful of salty air.

'It is not far now, monsieur,' whispered the weather-beaten individual who had collected them from the blacksmith's loft about an hour ago.

The sun had disappeared behind the horizon about an hour and half hours before they had been collected and the village church clock had struck ten as they passed, so Nathan guessed it was probably nudging toward midnight now. Having skirted the dark silent village, they had trudged a couple of miles through a woody area before reaching the dunes where they were now.

'I bloody hope not,' muttered Frobisher, as he limped along beside Nathan.

Although Frobisher's knee had improved, he still couldn't walk without the crutch and Nathan had to support him, so, much to the consternation of their wizened guide, they made slow progress towards their rendezvous point in the cove.

They crested the last dune and the sandy beach lay before them in the faint light from the waning moon. Keeping in the shadow of the sandbanks, they made their way towards the headland and then, splashing through the rippling waves, they entered a small cove. A rowing boat had been drawn up onto the beach and on spotting them the two men standing beside it came over.

'I was expecting you an hour ago,' said the older one, wearing a knitted hat and leather jerkin.

'Mon ami est blessé,' Nathan replied, removing his shoulder from under Frobisher's armpit.

He went to pull back the tarpaulin sheet lying over the boat's bench seats, but the other resistance fighter, a lean individual of about Nathan's age, stayed his hand.

'What's the bloody problem?' Frobisher snapped.

'I'm not sure,' Nathan replied, as incoming waves soaked his cord trousers.

'For God's sake.' Shrugging Nathan's arm off, Frobisher hobbled over to the side of the vessel. 'Hey, you!' He jabbed his finger at the Frenchman as he perched there. 'We haven't got all night, so be a good fellow and get a move on.'

Ignoring him, the Frenchman's hard eyes flickered onto the tarpaulin. A corner lifted and revealed the barrel of a British Lee–Enfield rifle. Nathan gave an almost imperceptible nod, and, turning to conceal his actions with his open jacket, pulled his service revolver from his belt.

'Halt!'

Nathan turned back.

Running down the cliff face from the coastal path, Sten guns on their hips, were half a dozen German soldiers, with a tall, slender officer a few paces behind them. The band of troopers stopped and, levelling their guns at the men around the boat, they fanned out either side of the officer, who, by the look of his insignia, was an SS lieutenant.

Looking rather pleased with himself and pointing his Luger at Nathan, he strode between them. 'Thank you, Monsieur Bernard,' he said to the old man who had led them from the blacksmith's house to the cove. 'Your service to the Führer will not go unrewarded.'

'Neither will yours,' shouted the Frenchman on the other side of the boat, pulling a revolver from beneath his jacket.

Leaping forward, Nathan pushed Frobisher to the ground as two men in working gear, brandishing British Sten guns, burst out from underneath the tarpaulin. The old man who had guided them down to the shore also pulled out a weapon.

With automatic gunfire ringing in his ears, Nathan threw himself on the shingle and then rolled behind a small protruding rock.

Although a couple of the troopers were already lying inert on the ground, the rest were returning fire, including the lieutenant, who aimed at their elderly guide, Bernard, and pulled the trigger. The old man fell to his knees, then flopped forward.

Mindful of the two resistance fighters who were now sheltering behind an outcrop of rocks, Nathan aimed his revolver and fired. This time it was the Nazi officer who plummeted into the surf.

Seeing their officer lying on the sand, the remaining troopers turned and dashed back towards the cliff and into a hail of bullets in the crossfire. As the last trooper crashed to the shingle, the clatter of gunfire ceased.

Nathan stood up and, after dusting himself down, splashed through the incoming surf across to the old man. Hunkering down, he rolled him over. The old man moaned as blood seeped from a gash in his trousers.

'He's alive, but has been shot in the leg,' said Nathan as a young man carrying a Sten gun reached him.

'We will take care of him, Monsieur,' he said, as a couple of resistance fighters helped Bernard to his feet. 'Now you must go.'

The older fisherman was already in the craft, at the oars, while the young one was gripping the vessel's stern as the tide tugged it back and forth.

Leaving them tending the old man, Nathan turned back towards the rowing boat.

Frobisher, having got himself upright, was standing staring at the bodies strewn across the beach.

'Get in,' Nathan yelled, shoving his revolver in his belt. He sprinted across the shingle.

When he was halfway across, something slammed into his back and pitched him face down in the frothy surf washing over the seashore as another short burst of gunfire rang out.

Gasping for breath, Nathan pressed his hands on the pebbles beneath him, but as he tried to rise to his feet he collapsed backwards onto the shingle. Black spots started popping in his peripheral vision. Feeling oblivion stealing over him, Nathan tried to rise again, but his strength was gone. Buffeted by the surging waves, he focused his failing consciousness on Effie so that his last thought in this life would be of her. However, as blackness enveloped him, someone grabbed his arm, hauling him up and bringing him back to the here and now.

With his head swimming, Nathan forced his eyes open, and found himself looking at Frobisher's face.

'Come on, old man,' the SOE officer lieutenant drawled, draping Nathan's arm round his shoulder and ramming his shoulder under him. 'You've got a wedding to get to, so don't cop it now.'

CHAPTER 34

Effie traced her index finger across the typed row until she reached the last column on the right. Noting the amount the dispatch clerk at Truman's brewery had written, she wrote £17 9s 3d in the appropriate box on the Ministry of Food form in front of her.

It was just after two on a Thursday afternoon and she was sitting at Florrie's drop-leaf table in the landlady's parlour. It was now almost two weeks since she'd returned to the Maid of Norway and, as it was the middle of August, spread out before her were the pub's monthly traders' bills. Through the open door leading to the public bar, gruff male voices and boisterous laughter sounded as the Maid of Norway's lunchtime customers enjoyed a midday pint before returning to work for the afternoon.

She turned the weekly beer bill over and placed it on the completed pile, but as she turned her attention to the next one on the pile there was a knock on the doorframe and Alice's head appeared through the beaded curtains holding a half glass of stout in her hand.

When they'd returned to their billet the day after her departure, her friends had been surprised to see her back in the Maid of Norway – and shocked, as Florrie had been, at the reason why. Although she was a little sad that she was no longer manning Bessie the barrage balloon, having them close at hand made her feel less alone in the world.

'Hello playmates!' Alice said, cheerily.

'You're very chipper today,' said Effie, leaning back in the chair.

'I have a forty-eight-hour pass,' said Alice, walking into the room. 'And I've been granted the same at the end of November for my youngest sister's wedding. This is for you.' She placed the glass in front of Effie. 'Florrie said it'll give you iron. How's the paperwork going?'

'Smoothly now I've got to grip with Florrie's somewhat unconventional bookkeeping system,' Effie replied as her friend unbuttoned the front of her navy boiler suit and sat on the dining chair opposite.

Florrie had been wrong when she said the Maid of Norway's accounts were in a bit of a mess. They weren't. They were in a colossal mess, so much so that it had taken Effie a whole week to sort them out. Having brought forth order from chaos, she'd now taken over the pub's accounts, leaving Florrie to do what she did best, which was run the bar and customer side of the business.

Florrie had been as good as her word, better in fact because, not only did she provide Effie with her bed and board, she also insisted on paying her two pound, three and six a week on top.

'And what did the midwives at Munroe House say about baby Fitzgerald this morning?' asked Alice.

'Everything is as it should be,' Effie replied. 'They're going to give me a certificate so I can claim my extra ration as a nursing mother from the Ministry of Food office.'

'Good, I'm glad to hear it,' said Alice. 'I can't wait to meet my new godson or daughter.'

'And I can't wait until I can have a full night's sleep without little feet dancing on my bladder,' Effie replied.

'If my big sister's babies were anything to go by, I think you can forget a full night's sleep until they're out of nappies,' said Alice. Her expression became serious. 'I don't suppose there's any news?'

She didn't have to clarify as to what news because Effie knew too well.

Although she now had a roof over her head and three square meals a day, the Nathan-size hole in her heart grew wider and deeper with each passing day. As she was not his next of kin, RAF command wouldn't notify her if there was any news, so she telephoned Tempsford every few days, only to be told there was no further information about Flying Officer Fitzgerald. The very small sliver of comfort she had was that, if he had been killed in action, he had left a precious part of himself with her.

Feeling the familiar ache in her chest, Effie shook her head.

Alice gave her a sympathetic look but said no more. After all, he'd been missing for eleven weeks, so what more was there to say that hadn't already been said.

Pushing aside the dark cloud hovering over her, Effie put on a bright smile. 'And what about you, Alice? Have you finally given in to their nagging and agreed to go dancing up west with the gang?'

'I'm still thinking about it,' Alice replied. 'I'm not sure I'm ready yet to put on my glad rags and dancing sh—'

The bead curtains parted and Daisy appeared.

'Scuse me barging in like this, Eff, but there's some foreign bloke in the bar asking for you,' she said, thumbing over her shoulder.

Nathan! Effie's heart leapt into her throat.

'D'you want me to show 'im through?' Daisy added.

With her mouth too dry to speak, Effie nodded.

Daisy disappeared back into the bar.

Fixing her eyes on the swaying curtain, Effie prayed silently until the young barmaid reappeared a minute later, followed by a tall air force officer with strawberry blond hair.

Although his uniform was air force blue, the insignia on his lapels and arm flashes were different to Nathan's. Effie stared at him for a moment, then she recognised him.

She stood up. 'Lieutenant Ostowicz.'

He pressed his heels together and bowed slightly. 'Good afternoon, Corporal Weston. I trust I find you well?'

'Very,' Effie replied, as the baby inside her shifted around. 'Have you come with news of Nathan?'

'I have.' His eyes flicked down to her swollen stomach before returning to her face. 'Perhaps it would be better if you sat down again, Corporal Weston.'

With her heart hammering in her chest and her blood rushing through her ears, Effie perched on the chair.

Rising, Alice came round and, taking her hand, squeezed it reassuringly.

The Polish officer smiled. 'I'm pleased to inform you that after crash-landing in enemy-occupied territory and evading capture for two months, Pilot Officer Nathan Fitzgerald was brought back to England two weeks ago.'

Her head swimming, Effie slumped back in the chair.

'Thank God,' she gasped. 'Is he all right?'

'Unfortunately, he was injured while escaping.'

'Is he badly hurt?' asked Effie, the anxiety that had started to ebb away rearing its head again.

'I am afraid I do not know the full details of his injuries or prognosis, but I can tell you he is being cared for in an RAF hospital outside Oxford. For operational reasons, I'm afraid you could not be informed sooner, but I have the address where he is.' He handed her a sheet of paper.

'Thank you, Lieutenant,' said Effie, beaming wildly at him. 'Thank you so much.'

He smiled. 'It is my absolute pleasure to be the messenger of such happy news.'

Effie stood up. 'I'm so sorry, Lieutenant Ostowicz, where are my manners? Can I offer you a tea or coffee?'

'Wiktor, please. And thank you kindly for the offer, but no,' he replied. 'I'm meeting an old friend in town for dinner. But perhaps we can share a drink together when you and my friend Nathan are reunited.'

He pressed his heels together, turned and marched back out into the bar.

Alice took her hands. 'I'm so pleased for you. And now you know where he is, you can at least write,' she added, indicating the sheet of paper Effie was holding.

'Write? I'm not going to write, Alice!' Effie replied. 'I'm going to be on the first train to Oxford tomorrow morning.'

Alice looked horrified. 'But you can't travel all the way to Oxford by yourself in your condition.'

Effie raised an eyebrow. 'Didn't you say you had a forty-eight-hour pass?'

∽

The warm and gentle presence that had entered his shadowy dreamlike existence raised Nathan's mind back to consciousness.

Propped up on what he assumed were half a dozen pillows and hovering on the edge of wakefulness, he listened to the sound of women's voices, squeaky wheels and purposeful footsteps tapping across wooden floors, then, as the smell of disinfectant drifted over him, he knew two things.

He was alive, thank God, and in a hospital.

Still drowsy and with his eyes closed, he lay there quietly, then a flowery perfume that he knew so well permeated the acrid smell of surgical spirit.

Effie!

Pushing aside the fog in his brain, Nathan forced his eyes open.

For a moment he thought he was still dreaming because there, curled on her side in the visitor armchair, with her knees tucked up and her hair in disarray, was Effie, fast asleep.

Love and joy burst through him, dispelling the last traces of lethargy from his mind.

The last thought he had, as he'd been tumbled into the French fishing boat, was of her, and now here she was beside him.

He couldn't have wished for a better sight to wake up to.

Giving himself over to the pleasure of gazing on the woman who he would love until his last breath, Nathan gathered moisture back into his mouth, 'Effie!' he croaked.

Her eyes flew open in an instant. 'Nathan!'

She swung her legs round, leant forward and grabbed his hand lying on the pristine white sheet. Pressing her lips on his knuckles, she kissed his fingers.

'Thank God,' she whispered, then turned in the chair.

'Nurse!' she shouted, taking his hand.

A young Princess Mary's RAF nurse with a white cap perched on her head appeared at the door. She took one look at Nathan and disappeared again, only to return a few moments later with a white-coated doctor with group leader stripes on his epaulettes.

Somewhere in his late thirties or early forties with dark blond Brylcreemed hair, the RAF doctor was a clean-cut individual who wouldn't have looked out of place strolling out to bat for England at the Oval.

'Officer Fitzgerald, good of you to join us at last,' he said in a cultured accent that could have cut glass.

Nathan was taken back. 'At last?'

'Yes, you've been out of it since you arrived here sixteen days ago,' the doctor replied.

Nathan stared incredulously at him.

'Doctor Ogilvie said you were in a bad way when you arrived,' said Effie, squeezing his hand.

'Your fiancée speaks the truth, Fitzgerald,' said Ogilvie. 'You had a bullet go clean through the bottom of your left lung, missing your liver by a cat's whisker and busting a couple of ribs on the way. On top of which by the time you'd bobbed about on the briny for a day you had double pneumonia as well. It was touch and go, I can tell you, for a few days, but thankfully you're young and fit, plus we've been issued with a new drug. Penicillin. It's only issued to the forces at present. But so far, it seems to be a bit of a wonder drug for this type of thing. Has to be given in a large syringe, which is why your rear might feel a bit tender for a few days when you sit.'

Nathan laughed and wished he hadn't as pain shot across his back.

'What's happened to Frobisher?' he asked.

'I understand he returned to Tempsford,' said Ogilvie. 'But he telephoned yesterday to see how you were faring.'

'And how long until I'm fit to fly?' asked Nathan.

'That depends on you and how quickly you can build up your strength again,' the doctor replied. 'But assuming there are no further setbacks, I'd say a month or two – but I expect we'll be kicking you out before that.' He glanced at Effie and one corner of his mouth lifted. 'Not a moment too soon, I imagine, given your fiancée's condition. Now if you'd excuse me...'

He swept out of the hospital side room with the nurse a step or two behind.

Nathan stared dumbly after him before his gaze shifted to Effie as a mischievous smile lifted her lips.

She slowly she rose to her feet and stood up straight.

Nathan's gaze shifted from her lovely face to her very rounded, very pregnant stomach.

'Oh, Effie!'

She laughed. 'Oh, Nathan.'

She sat on the side of his bed, took his hand and placed it on the thin summer fabric covering her swollen middle. He felt nothing for a second or two, then a small hand or foot pressed against his fingers and a joy he had never imagined could existed in this world flooded through him.

'When's our baby due?' he asked, delighting in the feel the slight movement of his baby's under his hand.

'Not for a few months yet,' she replied.

Alarm gripped him. 'Even so, shouldn't you be resting, not dashing around the country by yourself—'

'I'm fine and I'm not by myself, Alice is with me,' Effie replied. 'We're booked into a small B&B down the road from here.'

Nathan looked around. 'And where *is* here?'

'Goring RAF hospital in Oxfordshire,' Effie replied. 'I've got a lot to tell you but it can wait until you're stronger. There's nothing you should worry about now. I can stay for a few days, but then I have to get back to the Maid of Norway.'

Nathan frowned. 'You're still at the pub?'

'It's a long story,' said Effie. 'All you need to know for now is me and our baby are being well cared for, so there's nothing for you to worry about.'

'Except marrying you,' he replied.

'We can arrange that once you're back on your feet, Nathan,' said Effie.

Nathan's gaze ran over her as she sat there with their child large beneath her billowing maternity dress, and his heart swelled to bursting with love.

Ignoring the pain, he shifted round and looked at her. 'Effie, sweetheart, why don't we just get married right now?'

She gave him a puzzled look.

'What, right now, here in the hospital?' She laughed.

'Why not?' he replied, taking her hand. 'I know it's not what we planned and it won't be a fancy wedding but—'

'Yes, Nathan. Yes, let's get married now,' she cut in. Smiling, she leant forward and looked him in the eyes. 'And I don't give a jot about a fancy wedding. All I care about is marrying you.'

As her words filled his heart, all the pieces of Nathan's world fell back into place.

'I love you,' he said.

'I love you too,' she replied. Placing her hands gently either side of his face, she locked her gaze with his. 'I never doubted for even a second that you would come back, Nathan.'

'It was knowing you were waiting, Effie, that made me determined to,' Nathan replied.

There were lots of very practical reason why they should marry as soon as possible. A child born into the middle of a world war would have enough problems in life without having a birth certificate older than their parents' marriage certificate. Additionally, as a flying officer's wife, Effie would automatically receive a proportion of his monthly pay and, should he be killed in combat, receive a RAF widow's pension. However, truthfully the real and only reason he wanted to marry her as soon as possible was because he couldn't bear another second of not having her as his wife.

Nathan lost himself in Effie's lovely eyes briefly, then, ignoring his protesting ribs, he gathered her into his arms. Aching and tired, he surrendered to her embrace, savouring the feel of her arms round his neck and their child snuggled and growing between them, as she placed her mouth over his.

EPILOGUE

'It is now my pleasure to pronounce you man and wife,' said Reverend Jolliffe, beaming at Effie and Nathan. 'And now you may kiss the bride.'

Nathan turned to Effie and, taking her in his arms, pressed his lips on hers briefly.

'Hello, Mrs Fitzgerald,' he said softly, his blue eyes warm and full of love as they looked down into hers.

They were standing together in what had been the Goring family's private chapel in front of the RAF chaplain who had just conducted their wedding. The quiet place of family worship was situated in the west wing of the old country house and dappled in gentle colours by the late afternoon sunlight shining through the Victorian stained glass. It was a very beautiful place, but to be honest she could have been standing in a Nissen hunt ankle-deep in mud and she wouldn't have cared as long as she had Nathan by her side and his ring on her finger.

Two days had passed since they had been reunited at his bedside, and what a busy forty-eight hours they had been. Firstly, contacting the local church to arrange a special marriage licence, then finding something more suitable to wear on her wedding day than the second-hand maternity dresses she had brought with her.

Thankfully, Alice had managed to wangle a couple of extra days' leave so was able to go with her into Oxford. After an hour of going through the rails in Elliston & Cavell she found a lovely pink crêpe maternity dress with lace collar and cuffs. However, despite the sling supporting his right arm, in his RAF uniform Nathan looked every bit the handsome RAF hero. And he was a hero, officially, because a telegram had arrived the day before, telling him that for his actions in the field he had been promoted.

'Hello, Flight Lieutenant,' she replied, smiling up at him.

Lost in his eyes, she stood gazing up at her new husband for a blissful moment, then Alice and Wiktor joined them.

'Effie, I'm so pleased for you,' said Alice, hugging her. 'And you too, Nathan.'

'Thank you, Alice,' Nathan replied, as she pecked him on the cheek. 'I'm pretty pleased myself.'

'Congratulations, old man,' said Wiktor, slapping Nathan lightly on the back. 'And I hope you know how lucky you are having such a beautiful bride.'

'Thank you, Wiktor,' Nathan replied, shaking his friend's hand. 'I most certainly do.'

She and Nathan hadn't ever planned for a big wedding but even they hadn't envisioned it being quite so small. Their only guests were Wiktor, who had arrived the day before to act as Nathan's best man, and her bridesmaid Alice, both of whom doubled up as witnesses.

The only other people in the chapel were the nurse who had brought Nathan from his side ward and the RAF welfare officer who had come over from Brise Norton so Nathan could complete the necessary RAF paperwork.

There were other people who both she and Nathan would have loved to share their happy day with. Obviously, Nell,

Maeve, George and her other friends from 312 balloon site, but also Nathan's parents, who would only get the news of their son's marriage in the post. Of course, there were two people she'd always counted on being with her on her happiest day of her life: her father looking as pleased as punch as he walked her down the aisle and her mother dabbing away tears of joy beneath a ridiculously large hat. Despite their lack of response to her weekly letters, she had hoped that when they received her telegram inviting them to the wedding they might relent in their opposition to her and Nathan marrying and come. Alas, it was not to be.

Taking Effie's hand, Nathan drew her back to him, then took her in his arms.

'I most certainly do,' he repeated, looking deeply into her eyes.

He slipped his arm round her, held her close and kissed her again. Unhappy at being sandwiched between its parents, the baby kicked. Nathan tickled her waist, and they exchanged a private look, then he held out his arm.

Effie frowned. 'Perhaps you should let the nurse help you back to your room.'

Nathan shook his head. 'It was the thought of walking you down the aisle as my wife that kept me going all those weeks, Effie, so please...'

She took his arm, and Alice handed her the posy of summer flowers they'd gathered from Goring Hall's herbaceous borders.

Holding himself up straight and getting his balance, Nathan led her slowly down the aisle, but, as he reached the last pew, his resolute steps faltered and he stumbled.

Clutching his arm, Effie steadied him as the nurse sitting at the back grabbed the wheelchair by the door and hurried over.

'Nathan, sit in the chair,' said Effie, holding on to him.

'I'm fine,' he said, forcing himself upright.

'No, you're not, Nathan,' Effie replied firmly and looked

purposefully at him. 'And unless you want this to be our first married argument, I suggest you do as you're told.'

Nathan pressed his lips together and, letting out a sigh, gripped the wheelchair's arms and flopped down.

Looking less than pleased, Nathan, with Effie walking beside him and Alice and Wiktor bringing up the rear, was wheeled back to his room.

After stopping the wheelchair alongside the bed, the nurse started to help him, but Nathan held up his hand, gripped the armrest and, with a look of absolute determination on his face, rose to his feet.

The nurse moved the wheelchair aside and Nathan turned on the spot and sat on the bed. Crouching down, the nurse took off his shoes, and then she lifted his legs up and swung him on the bed. Letting out a long breath, Nathan sank back into the mountain of pillows behind him.

'Now,' said Wiktor as Effie sat on the bed next to Nathan. 'To the celebrations.'

'Celebrations?' said Nathan, with a wry smile.

'Of course,' said Wiktor. 'Is it not the custom in England for the best man to organise such things?'

'Well, yes,' agreed Nathan. 'But I hope you haven't gone to the expense of hiring a five-piece band. I don't think I'll be up to much dancing.'

His friend grinned and then disappeared out of the room, only to reappear a few moments later carrying a bottle of champagne in one hand and four hospital tumblers in the other.

'I beg you excuse the inappropriate glasses,' he said, placing the beaker on the bedside locker. 'But I'm sure the Dom Pérignon 36 will taste just as good.'

Nathan took Effie's hand as his comrade-in-arms popped the cork and then splashed a generous quantity of bubbly into each glass. He handed them out, then, standing at the end of the bed, raised his drink high.

'Mr and Mrs Fitzgerald.'

'Mr and Mrs Fitzgerald,' repeated Alice, smiling, as she toasted them.

'Wishing them a long and happy life together,' added Wiktor. 'And as you are apt to say in England on such occasions, may all their troubles be little ones. Although I think in this case it is a wish they will be experiencing in a few short months.'

Squeezing her hand, Nathan smiled.

'But now' – Wiktor took a large mouthful – 'I think it is time that Mrs Starling and I left you newly-weds alone.'

Alice finished her drink, then put her glass on the table, and Effie stood up.

'Congratulations again, Effie,' her friend said, hugging her.

Wiktor shook Nathan's hand and gave Effie a quick peck on the cheek, then he and Alice left, closing the door behind them.

'Alone at last,' said Effie as she sat back on the bed.

'Indeed.' Taking her hand, Nathan glanced around the whitewashed side room and gave her a wry smile. 'Not quite the honeymoon suite I envisaged for our first night together as husband and wife.'

'Perhaps not.' Shuffling up the bed, Effie wrapped her arms round his neck. 'Once you've recovered, we can start our married life properly.'

With the faint sounds of the hospital beyond their clinical cubicle in the background, Effie leant forward and pressed her lips onto his, then gave herself over to the unfathomable pleasure of his kisses.

After a moment, Nathan grinned up at his wife, tightening his arms round her. 'I couldn't agree more, Mrs Fitzgerald.'

Effie raised an eyebrow. They smiled at each other, then Nathan's expression grew serious as he drew her to him again, but this time his kiss was tender.

'I love you so much, Euphemia Fitzgerald. And I *am* going

to spend my whole life making you happy,' he said, the love glowing in his blue eyes underlying his every word.

Tears welled in Effie's eyes. The words *I love you* started in her heart but couldn't push past the swell of emotion clogging her throat. But it didn't matter really, as no words could adequately express the happiness filling her heart.

With their child growing inside her, Effie had lived hour by hour since Sergent Munroe told her Nathan was missing in action, hoping against hope that he was not lying dead in a French field or being held behind barbed wire in a prisoner of war camp, but now he was here. Nathan was here. And alive. That was all that mattered.

When she'd arrived cold and tired at Cardington eight months ago, little did she know how her life would be turned around. She now had lifelong friends in Nell, George and Maeve and especially Alice. She had never imagined, either, before having been taken under Florrie's motherly wing when everything seemed hopeless, that she would now regard the shattered streets of East London and the warm-hearted people who lived there as home.

But for all the joy now in her life, she couldn't forget they were in middle of a war, so who knew what tomorrow would bring? Whatever it was, Effie knew she had the strength to face it, because of the new life she'd built as a balloon girl but above all because she had Nathan beside her, the man she would love until her very last breath.

A LETTER FROM JEAN

Dear reader,

I want to say a huge thank you for choosing to read *The East End Girls*. If you did enjoy it, and want to keep up to date with all my latest releases, just sign up at the following link. Your email address will never be shared and you can unsubscribe at any time.

www.bookouture.com/jean-fullerton

I hope you loved *The East End Girls* and if you did I would be very grateful if you could write a review. I'd love to hear what you think, and it makes such a difference helping new readers to discover one of my books for the first time.

I love hearing from my readers – you can get in touch through social media or my website.

Thanks,

Jean Fullerton

jeanfullerton.com

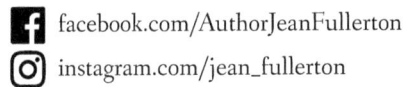

facebook.com/AuthorJeanFullerton
instagram.com/jean_fullerton

ACKNOWLEDGEMENTS

As always, I would like to mention a few books, authors and people to whom I am particularly indebted.

In order to set my characters' thoughts and worldview authentically to the harsh reality of Spitfire summer 1940, I returned to *Wartime Britain 1939–1945* and *The Blitz* (both by Juliet Gardiner) and *The East End at War* (Rosemary Taylor and Christopher Lloyd).

However, to tell Effie and her friends' story as balloon girls properly, I needed to have an understanding of their lives as wartime WAAFs. I was greatly helped in this task by a number of autobiographies, including *Our Wartime Days* (Beryl Escott), *Living Dangerously* (Betty Farley), *Spit, Polish and Tears* (Norman Small) and *We All Wore Blue* (Muriel Pushman). In addition to these personal accounts of life in the WAAF, I delved into *The Women Behind the Few* (Sarah-Louise Miller), *What Did You Do in the War, Mummy?* (Mavis Nicholson), *War World War II British Women's Uniforms* (Richard Ingram and Martin Brayley) and *Balloons at War* (John Christopher). I'm also grateful to the website *A History of RAF Cardington 1936–2000* (www.rafcardington.org.uk/).

For Nathan's experiences as a Barbadian who travelled halfway across the world to defend freedom, I drew on the excellent book by Stephen Bourne, *The Motherland Calls*, and *Jamaican Airman* (E. Martin Noble). There is also a fantastic YouTube video of British Empire soldiers working and speaking about their experiences (www.youtube.com/watch?v=ViGwx

Jlo170). To write Nathan as a pilot in the RAF, again I turned to *Fighter Pilot* (Paul Richey), *The RAF Battle of Britain Fighter Pilot's Kitbag* (Mark Hillier) and *The Royal Air Force 1939–45* (Andrew Cormack), and Major Robert Bourne-Patterson's *SOE in France, 1941–45* to ensure Nathan's involvement was correct. Plus I returned to Peter Wilkinson and Joan Bright Astley's biography *Gubbins & SOE* for the background to the operations.

Stuart Antrobus's *Life in Bedford during the Second World War* helped me set the scene for both Effie's and Nathan's off-duty time.

I have to give a special shoutout to the Shuttleworth Collection & Garden www.shuttleworth.org, who have an original SOE Lysander in their vintage aircraft collection. I would like to thank Debbie Land, the museum's Costume & Carriage Curator, for spending two hours of her time talking me through the aircraft and its role in the clandestine SOE operations, plus recommending Hugh Verity's autobiography, *We Landed by Moonlight*, documenting his time as an SOE pilot.

Lastly, I would also like to thank a few more people. Firstly, my very own Hero-at-Home, Kelvin, for his unwavering support, and my three daughters, Janet, Fiona and Amy, who listen patiently as I explain the endless twists and turns of the plot. Kate Burke, from Blake Friedmann Literary Agents, for her steadfast support and encouragement. A big thanks goes to Lizzie Brien for her detailed and insightful edits, and the rest of the wonderful Bookouture team for welcoming me into the fold and for all their support.

PUBLISHING TEAM

Turning a manuscript into a book requires the efforts of many people. The publishing team at Bookouture would like to acknowledge everyone who contributed to this publication.

Audio
Alba Proko
Melissa Tran
Sinead O'Connor

Commercial
Lauren Morrissette
Hannah Richmond
Imogen Allport

Contracts
Peta Nightingale

Cover design
Eileen Carey

Data and analysis
Mark Alder
Mohamed Bussuri

Editorial
Lizzie Brien

Copyeditor
Jacqui Lewis

Proofreader
Anne O'Brien

Marketing
Alex Crow
Melanie Price
Occy Carr
Cíara Rosney
Martyna Młynarska

Operations and distribution
Marina Valles
Stephanie Straub
Joe Morris

Production
Hannah Snetsinger
Mandy Kullar
Ria Clare
Nadia Michael

Publicity
Kim Nash
Noelle Holten
Jess Readett
Sarah Hardy

www.ingramcontent.com/pod-product-compliance
Ingram Content Group UK Ltd.
Pitfield, Milton Keynes, MK11 3LW, UK
UKHW040650280825
7616UKWH00014B/67

9 781836 185260